Close to t

Anna lives on the Isle of Wight with her husband and their chronically clumsy Labrador. An avid reader, she began writing around ten years ago and hasn't stopped since. Anna works as a freelance editor and loves helping out other authors. When not filling her head with stories, Anna enjoys baking (and eating) cakes and exploring rivers in her kayak.

Also by Anna Britton

Detectives Martin & Stern

CLOSE
TO THE
EDGE

ANNA
BRITTON

CANELO CRIME

First published in the United Kingdom in 2024 by

Canelo
Unit 9, 5th Floor
Cargo Works, 1–2 Hatfields
London SE1 9PG
United Kingdom

A CIP catalogue record for this book is available from the British Library.

Print ISBN 978 1 80436 526 7
Ebook ISBN 978 1 80436 527 4

This book is a work of fiction. Names, characters, businesses, organizations, places and events are either the product of the author's imagination or are used fictitiously. Any resemblance to actual persons, living or dead, events or locales is entirely coincidental.

Cover design by Dan Mogford

Cover images © Shutterstock

Look for more great books at www.canelo.co

Printed and bound in Great Britain by Clays Ltd, Elcograf S.p.A.

1

For Ben

Pull.

He tugs, digging his fingers between the rough strands of rope. Bending his wrists to unnatural angles, he pushes and twists. He doesn't know how long he's been doing this. If it's making any difference.

Try.

This is his chance to leave this place. He knows what he saw, what he can't be allowed to tell anyone. If only they'd asked, before they took him. He would have told them their secret was safe. He wouldn't say a word.

Breathe.

It's hard to draw in air through his clogged nose. The tight gag is wet with saliva, the blindfold clinging to his skin with tears and blood. There's a sharp ache along his left side. He tries not to focus on that. He presses his fingers between the knots of rope and strains.

Fuck.

It does nothing. All this effort is futile. He edges his fingers free and slumps. The position is more comfortable than the last time he gave up. His shoulders aren't dragged backward. His wrists have space to separate. He forces his fingers between the ropes with renewed vigour. He grits his teeth against the fabric that was forced into his mouth and yanks at his bindings.

Free.

One moment he is struggling, the next the knots loosen. He frantically jerks his arms apart. His heart leaping, his numb fingers struggle with the blindfold. He paws at it, then rips it off. He removes the gag and unwinds the rope from around his ankles. He blinks at the dim space. It's a small room. Doors stand open at one end, leading to neat bedrooms. A sofa looms to one side, a compact kitchen on the other. Cubbies and cupboards line the walls.

Listen.

At the top of a short staircase, there's another door. One that leads to freedom. As he waits for feeling to return to his hands and feet, he directs his attention outside. There were voices before. There aren't now.

Get up.

He crawls onto his knees first, then stumbles to his feet. It feels like he's swaying. He can't remember hitting his head. Maybe lack of oxygen is enough to make it feel like the whole room is moving from side to side.

Be brave.

He can either wait to be found or try to escape. He swallows, his spit tinged with copper, and places his hands on the railing either side of the short flight of stairs. His palms are slick with sweat and blood. His whole body feels like it's in unnatural motion. Gripping the railing, he takes one shaking step. He freezes at a clang from outside. The door flies open.

Day 1

Saturday, 25 April

Detective Inspector Paul Willis: Keith didn't have to leave.

Detective Inspector Juliet Stern: I don't need him here.

Detective Sergeant Nicole Stewart: It's up to you. Witness statement recorded with permission of the interviewee on the 25th April at 11:10 a.m. This interview is being conducted by Detective Inspector Paul Willis and myself, Detective Sergeant Nicole Stewart. The interviewee is Detective Inspector Juliet Stern. This interview is concerning the shooting of herself and Detective Sergeant Gabriella Martin outside Southampton Crown Court at 5:20 p.m. on the 24th April.

DI Paul Willis: Are you recovered enough to discuss your memories of the shooting?

DI Juliet Stern: I'm as prepared as I usually am to speak to you.

DI Paul Willis: Wonderful. Did you notice anything strange in the days before the shooting?

DI Juliet Stern: If that were the case, wouldn't I have raised the alarm?

DI Paul Willis: I'll take that as a no?

DI Juliet Stern: Indeed.

DS Nicole Stewart: Juliet, can you tell us about your arrival at the courthouse?

DI Juliet Stern: I drove in with Gabe. She said Maddy and some other officers were going to meet us, so we waited outside for a few minutes. In the end, we went in without them. We didn't want to enter the courtroom late.

DS Nicole Stewart: While you waited outside, was anyone milling around near where the shooting would take place?

DI Juliet Stern: There were smokers at the bottom of the steps. A man stood a little way from them. I assumed he'd distanced himself because of the fumes, but he would have been close to where we were shot.

4

DI Paul Willis: Can you describe him?

DI Juliet Stern: He was tall, about the same height as me. He was wearing a long tan coat. His shoes were shiny. Expensive.

DS Nicole Stewart: Anything distinctive about his face?

DI Juliet Stern: He was looking down at his phone most of the time. I didn't get a good look at him. He was white with dark brown hair.

DI Paul Willis: Alice is trawling through CCTV from around the shooting. I'll get her to look out for him as well.

DS Nicole Stewart: Did the man in the coat go into Karl Biss's trial?

DI Juliet Stern: Not that I noticed.

DS Nicole Stewart: Did anyone in the courtroom catch your eye?

DI Juliet Stern: I recognised a few people from the case. Melanie Pirt's grandmother was there, and Jordan Haines sat with Leonard Dunlow. Afterwards, they all waited in the courthouse lobby until the journalists cleared off. Like us.

DI Paul Willis: You can confirm Leonard Dunlow and Jordan Haines were in sight during the shooting?

DI Juliet Stern: Yes. I hope they were uninjured?

DS Nicole Stewart: They're fine. We've taken witness statements from them both. They helped Melanie's grandmother and her friend to safety after the shooting started.

DI Paul Willis: Commendable behaviour. Not everyone is as selfless in such a dangerous situation.

DS Nicole Stewart: Can we backtrack? You left the courthouse as a group?

DI Juliet Stern: Yes. Gabe and the others were chatting while I checked my emails.

DI Paul Willis: No one gave any indication they suspected something was about to happen?

DI Juliet Stern: No.

DS Nicole Stewart: You lost consciousness quickly after being shot, but did you notice anything directly before or after you were injured?

DI Juliet Stern: I barely had time to comprehend what was happening before I fell.

DI Paul Willis: What do you remember from those seconds?

DI Juliet Stern: The pain, obviously.

[Long pause.]

DS Nicole Stewart: Take your time.

DI Juliet Stern: I'm fine. I remember Gabe's face, when she realised I'd been shot. She was upset.

DI Paul Willis: She cares about you a great deal.

DI Juliet Stern: Have you spoken with her?

DI Paul Willis: Not yet. The curtains were drawn around her bed when we looked into the ward.

DI Juliet Stern: She'll be able to give you more of an idea of what happened after I was shot.

DI Paul Willis: We'll speak with her soon. She's going to be fine, by the way. Now, can you think of anyone who has a strong reason to want to hurt yourself and Gabe?

DI Juliet Stern: Not especially. We're heading up Operation Juno, but there had been no new leads for weeks.

[Knocking. Door opening.]

Keith Stern: Sorry to interrupt. The nurse said Juliet needs to sleep.

DI Paul Willis: Not a problem. We've got all we need. Rest up, Juliet.

DI Juliet Stern: It's not like I have much of an option.

Call connected at 12:01.

'999, which service do you require?'

'Police, please.'

'I'll put you through.'

PLEASE HOLD. PLEASE HOLD. PLEASE HOLD. PLEASE HOLD.

'Police, what's your emergency?'

'My son has gone missing.'

'Can you please tell me the circumstances around his disappearance?'

'Henry's a student at Solent University. No one has seen him since yesterday morning.'

'How old is Henry?'

'He's just turned nineteen. This is so unlike him. He's never done anything like this before.'

'I understand. Can I ask your relationship to Henry?'

'I'm his father. Jude Garside.'

'Okay, Mr Garside. I'm going to take a few more details from you, then have a member of the Southampton team give you a call.'

'Will someone come out soon? We need to find him.'

'An officer will be dispatched soon to take a statement from yourself and any other relevant parties before we launch a missing persons case. We'll do everything in our power to find your son. Can you tell me Henry's address in Southampton?'

Gabe

'It's a good job you've got small boobies,' the nurse said. 'It won't matter that you can't wear a bra for a while.'

The glare I levelled at her was interrupted when she pulled the overlarge T-shirt Ollie had brought into the hospital over my head. Her movements efficient, she threaded my injured arm through one sleeve. She left me to wrangle the other into place as she shook out a pair of jeans.

What she'd said was true, but I would have appreciated her not blurting it out with only a thin floral curtain separating us from the rest of the ward.

My cheeks heated as the nurse crouched, ready to guide my legs into the jeans. Despite the reddened skin of her knuckles and crumpled green scrubs, she was unfairly pretty. It should have been illegal to be tended to by someone who looked radiant even with heavy bags under her striking hazel eyes when I was at my most unattractive.

My feet pushed through the bunched fabric, the nurse tugged the jeans up over my knees and thighs. She didn't acknowledge my one-handed attempts to help her settle them around my waist, but secured the button and fly with the same cool competence as when she'd removed the cannula from the back of my hand.

'The clothes you were shot in were taken away as evidence.' She pulled a thick rainbow cardigan from Ollie's backpack.

I winced. I'd relegated the reason I was on this ward to the back of my mind. Stabs of pain from my shoulder each time I moved weren't enough to provoke me to relive the events of yesterday afternoon. I wouldn't unless I absolutely had to.

'A rude man came and took them,' the nurse muttered as she settled the cardigan over my bandage. She left me to struggle into the other sleeve while pulling a pair of boots from the bottom of Ollie's bag.

'Ginger?'

The nurse nodded, escaped brown curls from the high bun on top of her head bouncing as she loosened my laces.

David Rees was my least favourite colleague. The head of the forensic team was habitually brisk, but that wasn't what bothered me. Months before I moved to Southampton, David assumed Juliet's husband moving out of the city meant he'd left her. David asked her out and had never gotten over the rejection. He might have been less snide recently, but his eyes followed every move Juliet made.

In spite of this, David was the best at what he did. With him overseeing the forensics, the chances of finding whoever landed me and Juliet in hospital drastically increased.

I gripped the bed's side rail while the nurse eased on my boots. I whimpered when I attempted to hold on with my left hand, the movement sending a shockwave of pain through my shoulder.

The nurse looked up at me, one eyebrow raised. 'You don't get any points for being a hero here. How would you rate the pain out of ten?'

'Six?' I hedged. I'd woken several times yesterday from a haze of drugs and sharp aches, only to drown under the weight of more medication. I wasn't willing to lose myself like that again.

The curtain protecting me from prying eyes whipped back. Ollie held the bag of prescribed pills the nurse had sent him to collect while she helped me dress. His hair was unusually messy, the blond waves thatched in graceless tangles that gave way to shaved sides. His eyes were shadowed, his lips chapped. His long legs were encased in silver leggings and his tattooed arms swamped in a baggy jumper usually relegated to the inside of my maisonette.

The nurse gave one final tug at my laces and stood. She batted away wayward strands of hair curling around her face. Light brown eyes shot through with lines of dazzling green crinkled with a perfunctory smile. 'I know you're determined to brave it out, but we prescribe pain medication for a reason. You don't have to hurt constantly while your body is healing from trauma. At least consider taking something at night. It will help you sleep, and rest is the best thing for you right now.'

Suitably chastised, I took the medication from Ollie and slotted it into the vacated space in his backpack. 'Thank you for all your help while I've been here.' While I didn't want to dwell on the exact nature of the care she'd provided, I was grateful.

A genuine smile that brightened her heart-shaped face fought against the disapproval emanating from her in waves. 'Look after yourself,' she commanded, before striding off.

'Nurses are saints,' Ollie murmured as he picked up his bag. 'You should listen to her.'

'I will.' It wasn't a lie. I would take all the pain medication I could without lowering my IQ to useless levels. 'Did you catch her name at any point?'

'Mary Turner.' Ollie threw his bag over one shoulder and held out an elbow. 'Are you thinking of sending her a thank you card?'

I slipped my uninjured arm through his. 'Yeah. I might.'

That wasn't why I'd asked. I couldn't decide whether the nurse deserved censure or praise for how she'd treated me. My ego smarted over the comment about my breasts. Everyone on the ward would have heard. Or those capable of focusing on anything beyond their own bodies.

Ollie gripped my hand, a smile dimpling his tanned cheek. All thoughts of the nurse were banished. That this man, so kind and unbroken and whole, would look at me like I was precious was unfathomable. It never ceased to amaze me.

I'd been scared months ago when he suggested we date, convinced he'd grow bored of the harsh realities of closeness with me. That hadn't happened yet. Ollie wasn't deterred by my frequent nightmares and long working hours. He didn't push to know more about my past or demand I dredge up repressed feelings.

He was the person I wanted to see after a long and frustrating day at the station. I loved hearing about the petty arguments between his roommates. My weekends were filled with rambling dog walks and pub lunches, luxurious mornings in bed and evenings held close. My life was full of things I didn't think I could ever have, that I'd not allowed myself to dream of.

'Can we visit Juliet?' I slowed down as we reached the end of the ward. 'Is she on this floor?'

I'd woken from the operation to sew my shoulder together and demanded to know how my partner was. My relief on hearing Juliet was alive and would make a full recovery was a crashing wave. I was convinced I'd watched the beginning of her bleeding out as I laid on the cold ground outside the courthouse.

'She's got her own room.' Ollie steered me out into a wide corridor and down an offshoot lined with doors. He stopped before the third and knocked.

There was no window, no way to spy inside. A whiteboard proclaimed this was Juliet's room. I caught a glimpse of the end of a hospital bed when the door opened, then a man stepped out and it snapped shut.

'Hello?' Juliet's husband was as tall as she was in her most precarious heels, his brown hair lined with greys. He brushed his hands on worn jeans marked with small fingerprints in a rainbow of colours as his eyes crinkled with a smile. 'Gabe, is it? I'm Keith. I've heard so much about you.'

I didn't think that was likely, unless Juliet adopted a different personality at home. 'Nice to meet you.'

'Likewise. Although, I can't say I didn't wish it were in better circumstances.' Keith's short beard bunched with another tight smile, the hair covering his chin a lighter shade of brown than the strands falling over his freckled forehead. 'Juliet didn't say the investigation she'd been working on was dangerous.'

I frowned. I'd have to check with Ollie later, but I suspected a partner expressing gratitude and relief after an incident like this was more traditional than thinly veiled criticism.

I didn't have to ask which investigation Keith was referring to. One had dominated mine and Juliet's time over the last few months; a prolonged operation to bring down the leaders of a human trafficking ring discovered last October.

'We didn't know it was, or is.' I flexed my fingers inside Ollie's hold. 'Gathering evidence had been slow and unremarkable. At no point was there any indication we would come to harm.'

'I'm not sure I would have worried less if Juliet had told me the risk was low. I'm certainly not going to after this.' Keith braced one hand on the door. 'I find it hard to believe she wouldn't have suspected something was up.'

Worry was natural, but this felt like blame. Keith either had an overly high estimation of Juliet's detective skills, or he held her responsible for not identifying an unseen threat.

'We worked closely together for the whole investigation. There was honestly no warning anything like this might happen.'

'You know how Juliet is.' Keith sighed. 'She's not always adept at reading a situation. I wonder if someone else would have spotted the danger.'

'I was there.' Sharpness lined my words.

Months ago, Juliet had called her husband difficult. There wasn't a human alive she wouldn't claim was annoying at one time or another. Juliet didn't walk through life via the smoothest paths. Those she was closest to would rub against her rough edges most often.

Now I'd met Keith, I was inclined to agree with her.

Ollie looked between the two of us. The same smile he deployed when his mother complained about the lack of designer shops in her corner of Cornwall swept over his face. 'How is Juliet doing?'

Keith's hands wound together, concern for his wife finally evident. 'On the mend. Recovery will take a long while, but she's a fighter.'

He glanced at me. There was definitely an edge about him. It could be because I suspected something was awry in Juliet's home life and I felt fiercely protective of her, but I thought a small nudge would cause her husband's kind mask to slip.

'Can I pop in?'

Keith didn't spread his arms wide, but his exaggerated wince barred entry to Juliet's room all the same. 'I'm afraid not. The doctor said she needs as much rest as possible. Thankfully, your knock didn't wake her.'

His expression was apologetic, but his eyes hadn't shifted from mine. It was almost like he wanted me to challenge him, like he'd relish refusing a more forceful demand.

'Give her our love, won't you?' Ollie said.

Keith pressed his hands together. 'Thank you. Of course I will.'

Ollie turned toward the main thoroughfare. I looked back before we rounded the corner. Keith's head was bent as he fiddled with a phone.

I wished I was close enough to check whether it bore the damage of when Juliet dropped it. But even if it was her phone, that didn't mean anything untoward was going on. Ollie often grabbed my phone after placing his out of reach so he wouldn't play with it through the evening. My internet history was cluttered with his fact checking while we watched documentaries about his favourite kings and queens.

'How about soup tonight?' Ollie suggested as he tucked me into the corner of a lift, using his toned frame as a shield against accidental jostling. Beside him, a man held the hand of a young girl, their heads identically shaved. 'We can head home and get cosy. Tide ourselves over with biscuits until you're up for something more substantial.'

I shook my head. 'I can't go home yet. I have to go to the station.'

Ollie's lips flattened. He leant in and pressed them to the soft skin by my ear. 'Gabriella,' he whispered.

I didn't need to be full-named to know I was in trouble. This was the first long-standing joke I'd had with a partner, that materialised after Artie crashed into our lives. When walking into a living room littered with the remains of a cushion or when a burger mysteriously disappeared from the kitchen side, pulling out an Artemis felt appropriate despite the dog's wide-eyed innocence.

'I need to go in,' I murmured into Ollie's jumper. 'They need to hear my side of things.' The sooner I went to the station, the sooner I'd talk through my useless recollections.

Ollie slid his other arm around my waist. 'I don't like this. I want to take you home and bury you in blankets and feed you Hobnobs.'

'Tempting.' I touched my forehead to his. 'But I need to do this.'

The lift doors shunted open. Ollie kissed me as everyone else disembarked. The whisper of his dry lips on mine sent spirals of sensation down my spine.

'It's alright.' He straightened and guided me out of the lift. 'Significant others get a free pass for a fair amount of twattery just after they've been shot.'

The joke fell flat, all inflection lost in the tightness of his jaw. The skin around his eyes was sore, had been swiped at too often. He'd looked the same way when his dad went for tests about a prolonged chest infection two months ago, his whole body held taut over days of waiting. He'd wept when his mum called to tell him everything was fine, crumpling into my arms.

'Ol.' I stopped walking and pulled him into a hug even though it really fucking hurt. His arms tightened around me as crowds of patients and doctors darted past us.

'I'm okay,' I whispered, as he pressed his face into my neck. 'We're okay.'

I wished I could go home with Ollie, sink into his familiar warmth and forget the world. But he'd said it himself. I'd been shot. I couldn't laze around at home, doping myself against the pain.

I needed to find out who did this.

Unknown number. Sent 14:36.

You're not as good at this as you said you are.
You've made a total mess of a simple fucking job.

Unknown number. Sent 14:37.

I'm sorry. T.

Unknown number. Sent 14:37.

This is going to take some sorting out. It would be
grand if you could actually make yourself useful.

Call connected at 14:47.

'Superintendent Angela Dobson.'

    'Hi, it's Nicole. It's not good news, ma'am.'

    'Give me the overview.'

    'Henry Garside, a nineteen-year-old art student at Solent University, was meant to go over to Art for All gallery yesterday morning to set up a painting as part of a community exhibit. He never turned up. He was last seen by a fellow student, Rowan Lough, earlier that morning when they worked on their projects together at a studio on campus. Henry was captured leaving the art building just before ten a.m. yesterday on CCTV. He has not been seen since. His dorm mates say they haven't noticed him coming or going. A search of his room revealed no intention to leave; his clothes seem to all be there and there is no note of any kind. His parents have come down from Surrey and are extremely concerned. They speak to their son every evening and they say this is not like him.'

    'We've got a high-risk missing person on our hands?'

    'Afraid so, ma'am.'

    'Right. You'll have to take the lead on this while Paul investigates the shooting. You can have uniforms to search the area. Get a poster sorted and canvass all of Henry's known haunts. Arrange in-depth interviews with friends and family, and get someone looking at CCTV to track his movements after he left the art building.'

    'Will do, ma'am, but I'm afraid I can't work past five today. Lang is on shift tonight, and I have to look after the kids.'

    'Of course. Get the investigation kicked off and I'll step in for anything that can't wait until tomorrow.'

    'Thank you, ma'am.'

From: David Rees **david.rees@forensics.gov.uk**
To: Paul Willis **paul.willis@mit.gov.uk**
CC: Nicole Stewart **nicole.stewart@mit.gov.uk**
Date: **25 April, 15:14**
Subject: **Operation Orion – Forensic analysis of bullets and wounds**

Willis,

Attached are reports from the doctor who processed Stern and Martin last night at A&E, along with notes on the bullets found at the scene.

To summarise:

Stern was shot first. A non-fatal gunshot wound entered her left shoulder from the front, below the clavicle. The angle of entry was approximately twenty degrees, which suggests the perpetrator shot from an elevated position. No major arteries or bones were affected, but there is muscle damage. The exit wound is on her back, above the scapula notch. The gunshot wound was accompanied by significant blood loss. Despite this and the muscle damage, the prognosis is that Stern will make a full recovery with physio support.

Martin was shot second. A non-fatal gunshot wound entered her left shoulder from the front, above her clavicle. The angle of entry was similar to Stern's, suggesting the perpetrator did not change position between the two shootings. No major arteries, muscles or bones were affected. The exit wound is on her back, above the scapula notch. As there is only soft tissue damage, the prognosis is that Martin will make a full recovery.

Both bullets were retrieved untampered from the scene and have undergone initial analysis, which suggests they may have been fired from a long-barrelled weapon such as a hunting rifle. DNA samples taken from the bullets contained two profiles, which positively match Stern and Martin. There were no fingerprints on either bullet.

The bullets and the reports on the wounds have been sent off to the Firearms Lab for further testing, which may provide more information on possible firing positions. In the meantime, the forensic team is sweeping areas where the shooter could have been positioned for gunshot residue and casings. This includes several rooftops, which will suffer forensic compromise if the rain forecast for tomorrow falls.

I hope Stern is recovering. And Martin.

Rees

Gabe

'I don't think this is a good idea,' Ollie said as I unsheathed the seatbelt from my armpit. Wearing it across my shoulder during the drive from the hospital to the station was impossible.

'Noted.' I eased out of the car, biting the insides of my cheeks to suppress the grunts of pain each movement attempted to elicit. Leaning down, I gripped the edge of the Mini's roof to steady myself and raised a pinched smile. 'I'll get a lift home or give you a call, if that's alright?'

Ollie pursed his lips to the side. 'Give me a call any time and I'll come get you.'

'Thank you.' I straightened and fought the urge to roll my shoulder to ease the ache emanating from it. This wasn't a pulled muscle that could be stretched into submission.

Shutting the car door sent a jolt of pain down my back. I breathed slowly as I walked to the station's side entrance. We were only meant to use it when journalists made coming and going through the glass-fronted reception difficult, but it was closer to the car park and made avoiding the bulk of my co-workers possible.

I tapped my ID on the keypad and the door clicked open. I held my arm close to my side as I made my way through corridors to the bank of lifts. Inside, I avoided my reflection in the wall-to-wall mirrors. My clothes were more casual than my usual chinos and dark jumpers, but that wasn't what made me cringe away. My pale skin had been reduced to a stark white, my cropped brown hair lank over my ears and forehead. My eyes were sunken pits, evidence of a sleepless night and my refusal to take the prescribed pain medication.

The lift disgorged me onto the seventh floor, where the Major Investigations Team was housed. I kept my head lowered as I walked across the main part of the floor, the desks arranged in clusters of four across the wide open-plan room. A sparse handful were occupied, but I hurried on. I didn't want to be waylaid by curious colleagues. If enough time passed without a chance for them to pounce, new drama would unfold. I wouldn't have to relive what happened outside the courthouse yesterday more times than necessary.

'Gabe?' The voice of one of the only people I'd feel genuine remorse about ignoring rang out as I rushed toward mine and Juliet's office.

I stopped beside Maddy's desk and flashed her a toothy smile. 'Hi. Can you please send me all the files around the shooting?'

Maddy jumped up, her wavy brown hair swaying around her face and her bright pink fingernails dancing over the buttons of her cardigan. 'Gabe, I'm so glad you're okay.'

Maddy was one of the Major Investigations Team's admin assistants, the one we all gravitated toward because of her calm efficiency. Since I'd entered the station just over a year ago, she'd guided me through the intricacies of working with someone as prickly as Juliet and filled me in on the lives of our co-workers. While sharing gossip and enough chocolate to keep us afloat during dragging cases, we'd become friends.

She pulled me into a gentle hug, carefully avoiding my bandaged shoulder. Engulfed in her floral scent, I snapped from my mission to find sanctuary in my office and dive into the investigation.

My throat tightened. Maddy was there when I got shot. She'd helped me.

I wrapped my uninjured arm around her back. 'I'm so relieved you weren't hurt,' I whispered into her hair.

Maddy's eyes were glossy as we stepped back. Behind her, Paul chatted on the phone inside his office. A few heads were turned our way, lit by computer screens. A trickle of well-wishers could all too easily turn into a flood. There were few advantages to being as universally disliked as Juliet, but she wouldn't have to fear our co-workers prodding into memories she'd rather suppress once she returned to work.

'Get me those files, yeah?'

Maddy sniffed. 'I'll try, but I'm snowed under with a new missing persons case.'

I squeezed her arm and retreated to my office. It was one of two on the floor. While Paul's on the opposite side of the building was spacious and housed only his desk, mine and Juliet's was crammed with two. A bank of filing cabinets lined the wall behind her desk, and where a window could have looked out over the floor was bolted a huge corkboard.

That was why Juliet insisted I share the office with her. She liked to lay out evidence across the wall and she didn't want to constantly call me in to look over photos and transcripts and scraps of paper with her.

I'd not worked this way before, but I'd gotten used to it. Laying everything out and using brightly coloured twine to make connections was effective, if Juliet's arrest record was anything to go by. I'd do anything to become a better detective.

Currently, the wall was filled with evidence around the task force Juliet and I had been heading up for months. A human trafficking ring was uncovered last autumn and while we'd caught and charged several people guilty of working in the business of human slavery, we were all too aware we hadn't come close to taking down the masterminds.

We'd been gathering evidence against them but were no nearer to an effective arrest. The documents surrounding three photos on the board was so thick in places that Juliet had shoved in an additional pin or two to keep it from falling to the floor.

Tsambikos Galanis and his brothers, Alcaeus and Giannis, smiled down from the wall. They looked similar, their black hair gelled back from their foreheads and their light brown skin smooth. Tsambikos had the most flare; a diamond glinting from one ear and a hint of blusher highlighting his cheekbones.

No matter how polished they looked, they were mired in dirt. Although we hadn't found any irrefutable links, we were certain that for the last two years the brothers had spearheaded all major human trafficking, plus the movement of drug and weapons, across the city. Given how Juliet and I had been circling them for months and waiting for them to step out of line, they had to be suspects for our shooting.

I turned away from the wall and tucked my left hand onto my lap. If I stayed still while I worked, my arm shouldn't hamper me. I tapped my keyboard to bring my computer to life.

'Gabe?'

I flinched, then gasped at pain that felt far more like bone grinding on bone than the tug of torn tissue. It would be fascinating, if it wasn't so draining, how many different types of punishment it was possible to experience from one supposedly tidy wound. It was distracting enough that I hadn't noticed the rhythmic thump of Paul's stick as he crossed the outer office.

He leant against the doorframe, his mussed black hair decorated with greys. Although the purple bags under his eyes never lifted, an eagerness clung to him even after a long night of searching through documents to find the smallest incriminating detail. He'd used a walking aid since being injured in a poorly managed hostage situation years ago.

Paul walked over to Juliet's desk and sat down in her chair, leaning his stick beside him. If there was any chance of Juliet wandering in, he wouldn't have dared. He was a similar height to her, so at least wouldn't tamper with the chair's settings, but they were different in almost every other way. Where Paul was warm and invited me and Ollie over for dinner with his family at least once a month, Juliet was cold. The walls around her personal life were high and unrelenting.

Paul's eyes swept over me. I could feel, as his gaze roved, how lacking I must appear.

'I know I don't look great, but I'm ready to help out.'

Paul waved his hand. 'If anyone knows what it's like to be physically incapacitated but mentally raring to go, it's me.'

His words unravelled a knot in my chest. I'd been determined to help out with this investigation, but a small voice had wondered if I would be sent packing if I came to the station in less than perfect health. I should have known Paul would understand. He might not talk about his leg injury much, but he would remember what it felt like to want justice and the need to be one of the people who sought it.

'I'm fine.' I ignored the headache building behind my eyes. It reached from my shoulder, like concentrating all the pain in one section of my body was unsustainable.

Paul's gaze settled on the padding under my rainbow cardigan. 'Got yourself shot, then? The boys were beside themselves when I told them it would be stitched up. They were hoping for a hole to poke around in.'

I huffed out a laugh. Paul's sons were desperate to be detectives like their father. They'd fallen over themselves when I'd let them play with my official notepad and had cried when bedtime rolled around the time I'd brought over a pair of handcuffs. A real-life bullet wound would bring them untold joy.

'I'll have a scar.'

'They'll have to make do with that, although they're completely unimpressed by mine.' Paul swivelled Juliet's chair from side to side, his face sobering. 'You alright, Gabe?'

I'd known Paul before I moved down here. We both worked in north London, where he'd encouraged me to take the detective's exam. He hadn't ditched me when I was assigned to work with his least favourite colleague instead of him after I followed him to Southampton.

His gentle concern made me want to confess exactly how much pain I was in, but I squared a smile on my face. 'I'm fine. Ready to work.'

'Good to hear it.' Paul pulled an old-style Dictaphone from his trouser pocket. 'Before you do anything else, I need a witness statement.'

He tapped a button on the side and rattled off the essential information. I shifted my weight, searching for a position that wouldn't put unnecessary strain on my shoulder. I settled for hunching to my left, my arm pressed to my side. I'd only taken paracetamol and ibuprofen after leaving the hospital to keep my mind sharp. Pointless, since my brain capacity was being eroded by pain anyway.

'Please let me know if you need to stop at all.' Paul responded with a lopsided grin to my withering glare. 'Tell me about the days leading up to the shooting. Was there any indication of what would happen?'

I shook my head. 'Juliet and I were working on the same case we had been for months. There was no significant change. We had no new leads or information.'

'This was Operation Juno?' Paul twisted toward the wall crisscrossed with pink twine. 'The extended investigation following the discovery of a human trafficking ring?'

'Yes. We last spoke to the Galanis brothers a couple of weeks ago. They were as unhelpful as ever. Nothing they said made me think they had any particular ill will toward me and Juliet.'

'It wasn't a sad day when I was moved off Juno.' As much as Tsambikos Galanis and his silently hulking brothers rubbed me and Juliet up the wrong way, Paul had barely been able to control his anger when Tsambikos made regular enquiries about our families. 'They didn't give any indication they were violently inclined toward you and Juliet?'

'None at all. They had no reason to be. Although they have to be suspects for the shooting, I have no idea why they would have wanted to hurt us other than that Juliet and I were investigating them, and we'd been doing that for months.' Their smirking portraits mocked me from amongst the stacked evidence. 'Apart from uncovering the house where the women were held and arresting a few of their lackeys, we've not been able to touch them.' I wrinkled my nose. 'You know what Tsambikos is like. Last time we interviewed him, he was joking and going off on tangents. He thinks they're untouchable. If they were involved in the shooting because Juliet and I pissed them off in some unknown way, you'll find it hard to gather together anything to pin it on them. They're smart and sneaky.'

Paul leant his elbows on Juliet's desk and cradled his stubbled chin. I hoped he wouldn't move anything. Juliet would notice immediately. 'Anyone else you two have interacted with who might have wanted to hurt you?'

'No. Apart from Operation Juno, Juliet and I have only worked minor cases for weeks. Mainly burglaries. There's been nothing particularly violent and we've had no hate mail.' Juliet would have told me if she'd had any. She liked to read them to me, her lips quirking at the particularly gruesome bits.

'How about the Dunlows?'

My eyes flicked to the evidence board. Half a year ago, another case had occupied that space. At the time, it had been the most difficult I'd worked on. A selfie of a young Black woman occupied the centre spot.

Melanie Pirt. Murdered at seventeen years of age. She'd been visiting Leo Dunlow on his family's ancestral estate, who she had been seeing secretly for months. Due to his father's interference, Leo left Melanie to run out into the night alone. She was chased through the forest by a dog, then shot three times and left for dead.

I'd been convinced Timothy Dunlow was the killer. He'd been fixated on protecting his sons, to the extreme degree that it was believable he would shoot a young woman to disentangle his youngest from a relationship he considered unsuitable. His bad attitude didn't help. He cast himself in the role of uncaring upper class posho. As did his oldest legitimate son, Terence.

Timothy Dunlow was an innocent bystander. Melanie was killed by the groundskeeper, who we discovered was Timothy's unknown son, hellbent on punishing the family he believed had rejected him. Melanie was caught in the middle as Karl Biss lashed out at his father.

24

He'd confessed to the murder, but a full trial had been necessary as he'd pleaded innocence over a fire that destroyed half of Dunlow Manor, a hit and run against the younger son, and Terence's beating. With no one else in possession of such a strong motive and ample opportunity to lash out against the Dunlow family, Karl had been pronounced guilty on all counts.

'I don't know. Timothy Dunlow has access to guns, or at least he did when Melanie Pirt was killed. He's supposedly a good shot. So is Terence.'

'His son had just been convicted of murder,' Paul added.

'I'm not sure Dunlow would acknowledge Karl as his son. He wasn't at the trial and I'm not sure yesterday's verdict would have affected him.'

Timothy Dunlow's legitimate sons meant everything to him, but I didn't think his sorry excuse for a heart could grow to allow in another. More likely, Dunlow had swanned through the time of the trial unaware his recently revealed son was being sentenced to life imprisonment.

'Dunlow's someone we're going to look into. And Terence.' Paul fiddled with the edge of Juliet's mousepad. I resisted the urge to tell him to stop, aware the reminder of how precious Juliet was about her things would fuel childish rearranging. 'Can you talk me through the day of the shooting?'

I took a calming breath, which had the opposite effect when my shoulder throbbed. 'I arrived at the courthouse with Juliet. We were early, so waited outside for the others for a while before going in.'

'Was there anyone outside who caught your eye?'

Any memories of the wide plaza in front of the courthouse before the trial had been obliterated by the carnage afterwards. 'I can't recall anyone.'

'Was there anyone unusual inside the courthouse?' Paul asked.

'Jordan Haines and Leo Dunlow were sitting together, which was odd. Jordan beat up Leo during the investigation into who killed Melanie Pirt, so it was a shock to see them together. Other than that, I didn't notice anyone acting strangely.'

Paul stared at me for a beat. 'Take your time,' he said eventually, 'but can you tell me about the shooting itself?'

I bit my lip. I'd avoided thinking about this. I wasn't sure anything I remembered would be useful, but even the smallest detail could help solve a case.

'Myself, Juliet, Madison Campbell, Alice To, and James Knowles left the courthouse a few minutes after the main crowd. There were journalists outside and none of us wanted to talk to them.'

'Wise.'

'Leo and Jordan hung back as well, along with Ida Pirt and her friend Evie.' I frowned. 'I'm not sure we took her surname.'

Paul chuckled. 'Maybe she's like Madonna.'

'Same energy.' Ida Pirt, Melanie's grandmother, was rarely unaccompanied by her waspish neighbour. 'They left before us. When we went out onto the plaza, there was the usual amount of foot traffic passing by.'

'Did anyone stand out?'

'No. I saw nothing to indicate what was about to happen.' I suppressed a shudder. It would only make my shoulder clash with pain and wouldn't alleviate the chill inside of me.

I had to soldier through this. If I couldn't talk about the shooting, there was no way Paul would let me help find the perpetrator.

'What were you doing when the first shot was fired?' he nudged.

I pressed my lips together. My recollection of what had happened wasn't clear. I'd encountered these memory gaps with witnesses reeling in shock. It was a reasonable response to trauma, but I hadn't expected to be so unreliable.

'I was looking across the road,' I said. 'I'd planned to go for a meal with Ollie after the verdict was passed. He was trying to cross, but there was a lot of traffic.'

Ollie's smile when he spotted me morphed into tearstained horror as Alice held him and Artie back.

'Gabe?' Paul's face pinched with sympathy. 'Are you alright to carry on?'

'I'm fine.' Despite the sharp stab through my shoulder, I straightened my back. 'I initially thought the first gunshot was a backfiring car, but then Juliet dropped her phone and I realised something was wrong.'

I didn't tell Paul I'd panicked when I thought it was innocent. He didn't need to know my mind had taken to playing tricks on me since Karl Biss's arrest, loud noises sending my heart into overdrive.

'Did you notice where the gunshot came from?'

I hadn't thought to look. 'No. I didn't understand the nature of the situation until I saw blood on Juliet's top.'

The white cotton, staining with crimson.

'What did you do between discovering Juliet had been shot and when you were injured?'

Blush flooded my cheeks. 'Nothing. Alice and James were far more efficient than me, and Maddy was asking what was going on. All I did was stare as Juliet fell.'

Her face, always so controlled, draining of colour. Her eyes rolling. Her mouth slack.

'Hey.' The word was sharp. 'You work closely with Juliet and she gives off an aura of invulnerability. If anyone had a right to be blown away by what happened, it was you.'

I didn't need pity after proving to be useless in a life-or-death situation, but Paul was right. I'd seen members of the public gravely injured and I'd never been paralysed before. Seeing a detective I revered compromised had knocked me.

'Did you notice anything unusual after you were shot?' Paul's voice was gentle once more. It was strange to experience prolonged kindness in this room. The most Juliet managed was a single sentence of encouragement before she was back on her emails or snapping at someone on the phone. 'Maddy gave a witness statement earlier today. She said you didn't lose consciousness straight away.'

No, I didn't. There was more than enough time before I blacked out for images to imprint on my brain.

James performing CPR on Juliet's seemingly lifeless body. The desperation of people running away. Ollie's mouth curving around one sound over and over. Artie's flashing teeth.

'Nothing helpful.'

'Have you got everything you need?' Superintendent Angela Dobson asked as she marched through the door. I felt particularly scruffy next to her starched shirt and pressed black trousers. Her hair fell in carefully maintained cornrows down the centre of her broad back.

I twisted, and couldn't contain a groan. Two sets of eyes snapped my way, stormy grey and deep brown. A curl of dread licked up my spine.

Paul nodded as he pressed the button on the side of the Dictaphone. 'Yes, ma'am.'

'Good.' Angela waved a hand at me. 'Up you get. I'll arrange for someone to drop you home.'

'You need Angela to get rid of me for you?' I ground out, not moving from my chair. I'd have expected Paul to tell me he didn't want my help, rather than siccing our boss on me.

Paul stood, reaching for his stick. 'Angela asked me to let her know if you dragged yourself into the building. I called her when you came hobbling past.' His face was as immovable as when his sons tried to negotiate a later bedtime. 'You shouldn't be here, Gabe. You can't honestly think it's a good idea to work, not in the state you're in?'

'I can be useful. I can't lead on the investigation, but I should be here.' My face burned fiercely. 'I decide when I'm fit to work.'

'Do you?' Angela asked lightly.

Shame spread heat down my neck. 'I'm fine, ma'am.'

'You're not fine.' Angela clasped her hands, her uniform whispering as she rested her arms on top of her stomach. 'You were shot yesterday. You need time off to recover, and then a discussion will be had between yourself and occupational health over whether you are fit to return to desk duties.' She shook her head. 'There's no way you can be involved in the investigation into your own shooter anyway. It would compromise it completely.'

I'd been convinced the station was the right place for me to be and that my help on the case would be welcomed. Perhaps that was a sign my mind was addled by the medication I'd been pumped full of at hospital. We never let people consult on cases too close to home. It clouded their judgement and ran the risk that any evidence they gathered could be called into question due to personal bias.

'Fine.' I recognised defeat when staring it in the face. 'I can't be involved in that case, but what about the other one? Maddy mentioned a missing person.' I looked to Paul. 'You and Nicole were already going to be overworked covering the shooting and all your ongoing cases. You can't tell me you wouldn't appreciate me taking a new one off your hands.'

I bit my lip as his eyes darted to Angela. It may not be conventional to return to work less than twenty-four hours after being shot, but I couldn't sit at home with nothing but vague updates to keep me company. At least if I was here, I would know how the investigation into the shooting was going. I'd be around if Paul needed my opinion on a suspect or evidence.

'It would help, ma'am,' Paul said, twisting his stick from side to side.

Angela glared at him, then me. 'Up,' she commanded. 'You can work exclusively on the missing persons case. You'll be on light duties. No long days. But you can start in the morning. I will not have it said that one of my detectives didn't even have a full day off after they were bloody well shot before they were back at work.'

I stood up, my smile flickering as cramps spiked down my arm. 'Thank you, ma'am.'

Angela's face twisted with unwelcome sympathy. 'Go home and rest, Gabe.'

'I will.'

I jerked my head at her once but ignored Paul as I walked out of the office. He might have supported me taking over the missing persons case, but he was the reason I hadn't had a minute to look over the files around the shooting before I was turfed out.

Maddy was absent from her desk, so I didn't have to explain my abrupt departure. Eyes that had been trained on me as I crossed the floor earlier were lowered as I traipsed slowly to the lift. I wondered if they'd heard Angela's dismissal and reluctant invitation, who else she'd had posed to look out for my premature return to work.

I slumped when the lift doors shut. Breathing shallowly, I leant against the wall and carefully tilted my head back.

Investigating a missing person would be distracting, but I wasn't as cold as Juliet about cases other than the one I was primarily focused on. I would do everything I could to return them to their loved ones. Their disappearance had provided an excuse to be at the station, but not one I was glad of. It was cruel to view someone else's misfortune as a bright silver lining.

I would use lulls in the case as a chance to peek at the one I burned to launch into. It was unethical to be involved in finding my own shooter, but I didn't have to be meshed in the case to look over it. I was a victim and a detective; uniquely positioned to give insight into what happened yesterday afternoon.

One person would support me. Juliet might be stuck in hospital for now, but she would want to know what progress I'd made as soon as she got out. I couldn't let her down. I wouldn't.

From: Paul Willis **paul.willis@mit.gov.uk**
To: James Knowles **james.knowles@police.gov.uk**
CC: Nicole Stewart **nicole.stewart@mit.gov.uk**
Date: **25 April, 16:32**
Subject: **Operation Orion – Dunlows**

James,

You probably remember that Timothy, Terence, and Leonard Dunlow were persons of interest during Operation Chalice. As Melanie Pirt was murdered with a similar gun to the one used to shoot Gabe and Juliet just after Karl Biss's trial closed, it's worth checking Timothy and his sons weren't involved in Gabe and Juliet's shooting.

Can you please find the Dunlows' last known address and contact numbers? I'll also need the registration paperwork for their guns, including where they're stored and when they were last used. Contact the shooting ranges around the city to see if the Dunlows have visited at all.

Also, please contact the Prison Liaison Officer wherever Karl was being held prior to trial. Find out if the Dunlows visited him or if he communicated with anyone unusual. And can you start the process of getting a chat in the diary?

Thanks,

Paul

'Hello, Lock It Up Locksmiths. Frank speaking.'

'Hi. My name's Keith Stern. I need a new lock for my flat. It's urgent.'

'That's definitely something I can do. Let me have a quick look at my diary. I can pop over early this evening? I'm finishing up a job now, but could be with you in an hour or so.'

'That's great. Can you come collect the current key? I'm at the hospital. My wife was shot.'

'God. I'm sorry to hear that, mate.'

'She's pulling through, but that's the reason we need the locks changed. We have to make sure no one has access to our home.'

'Of course. Is this a good number to reach you on when I'm outside the hospital?'

'Yes, this is fine. The only reason I wouldn't pick up is if I'm talking with a doctor.'

'I don't have anything after you, so don't worry about it. I'll need ID to prove you own the property. Do you have anything like that with you?'

'I only grabbed my keys before I came here, but I've got my wife's driving licence. Is that alright?'

'That's fine, mate. I'll see you later, and good luck to your missus.'

Teddy. Sent 17:27.

I hope you're having fun x

Benny. Sent 17:28.

It's been lovely so far. How are you? x

Teddy. Sent 17:28.

Fine. Missing you x

Benny. Sent 17:30.

I miss you too, but this came at the right time. We both needed a break x

Teddy. Sent 17:30.

You needed one more than me. I've been a mess recently. I don't know what's wrong with me x

Benny. Sent 17:33.

Take some time to look after yourself. I've got a
couple more days here. Being apart will give us the
head space to think clearly about things. I have to
go. Dinner is on its way x

Teddy. Sent 17:33.

Okay. I love you. I'll try to be better x

Gabe

I woke in a groggy state of half-awareness, but full consciousness shoved into me when I stretched. Pain erupted from my shoulder. My eyes snapped open and I stilled, blinking against the fuzziness of drug-induced slumber.

I'd gotten home and remained upright long enough to down water and the strongest painkillers to hand. Ollie hadn't commented on the pathetic amount of time I'd spent at the station when he'd picked me up, then he'd fended off Artie so I could fall into bed without the help of an enthusiastic Alsatian.

I must have fallen asleep as soon as I'd lowered myself onto the soft surface. Ollie hadn't tried to move the duvet from under me. The thick blanket we'd bought from IKEA a couple of weeks ago was draped over the uninjured parts of my body.

My eyes trailed over the blind that let in too much light from the streetlamp outside, the chest of drawers topped with random scents Mum had given me and a pile of Ollie's clothes, the dying plant on my bedside table being kept from its ultimate fate by my sporadic attempts to care for it. This was a damn sight better than waking up in a hospital bed.

Ollie had tucked the blanket away from my injured shoulder, the bandaging a soft lump under my T-shirt. I wondered when I'd be able to remove the dressing. I wanted to see this clean shot, which felt more like the bullet had torn viciously through me.

Ollie appeared in the doorway, a steaming bowl in his hand and Artie peering around his knees. 'Are you awake enough for soup and company?'

'I think so.' If sleep abruptly claimed me again, Ollie would stop me faceplanting into my dinner.

He left the bowl on my bedside table and went to the kitchen for bread and butter, something he'd informed me was non-negotiable the first time we'd eaten soup together. My movements awkward to avoid stretching my shoulder again, I levered myself up to sit against the headboard. I angled to the right to avoid pressing my wound into the unforgiving wood.

Artie snuffled across the room and leant his head on my knee. Six months ago, he hadn't understood how to live inside a house. He'd tolerated sleeping beside the front door and bolted every time he got the chance. As he became comfortable with me and Ollie, he discovered the joys of carpet and my blanket-laden sofa. I couldn't be sure if Artie was in my bedroom now because he wanted to impart comfort or because he was eyeing up my bed.

'Hey, boy.' I reached over with my good arm to card my fingers through the soft fur behind his ears. 'I'm home now. I'm okay.'

'Glad to hear it.' Ollie walked back into the room and lowered himself onto the other side of the bed, settling a tray on his lap. His bowl of soup steamed beside thick slabs of bread slathered with butter. 'Oh, shit.'

He jumped up when he realised my soup was on the wrong side for me to grab it with ease, placing it gently onto my lap. Helplessness wasn't pleasant, but Ollie made it easier. He was certainly more tolerable than the nurse at the hospital. I'd take Ollie over a pretty stranger any day.

'You're the best boyfriend.' I blamed my soppiness on the combination of exhaustion, drugs, and pain fogging my mind.

'You're easy to please.' Ollie passed me a slice of bread. 'And you don't exactly have much of a subject pool to compare me to.'

'Don't need one.' I wiggled my fingers at Artie's nose when he sniffed hopefully at my dinner. 'Homemade soup and bread is top tier partner behaviour.'

Ollie insisted my opinion didn't count since my diet before we started dating consisted of takeaways and cereal. I didn't know how he stayed so slim with such quantities of delicious food on offer. His stomach was toned and his thighs pure muscle, always shown to great advantage at his photo shoots. Ollie assured me that while I worked, he adhered to a strict gym regimen that allowed for copious cheese eating.

We were quiet while we ate, the warm vegetables and creamy butter perfect after the dry toast and bright orange jelly offered at the hospital. I wondered how Juliet was coping. She wasn't picky, often too distracted to pay attention to what she was consuming, but surely even she would balk at the bland choices on the ward.

Maybe she wasn't eating yet. Juliet lost more blood than me. Her wound was clean too, but the decade or so she had on me meant her healing would be slower. Keith didn't think Juliet was up to visitors earlier today. Perhaps she couldn't manage sustenance either.

As we neared the end of our meal, my movements became sluggish. I slumped lopsidedly against the headboard while Ollie stacked the bowls and set them on his bedside table. We'd picked it up at a charity shop. My initial furniture purchases when I'd started renting hadn't included the luxury of two bedside tables. No one stuck around long enough to justify more than one.

'This is ridiculous. I slept most of the morning and again just now. How can I be so tired?'

'Gabe, you were shot.' Ollie lifted the blanket and helped me lay down underneath. 'That's going to take a while to recover from.'

I blinked up at him. 'You alright?'

He huffed a half-laugh, covering his face. 'Oh fuck.' The bed juddered with his uneven breaths. 'Fuck, Gabe. You were shot.'

I used my good arm to tug him down beside me. Ollie turned his face into my chest and shook with sobs. As well as I could, I held him close. I threaded my fingers through his hair and pressed my lips to his forehead.

'I'm so sorry you had to see that,' I said, once his tears subsided into irregular hiccups. 'It must have been awful.'

Ollie propped himself up on one elbow and mopped his face on the blanket. 'It must have been awful to see it? What about you? You had to live it.'

I shrugged, then instantly regretted it. Ollie's nose scrunched with sympathy as I grimaced through the pain. 'It wasn't much fun,' I ground out.

Ollie gazed down at me, his brows creased. 'Artie was going mad and Alice was screaming at me to clear off, but I didn't want to leave. You could have been dying and I didn't want to have one less moment with you than I could.'

'Ollie.' I pulled him close.

I felt the same. As I'd laid on the pavement and drifted away, my last thought had been of him.

36

'I looked at you,' I whispered, Ollie's nose pressing into my neck. 'I could see you shouting as I passed out.'

'I was screaming your name.' Ollie hooked his leg over mine. His tears trickled across my skin. 'Don't know what good I thought it would do. I just wanted you. Didn't want you to go.'

I blinked against the sharp sting behind my eyelids. 'I'm here.'

A soft sob wracked through him. I held him closer, my leg threading through his, trying to convey that if there was a way to keep myself here with him, that was always the option I'd take.

His breathing evened out and his arm across my stomach grew lax. I thought he was sleeping when he said, 'Do you want to call your parents?'

My eyes shot open. Months ago, I'd changed my next of kin to Ollie. I'd told him it made sense for someone nearby to be the first point of contact if anything happened to me.

I couldn't voice that removing my parents as my emergency contact had been a weight off my mind. I loved my mum and dad, but their reaction to any hint of threat caused by my job was maddeningly predictable.

They'd rush down here. They'd coddle me. They'd hide me away from the world so I could never be hurt again.

I brushed my fingers through Ollie's hair. 'I'll chat to them tomorrow.'

I wouldn't keep my injury from my parents, but I'd wait to tell them. When I was stronger and could fight off the stifling nature of their love.

Since Barnabas died, my parents had showered me with the attention and affection meant for two. It was suffocating, the pressure of being the only child left alive.

STUPID BITCH IS AS STUPID BITCH DOES

DETECTIVE REFUSES TO COMMENT ON VIOLENT BURGLARY

Detective Sergeant Juliet Stern was spotted leaving the site of a violent burglary in the early hours of yesterday morning. Blagden's has been conducting business in Southampton for the last eighty years, providing bespoke suits and evening wear for men. Three days ago the owner, Humphrey Winman, was knocked unconscious as he locked up for the night. His attackers proceeded to vandalise the shop and stole several thousands of pounds' worth of materials and finished garments.

On being asked for an update on the victim and the police operation, Stern told reporters to get out of the way. She said, 'You're useless, and you're stopping me from doing my job.'

I HOPE YOU CHOKE

MISSING PERSON

Appeal for information

HENRY GARSIDE

Henry was last seen on 24 April at ten a.m. leaving Solent University campus.

Aged nineteen, 5'8 tall, slim build, short blond hair, brown eyes, and a tattoo of a wave on the inside of his left wrist.

Henry was last seen wearing a red Solent University hoodie and dark blue jeans.

Henry is a keen art student, and his friends and family are eager to make contact.

If you've seen or heard from Henry since 24 April, please call the number below. If you see Henry, please ask him to get in touch with the local police as soon as possible.

Henry is not considered dangerous to members of the public.

Day 2

Sunday, 26 April

TWO DAYS ON AND NO LEADS – DETECTIVES LEADING THE CASE TO FIND THE SHOOTER OF TWO OF THEIR OWN ARE STUMPED…

Scroll.

COULD THERE BE A LINK? – KNOWN GUNMAN KARL BISS WAS SENTENCED MINUTES BEFORE TWO OFFICERS WERE SHOT…

Scroll.

WHAT PROTECTION IS IN PLACE? – DETECTIVE INSPECTOR PAUL WILLIS CLAIMS THIS WAS A CALCULATED ATTACK, SO HOW DO OTHER OFFICERS KNOW THEY WON'T BE NEXT…

Scroll.

Mum. Sent 8:32.

Hello, love. How are you? I was catching up on the news and saw that two police officers in Southampton have been shot. I hope it wasn't anyone you know and that they're okay. I'm praying for them xxxx

Gabe. Sent 8:40.

Thanks, Mum. Really busy trying to catch who did it. Talk soon x

Mum. Sent 8:41.

I'm here whenever you want to chat. Love you xxxx

Gabe. Sent 8:43.

Love you too x

13th February

Dear Mrs Stern,

Re: Child Arrangements

Thank you for coming in for a preliminary meeting on 4th February. I am writing to provide a summary of my advice following that meeting.

Background

The written background you provided ahead of our meeting was incredibly helpful. We discussed the ways in which Mr Stern's behaviour has been mentally and physically abusive toward you. We also discussed how Mr Stern is attempting to damage your relationship with your daughters by giving them false information about you.

Advice

Where it is safe to do so, the Court is keen for parties to reach an agreement outside of Court via mediation or negotiation with solicitors. As we discussed that it is not likely you and Mr Stern will be able to agree to arrangements for your daughters, one option will be for you to apply to the Family Court for a Child Arrangements Order. A Judge will direct where your daughters should live and the extent of contact they should have with their non-resident parent.

I understand you consider it would be in your daughters' best interests if the Court directed that they live with you full time, and any contact with Mr Stern be limited and/or supervised because of the concerns you've raised. However, it is the duty of the Judge to act in the best interests of your daughters, taking into account all of the facts before making a decision. While we can ask the Judge to make a particular order, there is no guarantee as to what the Judge will decide.

To present the strongest case possible, I advise you to keep a diary of all interactions Mr Stern has with you and your daughters. If it becomes necessary to apply to the Court for a Child Arrangements Order, you will then have a detailed record of incidents that demonstrate the harm and/or risk of harm Mr Stern poses to your daughters, either psychologically or physically.

I enclose my letter of engagement and our terms and conditions of business, which contain further explanation of my services and the potential costs and timescales. Please review, sign, and return these documents if you wish to instruct me to advise and assist further.

I suggest we meet again in three months' time to discuss your next steps, but please do not hesitate to get in touch if you have any questions.

Yours sincerely,

Missy Toon

Hart and New Solicitors

Gabe

Light drizzle dampened my face as I stepped out of Alice's car, making me wish I'd done up the coat I'd borrowed from Ollie since mine had been taken as evidence. It swamped me but I felt less like a child trying on their parents' clothes with the buttons open. Then the shape of my body wasn't lost to its bulk.

Alice and I hurried toward the reception of the Travelodge I'd stayed in for a few nights when I'd first moved down here. I ran a hand through my hair as I stepped into the familiar foyer, the movement twinging my shoulder. I'd dosed myself with paracetamol this morning after enduring Ollie's help with a sponge bath, feeling more like a patient than a girlfriend.

'I'll step in if you need support,' Alice whispered. She'd said variations of this on repeat the whole way over to our first interview of the day.

Our friendship had a rocky start. As the months passed and Maddy insisted Alice was fun, if in a heavy-handed way, I'd warmed to the young police constable. It was Alice I'd asked for help planning a special date for Ollie and it was my front door she'd turned up at when she found out she'd failed the detective's exam.

She'd practically been bouncing when I arrived at the station, bursting with the news she would be my partner on the missing persons case. I remembered what it was like to be ready to take on a different level of police work. I couldn't begrudge her excitement, but it meant I didn't have a minute to look over the shooting case before a quick run through of the missing persons investigation and we headed out to talk to Henry Garside's parents.

Alice trailed her fingers over her neat black hair, captured in a bun at the nape of her neck, as we waited for a lanky receptionist to finish discussing breakfast options with the family ahead of us. Alice's slim frame was bulked out by her uniform's padded vest. I didn't feel as scruffy next to her as I did Juliet. Ollie had helped me into a pair of chinos and a green jumper he said helped bring out the returning colour of my skin.

As the family moved on, I took a deep breath. I hadn't stepped up since Melanie Pirt's murder. That was an investigation full of twists and lies, which my inexperience and assumptions had slowed down. We'd found her killer, but I'd almost allowed him to escape due to misplaced compassion.

I'd learnt from that case. I didn't jump to conclusions, didn't liken myself too closely to suspects, trusted evidence rather than my gut. I'd been considering taking the lead again. Juliet being out of the picture had thrust it on me.

Flashing my ID badge in case Alice's uniform didn't make it clear who we were, I stepped up to the reception desk. 'Hello, I'm Detective Sergeant Gabe Martin. I believe you've set aside a corner of the dining room for us to speak to Mr and Mrs Garside?'

Usually, we would ask for a private room to discuss anything this sensitive. Maddy said Henry's parents were adamant that one of the hotel's largest public spaces was the right place to meet us.

The receptionist's eyes widened as he looked down the foot and a half he had on us. He hurried around the desk, the black curls perched on top of his head held static with crisp gel. 'Follow me.'

The hotel had been refurbished since my stay. Scuffed carpets had been replaced with laminate wood and the walls papered with subtle floral patterns. The receptionist led us through double doors to a large dining room. One side was taken up with a breakfast buffet, the platters of fruit and pastries being cleared by a waiter. Groups chattered as they finished off rashers of bacon and toast that I knew from experience could never be coaxed to the perfect shade of golden brown in the self-service machine.

An older couple sat in a far corner the receptionist held a hand toward. The woman's wrinkled white face betrayed the years her dyed brown bob tried to deny. The straight strands brushed the shoulders of a mustard jumper paired with bright red trousers. Orange framed glasses perched on the tip of her nose gave her the air of an eccentric headmistress, the effect deepening when she spotted us and her eyebrows lowered.

She whispered in her husband's ear. He'd been gazing out of a window, but all vacancy was packed away as he stood up from an electric wheelchair. He gripped one armrest, his back bowed as he glowered at us. White hair covered the sides of his head, leaving the pink top bald. His clothes complemented his wife's; a burgundy cardigan buttoned over a yellow shirt tucked into brown trousers.

He pointed a shaking finger at us. 'Who are you?'

I paused beside the table, checking my ID was on show. 'I'm Detective Sergeant Gabe Martin. This is Police Constable Alice To. I was told you were expecting us?'

Henry's father sat down, the skin around his eyes pinching as he settled his weight. 'We expected the detective we talked to yesterday. Not you.'

His wife rested a hand adorned with glinting rings on his arm. 'What Jude's trying to say is that we're surprised to see you here, rather than your colleague.'

'We know how this works,' Jude grumbled. 'You lot have decided Henry's disappearance doesn't need to be taken seriously. You're going to pass us from detective to detective, give lip service to finding him while you focus on flashier cases.'

I pulled out the chair opposite him and nodded for Alice to take the final seat at the square table. 'Nicole, who you spoke to yesterday, handled the initial stages of the missing persons investigation for your son. It's not unusual, after that point, for the case to be allocated to another detective.' I held Mr Garside's gaze as he breathed heavily through his nose. 'I promise that as a team we're taking the search for Henry incredibly seriously. I will personally be leading the investigation into his disappearance from now on, and I'll do everything I can to find him.'

Henry's father relaxed into the padded seat of the wheelchair, his wife raising a thin smile as she squeezed his arm. Neither seemed to notice that while I'd assured them I would do my best to find their son, I'd made no promises about whether that was likely. The number of missing people across the country was shocking to those blissfully unaware of the hordes who slipped away from their everyday lives, never to be seen again.

I pulled my notebook out of the pocket of Ollie's coat and placed it on the edge of the table. 'I know you've gone through a lot of this with Nicole already, but I want to make sure I have the whole picture. Can you please tell me your full names and what you do?'

Alice shifted beside me but kept quiet. Nicole had taken meticulous notes during her initial interviews with Henry's parents and his one close friend at university, but it was best to ease into the tougher elements I'd have to approach. Henry's parents were already hostile, convinced they understood the inner workings of the force after watching one too many TV series. I didn't want to alienate them by jumping in with probing questions about their son's mental health and the probability he would have absconded without saying a word.

'My name's Sheridan Garside.' Henry's mother dropped her hand from her husband's arm as she turned toward me. 'I work in our local M&S and volunteer at the library.'

'And yourself?' I tipped my biro toward Henry's father.

'Jude Garside. I don't work.'

He didn't elaborate. I looked down at my scribbled line of notes to avoid his heavy gaze. The one thing I was meant to be able to do without Juliet's support was build rapport with victims' friends and family. I couldn't assume Jude's unemployment was linked to his use of a wheelchair, but I should have realised I was storming into tactless territory Juliet usually occupied alone. I wondered if his reluctance to meet us elsewhere was linked to his limited mobility, but I'd leave the tally of thoughtless questions at one for today.

'Tell me about Henry.' I sat back from the table, sliding my notepad onto my knee. 'What's he like?'

A genuine smile spread across Sheridan's face. 'He's a lovely boy. Our only child. We had him when we were in our late forties. He was the most wonderful surprise.'

'He did well at school,' Jude added. 'He wasn't popular but wasn't bullied either. Left alone for the most part.'

'Did he enjoy art when he was younger?' I asked.

'Oh, yes.' His mum's face brightened. 'We took him to galleries each school holiday and he always asked for paints and pencils for his birthday. All he wanted to do was draw and create. He painted such beautiful things even when he was small.'

'We were surprised when he came down here to study,' Jude said. 'He hates the sea.'

Sheridan tsked. 'He doesn't hate it, Jude. He's explained this to you a hundred times.' She turned her exasperated gaze on me. 'Jude was desperate for Henry to study near home. There's a few universities nearer Surrey. Henry did apply to them, but he didn't tell us he'd

48

gone for Southampton as well. We were shocked when he accepted the place here, as he's always been afraid of water. When he was little, he refused to sit in the bath. Insisted on taking showers. He begged me to write a note to get him out of swimming lessons at school. But he explained it to us. He was tired of being afraid. On his eighteenth birthday, he got a tattoo on his wrist of a wave. He was determined to overcome his fear. That's why he came down here, to draw the sea and to show himself it was more than the horrible thing he'd built it up to in his head.'

'He sounds like an exceptional young man,' Alice said.

Sheridan beamed at her, and Jude raised a reluctant smile. 'He is,' he said gruffly. 'I might not like him being over an hour away, but his reasons for studying here show a strength of spirit not many young men his age have.'

'Was he enjoying himself down here?' I asked, piggybacking on the connection Alice had established with one simple statement. She might not be Juliet, but a tightness in my chest eased. I wasn't heading into this investigation solo.

'He was. He still feared water, but he wasn't as terrified as he'd once been.' Jude looked to the window, as though he could see the coastline rather than the brickwork of another building. 'He was doing well on his course. He liked where he was staying. He'd made a friend.'

'You said he wasn't popular at school?' I nudged closer to trickier questions.

'He wasn't,' Sheridan conceded, 'but he wasn't bothered by it. All he wanted to do was make art. Having lots of friends would get in the way.'

'He's friends with Rowan because the young lad is as into his painting as Henry,' Jude said. 'They've already been chatting about opening a gallery together when they graduate, or travelling and making art as they go.'

'That's why Henry wouldn't have wandered off,' Sheridan said, losing the fondness warming her voice. 'Having a piece in this local gallery meant so much to him. He wouldn't have missed that without a good reason.'

I flicked to a new page in my notepad. The tone of the conversation had shifted naturally, but exploring all the reasons Henry could have gone missing was no less unpleasant. 'Was Henry purely excited about having his work displayed publicly? He wasn't nervous?'

'He had a natural amount of nerves.' Jude's eyes fixed on me.

'Would you say Henry was generally happy?' I pressed on. 'He didn't have many close friends. Was he lonely?'

'He didn't want lots of friends,' Sheridan stated, gaze cold behind her glasses. 'He was perfectly happy.'

Wariness rose from Henry's parents in waves. I pressed my lips together. I'd worked missing persons cases with Juliet. Normally, she was the battering ram while I built a connection with concerned loved ones. Alice was too inexperienced to take on either role. She might chime in with helpful comments, but I couldn't expect her to ask the bulk of the questions or tempt Henry's parents' ire.

'I hope you understand I'm not jumping to any conclusions,' I said gently. 'When a person goes missing, we have to investigate whether their disappearance had anything to do with their mental state.'

'Henry's mental state was fine. Good,' Jude growled.

'That's not what you need to focus on.' Sheridan clasped her hands together on the table. 'Please, listen to what we're saying. We spoke to Henry the night before he went missing.'

'And he was fine,' Jude interrupted. 'Excited to go to the gallery the next morning.'

'Exactly.' Sheridan's eyes were wide, tears pooling above her short lashes. 'Displaying his work meant the world to him. He wouldn't have missed that unless something terrible happened.'

Jude gripped the wheelchair's armrests. 'You need to stop thinking about what Henry might have done. We know our son. He wouldn't have run off or hurt himself.' He sniffed, shaking his head. 'The only reason he missed going to the gallery, the only reason he's still gone now, is because someone has done something to him. You need to get your head out of your arse and find who's taken our son.'

This form is signed to confirm that the patient – Juliet Stern – has had her condition explained – bullet wound to left shoulder that resulted in significant blood loss – and doctors have made it clear it is strongly against their wishes that she would discharge herself at this time. Doctors have made it clear that should she experience any adverse symptoms – such as dizziness, blurriness in her vision and loss of consciousness – she should call an ambulance and return to hospital immediately.

Attached to this form are instructions for pain medication. The patient is strongly advised to keep her arm immobilised in a sling until a medical professional deems it no longer necessary.

Signed by patient: Juliet Stern

Attending doctor: Dr Pranav King

Date: 26th April

Detective Sergeant Nicole Stewart: Informal interview commencing at 11:05 a.m. on the 26th April. This interview is regarding the shooting of Detective Inspector Juliet Stern and Detective Sergeant Gabriella Martin on the afternoon of the 24th April. This interview is being conducted by myself, Detective Sergeant Nicole Stewart, and Detective Inspector Paul Willis at Tsambikos Galanis's home. The interviewees are Alcaeus, Tsambikos, and Giannis Galanis. None of you are under caution and you are free to stop the interview at any time. Thank you for agreeing to this interview.

Detective Inspector Paul Willis: Alcaeus, Tsambikos, and Giannis, please tell us your movements on the 24th April.

Tsambikos Galanis: As I've said to you and your colleagues before; let's dispense with the formalities. Please call me Tsam.

DI Paul Willis: Mr Galanis, please tell us your movements on the 24th April.

Tsambikos Galanis: Obstinacy is such an unattractive quality, Paul.

DS Nicole Stewart: Could you please answer the question?

Tsambikos Galanis: Very well. My brothers can attest that we were all at a spa for the entirety of the day.

Giannis Galanis: That's right.

DI Paul Willis: Where is this spa?

Tsambikos Galanis: It's one of ours. I'll have my assistant send over the details.

DS Nicole Stewart: What time did you go to the spa? When did you leave?

Tsambikos Galanis: We stayed at the attached hotel the night before. We'd had good luck with the horses, so went out to celebrate. My brothers' partners don't appreciate it when I bring them home worse for wear, so we went to the hotel to sober up. It only seemed right to make use of the spa the next day. We needed to re-beautify ourselves, and what's the point of owning a spa if you never use it?

52

DI Paul Willis: So your stay at the spa was impromptu?

Tsambikos Galanis: It certainly was. Have you ever needed a special day for yourself? It looks like one is overdue for the two of you. I'll have my assistant send over a few spa passes. On the house, of course.

DI Paul Willis: That won't be necessary. While you were at the spa, did you make any calls or send any messages?

Tsambikos Galanis: My brothers and I run a great number of businesses. Not a day goes by when we aren't contacted by some employee or another. On the day you're so interested in, we each made several calls. Nothing you need to worry about. Nothing that would lead to the injury of two upstanding officers of the law. I've become fond of Gabriella and Juliet during our acquaintance. I was distraught to hear they'd been hurt.

DS Nicole Stewart: When did you find out Detectives Martin and Stern had been shot?

Tsambikos Galanis: After we left the spa, I went home alone. I don't like to watch the news before bed as I find it interrupts my sleep cycle. I read the unfortunate news in the papers yesterday morning.

DS Nicole Stewart: And you, Alcaeus? Giannis?

Alcaeus Galanis: I heard about it in the morning too.

Giannis Galanis: Same.

DI Paul Willis: What did you do when you heard the news?

Tsambikos Galanis: I checked for the latest information, which told me that although Gabriella and Juliet had been injured, they were expected to make a full recovery. Then I finished my coffee. Went for a shower. Should I go on?

DS Nicole Stewart: It must be convenient for you that the two detectives running an investigation into your family's possible criminal activities were incapacitated. You didn't celebrate?

Tsambikos Galanis: How incredibly crass. Gabriella and Juliet's injuries would only be convenient if I or my brothers had anything to hide. We don't. Like I've told our absent friends countless times during our little chats, I'm an open book. I was deeply saddened by what happened to them.

Giannis Galanis: Tsam cancelled a couple of meetings that morning. He was shook up.

Tsambikos Galanis: Exactly. I imagine it must be terrible to be shot at and have no clue why. Which must be the case, since you're spending your no doubt valuable time talking to us.

DI Paul Willis: I see. It wasn't that Detectives Martin and Stern were close to uncovering something, and you needed them out of the way?

Tsambikos Galanis: What could they possibly have been getting closer to? As I said, my brothers and I have nothing to hide. We have been accommodating of all of Gabriella and Juliet's incorrectly directed investigations.

DS Nicole Stewart: It's suspected that you and your brothers head up a series of criminal activities across Hampshire. Human trafficking being primary amongst them. Had Detectives Stern and Martin made too much of a nuisance of themselves, and you needed them gone?

Tsambikos Galanis: What a lot of nonsense. My brothers and I are legitimate businessmen who do not enjoy being baselessly accused of wrongdoing. I think, if you don't have any other questions for us, we'll be getting on with our day.

DS Nicole Stewart: You've refused this request before, but we would like to take DNA samples from you all.

Tsambikos Galanis: I will tell you what I've told Gabriella and Juliet on numerous occasions; my brothers and I will not submit to invasions of our privacy without just cause. Return with a good reason for extracting our DNA, and we will gladly hand it over. Until then, we'd like to keep sensitive information off the police database.

DI Paul Willis: Before we leave, I wanted to warn you that we don't take the shooting of our colleagues lightly. If you thought you were under a spotlight before, prepare yourselves for much more rigorous questioning and surveillance if we get any hint you were involved.

Tsambikos Galanis: Your nonsensical warning is duly noted. If you want to waste time and money on pursuing three men who have clear alibis and no good reason to want to hurt Gabriella and Juliet, then have at it. Please pass on my well wishes. Good day.

Regulation of Investigatory Powers Act 2000 – section 32

REQUEST FOR INTRUSIVE SURVEILLANCE

REQUESTING OFFICERS:

Detective Inspector Paul Willis and Detective Sergeant Nicole Stewart

CASE NUMBER:

87049375

CASE DESCRIPTION:

Non-fatal shooting of Detective Inspector Juliet Stern and Detective Sergeant Gabriella Martin on 24 April near Southampton Crown Court

INDIVIDUAL/S FOR SURVEILLANCE:

Tsambikos Galanis, Alcaeus Galanis, and Giannis Galanis

REASON FOR SURVEILLANCE:

Detective Inspector Juliet Stern and Detective Sergeant Gabriella Martin were heading up the major crimes task force Operation Juno initiated after the discovery of a human trafficking ring last October. Over the course of their investigations, they identified Tsambikos, Alcaeus, and Giannis Galanis as the most likely heads of the organised crime group that spearheaded this human trafficking ring. It's likely the Galanis brothers lashed out at Detectives Martin and Stern due to the investigation. We would like to have the brothers' movements monitored, as this may shed light on both their involvement in the shooting and their suspected leadership of other criminal activities.

Gabe

Hazel from Student Services unlocked Henry's room and dropped a wedge between the door and frame. 'Without that, the door would lock every time it closes. Safety precaution.' She stepped back. 'I'll leave you to it, but if you need anything give me a shout. Please drop the keys off at my office when you're done.'

Before I could thank her, she scurried away down the narrow corridor. I exchanged a look with Alice as we walked into Henry's room. Hazel could not have been keener to escape our presence since we'd knocked on her door. It could have been general nervousness, but a couple of comments she'd made suggested she was anxious the university would be blamed for Henry's disappearance. She'd blinked owlishly when I'd asked if she'd met Henry, her effusive worries about his welfare falling flat after she'd admitted she had not.

The door whispered shut across the carpet tiles behind us, catching on the wooden wedge. I pulled on gloves as I turned full circle in the middle of Henry's room. It was as big as my bedroom, but made more spacious by a single bed pushed under the steamed window. Shelves above Henry's pillow housed thick sketchbooks and arty postcards. A desk and the top of a chest of drawers were littered with pens and pencils. Mugs held a mixture of abandoned tea and paintbrushes resting in murky water.

'It was intense with Henry's parents.' Alice pulled on her gloves.

She'd been quiet on the drive over. More than once, I'd berated Juliet for her ability to instantly brush off the vestiges of anger and sadness victims' loved ones threw at us. I'd not realised before how her callousness helped me take a step back. I would never be as impartial as her, but there were definite benefits to not carrying the emotional load friends and family attempted to pass on.

'They want us to find their son.' I moved to the chest of drawers. 'Do you mind starting in the bathroom?'

Ollie's stories suggested attending university involved sharing washing facilities with more cleaning-averse students than could ever be sanitary, but Henry's room had a cramped ensuite. A luxury that allowed him to sidestep a disgusting rite of passage.

Alice dithered in the doorway. 'Do you think what they said is true? That someone has taken their son?'

'There's no evidence of that at the moment.' I pulled open the top drawer, eyes flicking across piles of black boxers. 'No parent wants to believe their child would leave without saying a word.'

I waited until Alice's boots tapped on the bathroom's laminate floor before I shuffled through Henry's underwear. His parents were desperate for his disappearance to be taken seriously. I didn't know if they were inclined toward exaggeration or would say anything to make sure every possible resource was deployed to find Henry. I didn't doubt they genuinely believed what they'd said, but wondered whether it was based in reality or fiction.

My gloved fingers found nothing but pants and socks in the top drawer, then a mixture of paint-stained T-shirts and crumpled shorts in the second. Jumpers and jeans fought for space in the last. Half a glass of water gathered dust on Henry's bedside table next to a box of tissues. The shallow cupboard underneath was packed with a mismatched jumble of Lynx canisters, spare tubes of paint, and lecture notes. I settled cross-legged on the floor to read them, but they offered no insight into Henry's state of mind other than his preference for writing in capitals.

'This bathroom is surprisingly clean given that its primary user is a nineteen-year-old male,' Alice said.

'Ollie cleans my bathroom.' I rose onto my knees and ducked to look under the bed. My shoulder twinged, but I ignored it. I'd taken paracetamol on the car ride over to keep the worst of the pain at bay. 'He says the shower doesn't automatically clean the tub.'

'He's right,' Alice muttered. 'You animal.'

Underneath Henry's bed was cluttered with large sheets of paper and curling canvases. I pulled them out one by one, piling them in the middle of the floor. They all featured water. Waves lapped at the underside of a boat, the sun dipped behind the sea, crabs sheltered in rockpools.

'He was serious about conquering his fear.' Alice appeared in the bathroom doorway, her dark eyes roving over a peeling canvas.

White-tipped waves crashed into a seawall. She pointed her thumb over her shoulder. 'Zero in here.'

I bent to check I'd pulled out everything from under the bed. 'Nothing in the bin? Or tucked behind the toilet?'

'Nope.' Alice hopped around the pile of Henry's artwork and picked through the clutter on top of his desk. 'No used condoms, drugs, or anything interesting.'

Maybe not everything Henry's parents told us was true, but his focus on his art seemed to be. His room was well lived in, but he didn't seem to have any interests besides creating. My gaze snagged on the pile of art from under the bed. Creating and overcoming his fear. There was a brutality to the water smacking into defences created to contain it.

Careful not to damage anything, I slotted Henry's canvases back under the bed. I stood, cringing at the aches sitting on the floor for less than five minutes had awakened across my body, then lifted Henry's duvet. The cover was patterned with sprigs of lavender, matching the purple sheets across the mattress. I lowered it and picked up one of his pillows.

'Alice?' I set it down in the middle of the bed. 'Have you got an evidence bag handy?'

Bloodstained tissues rested on Henry's bottom pillow. A couple were almost covered in reddish brown. Others had swipes of diminishing thickness.

'Shit.' Alice handed me a clear plastic bag. 'Does this mean he was self-harming?'

Henry's parents' insistence about his steady mental state was weakening. I plucked the tissues from the pillow one by one.

'Can you go over the bathroom again? Look for anything linked to this. Razors, blades, more tissues.'

Alice hurried back into the bathroom. I sealed the evidence bag and wrote the details on the front. The second pillow hid no more secrets underneath.

The dorm room door swished across the carpet tiles. A young man stood in the doorway, one large hand braced against the heavy wood to keep it from swinging shut. A plaid shirt splattered with pinks and blues strained over his broad shoulders. Strawberry blond hair was twisted into a braid that draped around his neck and midway down his chest.

Blue eyes darted from me to the bloodstained tissues set on top of Henry's duvet.

'He gets nosebleeds.' His accent was thick, Scandi.

I pulled off my gloves as I stepped toward him. 'Detective Sergeant Gabe Martin. And you are?'

'Rowan Lough.' His gaze whipped around the room, settling on Alice's uniform as she walked out of the bathroom. 'I'm Henry's friend. Student Services said you were here.'

'Can I ask you a few questions?' As I spoke, Rowan tracked Alice plucking the evidence bag from the bed. She stored it beneath her stab-proof vest.

He swallowed. 'I spoke to the detective yesterday.'

'Did you tell Nicole about Henry's nosebleeds?'

Bright blush spread in circles on his cheeks. 'I didn't think it was relevant.'

I pulled out my notepad. 'His parents didn't mention them.'

The hand against the door bunched into a fist. 'They don't know. Henry loves them, but they worry about him a lot. Too much.'

Recognition flared, but I quashed it. I might be familiar with overbearing parents, but the panicked look hadn't left Rowan's eyes since he'd arrived. He was another person who wanted us to take Henry's disappearance seriously, who would bend or twist the truth to hide ways Henry may have instigated it.

'He told you,' I said.

Rowan dipped his head once. 'I'm his friend.'

'His one friend,' Alice added.

Rowan's brows lowered. 'He has other friends. But we are close.'

'Mr and Mrs Garside said Henry doesn't mind being alone.' I settled a gentle smile on my face. 'They said Henry is focused on his art, and that's why the two of you get along so well.'

My soothing tone seemed to relax Rowan. I didn't look at Alice, but I hoped she'd clocked how he'd reacted to her comment. He was as defensive as Henry's parents. If we wanted real answers, we needed to tread carefully.

'A lot of people aren't taking their first year seriously.' Rowan's hand relaxed against the door. 'They don't want to be artists. Not like me and Henry.'

'His parents mentioned a gallery?'

Rowan's face lit up. Despite his height and bulk, youthful exuberance shone through as he grinned. 'It's our dream. We're both inspired by water, but from different perspectives. I love it, and Henry fears it. A space celebrating the two would be beautiful.'

If Rowan's talent matched Henry's, it would be. 'You met on the course?'

'I live next door.' Rowan tilted his head, his long plait swaying. 'We met on our first day here and I knew he was special.'

I thought it was admiration that warmed Rowan's gaze, but I had to check. 'You and Henry are just friends?'

Rowan laughed, deep and throaty. 'Very good friends. Henry doesn't think about sex or anything like that. He's all about the art.'

I made a note. Friends, nothing more. Rowan was happy with this arrangement, but had Henry pined for him? Had the sadness of unrequited love driven him to self-harm, to abscond? 'You were working together the morning Henry went missing?'

All traces of levity deserted Rowan's face. 'Yes. We went over to one of the studios to put the finishing touches to our pieces for the gallery. We were due there at ten, but I wanted to get coffee beforehand so I left at about nine thirty. Henry wanted to spend a little more time working on his piece so he said he would meet me over there.'

'Henry was captured on CCTV leaving the art building at around ten,' I said. 'He didn't come to the gallery?'

Rowan's light eyebrows pulled together. 'I arrived as the doors opened. We had an hour to set up, which sounds like a lot but I wanted it to be perfect. Henry and I were meant to be displayed side by side. The two different ways of looking at water. But Henry never came.'

'What did you do when you realised Henry hadn't shown up?'

'I texted him. The guy at the gallery said that if Henry came over later, he should be able to include his piece in the exhibit.' Rowan raised his free hand to fiddle with the end of his braid. 'I was busy in the afternoon. My girlfriend had a gig that night and I helped her set up. I came back to my room late and didn't think about Henry until the next morning when he didn't show for our lecture. I came here afterwards and knocked on his door. He didn't pick up his phone, so I told Student Services what was going on.'

I tapped my pen on my notepad. 'You have no idea where Henry might have gone?'

'I don't think he went anywhere.' Rowan shook his head. 'I promise he gets nosebleeds and he genuinely likes being alone. Henry is eccentric, but he's not depressed and he wouldn't hurt himself. He was excited about seeing his piece in the gallery alongside mine. He wouldn't have missed that unless something stopped him from getting there.'

A similar sentiment to the one Henry's parents had shared. I wondered if Rowan and the Garsides had spent any time together since they'd rushed down to Southampton.

Rowan's jaw tightened as silence stretched between us. The hand against the door bunched into a fist. 'What are you going to do next?'

I flipped my notepad closed. 'We'll get the tissues off for testing, where our forensic team will be able to ascertain whether the blood came from a nosebleed or something else. Then we're going to go talk to the staff at the gallery.'

Alice shuffled beside me. 'We'll do all we can to find your friend.'

Rowan's gaze switched between us. Softness didn't return to features on the cusp of manhood as he stormed away, letting the door swish shut behind him.

You have one new voicemail. Voicemail left today at 12:27 p.m.

'Juliet, where are you? I popped to the flat to get a few things for you and when I got back to the hospital, they said you'd discharged yourself. Why would you do that? You have to know how dangerous that is. We're all so worried about you, me and the girls especially. You need to take better care of yourself. I don't know where you've gone off to, but come to the house and we can look after you. I'll take care of you. That little flat is no good for you at the moment. I did a quick tidy while I was there, so you don't have a mess to deal with when you go there. Anyway. Call me to let me know you're okay. I'll come get you from wherever you need me to. Love you.'

SUSPECTED HUMAN TRAFFICKING RING UNCOVERED

Late this morning, a call was placed to emergency services from a resident of Lark Estate concerned about the welfare of a young woman they had seen banging on an upstairs window of an adjacent block of flats. Emergency services arrived quickly at the scene. The door of the property had to be broken down as there was no reply from those inside. Several young women were taken into protective custody and two men were arrested.

Police have so far declined to comment on the incident, but it is believed a human trafficking incident has been uncovered. In the statement released by police, they have asked any members of the public with information about activity around Lark Estate to please come forward.

Local residents were shocked by the discovery of criminal activity occurring so close to their homes. 'You wouldn't have known,' said one woman who would like to remain nameless. 'Most of us work long hours. We're out all day and tucked up inside at night. There wasn't a chance to see anything.'

Most residents of the area made similar comments, which brings into question whether this location was specifically chosen because of the lack of neighbourly scrutiny.

Gabe

'Gosh. I'd heard the poor boy had gone missing, but I had literally no idea he was one of our artists. How absolutely terrible. I do hope you find him soon. His parents must be frantic.'

Joanna dabbed at her nose, her thick eyeliner unchanged no matter how many times she expressed her sorrow. The gallery manager had ushered us into her office when we explained who we were and had proceeded to alternately search the piles of paper on her desk and monologue about how horrible it was that Henry had gone missing, while Alice and I sat on gaudily patterned chairs.

'We love each and every one of our artists.' She tucked the tissue into her jumper's trailing sleeve as she tackled a particularly tall stack of folders and stapled receipts. Her dungarees were embroidered with sunflowers that matched her dangling earrings and a huge ring on her thumb. 'We're a family, really. I can't tell you how upset everyone will be when they hear one of our own has gone missing.'

I pressed my lips together. Alice moved her boots from side to side. There was a particular kind of person we encountered in this job who instantly pulled whatever tragedy they were faced with directly into their personal orbit.

'Here it is, here it is,' Joanna crowed in a way that would have been wholly inappropriate if she felt a genuine connection with the missing young man. She ran a finger down a column of dates on the crumpled piece of paper. 'Let me see who was on duty that morning.'

The community gallery was open to the public in the afternoons. In the mornings and evenings, they hosted groups and workshops in the mismatched rooms. Joanna couldn't remember who was working when Henry was supposed to drop off his piece for the student showcase and had held us hostage in her office until she found the rota.

'It was Terry.' She poked her finger midway down the page. 'Whom, if I remember correctly, is over in the blue room today. I'll take you there.'

Protests had been futile before, so Alice and I followed mutely as she swept into the gallery. While Joanna continued to lament about a young man she'd told us she'd never met, she led the way through a red room filled with misshapen pots and a green one with simple line drawings of nudes.

'Terry, darling,' she called out as we stepped into a room with bright blue walls, occupied with a clashing collection of paintings and sculptures. The quality varied between artwork close to the canvases stuffed under Henry's bed to those similar to drawings I'd received from Paul's sons.

A tall man turned around, and I stumbled. I threw out a hand to catch myself on Alice's arm, hissing as my shoulder jarred. Joanna rushed forward, jumper sleeves flapping as she explained why we were here. At least her echoing voice provided cover.

'That's Terence Dunlow,' I muttered to Alice, rolling my shoulder gingerly.

'I thought I recognised him.'

Alice had met Terence once or twice during the investigation to find Melanie Pirt's killer. She could be forgiven for not being able to place him, especially as Terence's once immaculate appearance had given way to something much more careworn.

His auburn hair fell back from his face in styled waves, but it hadn't been trimmed for a while. His expensive trousers were creased and his once form-fitting jumper hung from shoulders much bonier than when we'd last met. His brown eyes were bloodshot. They narrowed as he looked over at the two of us.

'We're understaffed so I can't spare you.' Joanna clasped Terence's upper arm and steered him toward us. 'You'll have to chat out here, but I've already told the detectives there's nothing we can do to help. If only we could.'

With one last dab at her eyes with the dry tissue, she breezed out of the room. The casual disinterest Alice and I had shown toward her displays of sadness meant she'd gone off to find someone else to pretend to cry on.

'Hello, Terence.' I pulled my notepad from my pocket. 'I believe you've met Police Constable Alice To.'

'Briefly.' His voice was as posh as ever. It set my teeth no less on edge now than when I'd suspected him of involvement in the murder of an innocent young woman on his family's ancestral grounds.

'I didn't know you worked here.' I looked at the student artwork surrounding us. 'I wouldn't have thought this was your scene.'

Blotchy blush rose up Terence's neck. 'Things have changed since we last spoke, Detective.' His eyes darted between my shoulders. 'I was sorry to hear about what happened to you. I hope you're well.'

'Well enough.' I thanked Ollie for insisting I take his bulky coat this morning. It concealed the site of my bullet wound from a man I didn't want to show any weakness in front of. 'How long have you worked here?'

'About six months.' Terence opened his mouth, closed it, then blurted out, 'I don't live with my father any more. We're estranged.'

I nodded slowly, my pen waiting above my notepad. Prying into Terence's private life wouldn't help our search for Henry, but the temptation to dig was strong. Terence had been rude and deceitful during the search for Melanie's killer, allowing me and Juliet to run in circles when he could have given us answers. I'd felt a small amount of kinship with him, especially after he was involuntarily outed, but his bad attitude always helped me to remember exactly who he was: an entitled brat.

'I live with my boyfriend now,' Terence went on unprompted. 'I want to pay my way, so I've been working here since I moved.'

'Admirable,' I said, as Alice wandered a couple of steps away to admire a painting so viciously red that I didn't want to examine it too closely.

The uneven blush on Terence's neck deepened. 'I don't want to be the kind of person I used to be.'

Hackles that had risen on seeing him softened. Terence used to be a bully, wielding his father's money to bend those around him to his will. But he said he didn't want to be like that any more.

I tapped my pen on my notepad. 'Do you enjoy working here?'

I thought I was offering an olive branch, but Terence spluttered. Beside me, Alice twisted on her heel to examine several bent clothes hangers welded together into an indecipherable shape.

Terence's gaze stuttered to the wide doorway behind me. The gallery wasn't busy, so no doubt our conversation could easily be heard by anyone nearby with an inclination to listen.

'It's a good job.' Terence's Adam's apple bobbed. He hadn't become a better liar in the months since I'd last seen him.

'As Joanna said, we're here because of a missing student.' I rummaged in my pocket then held out a missing persons poster with Henry's student ID photo printed at the top.

Terence took the piece of paper. 'Was he the one who didn't turn up?'

'He didn't come at all?'

'No.' Terence's attention fixed on Henry's picture. 'The rest of the students were keen, all came around ten when we opened the doors. I helped them set up, and near eleven one of them asked if their friend could come later. I said the gallery would be open, so they could pop in and drop off their piece. Joanna wouldn't want it added while the exhibit was open, but she'd given me the afternoon to make sure everything was in place.'

'And Henry didn't come later?' I checked.

'No one did.'

'Had you met Henry before?'

Terence looked up from the poster. 'No, but there was a buzz around him.' His eyes whipped over my head to the open doors. 'Joanna wasn't happy he hadn't brought his piece. It's supposed to be brilliant.'

'His friend, Rowan, said it partners his piece. Can you show us where it would have been put?'

Terence turned on his heel and led me and Alice around sculptures made of discarded cans. On the far wall, a canvas sat under a light. A wave danced, picked out in an unusual array of pinks and purples. It was joyful, like Rowan intended.

'Henry's would have been here.' Terence pointed to a painting beneath a similar spotlight. A single gull flew across grey skies.

Henry's would have matched his friend's painting much more closely than the one that hung in its place. The piece he'd been working on hadn't been left in the art studio where Rowan last saw him or in his room. It must have gone missing with him.

'Does the gallery have CCTV?' I turned from Rowan's bright wave.

Terence cringed. 'It does, but Joanna only turns it on when there's no one in the building. She says people don't want to feel watched when they're simply going about their business.'

How unhelpful. If Henry had turned up at the gallery later in the day, there would be no evidence of it.

'Do you have a sign-in sheet for the other students whose work is displayed here?' Perhaps one of them was jealous of Henry's talent. They might have waylaid him before he got here. The destruction or theft of his art may have tipped such a singularly focused young man over the edge.

'No.' Terence wound his hands together. His knuckles were dry. 'Joanna trusts the students to come back to collect their pieces.'

I bit my lip. It didn't seem like Terence was a major decision maker or influencer at this gallery. A series of choices had been made that hindered our investigation, but none of them had been controlled by him. Unlike the last time a case had touched on his life, Terence wasn't being deliberately unhelpful.

'That's all we need.' I tucked my notepad into my pocket. 'Thank you for your help.'

'I hope you find him,' Terence said, as we turned and walked away.

'He kept the poster,' Alice whispered.

Unknown number. Sent 14:55.

You're not going to make yourself useful?

Unknown number. Sent 14:57.

If you're going to keep pulling this shit, I'll have to seriously think about getting rid of you as well.

Called connected at 15:01.

'Hello, Lock It Up Locksmith. Frank speaking.'

'Why the fuck have you changed the locks on my flat?'

'Sorry, Miss. I'm going to need you to calm down. We don't tolerate abuse of staff.'

'And I don't tolerate fucking morons who change my locks without permission.'

'There's obviously been some kind of misunderstanding. Give me your name and I'll see if I can find out what's going on.'

'Detective Inspector Juliet Stern.'

'Mrs Stern? How are you? I spoke to your husband yesterday. Did he not tell you he'd arranged to have the locks changed? He was worried about someone gaining access to your flat.'

'The first I knew about this was when I tried to let myself into my flat and my key didn't work. One of my neighbours said they'd seen your van here yesterday.'

'That's right. Your husband came in and collected the new set of keys this morning.'

'What ID did he use to prove he lived at the flat?'

'Your driver's licence.'

'My driver's licence?'

'That's right. He didn't have any of his stuff on him, due to rushing into hospital.'

'You changed the locks of my flat and gave out the new keys based on another person's ID?'

'Look, Miss. I don't know exactly what's going on, but you've had a rough time of it. Your husband said you'd been shot and the flat needed to be secure. I thought I was doing the decent thing.'

'Let me tell you what's going on. You did your job poorly due to misplaced sympathy and, as a result, have effectively made me homeless. I need you to come here now and sort this.'

'I can't. I'm on a big job across the city. I'm really sorry, but I can't sort a new lock for you until tomorrow morning.'

'T-hat's the earliest you can do?'

'Sorry. There's only the two of us working and this contract—'

'Can you call me as soon as you've sorted the mess you've created?'

'Yes. I will.'

'When I'm recovered, I'll be coming into your office to have a chat with you and your employees about how to correctly ID customers.'

From: James Knowles **james.knowles@police.gov.uk**
To: Paul Willis **paul.willis@mit.gov.uk**
CC: Nicole Stewart **nicole.stewart@mit.gov.uk**
Date: **26 April, 15:39**
Subject: **Operation Orion – Dunlows' details**

Paul and Nicole,

I've updated the Dunlows' information on the system with their current addresses.
Terence is living in his boyfriend's house. Timothy is living in a rental property with
his youngest son as Dunlow Manor is awaiting repairs after the fire last October.
Timothy Dunlow no longer has a work address as he retired four months ago.

Without further information, I can't tell you whether or not Mr Dunlow has made
any trips back to the estate. According to the gun records, there are a number of
firearms stored on the property. They are consistent with the weapon we believe
was used to shoot Gabe and Juliet.

I spoke with the Prison Liaison Officer earlier today. He remembers Mr Dunlow
came to visit Karl Biss about a month ago. He's not sure when but is going to
check the visiting history.

I've started the process of a phone call with Karl Biss.

Please let me know if there's anything else I can do.

James

Gabe

'Anything?' Alice asked.

It was jarring to look up and see her sat at Juliet's desk. After several of Henry's dorm mates had popped into his room to tell us how much they missed him, we'd bagged up the sketchbooks on the shelf above his bed and decamped to the station to flick through them in peace. We hadn't found Henry's phone. He must have had it with him when he went missing.

'Nothing so far.'

I closed a sketch book from when he'd started university. Between tentative drawings of waves, Henry had written the odd line wondering if coming to Southampton had been a mistake. He missed his parents, missed his home, hated the sea. Since he hadn't shelved the sketchbooks in order, I already knew his homesickness and fear had lessened as time passed.

I pushed those I'd not looked through yet onto Juliet's desk. 'Do you mind checking the rest of these while I get a head start on the admin?'

Alice's eager nod caused a squirm of guilt as I breathed through the deepening ache in my shoulder. My unease didn't last long. It was nothing compared to the frustration that had built as I'd leafed through the random thoughts and drawings of a young man who had disappeared without a trace. There were no leads to follow, and my time could be used more fruitfully elsewhere.

Ignoring my emails, I searched for files around mine and Juliet's shooting. Witness statements filled my screen, alongside hundreds of entries from David Rees and the forensics team. All without a single DNA match.

I opened an interview with the Galanis brothers and clenched my teeth as I read through the transcript. Tsambikos had been as unhelpful as ever, while Alcaeus and Giannis barely said a word. They had a joint alibi for the time of the shooting, but that didn't mean much. If the Galanis brothers were involved, they wouldn't have gotten their hands dirty.

Despite how satisfying it would be to catch them out, they had no reason to hurt us. Juliet and I had been investigating them for months and were no closer to a breakthrough. If the brothers hadn't felt threatened when we first made contact, there was no new reason for them to have lashed out.

I huffed, then shot a tight smile across the desks. Alice was much more respectful of Juliet's space than Paul. The chair's height would cause her short legs to dangle above the floor, but she hadn't changed the settings.

I clicked through the other witness statements, pausing on Juliet's. Pain couldn't be blamed for her terrible attitude. She must have found it galling to be questioned by a detested co-worker while laying helpless in a hospital bed.

She'd noticed a man in a tan coat before we went into the courthouse. I couldn't remember anyone. I had been concerned about getting into the courtroom on time, anxious to hear Karl's sentence.

As Juliet had been shot first, that suggested she was the primary target. I could be collateral damage. Shot because I made myself a startlingly easy second victim. Time had moved slowly for me between the two gunshots, even though there couldn't have been more than a minute between them. If I'd been moving, perhaps the shooter would not have had the chance to take me down as well.

I was either of lower importance than Juliet or incidental. An opportunity not to be missed. A person who shot at one detective wouldn't have qualms about shooting another.

I could have been a footnote: take out if possible.

I clicked away from the files around the shooting and pulled up Juliet's personnel records. If she was the primary target, then I needed to look for someone with a specific reason to want to hurt her.

There was an impressive amount of public complaints and warnings over misconduct. I scrolled through her cases, looking for names that stood out. Anyone particularly violent or who had been released from custody in the last few days.

Juliet became a detective inspector ten years ago. Her promotion was preceded by a series of commendations for bravery. She'd have medals for them. I suspected they were stashed away in her flat or abandoned at the bottom of one of her desk drawers. Praise and censure bounced off Juliet without making an impression.

I kept scrolling, though the likelihood of anyone from this far in Juliet's past deciding to shoot her was small. The chance to delve into her history, even the highs and lows of her career, was rare. I wouldn't dare if she was sitting opposite, and she wouldn't divulge anything more personal than how she liked her coffee unless given no alternative.

She was promoted to detective sergeant fifteen years ago. I frowned when I reached a letter from the previous superintendent dated six months before her advancement. Douglas Frey had offered Juliet the position of detective sergeant. She'd declined. His letter accepting her decision was curt, citing no reason.

Juliet would let very little stand in the way of what she wanted. She'd taken the job as a detective sergeant six months later when Angela offered it to her, after Frey had retired. Why hadn't Juliet wanted it when Frey was at the station?

'Gabe?'

I slammed my hand on my mouse, clicking off Juliet's history. My shoulder sparking, I swivelled to grimace at Maddy where she stood in the doorway. I tried to give off the vibe I was simply surprised by her presence rather than that she'd caught me snooping.

A crease formed between her eyebrows. 'Angela called. She wants me to remind you that you're on light duties, which means heading home at a reasonable hour.'

Moving my mouse in a casual manner to close my search around the shooting, I checked the time on the screen. Just before five.

'She said it's non-negotiable,' Maddy added, her orange nails toying with the buttons of her matching cardigan.

My arguments fled. My presence here was at Angela's mercy. If she decided I was pushing too hard, then she'd send me home indefinitely. It would be worse to be shut out completely than to do half the job I wanted to.

'Fine.' I logged off and grabbed Ollie's coat from the back of my chair, my shoulder protesting every movement. 'Alice, can you go through the rest of the sketchbooks before you head home? And can you arrange interviews with Henry's tutors? They might be able to tell us if anyone was jealous of Henry, or if he was purely excited about displaying his art.' I pulled on the coat as Alice jotted down my instructions. 'It would be good to check in with Surrey police as well, get them to put up posters just in case Henry has fled close to home.'

Delegating work while I swanned off felt unnatural, but Alice raised a double thumbs up. 'I'll do this, then go through CCTV footage for Paul. Not all of us can have an early night.'

I opened my mouth to tease her about her loathing of CCTV, but Maddy snapped, 'Don't be a twat, Alice.'

Alice sighed as she leant back in Juliet's chair. 'You're not ready to joke about Gabe getting shot yet? Can you let me know when you regrow a sense of humour?'

'Ignore her.' I tugged Maddy out of the office. I wouldn't tell her, but I appreciated Alice's refusal to treat me differently because of my injury. 'I need you to do something for me before you leave.'

Maddy nudged my unbattered side. 'You know I'm not getting paid beyond the next ten minutes, so it better be good.'

I checked Paul and Nicole were out of earshot. They were both in his office, looking over papers spread across his desk. I leant close to Maddy. 'Can you please put together all the files around the shooting and drop them over to mine tonight?'

GG. Sent 16:52.

Someone's following me.

Tsam. Sent 16:52.

Darling, are you sure? x

Al. Sent 16:53.

Remember the delivery driver incident?

GG. Sent 16:53.

Don't take the piss.

GG. Sent 16:53.

I checked this time.

GG. Sent 16:53.

I think it's the pigs.

Tsam. Sent 16:53.

Interesting. I'll deal with it x

Al. Sent 16:54.

Need any help?

Tsam. Sent 16:54.

See if anyone else is being tailed x

GG. Sent 16:55.

Thanks. Both of you.

Tsam. Sent 16:55.

Of course, little brother x

DO YOU BELIEVE YOUR OWN DIRTY LIES?

DETECTIVE REWARDED FOR BRAVERY

Local Detective Sergeant Juliet Stern was awarded the Queen's Medal for bravery in the line of duty at a ceremony at Southampton Police Station. The medal was presented by Chief Constable Patrick Wells and the service attended by the Mayor of Southampton and pupils of St Mary's primary school.

Officers were dispatched to a disturbance at St Mary's primary school on 16 February, after several reports of shouting from the reception area. Detective Sergeant Juliet Stern arrived on the scene after the perimeter was secured and was told an unknown man was making threats to staff in the secured reception area.

Detective Stern used a taser to apprehend the man, Bert Vigh. He was upset about a custody hearing for his daughter attended earlier in the day. When breathalysed, Vigh was found to have exceeded the legal drink driving limit. He had several knives on his person.

Superintendent Angela Dobson said, 'We were impressed by Juliet's bravery in the face of extreme aggression to protect the lives of children and teaching staff. While we would not generally condone approaching a scene of this nature alone...'
[continued on page 16]

WHEN IS EVERYONE ELSE GOING TO REALISE WHAT A SELF-SERVING BITCH YOU ARE?

Gabe

Over the months we'd been together, I'd had many reasons to be thankful for Ollie's career as a model. He was gifted armfuls of clothes wildly out of my price range. As the sole person interested in the buffet carts at shoots, he often came home with enough food to dine on for days. Although I would have been attracted to him regardless, I enjoyed the feel of his toned stomach and gym-toughened muscles.

Now, I was glad of the nature of his job because it allowed him to be here. He had no bookings, so was home when I arrived. I didn't have to attempt to undress alone after announcing my desperate need for a shower.

'When they'd all stopped grabbing for their non-existent pearls and exclaiming about what the world was coming to, they actually asked about you.' Ollie finished the tale of how he'd told his flatmates about my shooting.

He eased my jumper over my head. There was no flicker of interest in his gaze as he pulled down my trousers and lifted off my crop top. I held onto his hand and I stepped into the tub.

'Shout if you need me,' he said, before the bathroom door clicked closed.

I wasn't in a fit state to do anything sexual, but Ollie's lack of attraction toward me in my current state made me want to shrivel up. Our relationship, mainly due to his efforts, was built on more than lust, but I didn't want to be a sexless being in his eyes until I was healed.

He might have joked about his flatmates' reactions, but maybe the shooting had flipped a switch in his head. He saw me as hurt and vulnerable. I'd have to help him view me as a partner again.

Another day, when my shoulder wasn't cramping. I couldn't get the dressing wet so had to keep it angled away from the showerhead, but the hot water flowing over the rest of my body felt heavenly. Standing sideways, I rubbed shampoo into my hair and scrubbed at my skin with Ollie's expensive body wash.

Wrapped in a towel, I brushed my fuzzy teeth. My skin still looked waxlike, but at least the shower had returned my cropped brown hair to more of a style rather than a violently assembled bird's nest.

Someone knocked on the front door as I arrived in my bedroom to find Ollie had laid out one of his softest jumpers and a pair of striped pyjama bottoms on the bed. His footfalls thumped along the hallway. For a man who achieved such grace at photoshoots, I would never want him living above me.

Ollie opened the door as I manoeuvred my injured arm into a crop top. 'Hi. Can I help you?'

I tugged on knickers, straining to hear the mumbled reply through the bedroom door. Getting the jumper on was painful, but worth it when the warm fabric fell across my skin. I hoped whoever was at the door would leave soon. I didn't want to wander past in my baggy pyjamas.

'Fuck,' Ollie shouted.

Moving faster than I'd have thought possible in my current state, I yanked my pyjama bottoms up over my thighs and threw open the bedroom door.

Ollie wasn't easily ruffled. His shouting out was unusual. I hadn't expected danger in my own home. I shouldn't have been so complacent.

I charged into the hallway and was so amped up that it took me a second to register what I was seeing.

Ollie had staggered back from the door. He clutched at a tall, blonde woman. She'd slumped into him, her legs bowed.

'Juliet?' I breathed.

Whatever temporary weakness had caused her to fall into Ollie's arms lifted. She grasped his shoulder as she straightened. Her normally perfect hair was pulled into a straggly ponytail, her habitual blouse and smart trousers exchanged for a paint-stained hoodie and grey tracksuit bottoms. A sling held her left arm close to her body.

As much of a shock as it had been when blood bloomed across her chest, it was startling to see her so dishevelled. If I put on armour before walking out into the world, Juliet's protection around herself was akin to a tank. Witnessing her this weak and unkempt was unprecedented.

'Hello, Gabe.' Juliet swayed in her trainer-clad feet, a couple of inches closer to my height without heels. 'I need your help.'

Detective Sergeant Nicole Stewart: Informal interview started at 5:25 p.m. on the 26th April in Mr Dunlow's home. This interview is regarding the shooting of Detective Inspector Juliet Stern and Detective Sergeant Gabriella Martin. The interviewee is Timothy Dunlow, who is not under caution and is free to stop this interview at any time. The interview is being conducted by myself, Detective Sergeant Nicole Stewart, and Detective Inspector Paul Willis.

Detective Inspector Paul Willis: Mr Dunlow, thank you for allowing us to drop in on you like this.

Timothy Dunlow: I didn't have a great deal of choice in the matter.

DS Nicole Stewart: Can you please tell us your whereabouts on the 24th April?

Timothy Dunlow: Although I retired from running my consultancy company several months ago, I retained a few clients. I'd planned to meet one of them on the twenty-fourth. I left for London early in the morning to beat the traffic. I browsed a few shops and had lunch, then met with my client. We spoke for a couple of hours, and I returned home late in the afternoon.

DI Paul Willis: Can anyone confirm your whereabouts?

Timothy Dunlow: I have receipts from the morning, and my client will be able to confirm I was with them for much of the afternoon. They have an assistant who would have noted when I arrived and left.

DI Paul Willis: Was anyone here when you got home?

Timothy Dunlow: Yes. My son, Leo.

DS Nicole Stewart: Did he say anything to you when you got home?

Timothy Dunlow: He said he'd gone to Karl Biss's trial, despite me telling him not to.

DI Paul Willis: Why didn't you want him to go to the trial?

Timothy Dunlow: Leo is incredibly close to his final exams and missing a day of school is foolish. He didn't need to distract himself with anything that would upset him unnecessarily.

DS Nicole Stewart: Why would the trial upset him?

Timothy Dunlow: Leo lost the girl he was infatuated with and finding out he has a deranged half-brother hasn't been easy on him. He blames himself for what happened.

DS Nicole Stewart: Leo told you he'd been to the trial. Did he tell you anything else?

Timothy Dunlow: He said the two detectives had been shot. Leo got himself to safety, and after that no one would tell him what was going on.

DI Paul Willis: What did you think when Leo told you who had been shot?

Timothy Dunlow: My dealings with the detectives were not always cordial, but they found the guilty party in the end and I have to be grateful for that. I obviously hoped they were not too badly harmed.

DS Nicole Stewart: You have no lingering ill feeling toward Detectives Martin and Stern?

Timothy Dunlow: None at all. What happened with the girl and everything that followed was a trying time for both myself and my family. I endeavour to put it all behind me.

DI Paul Willis: How does visiting Karl Biss factor into that?

DS Nicole Stewart: For the benefit of the tape, Mr Dunlow is shaking his head.

Timothy Dunlow: I don't know why I'd expect anything other than incompetence. This is exactly why I will not allow Leo to pursue his childish notion about joining law enforcement. He would be wasted.

DI Paul Willis: What does that mean?

Timothy Dunlow: I've never visited Karl Biss.

DS Nicole Stewart: Are you certain that's true?

Timothy Dunlow: Of course I am.

DI Paul Willis: We've spoken to the Prison Liaison Officer where Karl was held prior to sentencing. He says you visited about a month ago.

Timothy Dunlow: He's wrong. I've not been to the prison. I do not wish to see or speak to Karl Biss ever again.

DI Paul Willis: When was the last time you saw Mr Biss?

Timothy Dunlow: The morning he was arrested. Around six months ago.

DS Nicole Stewart: Mr Dunlow, we know you're a keen shot. Do you have access to any firearms?

Timothy Dunlow: In strictly regulated situations. The bulk of my guns are stored on the estate. I haven't been there for a fortnight. The one I use regularly is stored at my shooting range. There's a log there of every time I've used it, and I've not removed it from the premises.

DI Paul Willis: That's all we need for now. Thank you for your time, Mr Dunlow.

Al. Sent 17:42.

I'm being followed too.

GG. Sent 17:42.

Told you it was real this time!

Tsam. Sent 17:43.

My boys have noticed someone tailing me as well x

GG. Sent 17:43.

What do we do?

Tsam. Sent 17:44.

Nothing. We have to assume this is to do with the shooting. Have you two done anything since that we need to address? x

GG. Sent 17:44.

No. And as soon as I knew I was being watched, I stopped going out.

Al. Sent 17:44.

What a brilliant way to let them know we're onto them.

Tsam. Sent 17:44.

Don't squabble. It's not a problem so long as none of us has done anything they will be interested in x

Al. Sent 17:45.

I've been at the spa. All above board. I'll leave the project I'd started until we're left alone again.

Tsam. Sent 17:46.

Hopefully it will not be disturbed. We just have to wait until they get bored, and then we can get back to work x

GG. Sent 17:46.

Can you let me know when it stops? I don't like being followed.

Tsam. Sent 17:47.

Of course. I'll bring you dinner tonight x

Al. Sent 17:47.

Is this an open invitation?

Tsam. Sent 17:48.

Always x

Gabe

Lying beside Juliet on my bed was a novel experience.

I didn't need to lie down, but when Ollie decreed us unfit to be on our feet and ushered us into my bedroom I moved without protest. Juliet was far more likely to rest if I did too. If her falling into his arms and her dishevelled appearance weren't signs something was wrong, then her quiet submission would have been a flashing red light.

We lay on top of the duvet without speaking. Juliet's breathing was laboured. Her chest moved in the smallest possible increments with each inhalation, the arm strapped into a sling rising and falling. Her shoulder length blonde hair was lank and her usually spotless skin marred with uneven red blotches.

Her clothes were especially strange. I'd expect Juliet to look unwell after being shot, but not a full wardrobe upheaval. She'd worn jeans in my presence before, but nothing approaching the casualness of her current hoodie and tracksuit bottoms. The absence of a sharp jacket and punishing heels diminished her.

'Stop bloody watching me,' she growled. 'I had enough of that at the hospital.'

I whipped my head around to look at the ceiling. Juliet wouldn't tolerate heartfelt speeches professing how glad I was that she was alive. I'd have to settle for caustic wit and iron-clad efficiency. At least the normalcy was soothing.

'I know what you mean. I couldn't wait to get out from under my nurse's thumb.'

That was almost true. I'd not enjoyed my night in hospital, but it wasn't the nurse I'd wanted to escape. She'd been kind, underneath the harried efficiency and unwelcome comments about my body. I wondered what her hair looked like when it wasn't scraped into a lopsided bun.

'When did you get out?' Juliet asked. I chanced a quick glance at her. Her eyes were closed, the skin around them a puffy pink.

'Yesterday.'

'What have you done since then?'

I didn't need to ask what she meant. For Juliet, everything else was always trumped by whatever case we were working on.

'I went into the station. It went about as well as you can imagine.'

Maybe Juliet, with her ability to bypass rules and bend regulations, would have been welcomed as a consultant on the case. I didn't have nearly the heft she did, despite being far better liked.

Juliet's lips tipped up into a tight grin. 'Chucked out on your arse?'

'Not before Paul got a witness statement out of me.'

It stung that he'd kept me talking, kept me distracted, until Angela arrived and turfed me out. Nothing at work had affected mine and Paul's friendship before. I didn't think I'd be able to sit at his dining table while Joanie chattered and his sons demanded attention without glowering at him.

'He got one from me at the hospital.' Juliet winced as she prodded a round bulge in her trouser pocket. 'Insisted on giving me a portable panic alarm.'

They were linked directly to the control room. Press the button, and units would be dispatched immediately.

Paul hadn't given me one. I didn't know if he considered me safe under Alice's watchful eye at the station, or he'd concluded Juliet was the shooter's primary target as well.

'Angela let me back into the station today to work on a missing persons case.' I examined the pattern of swirls across the darkening ceiling. As expected, Juliet showed no interest in a case that wasn't her own. 'I've asked Maddy to drop over the files about our shooting on her way home.'

'Good work,' Juliet breathed. She readjusted her weight, the movement slow and pained. 'What are you thinking so far?'

'It's likely you were the main target.' I didn't bother sugar coating. Juliet would already have come to this conclusion, was probably getting me to talk this through because every word she spoke was costly. 'As you were shot first, we need to not only look for people who would be interested in hurting both of us, but you in particular.'

'Any ideas?'

'Two for someone who would want to hurt us both. One for you, leaving me as an added bonus.'

A laugh ghosted over Juliet's dry lips. 'Lucky you.'

I didn't pretend to smile, as her eyes were tamped shut. Both ideas filled me with dread. To be an intended target was horrible, but to have been shot for fun was similarly awful.

Neither possibility seemed to affect Juliet.

'The Galanis brothers have to be suspects for wanting us both out of the way, but I don't know if they're likely to have been involved. We hadn't uncovered anything new on them in weeks.'

'Maybe we were closer to a breakthrough than we realised.' Juliet's forehead wrinkled. 'Although, from everything we'd uncovered on them so far, if they'd wanted us out of the picture, we would be gone. And with much less fuss than a public shooting.'

The idea of being snuffed out in a quiet alley didn't seem to cause Juliet any disquiet. Feeling grateful for being shot was unexpected, but it was far better than being lost and never found.

Henry's face darted into my mind, but there was no evidence the Galanis brothers had anything to do with his disappearance. They had no reason to be interested in a first-year art student. The bloodstained tissues in Henry's bed pointed more toward self-inflicted pain than anything to do with an organised crime family.

'Unless the brothers needed us incapacitated for a little while. Or wanted to use us as an example?' I suggested. If the Galanis brothers could get away with shooting detectives, their enemies would think twice before getting in their way.

'I'm not sure violence like this is Tsambikos's style,' Juliet mused.

Despite gathering no irrefutable evidence yet of who headed up the criminal activity that swirled around but never quite touched the Galanis brothers, it was obvious that Tsambikos was the undisputed leader. His younger and older brothers deferred to him in every interview, letting him answer for them while they silently stood at his shoulders.

There was a reason the organisation headed up by this unswervingly annoying man had achieved such scope and influence over the last couple of years. Tsambikos, despite his penchant for flare, knew how to slip under the radar. The people he wanted out of the way disappeared. He wasn't prone to leaving messes.

We'd struggled to find any useable evidence to bring charges against him and his brothers. Witnesses came forward, then withdrew. Uncovering the human trafficking ring was a fluke, the luck of a nosy neighbour spotting something that shouldn't be. We'd arrested two men when the building was raided, but neither would talk. Tsambikos inspired a shocking amount of loyalty for someone I could barely stand to be in the same room as.

'Paul also thinks Timothy and Terence Dunlow are worth questioning,' I said. 'The timing of the shooting and the gun used are coincidental.'

'We don't like coincidence.'

'No.' I wrinkled my nose. 'I'm not sure about the Dunlows, but at least ruling them out will bring us closer to whoever did shoot us.'

'Who do you think could have it in for me?' Juliet asked, her voice a parody of what it usually was.

'I was searching for a case that would make sense or someone you'd worked with who might have a grudge.' I picked my words carefully to make it clear I hadn't been prying into Juliet's personal life. 'I saw you were offered the position of detective sergeant and declined, then the superintendent left soon after. You were then promoted by Angela. I wondered if there was a link between your refusal of the promotion the first time and the superintendent's departure?'

I was treading on dangerous ground liable to sink or explode spectacularly. One of the reasons Juliet and I worked so well together was our shared desire that our pasts be left well alone.

'I haven't thought of Douglas Frey in a long time.'

That gave no indication whether significant wrongdoing had hastened his departure or not. Juliet barely thought of a lot of people. Once someone lost their use, they were dismissed from her mind. I didn't think she was as cold as most officers at the station believed, but she always had a faint air of surprise when reminded of the existence of her husband and daughters.

I bit my lip rather than ask where Keith was. There had to be a reason Juliet was in my maisonette rather than with her family. I'd long suspected things weren't right at home. Her presence here could only be confirmation.

Coaxing her to share wouldn't work. I had to hope she'd tell me when ready.

'Do you think Douglas is worth investigating?'

'Possibly,' Juliet murmured. 'From what I'd last heard, he'd taken well to retirement. I might have been part of the reason he left the force, but I wasn't the only one. He didn't seem to resent it. I'm not sure he would shoot me over something that happened so long ago.'

I wanted to ask how Juliet was involved in Douglas's premature retirement, but the weary note creeping into her voice deterred me. There would be time, later, to delve into that. When I wouldn't feel like I was prodding an injured creature.

Juliet's breathing deepened and the ingrained concentration lines across her forehead smoothed. Her memories of Douglas Frey must not have been so troubling she couldn't fall asleep immediately after discussing him.

I took my fill of watching her now I wouldn't be told off for doing so. She barely resembled the woman who worked across from me day after day, but even a bullet through her shoulder hadn't extinguished the fire burning inside. She might be hurt and weakened, but she was like me; she didn't want to rest and recover if it meant our shooter walked free.

A crease ran between her eyebrows and her lips were chapped. Not all the damage was a direct result of the shooting. For years, Juliet had pushed herself too hard. I didn't know why she was so singularly focused on her work, but I trusted she had a good reason.

Despite the distance she maintained between us, I counted her as a friend. Her turning up here had to mean something, at least that she trusted me. I wouldn't take that for granted. Whatever help she needed, whether it was a place to rest or something more, she would get it from me.

From: Alice To **alice.to@police.gov.uk**
To: Paul Willis **paul.willis@mit.gov.uk**
CC: Nicole Stewart **nicole.stewart@mit.gov.uk**
Date: **26 April, 18:36**
Subject: **Operation Orion – CCTV findings**

Paul and Nicole,

I've attached a number of CCTV clips to this email that should be helpful in finding
Gabe and Juliet's shooter.

Clips 1 to 7:

When I retrieved the CCTV footage from around the area of the shooting, I was told
by several business owners that cameras had stopped working within the last week.
I asked for the footage from just before they malfunctioned, which is what you'll find
here. The lenses have been obscured with an almost impossible to remove mix of
black paint and superglue. These vandalised cameras are along a straight route
away from the courthouse.

Clip 4 is the most interesting, as there is a brief shot of the vandal. They appear
three seconds in, then go out of shot before destroying the camera. It's in black
and white and the quality isn't great, but by using 3D modelling of the scene we
can estimate the vandal was around 5'5 to 5'8 in height. They're wearing gloves
and a thick hoodie that obscures their face and body shape.

Clip 8:

This was taken from a camera mounted at the front of the courthouse. It shows
who we believe is a man standing for almost an hour on the spot where Gabe and
Juliet were shot. I believe this is the gentleman Juliet noted outside the courthouse
– he is wearing the same kind of coat she mentioned. He looks at his phone almost
the entire time and there is no clear shot of his face. His coat obscures most of his
body, but he is tall and slim. He has dark hair.

His appearance does not overlap with the shooter's, whose timeline we were able to establish in the clips below. I will continue trying to identify him, as it's strange he lingered for so long in the place where Gabe and Juliet were shot.

Clips 9 and 10:

These were both taken from the outward-facing camera inside a Wetherspoons. They show who we believe to be a man walking past at 16:43 with a large duffle bag – thirty minutes before Gabe and Juliet were shot. His face is turned away from the camera and obscured by a low cap. He is wearing bulky clothing and gloves.

He is then seen walking in the opposite direction two minutes after Gabe was shot. Again, there is no clear shot of his face. As we have not got a full body shot, it's impossible to estimate his height.

Clip 11:

We believe this clip narrows down where the shooter was positioned. It was taken from a camera mounted in the stairwell of an empty building opposite the court-house. It was tampered with, but a partial shot is available.

It shows who we believe is the same man who walked past the Wetherspoons climbing the stairs at 16:46 and then descending thirty seconds after Gabe was shot. There are two floors above this where they could have shot from. There is very little detail about the individual in this shot as it is so unclear. They are wearing bulky clothing and their face is obscured by a cap. There was no full body shot.

After clip 10, I have not been able to establish where the gunman went. I have contacted shops and businesses to ask for more footage, but none so far have reported anything unusual or any malfunctioning cameras. I have also not been able to find any more footage of the individual who vandalised the cameras or the man in the tan coat.

I'll keep looking,

Alice

Juliet. Sent 18:51.

Where were you at the time of the shooting?

Keith. Sent 18:51.

Where the hell are you? I've been worried sick x

Juliet. Sent 18:51.

Where were you when I was shot?

Keith. Sent 18:56.

Looking after our daughters. That can be my standard answer for most times, since I operate as a single parent.

Keith. Sent 18:56.

Are you happy now? Or were you hoping for a different answer?

Keith. Sent 18:59.

Juliet – don't you dare ignore me. Where are you?

Gabe

'This is incredible,' I said through a mouthful of gooey cheese and tomato.

Ollie laughed. 'Pasta bake doesn't usually get such rave reviews.'

I'd not eaten anything substantial all day. Woman could not live on biscuits alone. After the blandness of hospital food and a day of near starvation, Ollie's most basic meal was delicious.

Juliet's bowl steamed on the kitchen side. I'd left her sleeping when Ollie announced his culinary masterpiece was ready, my bedroom door ajar so we'd hear if she called out.

I'd shoved a colossal forkful of pasta into my mouth when someone tapped on the front door. Grinning, Ollie placed his bowl on the coffee table as he rose. He held up a warning hand to Artie, silently commanding him to stay put in his bed.

The dog laid his head on top of his paws and sighed. It had to be hard to have food theft and head pats denied.

'Hey, Maddy,' Ollie said, after fiddling with the locks. 'Hi, Paul.'

I froze, my mouth full. I didn't have time to do more than swallow and configure my face into a position that conveyed indifference before Ollie let both visitors into my living room. As far as he knew, Paul was the nice guy I worked with who I was always happy to see. I'd been too embarrassed about being kicked out of the station to tell Ollie any details.

I needed the files from Maddy, but she couldn't hand them over if Paul was here. I'd have to distract him so that she could give them to me.

She mouthed an apology before kneeling beside Artie's basket and showering him with attention. I tried to express with a look that it wasn't her fault Paul was here. He wasn't above inviting himself into people's homes, alongside his many other faults.

It was unlikely he and Maddy had spotted Juliet on my bed as they were ushered inside. Paul wouldn't keep quiet about it if he had. Juliet might not have minded Maddy seeing her so vulnerable, but she would want to keep Paul at a distance while she was feeling so far from her normal self.

He stole Ollie's seat on the sofa next to me. I took another bite of pasta, resisting the urge to glare like a petulant child. Paul got far too much of that from his sons, so was immune. I kept my eyes on the steaming swirls as he adjusted his weight, his long legs stretched out under my coffee table.

Ollie grabbed his bowl. 'I'll be in the kitchen.'

It was kind of him to give me space to talk to my co-workers. If I'd swallowed my pride earlier, he would have known time with Paul was entirely unwelcome.

'Don't be cranky.' Paul laid his arm along the back of the sofa and poked me in my uninjured shoulder. 'I come bearing gifts.'

He pulled a loaded case file from his bag and slapped it on my coffee table. Maddy had developed a sudden fascination with Artie's many stuffed toys. A mouthful of pasta prevented me from doing more than narrowing my eyes at Paul.

He poked me again. 'Did you think I wouldn't notice Maddy putting this together?'

I chewed slowly and swallowed. 'I don't know what you're talking about.'

Paul chuckled. 'You better hope you're never at the pointy end of an interrogation. You're a terrible liar. Worse than my boys. Remember when Joe said he hadn't pilfered any of the blue cupcakes before his birthday party? He didn't understand why poking out his tongue was an issue.'

I loved Paul's sons, but I didn't particularly want to be compared to them. I had enough of a poker face to deal with the criminals we encountered on a daily basis.

'He made me tell him why I was printing it,' Maddy piped up.

'If by that you mean I asked once and you let rip? Then yes, I made you.'

I set my empty bowl on the coffee table. 'Are you going to let me look at any of it, or are you here to warn me off again?'

Paul grabbed his stick and rapped my knee. 'Gabe, if one person understands how frustrating it is to be cut off from an important case, it's me.'

I glanced at Paul's leg. I'd never seen his wound, but his sons assured me the scar ran right from his knee all the way up to his hip. Paul had smiled indulgently as they argued over whether it was a reddish purple or purplish red. His injury was more significant than mine, requiring months of physical therapy before he could return to work.

I slumped into the sofa cushions. 'Why'd you help Angela relegate me to the missing persons case?'

'Because she's right. Of course you can't investigate your own shooting,' Paul said, swiping away any sympathetic feelings I might have been gathering toward him. 'But that doesn't mean you can't be useful. You can give insights into who might have wanted to hurt you and Juliet. It makes no sense for your skills to go to waste by not even letting you take an off-the-books look at the case files.'

I picked up the folder, ignoring the pained snap from my shoulder. My ability to have any meaningful insight into this case was entirely in Paul's hands. I couldn't show how much each movement hurt in case he decided sifting through paperwork was too much for me on top of Henry's case.

For a second, I questioned leaving Juliet undisturbed in my bedroom. She would want to be as involved as me, but her aversion to being seen as anything other than put together had to be stronger. I would tell her everything I discussed with Paul after he left and we could read the file later.

'Drinks.' Ollie appeared with a tray of steaming mugs.

Paul beamed. 'Good lad.'

Ollie retreated to the kitchen after he'd set out our cups and a plate of biscuits. The boiler clunked to life as our pasta bowls clattered in the sink. Unease crept across my ribs as I settled the file on my lap. I'd tried to keep Ollie and my work separate. I didn't want him around while we delved into this, but currently had no other option.

'Have you got much to go on?' I opened the file and rested my fingers on a witness account of the shooting. The word *blood* jumped from the page.

'Some.' Paul dipped a custard cream into his milky tea. 'The CCTV around the area was tampered with. There are stills of the damage in the file.' He gestured at it, a drop of tea teetering on the corner of his biscuit. 'We're not sure if it was the shooter or someone else, but it's in such a select area that it has to be related. I've got Alice looking through footage for anything to identify the vandal, but no luck yet.'

'I bet she's loving that,' I said. Alice's CCTV grumbles were legendary.

'That she is.' Paul grabbed a bourbon. 'Despite the damage, we've got several shots of the vandal and gunman.'

'It was a man?' I cupped my decaf coffee between my hands.

'Most likely. None of the images are clear, but the build is more consistent with a male frame.'

A man fit with the suspects I'd identified. 'Have you got any idea of who it might be?'

'Nicole and I chatted with your mate Tsambikos and his brothers this morning.' Paul grimaced as he selected another biscuit. 'He was as helpful as ever.'

Over the months Juliet and I had been working on Operation Juno, I'd come to dread our interviews with the suspected crime boss. Tsambikos was always full of smiles and greasy charm. All obviously fake, like plastic flowers wedged in a garden. He never failed to ask after my parents and Juliet's daughters, the subtext blazingly clear.

I know who you love. I know where they live. I have the power to make them disappear.

Cutlery clanked in the kitchen. My fingers tightened around my mug, my shoulder giving a sympathetic throb toward the clench in my heart.

'Do you think they're involved?' I asked. If they were, the Galanis brothers wouldn't have pulled the trigger themselves. They'd have a minion for that, easy to throw under the bus or discard if things went sideways. Someone with people they loved, people they would lie to protect. The clinging strands of the Galanis brothers' web ran wide, while they sat hidden at one edge.

'At this stage, I'm not sure.' Paul's hand hovered over the biscuits until Maddy edged the plate out of his reach. He nodded, like removing temptation was the wisest choice. 'I've had a look over Operation Juno's latest findings, and there doesn't seem to be anything that would make the brothers nervous. I've put them under surveillance, so we'll pick up if they're doing anything strange.'

'I don't think we were close to something important,' I conceded. 'Do you have anyone else in mind?'

'Nicole and I visited Timothy Dunlow this afternoon.'

I wrinkled my nose. 'What did he have to say for himself?'

'He claims he has an alibi,' Paul said. 'We're checking it and if it's solid, he couldn't have been involved no matter how much he dislikes you and Juliet.'

One thing didn't fit, even if his alibi fell through. 'Dunlow wouldn't do anything to endanger his sons. Leo was nearby when Juliet and I were shot.'

'Unless he's such a good shot that he knew his son wouldn't be in danger,' Paul countered.

Dunlow was arrogant, but I didn't think it would stretch that far. Behind his cold demeanour was a burning desire to see his sons safe and well.

'James asked the Prison Liaison Officer to set up a chat with Karl Biss, and he mentioned Karl had a visit from Dunlow about a month ago,' Paul said. 'When we asked about it, Dunlow denied it had happened.'

'He wasn't concerned about lying during Melanie Pirt's case, but he didn't carry on once we had evidence.' Dunlow's omissions and half-truths had tangled an already complex investigation. 'I wonder why he's being stubborn this time?'

It indicated guilt. Lying past the point of plausibility was out of character, the kind of action Dunlow would take if he'd messed up. Maybe he didn't think we would be able to access the prison visit records, or had decided we were so incompetent that we wouldn't think to.

'Is there anyone else you've thought of? Juliet was shot first, so it's likely she was the primary target, but it could have been someone interested in incapacitating both of you.' Paul didn't throw out his theories as casually as Juliet. His voice was sharp, like whether I'd been a target or not brought him disquiet.

'I wondered about ex-Superintendent Douglas Frey.'

Maddy's hand stilled under Artie's chin. 'Juliet's old boss?'

'Poor chap.' Paul gazed longingly at the biscuits. 'Name doesn't ring a bell.'

Paul had no historic connection with the city. His wife wanted to live nearer the sea, so he'd jumped at the chance to move to Southampton when the detective inspector post opened up.

'I've not heard much about him.' Maddy resumed her chin scratches after Artie nudged her. 'Years ago, Juliet was offered the promotion to detective sergeant but she refused it. Soon after, Douglas Frey took early retirement. There aren't many people around who worked with both of them. No one seems to know what happened. If anything did.'

'Has Juliet ever mentioned him?' Paul asked.

'No.' It was the truth. If I hadn't brought up Douglas, Juliet might never have thought of her old boss.

Paul pulled his phone out of his pocket. 'I'll note down the name, but most likely it was a clash of personalities. We can't go chasing down every co-worker Juliet didn't get along with. If we did, we'd have to consider almost everyone in the station a suspect.'

I took a sip of coffee. Juliet's unpopularity bothered me but she was oblivious to the opinions of our co-workers, or so uncaring that it didn't affect her. She and Paul were particularly unfriendly. They clashed over allocation of resources, taking the lead on cases, their favourite mugs. On Paul's side there was an undercurrent of teasing. Juliet couldn't understand why he wouldn't stay out of her way when she had a job to do.

'Let's be off.' Paul used his stick to haul himself to his feet. Maddy patted Artie once more before she stood.

'Thank you for bringing the file.' I set it down beside the remaining biscuits and eased myself off the sofa.

At my front door, Maddy gave me a gentle hug. 'Look after yourself,' she whispered, before hurrying off to her car.

Paul paused in the doorway. I resisted the urge to check how much of my bedroom was visible behind me. He rummaged in his pocket, then pulled out a portable panic alarm.

'Take this,' he said. 'From what we've gathered so far, the shooting was planned and premeditated. The gunman came to hurt Juliet, then you. No one else.'

This was the conclusion I'd come to, so I didn't know why shivers skittered across my skin at Paul's words. I gripped the black plastic oval he'd passed to me.

Paul squeezed my uninjured shoulder. 'It's unlikely they'll try again, but look after yourself, alright?'

I closed the door after him, then leant back against the strong wood. I'd known Juliet and I had been targeted. I'd known whoever did it was out there. But I'd not equated that with our lives still being on the line. We hadn't escaped danger, but were in the midst of it. Paul was concerned enough to give me an instant way of calling for help.

This wasn't over and done with. The possibility of more damage to myself and those around me was present now.

'You okay?'

I flinched, then gasped as pain exploded from my shoulder. Ollie hurried to my side, face twisted with concern as he dried his damp hands on a tea towel.

I pressed my forehead into his chest for one moment, breathed in his familiar warmth, then stepped away. As much as I wanted to fall into his comfort, I needed to find mine and Juliet's shooter more.

'Is it alright if you head off as well? I think Juliet will ask to stay.' I slipped the portable panic button into my pyjama pocket before he could ask what it was. 'She'll take the bed, and there isn't room for the two of us on the sofa.'

'That's fine.' Ollie's eyes tracked over my face. 'Please look after yourself.'

I leant on the front door while he chucked the tea towel in the kitchen and grabbed his coat and phone. He didn't give me a chance to straighten before kissing me, hands cupping the sides of my face. I chased his lips when he pulled back, the pained tug from my shoulder stopping me short.

My good hand clung to his coat collar as he eased the door open. I didn't want him to leave, but I needed him gone. I couldn't work with him here.

The hinges of my bedroom door creaked as Ollie walked down the street.

'Have they all left?'

I nodded at Juliet as I closed the front door. Her hair was a mess, her untidy clothes hanging off her slim frame, but a light to her eyes that had been missing when she'd stumbled into my flat had reignited.

'How much did you hear?' I led the way to my living room.

'Everything.' Juliet lowered herself onto the sofa and flipped open the file. One of the perks of my tiny home was that all conversations could be heard throughout. 'Do you have a wall we can wreck?'

'Yeah.' I walked through to the kitchen to reheat her pasta. Since adopting Artie, my security deposit had been irretrievably lost. He'd been raised in a barn, so had little understanding of plaster or carpet. Thankfully, his first forceful explorations had calmed as he'd accepted that living inside was vastly preferable to outside.

I presented Juliet with the steaming bowl after it had spun in the microwave for two minutes. She thanked me but didn't ask how the meal had come to be.

Ollie leaving held no significance for her. It hadn't left an ache in her chest.

From: David Rees **david.rees@forensics.gov.uk**
To: Paul Willis **paul.willis@mit.gov.uk**
CC: Nicole Stewart **nicole.stewart@mit.gov.uk**
Date: **26 April, 20:49**
Subject: **Operation Orion – DNA samples collected from empty building**

Willis,

Following the identification of the site of the shooter to either the second or third floor of an empty building across from the courthouse, my team and I did a thorough forensic sweep of these areas. We were unable to recover any bullet casings or other materials that would confirm the shooting position, which suggests a high degree of preparedness.

However, we have taken a large amount of material from around the windows facing the site of the shooting and the stairwell. Once DNA is taken from suspects, we will have a wealth of materials to test against.

None of the material collected is a match for anyone currently on our system.

Rees

Rowan. Sent 20:59.

Have you had any contact from the police since they took our statements?

Flea. Sent 21:05.

Good evening to you. And no.

Rowan. Sent 21:06.

I tried to call. They asked if I had any new information then said they had nothing to tell me. I don't think they're taking Henry's disappearance seriously.

Flea. Sent 21:08.

I got the impression they weren't sure anything was wrong. Like he might have wandered off and would come back in his own time.

Rowan. Sent 21:09.

That's so stupid. We actually know Henry, and we're saying he wouldn't do that.

Flea. Sent 21:10.

Since we could barely convince him to go for a night out, it seems unlikely he's gone off on his own for days.

Rowan. Sent 21:11.

We need to do something. Can I come over? We can make a plan, then get other people involved. If the police aren't going to help Henry, then we need to.

Flea. Sent 21:12.

So long as you don't mind hatching a plan while I'm in my pyjamas, I'm game.

Gabe

Neither of us had the energy to decorate one of the walls of my maisonette. Instead, Juliet and I sat on my sofa and read through the thick file. Artie crept forward until his chin rested on Juliet's foot. I wasn't sure she'd noticed his quiet affection.

Juliet piled everything to do with Timothy Dunlow on my knee, while evidence around Tsambikos Galanis and his brothers went on hers.

Each stack was dispiritingly small. The bulk of the folder was taken up with largely useless witness accounts and reports from the medical examiner about mine and Juliet's wounds. I'd placed the photographs of our bleeding bullet holes face down on my coffee table.

'We need to look at what we were focused on with Operation Juno in the week before the shooting.' I gestured at the neat pile on Juliet's knee. 'If the Galanis brothers were involved, it means we were close to something. I'll ask Maddy to put together another file.'

Juliet relaxed into my IKEA sofa cushions. I didn't think she judged my furniture choices. She probably had better stuff than this, but neither cared nor noticed.

'I don't remember anything other than one of Tsambikos's shopping sprees,' she said.

Every few weeks, Tsambikos broke from his normal pattern of loitering at his various businesses to throw money around. His purchases were varied and extravagant, and none had led to any significant information. When he paid in cash for huge vases and strange artwork, the money was squeaky clean. Juliet theorised he was flaunting that he could spend his ill-gotten gains and there was nothing we could do about it.

I wasn't sure Tsambikos was merely showing off. Operation Juno had included a deep dive into the pasts of the Galanis brothers. Their father left when Giannis wasn't yet two years old, and their mother cared for her three sons alone. She'd had several jobs, and the boys had started earning as young as possible.

They'd bought their mother a five-bedroom house on the edge of the New Forest and made sure she wanted for nothing. Giannis and Alcaeus were more reserved with their spending, occasionally heading off on spur-of-the-moment holidays with their partners and splashing out on new cars.

Only Tsambikos indulged in wild spending sprees. I felt a degree of sympathy for him. I'd not grown up destitute, but my parents' care work and carpentry meant there was enough for the basics. Our holidays were on camp sites around the coast and my school shoes were hand-me-downs from people at church. If I came into huge sums of money, I wasn't sure I'd be able to resist spending for spending's sake either.

'Someone else will have to follow up on his purchases, since I'm on light duties.' I didn't mention when Juliet might return to work. Hypocritical, but I wanted her to rest.

'One of the many and varied benefits of getting shot,' Juliet murmured, her eyes slipping closed. 'What do you think of Dunlow?'

'I understand why Paul has him in the picture but even with a strong motive, which I'm not sure disliking us counts as, I can't see him shooting a gun when Leo was nearby. Plus, he claims to have an alibi.' I looked down at the scant evidence stacked on my knee. 'That said, Dunlow is arrogant enough to believe he could shoot us and hit no one else, and he definitely thinks himself clever enough to get away with it.'

'The visit to Karl is suspicious, especially as he's denying it happened.'

'Maybe.' I shuffled to lean more comfortably on my good shoulder. 'Dunlow would never admit it, but guilt is a powerful motivator. He can't honestly feel wholly blameless about everything that went down. If he'd been less of an arsehole, Melanie Pirt would be alive.'

'I don't think he'd see it that way.' Juliet's eyes drifted open. 'He obviously enjoys influencing those around him, but he wouldn't take responsibility for their poor actions. Do you seriously think he accepts culpability for Leo hiding a young woman on the estate, or Terence concealing his sexuality?'

The interview transcript confirmed Dunlow was an unchanged man. 'You're saying he's not likely to feel guilty about any of it?'

'He's probably angry.' Juliet's jaw tightened. 'And we've witnessed exactly what Dunlow would do to protect his sons. Karl is part of his family now. What if shooting us was all his neglected son asked of him? How could he say no?'

I wrinkled my nose. 'That's assuming Dunlow would consider Karl his son. And do you think Karl would want us hurt? He didn't seem to have any particular animosity toward us, not even after we caught him.'

Karl Biss was the same man at the start of Melanie Pirt's investigation as he was at the end. When the evidence stacked against him, he came quietly. He didn't lash out at Juliet or me, but sat across from us in the interview room and calmly explained how he'd killed a young woman so his daddy would pay attention to him.

'Prison changes people,' Juliet stated.

'Paul will talk to him soon. Hopefully Karl will be more open about the visit.'

Juliet huffed. 'And we'll find out about it second-hand.'

'Dunlow might have an alibi.' I rerouted Juliet from a diatribe about Paul's benevolence in letting us help out passively with the case. 'But Tsambikos and his brothers' alibi isn't brilliant.'

'How horribly familiar.' A wry smile twisted Juliet's dry lips. 'They were in a spa they own. I doubt there's CCTV, and anyone who can corroborate is on their payroll.'

'Not that it matters where they were at the time of the shooting. If they were involved, none of them would have pulled the trigger.' The whole reason we'd had such trouble pinning anything on the brothers was their ability to keep their distance.

'There's someone else we should consider.' Juliet sat up, her grey eyes sharp. 'I would prefer this was kept between us. I don't want Paul or anyone else involved.'

'Why?' I'd need a good reason to keep anything to myself.

Juliet looked toward the wall where evidence would be pinned once we summoned the energy. 'It's personal. Until we know if it's a good lead, I don't want anyone else poking around in my business.'

'Who is it?' I asked, in place of agreeing. I wouldn't break Juliet's confidence lightly, but there was only so much I could do without endangering the investigation.

'Douglas Frey,' Juliet said.

'What?' I leant against the arm of the sofa to look at her face on. 'You made it sound like considering him would be a waste of time.'

'It might be, and until we know I don't want Paul or anyone else to talk to Douglas. I want you to.'

'Why?' I wanted to help Juliet, but Douglas could be dangerous. Talking to him could mess up Paul's investigation.

A whisper of guilt threaded through me. I'd already mentioned Douglas to Paul, but he hadn't taken my suspicions around Juliet's ex-boss seriously. The most he was likely to do was search Douglas's name, look through the files I'd already read.

Juliet took a breath, her gaze pinned on the mismatched frames Ollie had hung on the wall above my TV. He'd printed selfies; one at the beach with our hair wild and another of Artie photobombing.

'I don't want to explain my history with Douglas to Paul.'

'Why did Douglas retire?' It wasn't enough that Juliet trusted me to talk to him. No matter how flattering that was, I had to know the reasons and assess them for myself before I did this.

Juliet considered me for long seconds. I pressed my lips together, resisting the urge to fill the silence with assurances she could depend on me. She already knew that.

I suspected it wasn't that Juliet was weighing up my trustworthiness, but more she was hunting for reasons not to share any of her history with me. She was an incredibly private person. I understood, but there were times to open up. One of those was when asking someone to cut across an investigation.

'I'd passed the detective's exam and was doing well on the cases I was assigned.' Juliet's eyes darted away from me. 'When an opportunity for promotion came up, Douglas asked me into his office to discuss it. He said I showed promise, but there were lots of other officers who wanted the position as well. He made it clear I needed to do something special to stand out from the crowd.'

Pasta churned in my stomach. 'What did he mean?' I asked, hoping I'd misunderstood.

'He wanted me to give him a blow job,' Juliet stated baldly. 'As soon as I realised what he was angling for, I played the part of a confused innocent. He said the actual words in the end. It didn't occur to him I was letting him entrap himself. I walked out of his office and went straight to HR.'

I opened my mouth to issue a useless apology, then snapped it shut. Juliet didn't need that. She needed me to listen and understand. She shouldn't have to deal with my guilt for assuming things like this didn't happen to women like her. I should have known there was no defence against terrible men.

'After news spread of what I'd done, other women came forward. With all of us speaking out against him, Douglas couldn't deny it. Instead of a lengthy trial that likely wouldn't result in a conviction, we all agreed early retirement was the best course of action.'

'Would he want revenge?' Rage burned inside me. Douglas may be elderly now, but that didn't undo the wrongs he'd committed when more able and powerful. 'Why would he lash out after all this time?'

Juliet looked at the photos again. I would have been impressed if she'd been able to tell me who I was posing with. Details of my personal life were of no interest to her. It wasn't the kind of thing she wanted us to share, but her hand was being forced.

Juliet scrunched her nose. 'I don't think so. I might have been the first to tattle on him, but I was quickly joined by others. Douglas has never reached out to me, hasn't done anything but settle into quiet retirement.'

Funded by tax payers. The loss of his position scraped the surface of what Douglas Frey deserved, but after he was deposed he was allowed to live on in comfort.

'Why do you want me to go see him?' I asked. If Juliet didn't think Douglas a likely suspect, then stepping across Paul's investigation wasn't necessary.

'Because we need to know. If Douglas is a dead end, I'd much rather you figure it out than Paul.' Juliet's jaw jutted. 'I asked for it all to be hushed up at the time. I don't want it being dug up now. My career was not built on the back of a monster or what he tried to do to me.'

Even more unexpected than Juliet sharing her history was this insight that she cared what other people thought of her. She appeared to march through life, disregarding the opinions of others. But she would let a man's horrible deeds slip into forgotten history if it meant she could rise through the ranks unblemished.

'I want you to question Douglas and remove him quietly from the investigation.' Juliet searched my face. 'Find out where he was at the time of the shooting. If you get anything you can work with, go to Paul and tell him everything. But if not, don't tell anyone. Please.'

Juliet didn't need to beg. 'I'll do it,' I said. 'I'll help you.'

Juliet was a brilliant detective, but she didn't always have the same eye for danger I did. One pensioner might be doddery, while another could be strong. I wasn't about to put myself in harm's way to preserve Juliet's privacy.

I wouldn't tell Paul, but there were other people I could take with me. People I could trust to keep a secret.

'Thank you.' Juliet relaxed into my sofa cushions.

She'd clearly been uncomfortable asking for help. I didn't want her to throw up protective walls again, but I needed to know something else.

'Juliet, why are you here? I don't mind, but why aren't you at home with Keith?'

She stiffened. The action must have pulled on her wound, since her face creased with pain. She took a breath, then regarded me with unreadable eyes.

'I heard you at the door. At the hospital. When Keith came back into the room, I asked him to go get you.' Juliet pressed her lips together so hard they practically disappeared. 'He refused.'

A chill washed over me. I'd felt helpless enough on the ward with a partner who would do anything I asked. Juliet's side room must have felt like a closed trap.

'I would have come back,' I offered uselessly.

Her expression softened. 'I know you would have.'

Juliet hadn't explained why she was here, but she'd given enough. I wouldn't want to be around anyone who would deny my basic requests while I was hurt. 'You can stay here as long as you need to.'

'I'll be able to get into my flat tomorrow,' she murmured, turning her attention back to the file on her lap. 'Just the one night will be sufficient.'

Day 3

Monday, 27 April

OFFICERS NAMED – JULIET STERN AND GABRIELLA MARTIN WERE THE DETECTIVES SHOT OUTSIDE SOUTHAMPTON CROWN COURT…

Scroll.

SEXIST SHOOTER? – TWO FEMALE DETECTIVES SHOT IN A TARGETED ATTACK…

Scroll.

POLICE FINALLY RELEASE DETAILS – WITH THE DETECTIVES NAMED, WILL THE NEXT STEP BE ACTION TO KEEP THEIR COLLEAGUES SAFE…

Scroll.

Call connected at 9:52.

'999, which service do you require?'

'I found him. I fucking found him.'

'I'm sorry. It's hard to understand you. Have you found someone?'

'Henry. I—'

[Sounds of sobbing.]

'Take a deep breath. Can you tell me where you are?'

'I'm down at the docks. Behind the casino.'

'And you found someone?'

'Yeah, my friend. Henry.'

'Is Henry okay?'

[Sounds of sobbing.]

'No. He's dead.'

'Okay. I'm sending an ambulance and police your way. They'll be there in eight minutes. Are you near Henry?'

'He's inside a container. I'm outside.'

'It's better if you stay outside so the teams can find you. Can you tell me your name?'

'It's Rowan.'

[Sniffing.]

'I wanted to find Henry, but not like this.'

Gabe

'How does Henry know Mr Frey?' Alice asked as we walked up the paved path to a cottage that had been well looked after twenty years ago. Knee-high grass swayed under windows painted a flaking blue. Smoke puttered from a leaning chimney set atop a mossy slate roof.

I turned to face Alice. 'You can go back to the car if you want to.'

'What?' Her hand twitched reflexively toward the taser attached to her hip. 'Gabe, what's going on?'

'I wasn't sure you'd agree to come if I told you.'

If Alice refused to enter the cottage, she would at least be close by. I didn't want to walk into Douglas Frey's home alone, but back-up within shouting distance might have to suffice.

'What's going on?' she repeated.

'Douglas Frey doesn't have anything to do with Henry's disappearance.' I'd toyed with telling Alice the truth the whole way over to the dilapidated cottage in the north of the New Forest, but had bottled it. I couldn't risk her recognising that talking to a person related to Paul's investigation was inadvisable and turning the car around. I couldn't let Juliet down.

'Why are we here, then?' Alice lowered her hand.

'Juliet asked if I would speak to Douglas, as there's the smallest chance he was involved in our shooting.' I gripped the cuffs of Ollie's coat. 'It's unlikely he had anything to do with it, but I'd rather not go in alone.'

I was leaning heavily on our friendship. Alice's eyes darted between me and the cottage.

'Juliet asked you to do this?'

I nodded. 'She doesn't want her past dragged into the investigation unless it has to be.'

Juliet was asleep in my bed as I'd left my maisonette and climbed into Alice's car. I didn't enjoy being ferried around, but the strain of changing gear yesterday ached through my arm and back this morning.

Alice's stab-proof vest rose and fell. 'Let's get this over with.'

'Thank you.' Whether going in with me was the lesser of two evils or if Juliet's request motivated her, I was grateful not to face this alone. Douglas Frey may be older, but that didn't mean he would be harmless.

'Any sign of trouble, anything suspicious at all, and we're out of here. No arguments about calling Paul,' Alice said as I tapped on the stained red and blue glass set at the top of the cottage's front door.

I attempted a reassuring smile. 'I promise.'

She grimaced, kicking the edge of a paving stone. The sun shone on her black hair as she turned her light bronze face toward the ground. Even though her uniform and Ollie's borrowed coat bulked us out, I hoped facing two small women would disarm Douglas enough that he would lower his defences quickly.

The glass coloured as someone arrived on the other side of the door. Locks clicked and scraped. I looked back at Alice when it hadn't opened after half a minute of noisy tinkering, the movement pulling on my shoulder. It was stiff this morning. A night on the sofa was not the best idea when recovering from a bullet wound, but I couldn't chance sleeping in my bed with Juliet and waking her with one of my nightmares.

After a loud clang, the door swept inward to reveal an elderly man. His stooped back lowered his bald head to the same level as mine and Alice's.

I'd rooted out a picture of Douglas Frey last night. A headshot from his time on the force didn't elicit sympathy. In middle age, sandy hair had flopped over his forehead and his light brown eyes had lines of mirth carved around them. The picture was taken on the day he'd won an award for bravery so his uniform was pressed, the buttons shining. I wondered if that was before or after he'd begun using his position to harass women.

The man standing before me barely resembled his younger self. The hair left around his ears was white and his mouth was permanently downturned. A checked shirt hung from his bony shoulders, the ends tucked messily into brown trousers. His slippers were grey, almost camouflaged against the flagstones of the cottage.

In the still image, Douglas Frey had looked sharp and clear. Now, his face sagged with vague confusion.

My heart sank. Unless this was an incredible act, he clearly wasn't the same man who'd tried to take advantage of Juliet or been capable of shooting us.

'Mr Frey?' I checked. 'I'm Detective Sergeant Gabe Martin. I wonder if we might come in and ask you a few questions?'

I didn't introduce Alice. If everything went to shit and word of this interview made its way to Paul, she didn't need to get in trouble. Without her name, it would be harder to categorically prove who'd come here with me.

Not that the precaution was necessary. Douglas's eyes wandered unsteadily between us. I would have been surprised if he'd retained half of what I'd said.

'Of course. Of course.' He nodded jerkily, then shuffled down a short corridor. His whole body swayed with each step. More than once, he placed a wrinkled hand on a bare spot on the wall to prevent himself from toppling over.

The hallway was decorated with flowery wallpaper curling near the ceiling and framed family photos. Most showed four people; Douglas and a woman I presumed was his wife, with their arms around their son and daughter in various scenic spots. The children were in their mid-teens when the photos tapered off, faces sullen behind dust-encrusted glass and their overgrown curly hair.

In a cramped living room, Douglas settled heavily into an armchair angled toward an ancient TV. Alice and I sat down on a sofa shoved against the wall, the distinct smell of mildew wafting up as it took our weight. A fire blazed behind a blackened grate, swamping us with waves of heat.

The cottage was the same inside as it was outside; the bones were good, but neglect was beginning to take its toll. It was the kind of place Ollie dreamed of doing up, his hands waving as he described the renovations he'd do to the outhouses on his parents' farm in Cornwall if they'd listen to him.

'Do I know you?' Douglas looked more reduced when sat, his body hunching into itself. He peered across the gloom, his eyes filmy. All the training we did about how the elderly could be vulnerable became starkly apparent as he regarded us with helpless curiosity.

I shook my head, pity battling with revulsion at his younger self. 'I started at Southampton about a year ago.'

Douglas nodded absently, content to overlook Alice. 'Well after my time.'

'Do you live alone, Mr Frey?' I asked.

'I live with my son.' His gaze swung around the room in lazy arcs and his speech wasn't slurred, but it was like the words were said without conscious decision. Automatic responses, rather than anything he had to think about. 'I don't think he's here right now.'

The cottage couldn't have more than two rooms downstairs, and a couple of bedrooms above. It was strange that Douglas couldn't be sure of the whereabouts of his son.

'Does he work?'

Douglas's focus flicked across the room. 'I don't think he's working at the moment.'

I didn't think he was lying or being difficult. He genuinely didn't recall whether the person living with him had a job or not.

Coming here had been a bad idea, but I'd done it because Juliet asked. She requested so little help, revealed such miniscule parts of herself, that when she did it was almost impossible to say no. But being here felt messier now it was clear Douglas was unwell. He was vulnerable and couldn't have been involved with the shooting. We were intruding on his life for no reason.

I pulled my notepad from my coat pocket and set it on my knee, determined to ask all the necessary questions and clear out. 'What's your son's name?'

Douglas's eyes settled on the fresh page before skittering away. 'Thomas. Tommy.'

'And your daughter, where does she live?'

'Maria lives with her husband in the city. They work there.' Douglas didn't seem concerned by my questioning, didn't want to know how I knew he had a daughter. His limited attention was reserved for finding the right answers. 'She has children.'

'What does Maria do?' I asked.

Douglas swallowed. 'She was at university. She works in the city. She's busy.'

'You must be proud,' Alice said.

The distress Douglas felt at not being able to answer my question lifted, a smile fighting through the folds of his face. 'I am. Tommy makes me proud. He lives with me.'

I tapped my pencil. At least part of the old Douglas was alive and well, happy to overlook his daughter in favour of his son. 'And your wife? Where is she?'

Douglas's face fell back into deep lines. 'She left me.'

'Oh.' I'd assumed the abrupt end to the family photos was precipitated by death.

Douglas picked at a loose thread on the arm of his chair. 'She jumped ship like the rat she was.'

His pronouncement was delivered in the same dull way he'd said everything else. He'd said it many times before, had learnt by rote.

'I'm sorry to pry into a delicate subject, but when did she leave?' I had an inkling of why his wife would have walked away, but I wanted to take a whole picture back to Juliet so that we could rule him out completely.

'After I left the force.' Douglas tugged on the thread. 'She took the kids. Left me here to rot. They only came back when she found someone else to look after her.'

I forced my face to impassivity. Through the curtains time had drawn around this man, we were getting a taste of what a younger Douglas Frey was like. He'd thought he'd get away with coercing women at work and had been shocked when that had blown up in his face. The timing of his wife leaving couldn't be coincidental and had probably blindsided him too.

'I wanted to ask about your retirement.' I kept my voice low and soothing. 'What made you decide to leave?'

Douglas's gaze darted around the room, no longer an absent sway. 'It was time to step down.'

'Did anything in particular prompt the decision?'

His eyes snapped to mine, the hatred behind them scalding. 'I left because that blonde bitch lied about me. Told everyone I wanted to fuck her. Who would want to fuck something like that? Ugly cunt. No one would want her. Not me. She ruined me. Fucking stole my life.'

Silence stretched after Douglas's rant. I breathed through the blood thundering in my ears. Alice's fingers dug into the sofa cushion.

There was no doubt who Douglas was referring to. Pushing him to talk about Juliet had awakened something buried under layers of doddering confusion. It was like a bumbling hedgehog had opened its mouth and bared fangs.

'It was time for a change,' Douglas muttered. All the fight left him, all hateful energy draining away.

The front door bounced off the cottage wall as someone far stronger than Douglas shoved it open. 'Dad? Why's the door unlocked? You know you're meant to stay in when I'm not here.'

'Tommy?' Douglas called, his voice weak when not spewing bile about Juliet. 'I'm in here. We've got visitors.'

Thomas Frey popped his head into the room. His resemblance to a younger Douglas was more pronounced than the fading image sitting beside a blazing fire. His sandy hair stuck up in many directions, his shoulders broad and his head an inch from the wooden bar as he stood in the doorway. His clothes were splattered with paint and a pair of sunglasses sat on his straight nose.

His arrival wasn't ideal. Douglas may have had a vague recollection of our visit, but Thomas's memory would be sharper. We needed to get out before he could delve into our reasons for coming.

Thomas's frown was unmistakable even behind the black frames. 'Who have you got here?'

His voice was loud and bright, at odds with his wary expression. It spoke of someone used to dealing with Douglas's vague answers and half-attention. Thomas's face settled into resignation as his father's turned blank. I wondered how often Douglas let strangers into their home.

'I'm Detective Sergeant Gabe Martin.' I jumped up from the sofa, the adrenaline Douglas's rant awakened powering a movement much more energetic than any other I'd trialled today. My shoulder shouted its protest. 'We needed to ask your father a few questions, but we're done now.'

I wished Thomas would take off his sunglasses. It was hard to tell who he was looking at behind the dark lenses.

'Is there anything else you need?' He stepped into the room to rest a hand on the back of his father's chair, leaving the doorway clear. 'Dad can get confused.'

'He's been helpful.' I took a step toward escape from the stifling room. 'Can I ask where you and your father were on the afternoon of the 24th April?'

Thomas lifted his shoulders. 'Most likely here. I work occasionally, but not in the last week or so. I'm Dad's carer. We don't get out much.' His eyebrows disappeared behind his glasses. 'Is that day important?'

'Thank you for your time.' I nodded at the two men, before hurrying out of the cottage and into the cool spring air.

The pressure of being too close to an unnecessary fire fell off me, along with the weight of doing something I shouldn't have. Douglas clearly wasn't our shooter so there shouldn't be any unpleasant reper-cussions from this chat but prodding an unwell man, even one who had been a monster when able, was uncomfortable.

'You get what you needed?' Alice asked as we walked over to her car.

I nodded, gripping my notepad. I'd jotted down barely anything: the names of Douglas's children and his living situation. Despite the lack of tangible evidence, this conversation had removed Douglas from the pool of suspects.

My phone buzzed furiously in my coat-pocket, like it had received several messages at once. I'd assumed the cottage's roof was slate but perhaps it was lead lined, creating a signal dead spot.

I pulled my phone out and stopped walking. I had several missed calls and a series of messages from Paul and Nicole. I flicked through the most recent.

'Shit.' I rushed over to join Alice at her car. 'You're going to have to put the lights on. We need to get down to the docks.'

Detective Sergeant Nicole Stewart: Witness statement taken on Monday the 27th April at 10:50 a.m. This interview is being conducted by myself, Detective Sergeant Nicole Stewart. The interviewee is Rowan Lough, whose girlfriend Emelia Fleason is also present. We are near the container where Henry Garside's body was discovered earlier today. Rowan, I'm going to keep this brief because you've had an incredibly distressing morning. Can you please tell me your actions leading up to finding Henry's body?

Rowan Lough: I was upset. I didn't think you, the police, were doing enough to find Henry.

[Sniffing.]

Emelia Fleason: Rowan chatted to me about it. We made a plan with a group of mates to search the city.

DS Nicole Stewart: How did you decide where to search?

Emelia Fleason: We split the city up into chunks, and focused on places Henry had been recently or that we thought would be somewhere good to hide someone.

[Sniffing.]

Rowan Lough: I took the section by the sea. It was unlikely Henry would come here voluntarily, since he's so afraid of the water. I thought he would only be down here if someone had taken him. I wish I was wrong.

DS Nicole Stewart: What made you feel so certain Henry had been taken?

Rowan Lough: I know— I knew Henry. He wouldn't have run away. He was excited about the exhibition at the gallery, and he wouldn't have missed that unless someone stopped him from coming.

DS Nicole Stewart: When did you start the search?

Emelia Fleason: Early this morning. The plan was to search before any lectures and stuff, then go out to our sections again whenever we could.

Rowan Lough: I couldn't stop searching once I'd started. I missed a seminar, but I couldn't stand the idea that Henry could be somewhere in need of help and I'd let him down.

[Sniffing.]

DS Nicole Stewart: You're doing really well, Rowan. I only have a few more questions. How did you gain access to this section of the docks?

Rowan Lough: I climbed the fence. The other places I'd searched were easy enough to get around. I couldn't not check here just because it wasn't open to the public.

DS Nicole Stewart: Have you been here before?

Rowan Lough: No. I go to the seafront. Sometimes Henry came with me.

DS Nicole Stewart: Did you break into other containers?

Rowan Lough: No. Lots of them aren't locked. I went into the ones I could. Most of them were empty.

DS Nicole Stewart: What made you decide to break into the one where you found Henry's body?

Rowan Lough: The lock was different to the others. New and not as bulky. I had a crowbar with me. I used it to break the bolt. And I know it will sound strange, but I had a feeling about it. I'd been freaking out the whole morning but when I saw the container, everything jumped up a notch.

DS Nicole Stewart: I'm not going to ask you to talk in detail about what you found inside the container, but was there anything you noticed before or after you discovered Henry's body?

Rowan Lough: The door opened easily. Some of the others were hard to get into. Inside, there was nothing but the big black bag. I used my phone to light the way, so I couldn't see much around me. The bag—

[Sniffing.]

Emelia Fleason: Have you got enough?

DS Nicole Stewart: Almost. Rowan, what were you going to say about the bag?

Rowan Lough: It looked new.

DS Nicole Stewart: That's all my questions, but do you have anything else you'd like to tell me?

[Long pause.]

Rowan Lough: It won't make a difference, but I wish you and the other detective had listened. I told you Henry wouldn't have run away. If you'd searched for him before, had taken this seriously, then maybe there was a chance—

[Sniffing.]

Rowan Lough: Maybe my friend could have still been alive.

Items missing from my flat:

- Phone charger
- Letters from solicitor
- Diary of behaviour
- Address book
- Work ID
- Mum's bracelet
- Painting from fridge
- Cactus

FUCKING BASTARD

You have one new voicemail. Voicemail left today at 11:51 a.m.

'Gabriella, you need to call me. Are you alright? I'm so cross with you, I could scream. I cannot believe you didn't tell us you'd been shot. I can't see how the newspapers could have gotten it wrong, so you must have lied when I asked if you were okay. I don't know why you'd do that. Call me, please, as soon as you can. It's Mum.'

Gabe

A fresh breeze coasting in off the sea greeted me as I stepped out of Alice's car. Gulls cried overhead, wheeling across a narrow strip of pale blue sky. The area I'd directed Alice to was surrounded by towering stacks of shipping containers, their bright paint speckled with rust.

Hand shaking, I slotted my phone into my coat pocket. I'd read Paul and Nicole's messages as we'd rushed over. They'd become increasingly frantic, but they hadn't affected me nearly as much as my mum's name flashing across the screen. She'd called three times, then left a voicemail. I'd tried to keep my face neutral as I listened to her trembling voice.

I'd been so involved in finding my shooter and discovering what had happened to Henry that I'd forgotten to tell my parents about my injury. Or maybe not forgotten, but shoved to the back of my mind. Mum's indignation and worry were the tip of the iceberg. I couldn't deal with everything else she and Dad would hurl at me, but that didn't stop guilt sliding through my guts. I hadn't meant for them to find out in such a careless way.

The bare concrete between the shipping containers was crowded with police cars and forensic vans. Uniformed officers milled around them. At the open latch of one container, flapping tape barred idle entry.

'You don't have to come in,' I murmured to Alice after we gave our names for the log. 'Paul said it's unpleasant.'

She squared her shoulders. 'I can handle it.'

Scenes like this might affect her less the more she was exposed to them. It had the opposite effect on me. If my colleagues' nerves were dulled, mine were flayed open.

Alice lifted the tape and we stepped inside the shipping container. The long rectangular space was lit by a series of leaning lights powered by a generator buzzing outside the door. Three figures gathered at the far end, two in full forensic suits.

Mine and Alice's footsteps echoed as we neared them. Nicole raised her head and walked to meet us, leaving David Rees and a member of his team crouched beside something hidden in the patchy gloom.

'Gabe.' Despite the hint of a smile, Nicole's dark eyes bored into mine. 'Paul had to head back to the station.'

She didn't ask where we'd been, but the subtext was clear. We'd been so delayed in getting here that the only detective inspector currently at work hadn't been able to wait.

'We were following up on other leads,' I muttered, the best I could offer without lying outright.

Nicole nodded. Her cropped black hair accentuated the roundness of her face, her brown skin turned grey by the sporadic lights. Despite her casual friendliness, she always made me feel like a younger sibling playing catch up. She was the other detective sergeant at the station, so was my unacknowledged competition. Married with a kid, juggling a career and a normal home life, Paul regularly gave her the lead on cases and her success rate rivalled Juliet's. It didn't matter that Nicole had at least five years on me and had been promoted long before I was.

Squaring my shoulders despite the pain, I chased the juvenile bull-shit from the forefront of my mind. 'What can you tell me?'

Nicole turned so we could watch the two white bodysuits moving around a dark shape at the end of the shipping container. 'Rowan Lough and other students from Solent University decided we weren't putting in enough effort to find Henry. They took it into their own hands.'

We wouldn't have found Henry without their help. Everything had pointed toward a missing persons case, one with possible elements of self-harm. Our search was focused on places where a young man would run and hide, not where a body could be stashed away. Even if we'd been looking in the right places, I'd been interviewing a harmless old man when I should have been focused on my job.

'Rowan found him.' Nicole walked slowly toward David and his colleague. 'He'd been out all morning around the docks, searching hundreds of containers like this. He was about to give up, but then he spotted this hatch had a different kind of lock than the others. He broke in and found Henry's body.'

'Is Rowan around?' I asked.

Nicole shook her head. 'I questioned him after we couldn't get through to you. The poor guy was devastated. His girlfriend picked him up.'

I hoped the shamed blush staining my cheeks was washed away by the angled lighting. Juliet couldn't have known Henry's body would be discovered while I spoke to Douglas Frey, but her request had the worst timing. My visit might not have endangered Paul's investigation, but it had hindered my ability to oversee my own.

'We've run a check on the container,' Nicole carried on. 'No owner, no history at all.'

The ownership may not have correlated with whoever was using it anyway, but the lack of leads in any direction was frustrating.

'Martin.' David stood up. His light blue eyes flicked to Alice but dismissed her once they alighted on her uniform. 'Nice of you to show up.'

'What have you worked out so far?' I ignored his jab and pulled my notepad from my pocket.

'The young man who discovered the body told us this is Henry Garside, who was reported missing on the 25th April,' David said in a bland drawl. He would have rattled off this information once already to the detectives able to rush to the scene when called. 'His face is relatively untouched so it's likely he's right, but I've sent samples off for DNA matching so we can be sure.'

David stepped to the side. I walked forward to stand beside him. One controlled breath, and I moved my notepad out of the way.

Henry's body sprawled from a thick black bag, the material similar to a weatherproof coat. He was naked, exposed to where his thighs and lower legs hid beneath the fabric. Bruises and scrapes littered his skin. His blond hair was matted with blood and more caked around his nose and mouth. Despite the damage, this was unmistakably the same face as those on missing persons posters throughout the city.

One of Henry's arms crooked awkwardly around his back, but the other reached across the floor. Each finger was shortened to a bloody stump below the first knuckle.

I swallowed the gorge rising in my throat. 'This looks professional.'

'It does,' David confirmed. 'The fingers were likely taken because there was a struggle. Whoever killed him didn't want stray DNA showing up under his nails. He's been stripped and cleaned, except for his head.'

'Our theory is that whoever was working on him was disturbed,' Nicole said from behind my shoulder. 'They stashed the body away and planned to finish the job of cleaning him at another time.'

Then they would have taken him to a far corner of the country and dumped him. He'd have become an unidentified body, if his remains were ever found.

'How did he die?' I gripped my pen tight in one fist. 'And when?'

'Head trauma, most likely. Days ago.' David squatted next to the body, putting his face level with Henry's. 'He's got a cracked skull. There's a lot of blood around the back of his head. Looks like he hit a flat surface.' He gestured at Henry's exposed torso. 'The other injuries were sustained before he died.'

Vivid bruising stood out along the side of Henry's ribs. More marks darkened his wrist, like he'd been tied up before he died. Blood pressing toward the surface of his white skin cut through a tattoo of a cresting wave on his arm.

'I'll leave you to it.' I turned on my heel and smiled tightly at Nicole. 'Alice and I can take over here.'

Her mouth pinched. 'Actually, Angela asked for you to head to the station.'

'Did she say why?' Anxiety and annoyance spiked. Angela couldn't have figured out where Alice and I were this morning, but there was no other reason to recall me to the station when a crime scene needed managing.

'She did not.' Each word was distinct. Nicole shrugged. 'I asked, but she just said to send you there as soon as possible.'

'Fine.' I flashed Nicole a quick smile. 'Thanks for asking.'

'I'll make sure you get all the information from here as soon as I do,' Nicole promised.

'Thank you.' My smile was more genuine this time. It wasn't her fault I felt like a child called home.

Alice led the way out of the shipping container, boots thumping on the metal floor. We ducked under the tape at the door and walked to her car.

I paused before climbing in. I looked back to where Rowan found his friend's body. It was the kind of thing that would haunt him for a lifetime, but it was because of his dogged diligence that we'd found Henry. Without Rowan's intervention, his friend would have remained lost.

Guilt crawled over my skin. I'd considered Henry a missing person so hadn't extended the search to places like this, but if I'd taken Rowan and Henry's parents seriously I could have spared his friend the trauma of finding his mutilated body. I'd assumed they spoke out of defensive love when they said he would never have run off.

Shaking my head, I got into the car. Henry had been dead the whole time we'd been searching for him. Murdered.

Alice sniffed. 'God.'

'Hey.' I rested a hand on her shoulder. 'It's okay.'

'It's really not, is it?' She pressed her palms over her eyes, but tears leaked around them. 'That poor boy.'

I squeezed her arm. Soon, we would call on Henry's parents. Telling them they were right, that someone had caused their son's disappearance, would be a whole different kind of hell to seeing his broken body abandoned in the darkest recess of a shipping container.

Unknown number. Sent 13:21.

The second payment hasn't come through.

Unknown number. Sent 13:35.

You thought you'd get paid in full for doing half a job?

Unknown number. Sent 13:36.

I need that money.

Unknown number. Sent 13:37.

Count yourself lucky that a bit of money is all you're losing out on.

From: James Knowles **james.knowles@police.gov.uk**
To: Paul Willis **paul.willis@mit.gov.uk**,
Nicole Stewart **nicole.stewart@mit.gov.uk**
Date: **27 April, 14:39**
Subject: **Operation Orion – Dunlow's alibi**

Paul and Nicole,

Just had a call from the client Timothy Dunlow met with on the afternoon of the shooting. Grant Olsen has multiple ways to prove he and Dunlow were together from two p.m. to four p.m. on the afternoon of the twenty-fourth – sign-in records, CCTV for the building, diary entries for their meeting, and an email they sent together at the end of the meeting.

Along with the receipts Mr Dunlow has already provided for the morning, it would have been difficult for him to be in the vicinity of the shooting at the time it occurred.

Although Mr Dunlow has an alibi, I thought you would like to know he's been visiting a local shooting range every two weeks for the last few years. The most recent time was one week before the shooting. A copy of the sign-in sheet is attached to this email.

I hope this is helpful,

James

ONE ATTACHMENT

DATE	NAME	SIGN-IN	SIGN-OUT
17th April	Ursula Jones	2pm	3pm
17/04	B BRIGHT	14.10	16.40
17/04	Timothy Dunlow	14.30	15.40
17th April	Jim Hunter	14.35	15.15
17/04	M Turner	14.45	15.30
17 APRIL	J PATEL	3	4
17.04	K Patel	3pm	4pm

Gabe

I spat into the toilet bowl, then pushed the button to flush. Slumping against the wall, I closed my eyes and breathed shallowly across my acidic tongue.

Roadworks had forced Alice and me on a winding route back to the station. Bile was bubbling up my throat as I made my excuses and rushed away.

Alice wasn't as perceptive as Juliet. She wouldn't figure out where I'd gone or why. I hoped Juliet thought this was a reaction to the horrifying sights we dealt with, rather than an involuntary weakness I couldn't seem to shake.

Tears prickled against my closed eyelids. Faced with a murder victim, I found it impossible to keep thoughts of my lost brother at bay. I'd not seen his body, I'm not sure I'd asked to, but the knowledge that his life had been torn away was a brand I could never erase. I carried his death with me always, but it was only after facing a new murder victim that I reacted like this.

I leant to spit again. Juliet and I hadn't investigated a murder since Melanie Pirt was killed, so I hadn't needed to make urgent use of the lone toilet in the station separated by two doors from any prying co-workers. The air freshener I'd stashed behind the cistern was untouched. I filled the cubicle with floral mist and escaped to the outer space.

Swilling water around my teeth, I splashed my face. Nothing could be done about the unhealthy yellow tinge to my skin, but that could be blamed on the shooting. I popped an extra strong mint in my mouth, smoothed a hand over my cropped hair, and unlocked the door.

No one waited in the corridor. I hurried along toward the lifts, keeping my head down near open office doors. This momentary weakness had to be tolerated, but I didn't let it affect my work so no one needed to know about it.

I rested on the mirrored wall of the lift as it rose upward, eyes fixed on the ceiling rather than my ghostly reflection. Now I'd gotten this over and done with, I had a lot of work to do. The investigation needed to switch from a missing persons case to murder. Alice and I would need to reinterview Rowan and the other students on Henry's floor, talk to his parents, and scour the CCTV around his disappearance.

The seventh floor was quiet as I walked to mine and Juliet's office. It was empty. I couldn't assume Alice would continue as my temporary partner now the nature of the investigation had changed. She'd been affected by Henry's broken body. The question was whether she could control that reaction and do what needed to be done, or whether she would let it rule her.

I leant on my desk and stared at the packed evidence wall. The Galanis brothers looked blankly back at me.

The partial clean-up of Henry's body looked professional. I'd get more information once he was moved and the results from samples David had taken poured in, but assuming Henry had been murdered by someone who had done it before and knew how to dispose of a body was a good place to start.

Henry didn't fit the profile of the others we believed had been killed by the Galanis brothers, but his death did. They were adept at making people with no family and friends vanish. I wasn't sure why they would murder an art student, but they were at the heart of organised crime across the city. Whoever had partially cleaned Henry's body had likely done so at their order.

Henry had been brave to move down to Southampton. His sketch-books and artwork showed a young man determined to conquer his fear of water. Whatever happened to him before he died, I hoped it was swift, that he hadn't been too afraid.

Alice appeared in the doorway, and I tore myself from a staring contest with Tsambikos's smirking portrait.

'You ready to get to work?' I asked. 'We need to organise an interview with Henry's parents and Rowan as soon as possible, and we need to establish where Henry went after he left the art building the morning he disappeared.'

Alice stepped into mine and Juliet's office. 'We're not going to have time for any of that.'

I pushed away from my desk, my shoulder grinding. 'What?'

Angela walked into the office. Her eyes raked over my sickly skin and the oversized coat Ollie had lent me, which didn't hide the lopsided slope of my back.

'Gabe, you need to head home.'

My organs migrated several inches toward the floor. 'I need to be here.'

'The deal was you came back to work so soon after the shooting with a lighter case load.' Angela crossed her arms, the front of her shirt creasing over her rounded stomach. 'How does that fit with investigating a murder?'

I opened my mouth, then snapped it shut. It wasn't possible. To find Henry's killer I'd need to stay late at the office, searching for the smallest detail to bring them to justice.

'I can do it.' I straightened my spine despite the ache trailing down it. 'My shoulder is barely bothering me. I don't need to be on a lighter caseload, and the whole point of letting me back was to take pressure off Paul and Nicole. Are you going to throw a murder case at them on top of trying to find mine and Juliet's shooter?'

Angela's nostrils flared. 'That's not your concern.'

'But it does concern me. Ma'am,' I tacked on, when Angela's eyes widened. 'Henry's parents won't like being passed to another detective.' I scrabbled for reasons to stay. 'I know this case. I'm best placed to find Henry's killer.'

I stopped talking. Angela regarded me coolly, her full lips pressed together. She knew everything I'd have to say. Pleading wouldn't persuade her to let me stay.

'I'm not taking you off the case.' She finally broke the loaded silence watched over by a fidgeting Alice. 'But I do need you to head home for now. I have to assess whether this is the right investigation for you to be leading on so soon after being injured, and you agreed to shorter days. Paul and Nicole will kick start things for now, and you can take over tomorrow if I decide it's in your best interest to continue.'

I wanted to punch something. It wasn't my fault I'd been shot. My mind was perfectly functional, but I wasn't allowed to do my job because some idiot decided to take a pop at me as well as Juliet.

'Alice will give you a lift home.' Angela stepped to one side, leaving the door wide open for my exit.

'Fine.' I glared at the floor as I stalked past her.

Maddy was hovering beside her desk as I stepped out into the main part of the floor. I grabbed her hand and dragged her along with me.

'I need you to bring everything from the office wall to my house after you finish work,' I whispered, in case Angela was following. 'Bring everything you can to do with the Galanis brothers.'

I let go of her arm and marched toward the lifts. Alice managed to hop inside before the doors slid shut. She wisely didn't speak as we descended.

I ground my teeth together. Angela might have decided I was too fragile to be at the station, but I wouldn't let her stop me from doing everything I could to find Henry's killer. If the Galanis brothers had anything to do with his death, I'd catch them.

Call connected at 16:04.

'Gabriella, darling. Are you alright?'

'Yeah, Mum. I'm fine. I promise.'

'Why on earth didn't you tell us you'd been shot?'

'I don't know, Mum. I'm sorry.'

'You promise you're okay?'

'Yes. It was a clean shot. No permanent damage.'

'Are you resting? Do you need us to come down? Or you could come home?'

'No, I don't need any of that. Work is keeping me busy.'

'Work? Gabriella, what are you thinking of going back to work so soon after being shot? You need to rest.'

'I don't. I'm fine.'

'You can't be fine, darling. Look, me and Dad will come down tomorrow and we can see what you need. We can bring you back home for a proper rest and—'

'No.'

'Gabriella, you're clearly not looking after yourself.'

'I don't need looking after. My shoulder might hurt, but it's manageable.'

'If your shoulder is hurting, you shouldn't be working.'

'That's blatantly not true. This is why I didn't want to tell you.'

'What do you mean?'

'You and Dad don't get that working is the best thing for me. I need to be here. I need to get on.'

'We want to look after you, love.'

'I don't need looking after.'

'It's not weak to take time after you've been hurt to care for yourself, to let other people care for you.'

'That's not what this is. I don't need to take time off. Look, I've got to go. Bye.'

'Gabriella, do not hang—'

ARE ALL WOMEN THIS STUPID?

Clara the Clothes Lover @ClaraClothesLover

Babes I don't know about you but the only thing I've been interested in with this whole trial is my ICON Detective Stern's outfits. Queen is on FIRE!!

BITCH USES CLOTHES TO DISTRACT FROM THE FACT THAT SHE'S A USELESS ARSEHOLE

Gabe

A soft knock on my front door was followed by a booming bark as Ollie slotted a risotto into the oven.

'I'll get it,' I called.

I unpicked myself from between the piles of notes I'd strewn on the sofa. I didn't have anything to do with Henry's case at home, but I'd used the rage burning through me after my conversations with Angela and Mum to dive into the file around mine and Juliet's shooting with renewed vigour.

I'd simmered down as I'd searched through transcripts and high-lighted key details. Ollie supplied me with coffee and raised his eyebrows when I started sticking things to one wall, but relegated himself to the kitchen.

'Don't be a berk.' I patted Artie on the head as I joined him at the front door, his tail thumping against the wall. Maddy loved him, but he was almost as tall as her when he bounced to give a particularly enthusiastic greeting. Using my legs as a barrier against my dog, I tugged open the door.

Juliet stood on my path. Gone were the tracksuit bottoms and ill-fitting top. Pale green trousers and a matching jacket rested over a baby-blue blouse. Shiny navy heels complemented her polished nails. Apart from the slight padding to her shoulder and the sling holding her left arm close to her chest, there was no indication she'd been involved in a shooting days ago.

'Evening.' Her lips curved into a small smile.

'How are you?' I let her inside, barring Artie from licking her.

'Fine.'

The high walls Juliet built around herself were back in place. I couldn't act on the impulse to draw her close, to show her she wasn't alone. I couldn't ask questions about where she'd been today, if she'd had enough rest, or had seen her husband.

Instead, I offered her what she'd accept. 'Douglas couldn't have shot us, so I've been taking another look at the files Paul brought over. Maddy's bringing more about the shooting and Operation Juno later.'

Juliet's eyes lit up, unaffected by the mention of her previous superintendent. 'Perfect.'

I led Artie into the living room and straight to his basket, unwilling to watch a much more aware Juliet reject my dog's affections. She walked to the information tacked to one wall, while I looked over the files spread across the sofa.

I was uncomfortable with Ollie being here while I worked, but I couldn't see any way around it. I wanted his warmth and kindness, despite how cranky I'd been when I'd slammed through the front door. It shouldn't have been a surprise to find him here when Alice dropped me off. Our pattern had become spending every evening together. Ollie wasn't to know that to get my job done, I needed space.

I'd asked him not to look at anything. He'd promised, but I couldn't help checking the angles of the papers. It didn't look like he'd taken a peek. He wasn't as curious as me, wasn't professionally obligated to stick his nose into other people's business.

'Juliet.' Ollie wiped his hands on his apron as he came out of the kitchen. 'It's great to properly meet you.'

Juliet accepted his outstretched hand. Watching two people I cared for interact was bizarre considering their vastly different reactions to one another's presence. Juliet was a staple name in the work stories I deemed safe to tell Ollie, so he'd been excited to meet her for months. If Juliet remembered I had a boyfriend, she'd shown no inclination toward getting to know him.

'You remember Ollie,' I said, dodging any awkwardness in case Juliet had forgotten the name of the man whose arms she'd fallen into yesterday.

Juliet pulled her hand back and nodded, her attention reverting to the evidence-covered wall. Dodging Artie's attempt to slip his head under her fingers, she stepped closer. I scrunched the fur between his ears.

If I ignored the dog at my side and the homecooked meal and Ollie's presence, I could pretend we were at the station. Wearing one of my boyfriend's jumpers and a pair of leggings didn't ruin the illusion. I was far too used to feeling underdressed compared to Juliet.

Her eyes roved over the information I'd pinned to the wall. 'We need wool.'

She didn't ask about my visit to Douglas, disinterested now he wasn't a possible suspect. Juliet either trusted my abilities so highly that she didn't need any details, or hadn't considered she could have been sending me into a potentially volatile situation.

'Maddy's bringing it.'

Juliet dipped her head at the wall. 'Shall we talk through what we've got so far?'

'Do you want a drink?' Ollie asked.

'Black coffee, please.' Juliet didn't turn.

I offered Ollie a smile. He raised an eyebrow at Juliet's back while holding up my favourite mug. I'd told him Juliet was brilliant at her job and how much I admired her, but I'd been sure to furnish him with stories of her harsher side too.

I was glad when he retreated to the kitchen. I didn't want him to see or hear anything he shouldn't.

'Now Douglas is out of the picture, the Galanis brothers are top of the suspect list.' I spoke softly, hoping Juliet would follow my lead and keep her voice down. 'They have means and opportunity in abundance, and their alibi means next to nothing since one of them wouldn't have pulled the trigger anyway.'

Juliet frowned at Tsambikos, Alcaeus and Giannis's pictures. 'What would have prompted it? They hadn't done anything different, and we weren't chasing any new leads.'

I steered my mind from worrying about how her voice would carry through my tiny maisonette and focused on the words she'd said. The investigation into the Galanis brothers had wielded a frustrating lack of convictions thus far. The brothers ran a tight and faithful ship. Any underlings we apprehended were unwilling to speak out against their leaders and ready to take the fall for any crimes we asked about.

'The university student who went missing has been found dead,' I said.

Juliet had no visible reaction. 'And?'

'Henry Garside disappeared the morning before we were shot. He doesn't fit the profile of the brothers' typical victim, but the clean-up of his body looked professional.' I flinched away from the memory of Henry's mangled hand. 'Because of that and the timing, there could be a link.'

As soon as I said Henry's name, Juliet whipped her phone out of her pocket. A deep crack splintered the centre of the screen, bisecting his missing persons poster. 'You're right. He isn't who the brothers would usually go for.'

I didn't know if that was dismissal of my hunch or not. 'There's also Timothy Dunlow.'

Juliet's head tipped to the side to take in his sparse section of wall. 'The denial of his visit to Karl is intriguing, but he's prone to lying to the police.'

During the investigation into Melanie Pirt's murder, Dunlow not only lied about his own actions but encouraged his sons to do the same. It made an already tangled case more difficult to unpick.

'Paul will chat with Karl soon.' Whenever the Prison Liaison Officer could arrange it. Getting inmates to cooperate with investigations outside their prison walls was notoriously tricky. 'Maybe he will be more forthcoming about their chat. Although, I'm not sure that will make Dunlow more of a contender. He could have an alibi and Karl didn't seem to have any ill will toward us.'

A hand landing on my uninjured shoulder made me jump. Pain jolted through my other side. I raised a smile for Ollie while calculating exactly how much he may have heard. Too much. Having him here while Juliet and I talked through a case was unnerving. Especially as we were debating who may have had good enough reason and chance to shoot us.

He gestured at the drinks he'd placed on the coffee table. 'I know you're both keen to talk through the case, but maybe you could do it from somewhere you can rest as well?'

Juliet finally turned away from the wall. Her eyes were flat as she regarded Ollie and the steaming coffees. 'Do you live here?'

Ollie's cheeks flushed. Corresponding warmth rose to my own. I studiously avoided talking about our living arrangements. Ollie stayed here more often than not, slept in my bed and filled my evenings with his gentle laughter, but I wasn't ready to live with him. It didn't feel like the next step in our relationship, but rather a flying leap into the unknown.

'No,' Ollie spluttered out through a forced smile.

'Why are you here, then?' Juliet asked.

The heat slipped from my face. Words caught in my throat.

Ollie's kindness was always going to be too much for Juliet, but I didn't know she would pull a move like this. She wasn't rude to Maddy when she forced us to eat or shouted the time when she left the station as a reminder to go home soon.

'I came to make dinner.' Bewilderment made Ollie's words slow. All the warnings in the world couldn't prepare him for Juliet's ruthless efficiency. When there was a job to be done, she would kick anything and anyone out of the way that threatened to slow her down.

'Did Gabe ask you to do that?' Juliet's voice was toneless. She didn't revel in ousting Ollie, but her goal was clear. She wanted to investigate our shooting unimpeded by his ministrations.

He turned to me, clearly looking for back-up. I opened my mouth, then pressed my lips together and tried not to combust with the shame twisting through my guts. I didn't want Juliet to be rude, but I wasn't able to do what it took to make him step out of our way. If I wanted to work, to find our shooter and Henry's killer, then Ollie had to leave.

His face settled into unfamiliar lines of resignation as the silence stretched. I hated the creases at the edges of his eyes, the slope of his mouth. He stepped forward and kissed my undeserving forehead.

'Leave dinner to sit for ten minutes out of the oven once the timer goes off,' he murmured.

Too quickly for me to stop it, to reconsider, he gathered his things. Mutely, I trailed after him, only to watch the front door swing shut in his wake. The click of the lock felt overloud. Shellshocked, I returned to my living room.

Juliet had gone back to perusing the evidence like nothing had happened. She flicked through the papers I'd pinned to the wall, deftly sidestepping Artie's questing nose.

A small part of me thought I might hate Juliet. She'd ripped away my source of support and would offer nothing to take its place. Because she stood alone, she expected me to do the same.

It was an effort to remind myself that I had a job to do, one I couldn't concentrate on fully with my boyfriend around. I'd always assumed I would do something to chase Ollie away, but maybe not. Perhaps the absence of action would finally open his eyes to the reality of being with me.

Call connected at 17:10.

'Hello?'

  'Hi. This is Sally Bull. Is that Keith Stern?'

  'Yes, that's me.'

  'Great. I'm returning your call to Children's Services. I'm a social worker in the Child in Need team. Lara and Ellie have been allocated to me for a section 17 Child in Need assessment.'

  'Oh, thank you.'

  'That's quite alright. You mentioned your wife is acting erratically and you're concerned for your daughters?'

  'Yes. My wife, Juliet, was recently injured. Since then, she's been strange. Well, I have to admit, there were signs before she was hurt. But it's gotten worse.'

  'Do you think she poses a physical threat to your daughters?'

  'God, I don't know. I'd hate to think that.'

  'This can be a difficult thing to confront. Perhaps the best next step would be a home visit. I can meet you and your daughters and we can chat through your situation in more detail, plus make sure your steps for getting help are clear.'

  'That would be brilliant.'

  'It would be best to chat when your wife is absent. Would tomorrow morning work?'

  'Yes, that's fine. Juliet won't be here.'

  'Great. I have your address already. In the meantime, please call 999 if you become concerned for your own or your daughters' safety.'

  'Yes, I will. Thank you so much.'

Call connected at 17:48.

'Hello, Detective Inspector Paul Willis.'

'Hello, it's Ryan White here. I've got Karl Biss with me. Are you ready to talk?'

'Absolutely. Pass him over.'

'Will do. Just a reminder; Karl is free to end this conversation whenever he wishes. He's been offered legal counsel but has refused. If he changes his mind, I'll sort it before you speak again.'

'Great stuff.'

'Right. Here you are.'

'Hi. This is Karl.'

'Hello, Karl. Thank you for agreeing to speak with me. My name is Detective Inspector Paul Willis. I have some questions for you about a shooting that occurred after you were sentenced.'

'It was Gabe and Juliet, right?'

'It was. How did you hear about it?'

'We get newspapers in here. Are they alright?'

'Both of them sustained serious injuries, but they'll recover. Any idea who might have shot them?'

'Oh, I see. You think I had something to do with it?'

'I find it strange the two detectives who worked Melanie Pirt's case were shot minutes after you were sentenced with a similar gun to the one you used to commit murder.'

'How would I have had anything to do with it from in here?'

'You had a visit from Timothy Dunlow. Can you tell me about that?'

'Dunlow hasn't visited me.'

'There's no point in lying. We've spoken to Officer White about it.'

'Well, he's wrong. Dunlow didn't come to see me. I don't know why you'd think he would.'

'Karl, you've had one visit since you entered prison and it was from Timothy Dunlow.'

'You haven't considered that Officer White could be mistaken about who visited me?'

'Who was it, then?'

'He's right about one thing. A Dunlow did come to see me.'

'Leo?'

'Third time's the charm.'

'Terence Dunlow visited you in prison?'

'Yeah. About a month ago.'

'What did you talk about?'

'He was quiet at first. I wondered if he was going to explode like his dad would. I thought he might blame me for how he can't dip into the endless daddy money pot any more. But he didn't want to talk about that. He asked what it felt like to shoot someone.'

'What did you tell him?'

'That it was very different to the shooting he did with his daddy down at the range. That he likely didn't have the stomach for it.'

'Did he say anything about Detectives Martin and Stern?'

'He was angry at them. He blames them for what's gone wrong in his life. He said they'd ruined it.'

'Right. Thank you for talking to me, Karl. I'll be in touch if there's anything else.'

'I'll be here.'

Gabe

'Thought I'd give Maddy the night off,' Paul said.

I'd hoped it was Ollie at my front door. He didn't like being sent away and was here to do something about it. It could have been him if I'd given any indication that what Juliet said didn't tally with my thoughts. Or if he wasn't so consistently respectful of my wishes.

Paul shrugged off his coat. 'That's everything about the shooting from today, plus all your recent findings from Juno.' He raised his head and sniffed. 'What's cooking?'

'Cooked,' I corrected, holding the file he'd given me to the uninjured side of my chest. 'Ollie made risotto.'

'He's a saint.'

Paul's words compounded the unignorable guilt I'd been carrying since I'd allowed Juliet to oust my boyfriend. I'd forced down my portion of creamy rice, each mouthful a reminder of how lovely Ollie was and how rotten I'd been to him. Yet each time I reached for my phone to beg him to come back, I reminded myself this was necessary. Distancing myself from him would only last a short while. I had to get this job done.

'Juliet.' Paul tensed when he walked into my living room.

I scooted past him and passed the file to Juliet. 'You want any risotto?'

That distracted them. Their nonsense was tolerable at the station but the thought of them sparring in my cramped living room gave me the beginning of a tension headache. With Juliet poring over the day's work on the sofa beside me and Paul digging in to the last remains of risotto on a ratty armchair Ollie had carried home from a charity shop, they didn't snipe at each other for several blessed minutes.

'Sorry Angela sent you home.' Paul chased grains of rice around his bowl. 'Where were you this morning?'

My eyes snapped to Juliet, but she continued leafing through the file. 'Following other leads. Do you think Angela will let me back?'

'I've made an argument for it.' Paul grimaced. 'Not up to me, though, and she isn't happy with you working a more complex case while recovering.'

I bit my tongue, telling myself not to bristle. Paul didn't agree with Angela. He understood physical harm didn't equate to mental ineptitude. It was gutting to be powerless, but I had to wait for Angela's decree before I knew whether or not I'd be working Henry's case officially.

'Did you speak to Mr and Mrs Garside?' That couldn't be delayed. When a body was found, their loved ones needed to be informed quickly regardless of whether the person leading the case had been sent home.

Paul nodded heavily. 'They were heartbroken.'

I didn't ask whether they'd been cross about another detective change. That had likely seemed inconsequential once they heard what Paul had to say.

I peered at the transcript of Paul and Karl's chat that Juliet was speed-reading, keen to move on from distraught parents I currently had no way to help. 'You talked to Karl about Terence Dunlow?'

'Indeed.' Paul set his empty bowl on my coffee table, his hands instantly occupied by a seemingly touch-deprived Alsatian. 'Timothy wasn't lying about ignoring Karl. It was Terence who visited the prison. The Prison Liaison Officer got the names mixed up. Terence asked what it felt like to hurt someone. Karl said Terence blames you two for how his life has changed.' Paul scratched between Artie's ears. 'I tried calling and popped over to his boyfriend's house before I came here, but no joy. I'll try again on my way back to the station.'

I wished I had notes or a needy dog to keep my hands busy. I twisted them in the hem of Ollie's jumper, my shoulder pulsing as I considered the possibility Terence Dunlow had shot me and Juliet.

Terence could blame us for his changed circumstances. His father certainly did. I wondered if Terence had enough oomph to take violent action against us. He'd always seemed passive to me, cowering under his father's moneyed protection.

Juliet flicked through Paul's notes about his interview with Karl. 'Do you think that puts Terence in the running?'

Paul rocked his head from side to side, hands buried in Artie's fur. 'Maybe. The Galanis brothers are the main suspects, but the timing of the shooting and the visit to Karl have to be taken into account. According to Karl, Terence is pissed at you.'

'Karl could be lying and if this is anything like Melanie Pirt's case, the Dunlows being cross at us isn't an indication of guilt,' I said. 'Timothy and Terence in particular consider themselves above the law. It was unbelievable to them that we would consider them suspects back then. I reckon you'll come up against that attitude again.'

I'd already encountered it at the gallery, but Terence's disinclination to talk to us didn't mean he'd had anything to do with the shooting or Henry's death. Yet what were the chances he was mixed up in two high priority cases and had no involvement in either?

Juliet flipped the file shut and rested it on the arm of the sofa. 'Being standoffish because they're arses or because they're guilty looks deceptively alike.'

'I agree,' Paul said.

I blinked at them. Normally, accord between Paul and Juliet was reached with far more reluctance. I narrowed my eyes at him. Paul could be being kinder because she'd been shot. I wondered if that pity extended to me.

'We'll talk with Terence tonight, if we can find him. Nicole wanted to pop home to see the little one, so I thought I'd drop in on you while I waited.' Paul nodded at the files. 'I'll look through Juno too.'

'Do you think we've missed something?' Hardness wound through Juliet's words.

'We have to consider whether we did anything in the last week or so that upset the Galanis brothers,' I rushed to keep the peace.

'What about Douglas Frey?' Paul winced as he extended his foot back and forth. 'Is he worth pursuing?'

'He's an unlikely culprit,' Juliet said without missing a beat. 'We've had no contact since he left the force and he would be in his seventies now. I'm not sure he'd be physically able.'

Paul nodded. 'Could Karl have influenced Terence into hurting you?'

I tried not to obviously unclench as the conversation moved on from Douglas. 'I don't think so. Even after we caught Karl, I didn't get the sense he fostered any particular ill will toward us.'

'I'm not sure I agree,' Juliet said. 'Karl can't have been pleased we figured out he killed Melanie. He might blame us, instead of himself, for his current living arrangements. He's capable of pretending to like us, then feeding poison to Terence. Karl has a twisted mind.'

I pinched the hem of Ollie's jumper. I feared people would dismiss me as broken, decide I was less capable or logical, if they knew my past. But that wasn't what Juliet was doing. She wasn't judging Karl because of the trauma he'd suffered. She deemed him a monster because of what he'd gone on to do.

'Terence is more likely to fall for manipulation than his father,' I mused. 'He's just as entitled, but not nearly as savvy.'

'I'll find out what he was talking to Karl about soon.' Paul removed his hands from Artie's fur and planted them on the arms of the chair to push himself up. Grabbing his stick, he gestured for me and Juliet to stay on the sofa.

'I can see myself out.' He headed for my short hallway. 'You two rest.'

Juliet wrinkled her nose, but Paul missed it as he walked from the room. We waited quietly while he put on his coat and unlatched the front door, turning to look at one another once it clicked shut.

'Thank you for dealing with it when he mentioned Frey.' I didn't like lying to Paul, and Juliet had removed the necessity.

She shrugged, then winced. 'He didn't need to know.'

Detective Sergeant Nicole Stewart: Informal interview recorded with permission of the interviewee, Terence Dunlow, on the 27th April at 7:30 p.m. at his home. The interview is being conducted by Detective Inspector Paul Willis and myself, Detective Sergeant Nicole Stewart. Terence can stop this interview at any time and is free to seek legal counsel. This interview is regarding the shooting of Detective Inspector Juliet Stern and Detective Sergeant Gabriella Martin, and the disappearance of Henry Garside.

Detective Inspector Paul Willis: Thank you for making the time to talk to us this evening.

Terence Dunlow: It's fine, but I'm not sure what you think I'll be able to tell you. The first thing I knew about the shooting was when Leo called me that evening and I've never met Henry.

DS Nicole Stewart: Can you tell us about Leo's call?

Terence Dunlow: He was upset about seeing the detectives get hurt, especially since Dad told him off. Leo almost forgot to tell me what the verdict was, until I reminded him.

DI Paul Willis: How did you feel when you heard Detectives Martin and Stern had been shot?

Terence Dunlow: Concerned. I have to say, I didn't know the detectives well so I was more upset for Leo. He's been disturbed by what happened with the girl last year. He didn't need for this to happen. And he didn't need Dad to be an arse about it as well.

DS Nicole Stewart: How did you feel when Leo told you Karl Biss had been found guilty?

Terence Dunlow: Relieved. Leo had been following the trial obsessively. Now it's over, he can move on with his life.

DI Paul Willis: How did you feel about the verdict itself?

Terence Dunlow: It was a forgone conclusion. Karl confessed.

DI Paul Wills: How do you feel about Karl?

Terence Dunlow: I don't feel anything about him.

DS Nicole Stewart: When did you last see Karl?

Terence Dunlow: Must have been before he ran off last year. I'm not sure exactly when.

DI Paul Willis: I spoke to Karl earlier today.

Terence Dunlow: Ah.

DI Paul Willis: Ah, indeed. Would you like to amend your previous answer?

Terence Dunlow: I visited Karl in prison. Once. It wasn't important.

DS Nicole Stewart: Can you tell us about this visit?

Terence Dunlow: It was short. We didn't have much to say to one another.

DI Paul Willis: Can you tell us what you did say?

Terence Dunlow: The things the detectives said about why Karl killed that girl gnawed at me. I wanted to know if it was true.

DS Nicole Stewart: For clarity, 'that girl' Terence is referring to is Melanie Pirt, the young woman shot and killed by Karl Biss last year.

DI Paul Willis: What did you say to Karl when you visited him?

Terence Dunlow: I asked if he'd killed Miss Pirt because of us. Or, at least, because of how we'd treated him.

DI Paul Willis: What did Karl say?

Terence Dunlow: Not a lot. I talked to my boyfriend, Benedict Hogan, when I got home and realised I'd gone to see Karl to try to get rid of misplaced guilt. I didn't need to feel responsible for what happened because I'd treated him badly in a very mild way. That didn't mean I was guilty of murder.

DS Nicole Stewart: Is that all you talked to Karl about?

Terence Dunlow: I asked him why he was so adamant, before I was outed, that I should tell Dad I'm gay. That was the only time Karl smiled. He didn't say anything, but it was pretty clear why he'd been pushy. He was looking for any way to cause trouble between us, that was all he was ever interested in. After it became clear he wasn't going to give me any answers, I left.

DI Paul Willis: Karl has given a different account of your visit.

Terence Dunlow: What's he said? You know he's a liar.

DI Paul Willis: It's interesting you call him a liar. I guess brothers really are alike.

Terence Dunlow: We're not.

DI Paul Willis: Karl said you were angry when you met with him. He said you asked what it was like to kill someone.

Terence Dunlow: What? I can't. No. I didn't bloody say anything like that.

DI Paul Willis: He said you were angry at Detectives Martin and Stern, that you blamed them for being cut off from your father. Karl said you claimed the detectives ruined your life.

Terence Dunlow: That's not true. None of it is true. I'm not angry at the detectives. Honestly, I don't feel much toward them except gratitude for putting Karl in his rightful place. I wouldn't say any nonsense about them ruining my life, because it's simply not true. Since being outed and becoming estranged from my father, my life has gotten better. I'm free now.

DS Nicole Stewart: Why do you think Karl gave such a different account of your conversation?

Terence Dunlow: Because he's a bloody freak who's looking for any way to hurt me and my family. He killed a girl to get back at us for not welcoming him into the fold, when we didn't know who the hell he was.

DI Paul Willis: Terence, where were you on the afternoon of the 24th April?

Terence Dunlow: I finished work at about three p.m., then I came home.

DS Nicole Stewart: Can anyone confirm that?

Terence Dunlow: No. Benny has been away the last few days.

DI Paul Willis: No one can confirm your whereabouts on the twenty-fourth after three p.m.?

Terence Dunlow: No, they can't. But that doesn't mean I was off shooting anyone.

DI Paul Willis: How about pushing someone?

Terence Dunlow: What?

DS Nicole Stewart: The body of Henry Garside was discovered this morning. He has severe head injuries, possibly resulting from a fall.

Terence Dunlow: God. That's terrible. But I had nothing to do with it. I didn't know him. Never met him.

DI Paul Willis: That's what you said when you spoke with Detective Martin before. I wondered if you wanted to amend your statement.

Terence Dunlow: There's nothing to amend. I'm sorry about what's happened to him, but I know nothing. I did nothing.

DI Paul Willis: It's interesting that at the time of two violent crimes, you have no alibi.

Terence Dunlow: I don't think it's interesting. Have you got any more questions? I've got to be up early tomorrow morning.

DS Nicole Stewart: One more. Will you submit your DNA for testing? We'd like to rule you out as a suspect.

Terence Dunlow: Yes, that's fine.

You have one new voicemail. Voicemail left today at 8:26 p.m.

'Benny, I know the plan was for you to stay at the spa tonight, but can I come get you? Please? I need to talk to you. God. It's pathetic, but I can't stop crying. Some detectives came and questioned me this evening. I barely held it together. Everything's gone wrong. I've done something stupid, and I don't know how to fix anything. The guilt is eating me alive. Please, call me when you get this.'

Regulation of Investigatory Powers Act 2000 – section 32

REQUEST FOR INTRUSIVE SURVEILLANCE

REQUESTING OFFICERS:

Detective Inspector Paul Willis and Detective Sergeant Nicole Stewart

CASE NUMBER:

87049375 and 87049422

INDIVIDUAL FOR SURVEILLANCE:

Terence Dunlow

REASON FOR SURVEILLANCE:

Terence Dunlow has given insufficient reason to discount him as a suspect for the shooting of Detective Inspector Juliet Stern and Detective Sergeant Gabriella Martin on 24 April. Terence has no alibi for the time of the shooting. He is competent in handling the type of gun we believe was used in the attack. Terence has been in contact with Karl Biss, who has reason to resent the detectives and may have manipulated Terence. Since October of last year, Terence has been estranged from his father and may blame the detectives for this.

Terence is also a person of interest in the murder of Henry Garside. He works at the gallery Henry was on route to when he disappeared. Terence claims he did not know Henry but has no alibi for the afternoon following his disappearance.

We would like Terence's activities monitored so that any strange behaviour can be investigated. Terence has lied to the police before, and we do not believe he would come forward with information. As the gun and clothes of the shooter have not yet been discovered, I'd like Terence to be monitored to see if he disposes of these items, or anything to do with Henry's murder and subsequent cleaning of his body.

Day 4

Tuesday, 28 April

BODY OF MISSING STUDENT FOUND – NINETEEN-YEAR-OLD HENRY GARSIDE WAS DISCOVERED DEAD YESTERDAY MORNING BY HIS BEST FRIEND...

Scroll.

COULD HE HAVE BEEN SAVED? – HENRY'S DISTRAUGHT PARENTS BELIEVE POLICE DID NOT TAKE THE DISAPPEARANCE OF THEIR ONLY SON SERIOUSLY...

Scroll.

WHAT HAPPENED TO HENRY? – HE WAS QUIET AND HAD NO ENEMIES, SO WHO HURT THIS INNOCENT ART STUDENT? ...

Scroll.

'Hello?'

'Hello there. This is Detective Inspector Paul Willis. Can I please speak to Douglas Frey?'

'I'd rather you didn't. He's asleep.'

'Right. Can I ask who you are?'

'I'm Tommy. His son. I live with him as his carer.'

'I didn't realise your father's health had deteriorated.'

'He's got Alzheimer's and he's easily tired out, which is why I'd rather leave him for now. Talking to the police again so soon would be too much for him.'

'I'm sorry, what? Why has he talked to an officer recently?'

'I wasn't here, so I'm not sure. Two women visited him yesterday morning.'

'Did they give their names?'

'One of them did. Gabe, or something like that. I came home as they were leaving, but I was more focused on Dad. He doesn't have a clue who they were.'

'Can you describe the other woman?'

'She was Asian. Small, black hair.'

'Okay. We'll need to talk to your father, but we can arrange that for a couple of days after he's recovered. We'll make it as easy as possible for him.'

'Did the other officers not get everything you need? Dad said they talked to him about a case. He can't remember which one. If you need him to consult, I'm not sure he's going to be much use.'

'Oh, no. It's nothing like that. This is more of a formality. Nothing to worry about, but we will need to pop over again. You could help by telling us your father's whereabouts on the 24th April.'

'He was here all day. With me.'

'That's brilliant. Thank you. I have to run. Something urgent has come up.'

GG. Sent 8:21.

AI, were you careful with the project?

AI. Sent 8:22.

What do you take me for? Of course I was fucking careful.

Tsam. Sent 8:23.

We know you were. I'm sure GG only asked because he's worried for you x

GG. Sent 8:24.

We're being watched. We can't do anything stupid.

AI. Sent 8:25.

I'm not the one we need to worry about.

Tsam. Sent 8:25.

None of us is going to do anything stupid. This will blow over soon x

Gabe

I patted Artie on the head and his tail threatened to muddle the papers spread around us on the floor. I hadn't had the go ahead from Angela to return to the station, but I'd gotten up and dressed anyway. In the absence of anything else to do, I'd reread the files Paul brought over yesterday.

There had to be something in these piles of paper to pin our shooting or Henry's murder on the Galanis brothers. Paul hadn't included any information about Henry, but I'd grabbed my notepad and added the highlights. Although he was distinctly different to the other individuals we suspected the Galanis brothers had made disappear, he had gone missing at a pivotal time. Henry's murder could have been the reason the brothers needed me and Juliet incapacitated. They'd made a misstep and needed us out of action while they cleaned up their mess.

I sighed and leant against Artie's cushioned bed, triggering another volley of furious tail-beats. My arm ached this morning, the stiffness of the day before ramping up. The whole left side of my back was frozen. My shoulder creaked as I reached for a piece of paper I'd read twice before.

I'd trawled through all the information, checked every receipt and report and transcript. Nothing stood out.

It wasn't like more words would have magically sprouted, but I had to do something while I waited for Angela's call. If the Galanis brothers were behind our shooting, they couldn't be allowed to get away with it. They orchestrated half the crime across the city and I suspected they had a hand in Henry Garside's murder. The timing couldn't be coincidental, and the cleaning of his body pointed toward experienced killers.

I scanned the documents from Tsambikos's latest spending spree. This time, he'd bought a race horse and two works of art by artists who, according to a quick Google search, were up and coming. I couldn't make head nor tail of what they'd created. I much preferred paintings similar to what Henry had tucked under his bed, or the joyful wave Rowan had hung at the gallery.

Evenly spaced taps on my front door distracted me from another search through properties recently bought by the brothers. With a bark, Artie bounded over the papers on the floor. He didn't dislodge a single one.

Holding my shoulder, I followed him into my short hallway. My heart sunk as I peered through the glass at the top of my front door. The person on the other side didn't have Ollie's blond hair. I tucked my fingers into Artie's collar and undid the locks.

'Alright, Gabe?' Nicole was dressed in her standard work blouse and trousers, each ironed but nowhere near the crisp perfection of Juliet's. She stepped forward, forcing me to dodge out of the way, and veered toward my living room with Artie snuffling around her knees.

Paul followed like an angry storm cloud. It took a lot to make him cross, but his rage was impressive once he got there. It made Juliet smirk when we heard his raised voice across the open-plan floor chewing someone out. He'd always offer them a biscuit later. His anger was explosive but short lived.

'Morning.' Cool dread crept up my spine as I pushed my front door shut.

'Been doing a little investigating of your own?' Paul threw over his shoulder as I trailed behind them.

I wasn't sure what had made him cross, but it couldn't be anything he'd find here. 'This is the information you gave me.'

Nicole pulled evidence from the wall. Her hourglass figure swayed as she placed pictures and notes into an open file on my coffee table. Artie sat in his bed, nose twitching as he followed her movements.

'What are you doing?'

Paul leant heavily on his stick as he glowered at me. 'Righting a wrong. I don't know how bloody stupid I was to think allowing you and Juliet to look at evidence around your shooting was a good idea, but I expect the answer is unflattering.'

'It's not,' I butted in. 'We can help.'

'I told myself,' Paul went on like I hadn't spoken, 'you know how frustrating it is to be left out of the loop. But there's a good reason we don't investigate anything too close to home. It clouds our judgement. Makes us stupid. Prone to terrible decisions.'

I gripped my hands into fists despite how my shoulder ached. I thought I knew what this was about, but I wasn't going to say anything to tip Paul off.

'It's a good idea to let us look.' I refused to be cowed by his dark scowl. 'We're brilliant detectives. There's no reason I shouldn't be at work.'

Paul barked out a harsh laugh while Nicole continued calmly unpinning evidence from the wall.

'You might be brilliant, but you've spent too much time with Juliet,' Paul ranted. 'She's rubbing off on you. Do you honestly think, even a couple of months ago, that you would have pulled the kind of shit you did yesterday with Douglas Frey?'

I hoped the chill racing down my spine wasn't obvious. I'd known visiting Frey was a bad idea, but I'd thought it would fly under the radar while Paul chased more likely suspects.

'You can't blame Juliet. I'm the one who talked to Douglas. And have you considered that I had a damn good reason?'

Paul's eyes narrowed. 'What good reason?'

My cheeks coloured. I couldn't tell Paul why I'd gone to see Douglas Frey without breaking Juliet's confidence, and that was too high a price to pay to get back in Paul's good books. His anger was a flash fire, whereas Juliet's would smoulder.

'I can't say,' I muttered, tracking Nicole as she bent to pile papers together on the floor.

Paul heaved a sigh. 'What happened between Juliet and Douglas?'

My face burned brighter, but I kept my gaze averted. I struggled for an answer that wouldn't reveal there was something to know, something it wouldn't be too difficult for Paul to figure out.

He shook his head. 'Did you find out anything useful while basically shitting over any chance anything Douglas says would stand up in court?'

The burn migrated to my chest. I'd known what I'd done yesterday wasn't entirely by the book, but I'd not thought through the full ramifications. I was too caught up in Juliet trusting me.

I bit my lip as a disconcerting thought busted into my mind. Juliet encouraged me to go see Douglas alone and behind Paul's back. She often bent the rules, but why would she ask me to do something so clearly beyond the pale? Was she so determined to keep her past a secret that she would jeopardise an investigation?

A voice whispered she'd used me. I had chosen to visit Douglas, but did Juliet know the right pressure to apply to get me to agree? I'd seen her manipulate suspects before. I didn't think she would turn on me.

'You have to know interviewing an unwell old man is far over the line.' Paul didn't seem cross any more, but weary.

'I didn't know Douglas was unwell before I went.' My voice was far too small, but the weight of the investigation being snatched from me and wondering if Juliet had used me was too much. I wanted to be small. Wanted to curl up into a ball and hide.

'That's one reason why it's a bad idea to go running off on your own.'

Keeping Juliet's secret had seemed a good enough reason to trample all over this rule. She wanted her past hidden, but that didn't mean it could be. I, of all people, knew how hard it was to live with your terrible history as public property. I had to suck it up. I should have expected Juliet to do the same.

'I don't think Douglas shot us,' I said. 'He doesn't have the mental or physical capacity.'

'All done.' Nicole patted Artie on the head, then grabbed the bulging files. 'See you at the car, boss.'

She offered me a sympathetic smile before she swept from the room. Her absence was a relief. Bad enough Paul was chewing me out for being a twat, I didn't need it witnessed by someone I already felt permanently on the back foot with.

At least Nicole wasn't one for gossip or pettiness. If I bought her a fancy coffee, all would be forgotten. Another way she was a proper adult while I floundered. She could let things go. I was constantly bothered by my past.

'You're off the case and you're not welcome at the station,' Paul said. 'I talked to Angela and she agrees you're obviously not in a fit state to investigate a murder. Nicole will be taking over Henry's case.' Paul leant heavily on his stick. He'd probably stormed through the station and up my path, ignoring the complaints of his leg. 'I know you idolise Juliet, but let this be a moment to stop and think. Yes, she's good at her job, but she often doesn't go about things in the right way. I don't know what she said to make you think lone wolfing was a good idea, but police work is a team effort.' His lips drew downward. 'You can learn from Juliet without doing as she does. Take the best bits from her but keep the best bits of you too.'

Shame burned white hot inside me as I followed Paul to my front door, not least because of his uneven gait.

'Paul?' I called out before he walked through the front gate. 'I'm sorry.'

I knew visiting Douglas Frey was wrong, but I did it anyway. I was distracted by Juliet's story and her rare request for help. I didn't know yet whether she'd been calculating or desperate, but she shouldn't have asked me to do it.

'I know you are.' Paul's smile was like a ray of sunshine during a thunderstorm. 'Don't let Juliet turn you into an arsehole.'

With that parting shot, he limped out of sight. I shut my front door and slid down to the floor, closing my eyes against the sharp twang of pain from my shoulder.

Under the embarrassment crawling through me loomed a hot lick of annoyance. Juliet had convinced me to talk to Douglas Frey. She said she needed my help, trusted me to keep her secret. She had to know how that would play on me.

My chat with the old man had yielded nothing of use. It only resulted in me being shut out of our case and thrown off of Henry's.

From: Paul Willis **paul.willis@mit.gov.uk**
To: Alice To **alice.to@police.gov.uk**,
Madison Campbell **madison.campbell@mitadmin.gov.uk**
Date: **28 April, 10:47**
Subject: **Operation Orion – Gabe and Juliet's involvement**

Alice and Maddy,

Where we had been sharing elements of this investigation with Gabe and Juliet as their insights could have proven helpful, we have moved on to a stage where they will no longer be consulting.

Please inform me if either of them asks for your assistance.

Paul

From: Sally Bull **sally.bull@hampshirechildrensservices.gov**
To: Keith Stern **sternkeith@thesternfamily.co.uk**
Date: **28 April, 11:31**
Subject: **Initial visit notes**

Dear Keith,

We met this morning to discuss your wife's – Juliet Stern's – behaviour. She has been living separately to the family during the working week for a couple of years and her absences at weekends have become more frequent. When she is with yourself and your two daughters, she is prone to foul moods. Since her injury, you've noticed an uptick in this.

However, she has not lashed out physically at yourself or the children. You are not concerned this is a possibility and so do not see a need to take further action at this time. We discussed that once Juliet heals, it may be worthwhile seeking couples counselling to minimise the impact of her mental health struggles on your marriage and children.

We discussed the following action points:

- You will keep a detailed diary of Juliet's actions toward yourself and your daughters so that you have a clear record of behaviour escalation if this occurs. This will be a fair account – making sure to note both negative and positive behaviours

- You will make sure to remove yourself and your children from any situation where you believe they could come to harm

- You will not challenge aggressive behaviour if it arises, but instead remove yourself and the children to safety and call emergency services.

I wish you and your family all the best in the future. If there are any developments or you are concerned, please do not hesitate to get in touch.

Best wishes,

Sally Bull

Senior Social Worker

Hampshire Children's Services

Ollie. Sent 12:52.

How are you feeling today? xxx

Gabe. Sent 12:53.

Achy. I'm sorry about Juliet x

Ollie. Sent 12:54.

It's fine. From what Paul told me, I should have
expected it. What do you want for dinner tonight? xxx

Gabe. Sent 12:57.

Juliet might be here again, so it's probably not a
good idea for you to come over. It would be best if
you kept your distance until this is sorted x

Ollie. Sent 12:58.

I can understand not wanting to throw me in front of
Juliet again, but are you going to make me stay
away until you've found the shooter?

Gabe. Sent 13:01.

It's for the best x

Ollie. Sent 13:01.

It's really not.

Gabe

I shoved my phone into my borrowed coat pocket and kicked open the car door. I stomped to the boot and let a wiggling Artie jump free. Ignoring the ache in my shoulder and the sadness clogging my throat, I slammed the boot closed.

I'd leapt into action after a couple of hours of stewing in my maisonette. I'd wondered if Juliet would show up, and I couldn't decide if I should liken her to a bad penny. Pounding along the familiar trails of the New Forest would help me work off my frustration before I saw her again.

A car had pulled up after me, so I headed for the furthest path in the hope I could go for an entire walk without any human interaction. The argument with Paul and fraught texts from Ollie and the persistent pain from my arm and my doubts about Juliet made me feel like I was fighting on all fronts. I needed time to myself. I wanted to escape the mire surrounding me.

Artie dancing around my feet, I left the car park behind and plunged into the cool darkness under the canopy of trees. Every step throbbed through my wound, punctuation to the thoughts pounding in my head.

I'd blown it with Ollie. I wasn't capable of explaining myself, and this was what would finally make him leave. He would go find a partner who wouldn't push him away or allow their co-workers to be rude to him.

Juliet wasn't answering my calls. Probably off interfering in Paul's case in another way that would come around to bite me in the arse.

I couldn't call my parents because things were messed up between us. By me.

Paul was angry. He wouldn't invite me over for dinner for a while. I'd miss the boys and Joanie.

Maddy and Alice were probably annoyed too. I'd dragged them down with me.

I'd disappointed Henry's loved ones. I'd abandoned all those hurt by the Galanis brothers.

Artie placed a stick in the middle of the path and I kicked at it, grimacing as pain cracked down my arm.

I couldn't distract myself with work because it had been stripped from me. All I could do was sit in my crappy maisonette and wait for someone else to figure out who killed Henry and shot me. Or wait for the shooter to take aim again. Either option made me feel like spikes were poking under my skin.

It felt like perfect timing when Artie squatted in the middle of the path. My whole life had turned to shit, so it made sense I should pick some up too.

I searched through the assorted debris in the pockets of Ollie's coat. My fingers caught on my notepad and a pair of gloves, before alighting on smooth plastic. I opened the bag and crouched to retrieve Artie's gift, a shoulder spasm making the whole experience much more enjoyable.

Anger fuelling me, I continued marching through the forest. Artie skipped alongside, aware I was unhappy but confused by this state of being while on a walk, his favourite activity bar stealing biscuits. Avoiding the grassy plains where the most talkative of dog walkers lurked, I wound in loops between the trees.

Despite the distance covered, my mind refused to clear.

I wasn't good at my job. I wasn't a good girlfriend. I wasn't a good friend. I wasn't a good daughter.

All the evidence added up: I wasn't a good person.

My pace eventually slowed. The ache in my shoulder refused to be ignored and my thighs protested in a way they usually only did after a weekend spent solely in Ollie's company. Sticking to the treeline, I headed toward my favourite log. It looked out over a patch of grass where wild horses wandered. I'd take a break, see if sitting made a difference to my state of mind, then keep walking if I could.

The log came into view. So did a person. They were bent over, their face obscured by a black hoodie.

I stopped. I was still in no state to make idle conversation with a stranger. Turning on one heel, I froze when I spotted red on their fingers.

'Hey,' I called out, reversing the motion and hurrying toward them. 'Can I help you?'

They straightened, their head whipping around. The red wasn't on their hands, but on the log.

Annoyance spiked. I wasn't going to get away with shouting and not explaining myself. But before I could get close, they dashed down the path.

Artie barked and gave chase.

'No,' I called out. 'Artie, come.'

It was testament to the hours of training me and Ollie had put in that Artie returned to my side, rather than terrorising someone even more averse to talking to strangers than me. I shuffled over to the vacated log. Hopefully the red thing would be easy to move out of the way so I could sit down.

It was square. Card. Not the lost scarf or hat I'd expected. Papers stuck out from beneath the cover at odd angles.

A file. Scrawled on the front were two words.

DETECTIVE MARTIN.

My heart jumped in my ribcage as I spun round. I looked down at Artie. 'Chase.'

He got the idea soon enough as I hobbled along the path. I couldn't call what I was doing a jog. It was barely faster than walking. We followed the quickest route to the car park. The person in the hoodie was at least half a minute ahead of us, but I had to try to stop them before they left. Artie caught their scent and ran off down the path.

His bark bounced through the forest, giving me a brief spurt of energy to put on extra speed and break from the trees.

In the car park, the person in the hoodie was almost at their car. They couldn't be very fit, if I'd caught up with them. Artie circled them, his head low.

They kicked out at him. I couldn't contain the inarticulate shout that punched out of me.

They turned their head, but they were no closer than they'd been at the log. I couldn't define their features.

Their eyes stood out. Wide with fear.

My shout distracted Artie. He raced across the car park to me. The person in the hoodie climbed into their car.

I attempted to run, but pain ricocheted through my shoulder. Panting, I watched helplessly as they reversed out of their space.

My eyes widened as the back of their car pointed toward me. Their number plate was covered.

I'd not noticed anything strange about their vehicle before. Rage had clouded my vision. I was lucky they only wanted to drop off a file, rather than hurt me.

They sped away. There was no point trying to follow. I fumbled through my coat pockets but by the time I grabbed my phone and flicked to the camera, the car had disappeared around a tree-lined bend. If I called for back-up, they wouldn't find anything. There were too many lanes they could hide along.

Breathing hard, I pulled out my notebook and jotted down what I could remember.

Black hoodie. Bulky.
My height? Maybe taller
Jeans
White – pale
Brown hair. Brown eyes?
Unfit?
Blue car – older
Left a red file with my name on it on a log
Followed me here?

The last line made the sweat coating my skin chill. I'd been distracted the whole way here. My paddy made me sloppy, vigilance dropping to a dangerous low.

Further evidence I wasn't getting anything right. A car with covered plates was pretty fucking strange. That shouldn't have passed me by.

Walking as fast as my shoulder allowed, I returned to the log. I couldn't have a walker stumbling across the file. At best, they would contaminate it. At worst, there could be something more dangerous than paper inside.

My chest unclenched as the log came into view. The red file lay on top. Unchanged.

I edged closer. The cover was uneven red card. It looked old, patches of crimson and pink evidence of time spent under other objects or exposed to the sun. A collection of papers was contained within.

It was flat. I didn't think there was anything else inside.

I could call Paul, but I couldn't be certain there was only paper in there. I would have been horrified if a dog walker had been hurt by whatever was in this file, and I'd be heartbroken if one of my colleagues was injured. Or humiliated if I called them here and it was something random. They were already stretched between two major cases. They didn't need to deal with this too.

Checking Artie was occupied by sniffing along a badger trail, I pulled the plastic gloves from my pocket and tugged them on. Paul's warning rung in my ears. I wasn't about to do anything to mess up his or anyone else's investigation.

I pushed one finger under the file lid. It flipped open easily, like the spine was used to bending backward. Hands shaking, I gripped the edge of the stack of paper and flicked through them until my fingertips were empty.

Nothing but paper. I took a deep breath and read the one on top.

TWO OFFICERS INJURED IN NON-FATAL SHOOTING OUTSIDE SOUTHAMPTON CROWN COURT

Underneath the headline, a handwritten note filled the space alongside the journalist's name.

BITCH DESERVED IT.

Underneath was another clipping, this time about an investigation Juliet led before I moved to Southampton. She stood beside a business she'd helped find justice against the gang repeatedly stealing their takings.

Red pen created a crude moustache and curled horns reaching out from her grainy blonde hair.

I carefully lifted paper after paper. They centred on Juliet, but a few included me. All had comments added.

ONE DAY, YOU'LL GET WHAT'S COMING TO YOU

I HATE YOU.

FUCKING BITCH. I HOPE SOMEONE LIGHTS YOU ON FIRE.

With a shudder, I let go of the papers. I checked over my shoulder, but the path was empty. Whoever had left this plethora of hate was long gone.

I struggled to picture them beyond the hoodie and panicked expression, but something about them kept catching in my mind. I didn't know them, but maybe I'd seen them somewhere.

It didn't make a lot of sense for them to be the note maker, but I didn't pretend to understand the strange ways that criminals' minds worked. Mine and Juliet's shooter could have been cross at the lack of attention they were getting now the media was more interested in Henry's murder. Maybe they wanted Juliet to know how reviled she was, wanted me to know I was an unlucky bystander.

That was the truth, if whoever wrote these notes had anything to do with the shooting.

Juliet was the detested target. I was there. Hurt because of my proximity to her.

Call connected at 15:49.

'Hello, this is Benedict Hogan.'

'Hello, Mr Hogan. This is Detective Inspector Paul Willis. Is this a good time to talk with you about an ongoing investigation?'

'Yes, of course.'

'Can you tell me about your relationship with Terence Dunlow?'

'We've been together officially for half a year. But we were in a relationship for years before that. Teddy was scared of coming out because of his father. I have to say, he wasn't wrong to think his father would turn his back on him.'

'Has Terence talked to you about his estrangement from his father?'

'Yes. A lot. Teddy saw it coming, but it's like he can't get his head around it.'

'Did he mention blaming anyone for his changed relationship with his father?'

'He's angry at the magazine who outed him. It wasn't fair, what they did.'

'Terence hasn't mentioned anyone else?'

'He's cross at his father, if that's what you mean?'

'He's not mentioned Detectives Juliet Stern or Gabriella Martin?'

'What? The two women who were shot? Oh, God. You don't think Teddy had anything to do with that? I know Teddy has been acting strangely, but he's not capable of killing. He's got a good heart.'

'Terence has been acting strangely?'

'Yes, but not violent.'

'Can you explain what's changed about his behaviour?'

'When he first moved in with me after everything that went on, he was happy. We both were. Our relationship had to exist in snatched, secret moments before. It was wonderful to see so much of each other, to not worry about hiding. Everything seemed perfect.'

'What changed?'

'I don't know. Terence would stay late at work and when I asked what he was doing, he would ignore me. I'd catch him crying when he thought I wasn't home. He's had days when he's not gotten out of bed, when I can't seem to say anything to get through to him.'

'That sounds difficult.'

'It was horrible, especially after we'd finally gotten everything we wanted.'

'Where were you on the 24th April?'

'I was meant to meet Teddy in the morning before I went off on a mini-break with my sister.'

'What do you mean?'

'He had gone off to work, but he texted early to ask if we could meet up. I waited for him for over an hour near a café we like, but he never showed. So I went off to the spa. Teddy left a voicemail to apologise. Apparently, work got busy and he couldn't get away.'

'You didn't see or hear from Terence that afternoon?'

'No. I went to a spa with my sister.'

'Have you heard from Terence since?'

'Yes. He called last night and asked if he could pick me up. He was upset after being questioned about the shooting and a young man who's been found dead. I've been home with him since then.'

'Has Terence spoken to you about the shooting or Henry's death?'

'Not much. He's either been crying or in bed since last night.'

'Thank you, Mr Hogan. This has all been really helpful.'

'I know things between me and Teddy aren't ideal right now, but you're honestly barking up the wrong tree if you think he had anything to do with the detectives getting shot or that boy being hurt. He's such a gentle soul. He couldn't do anything like that.'

'I appreciate that you believe that.'

Call connected at 15:58.

'Detective Inspector Juliet Stern.'

'Do you have to answer the phone like that even when you're off sick?'

'What do you want?'

'My wife was shot. She then leaves hospital earlier than is medically advisable. She hides away in her dingy flat in the city. None of that sounds like a good enough reason for a husband to check in?'

'You changed my locks.'

'I had to. You needed clothes.'

'You didn't take any clothes though, did you?'

'Sweetheart, I don't know what you're talking about. By the time I gained access to your hideaway, I had a call from the hospital to say you'd discharged yourself. I was frantic with worry, and there was no point taking anything.'

'I've changed the locks again. You won't be getting back in.'

'I won't need to.'

'I want you to return the things you took.'

'Juliet, I have no idea what you're talking about. The girls are okay, by the way.'

'Why wouldn't they be okay?'

'A normal mother would ask after their children if they hadn't seen them for over a week.'

'I asked you to bring them to the hospital.'

'A silly request. It would have scared them.'

'What do you want, Keith? I have things to do.'

'I wanted to let you know I've sorted a car for you.'

'What? Why?'

'When you move here, you'll need a car to get back and forth to the station.'

'I am not moving.'

186

'You are. If you want to have any contact with our daughters and keep your precious job, you'll start packing right now.'

'What are you talking about?'

'I had a visit from a social worker today. I explained you've been acting strangely and I'm concerned you might do something to hurt the girls.'

'What the fuck? I would never hurt them. Are you doing this because you saw the letter from the solicitor?'

'I have no idea what you're talking about. It's a Vauxhall Corsa, by the way.'

'Keith, I'll drop everything if you stop this. I can't move.'

'You can, and you will. One word from me, and social services will make sure you never see our daughters again. And what police officer would keep their job if accused of endangering their own children?'

'Please, Keith. Don't do this.'

'You know what you'll lose if you don't move; everything. So get on with it. I'll give you a few days to get started. I know you need to rest. But don't let me down.'

Nicole. Sent 16:09.

Hey boss. Full forensic sweep of Henry's room is done and I've re-interviewed his friends and family.

Paul. Sent 16:13.

Any joy?

Nicole. Sent 16:15.

Nothing. We'll get DNA results soon but no one has anything new to add.

Paul. Sent 16:16.

Bollocks. Come back in and we can talk next steps.

Paul. Sent 16:20.

Was I too harsh with Gabe earlier?

Nicole. Sent 16:22.

She knows what you're like.

Paul. Sent 16:22.

What am I like?

Nicole. Sent 16:23.

You puff up, then deflate almost as quickly.

Paul. Sent 16:23.

How flattering. Get me coffee on your way in to make up for such insubordination.

Gabe

Juliet pulled off her coat and hung it on one of the pegs my landlord had allowed me to add to the wall. Her movements were stiff, her face unmoving. She'd ditched her sling. I wanted to ask if that was wise, but restrained myself. It would get her back up, and I didn't need extra tension between us until it was unavoidable.

I'd stopped calling her about an hour ago and texted to say I needed to show her something important to do with the investigation. I should have known that was the way to get her attention.

'What's this about?' Juliet asked as I led the way to the living room. 'I can't stay long.'

If I didn't know her, I might have worried she was annoyed at me. As it was, I could tell she was distracted. Something else had captured her interest. Being here was a road bump on the way to getting to where she wanted to be. Which was strange. Normally, Juliet focused solely on a case to the detriment of every other aspect of her life.

She tugged at the cuffs of her blouse as she sat on my sofa, her gaze sharpening when she spotted the undecorated wall. Pockmarks ringed with Blu Tack decorated the magnolia paint. Her eyes widened as she looked at me and caught whatever stray emotions I wasn't able to shut down.

'Paul came over this morning and took everything away.' I stayed standing and petted Artie behind his ears, heading off any mourning at being ignored by a newcomer. I checked the file was where I'd stashed it behind the TV in an evidence bag. No one could have moved it, but since bringing it home I'd been paranoid it would disappear. 'He wasn't happy about my chat with Douglas Frey.'

Juliet rolled her eyes and settled into the sofa cushions. 'He didn't consider Douglas a real suspect. He's just getting territorial.'

'Actually, he isn't.'

Juliet's focus snapped to me, her body stilling even as she lounged. 'What's up, Gabe?'

'You didn't want to share your past with Paul, but you had to know that doesn't matter during an investigation. You encouraged me to act in a way we both should have thought better of.' I tried to keep my voice level, but it was hard when every aspect of my life was trashed and one of the instigators sat before me. 'My visit to Douglas Frey means any statement Paul takes from him could be compromised. As a result, we're no longer consulting on the case and I've been barred from the station.'

'If you thought talking to Douglas was such a bad idea, then why did you do it?' Juliet's voice was cold in a way that had only been turned on others in my presence before.

'Because you asked me to,' I half-shouted. I caught myself, smoothing my fingers through Artie's fur when he whined. 'You said you needed my help.'

Juliet had never asked for anything like this before. She had to know how it would affect me.

She shook her head. 'Do you think Douglas did it?'

I swallowed, pressing into Artie's fur to ground myself. 'No. He's not physically or mentally able.'

'It doesn't matter that you talked to him then, does it?' Juliet sat up. 'Are we done now? Because I have infinitely more important things to do with my time than be guilt-tripped by you.'

I breathed heavily through my nose. Not all of my frustration was directed at Juliet, but the temptation to let rip was hard to resist. She was well known for doing things her own way, for taking steps no other officer would and getting away with it because of her arrest and conviction records. But Paul was right. Her way of working was dying out. I wouldn't agree Juliet was turning me into an arsehole, but I didn't want to conduct myself like her.

'I went for a walk with Artie earlier.' I extracted the evidence bag from behind the TV, my fingers clammy against the plastic. 'Someone left this on a log and ran away when they saw me.' I turned the file to show Juliet the front. 'It has my name on it, but it's full of newspaper clippings about you. There are aggressive notes written on them.'

At the hunger in Juliet's eyes, I held the file close to my chest. I wouldn't put it past her to launch across the coffee table to get it.

'What's written on them?' she asked.

'Do you want to take a look? We could read them together.'

Juliet's face fell into lines of slack disbelief, the ever present purple bags under her eyes sagging. 'You haven't already?'

Her answer told me everything I needed to know, but everything I'd been hoping I was wrong about. This was a test. She'd failed. I slotted the file back behind my TV.

'What's wrong with you?' I folded my arms over my chest. 'I looked at enough of the clippings to check what was in the file, but you truly think we should go through the rest?'

Juliet's eyes widened, then the shutters crashed down. She wore the same mask of impassivity around Paul and David. I'd never thought she'd use it on me. I hated her cutting me out so thoroughly, but this was necessary. I needed to draw a line, make it clear how far I would go and no further.

'I'm sorry?' Juliet said with studied blankness.

'I told you Paul took away the courtesy he'd been extending to us because I went behind his back and interviewed Douglas Frey. I can't go into the station any more, can't search for Henry Garside's killer.' My heart beat loud in my ears and through my injured shoulder. I didn't want to confront Juliet like this, but I couldn't do the things she did. I wasn't like her. 'But you think it's a good idea to go ahead and tamper with evidence?'

Juliet's jaw tightened, then she stood in one fluid motion. The pinched skin between her eyebrows betrayed that the movement wasn't as painless as she wanted me to believe.

'Fine.' She walked to the hallway. 'We're off the case and we'll wait around for Paul to figure out who shot us. I'm sure that will go incredibly well.'

Fire burned inside me for a second; that Juliet would take a jab at Paul, that she clearly still thought her way was right, that if I was more naïve then she would have led me into more trouble. But it fizzled out. I didn't hate Juliet, and I couldn't blame her. She was who she was. I was an adult, like she said. I'd chosen to go to Douglas. Being thrown off the case was as much on me as on her.

'Juliet. Wait.' I followed her into the hallway where she was tugging on her coat. 'You don't have to leave. I'm frustrated, but not just at you. There's other stuff going on.'

'I'm sure there is.' Juliet straightened her collar and yanked open my front door. 'Have fun with your boyfriend. I'm sure he'll brush your hair and bake cupcakes while you wait for someone else to do the work of finding our shooter.'

It felt like Juliet had lashed out physically, her parting words stealing my breath. I couldn't believe that was all she was taking from this.

'I'm sorry I won't do what you want me to,' I said as she strode down my front path. 'I'm going to work with Paul, not against him.'

Juliet didn't reply. Her hands were steady as she slammed my front gate and marched down my street. Trees opening their buds stretched ghostly fingers across the streetlamps, casting her into shadow. I closed my front door with more force than necessary rather than wait to see if she would look back.

Despite how terribly that had gone and how much I wanted to race as fast as my shoulder would allow after Juliet to check everything would be okay, I knew I'd done the right thing. Juliet was brilliant, but she wasn't flawless. She was too fixated on getting the job done regardless of the cost. I couldn't let her drag me down the same path.

I let out a stuttering breath as I buried my hands in Artie's fur. He'd joined me in the hallway after I slammed the door, his tail curled between his legs. He perked up as my fingers wound around his ears.

I wished Juliet was right, that Ollie was here with me. I looked down into Artie's deep brown eyes. Juliet clearly thought Ollie would be around. She had a family to go home to. So did Paul and Nicole.

I couldn't work any more, so there was no point in keeping Ollie at a distance. I wouldn't have wanted to, not even if Nicole hadn't packed everything away. If there was a way to fix our relationship, I wanted to do it. I didn't want Ollie to disappear from my life too.

Gabe. Sent 19:29.

I've got something I need to give to you for the case.

Paul. Sent 19:35.

Can it wait? I'm at home with the monsters this evening. I can swing by before work tomorrow.

Gabe. Sent 19:36.

That's fine.

Gabe. Sent 19:38.

I've heard sugar is great for getting kids to sleep.

Paul. Sent 19:39.

I'll give that a go after our horror film marathon and water chugging contest.

Gabe. Sent 20:21.

I was wrong earlier x

Ollie. Sent 20:30.

You're going to have to be more specific.

Gabe. Sent 20:31.

I'm sorry, Ol. I shouldn't have pushed you away or let Juliet be so rude to you. Will you come over tomorrow? x

Ollie. Sent 20:35.

I have a shoot. I'll come over after.

Gabe. Sent 20:35.

I miss you x

Ollie. Sent 20:39.

Fuck it. I miss you too x

From: Alice To **alice.to@police.gov.uk**
To: Paul Willis **paul.willis@mit.gov.uk**,
Nicole Stewart **nicole.stewart@mit.gov.uk**
Date: **28 April, 20:52**
Subject: <u>**Operation Orion – man in coat**</u>

Paul and Nicole,

I wanted to ping you a quick email before I head home to let you know I've gotten no further with identifying the man in the tan coat. He stood where Gabe and Juliet were shot for over an hour, then left on foot via a route with minimal CCTV coverage.

No other witnesses remember him and there are no clear shots of his face to run through recognition software.

Sorry to add to the things we don't know. I'll keep searching when I get in tomorrow.

Alice

Gabe

A knock on the front door.

I opened my eyes. Stars shone on the ceiling. The world beyond our dinosaur print curtains was inky black. I curled my toes under my warm duvet. Mummy or Daddy would see who it was.

Another knock.

No heavy footsteps or sleepy murmurs. Across the room in a bed identical to mine, Barney slept facing the wall. His shoulders rose and fell with each breath. His brown hair tangled over his pillow.

Another knock, and another.

Tears gathered in my eyes. I pulled my covers snug beneath my chin. I didn't want to open the door. Mummy made me sometimes. It was hard talking to the postman. I didn't think it would be him this time.

The knock changed to a thump.

My lower lip trembling, I slipped out of bed and padded into the hallway. The front door was visible at the bottom of the stairs. A dark shadow pressed against the blurred glass.

Thump thump. Thump thump.

It felt like the knocking was inside me. There was no sign Mummy and Daddy were awake. Barney was still sleeping. I rebelled at the thought of waking him.

I didn't want Barney to come downstairs. I needed him to stay in bed. Stay safe.

THUMP THUMP THUMP.

The door shuddered. I scurried downstairs. Sucking my thumb, I reached for the latch. I stretched on my tippytoes. The door unlocked with a click, then swung open.

A man stepped inside. I yelped and jumped back, but he caught my arm in his fist.

He had stained boots. Rough jeans. A barrel chest.

He gripped my arm. It hurt, worse than anything I'd felt before.

I opened my mouth,
and screamed.

I shot upward in bed. My shout stuttered as my shoulder flamed into unholy agony. I sobbed and scrunched over myself.

What was this? What had I done? Where was the bad man?

I couldn't let him in, couldn't let him hurt me, couldn't let him have my brother.

I lifted my head. Nothing in the room was right. No curtains covered the window, only blinds barely keeping out the light of a streetlamp. No stars dotted the ceiling.

No Barnabas across the room.

'No,' I moaned, then stifled the sound against a clenched fist.

I no longer lived at home. I wasn't small and defenceless, but grown. It had been many years since I'd fallen asleep to my brother's soft snores.

Heart hammering, I listened for noise in the maisonette above. Ollie usually woke me before I shouted out. Hopefully it had been short, unheard or dismissed as an animal.

I scooted backward to sit against my headboard. Despite the sweat coating my skin, I gathered my duvet around me.

A futile act of comfort. I was alone. The bad man had come in a nightmare, and there was no one to help chase him away.

I gasped when the bed dipped, wondering if I'd conjured Ollie by sheer need, but then I had a lapful of Alsatian.

Artie was warm. Present and alive.

I gripped handfuls of his fur, heedless of his scratching claws and the pull in my shoulder.

'I hate this,' I whispered into his neck. His fur grew damp with my tears. 'I hate this. I hate this. I hate this.'

Day 5

Wednesday, 29 April

News – Solent University

Staff and students may be aware that Henry Garside, a nineteen-year-old art student in his first year at Solent University, was found dead yesterday morning. This has prompted local and national media coverage.

Henry's close friends and family are receiving support from the university, and we will continue to liaise closely with the police.

Professor Naomi Dodge, University President said:

'We are deeply saddened to learn of Henry's death. He was a keen student and his friends are shocked by what has happened. Our condolences go to Henry's family and loved ones. Anyone who has information about Henry's movements on 24 April should contact the police or Student Services urgently.'

The university has several pastoral services for students affected by Henry's death. We would urge them to make use of the support available within our university community.

Gabe

I flinched at the knock on my front door, even though Paul had texted to say he was headed over.

I hadn't regained my equilibrium since the nightmare. The bad man had never come to my childhood home, but the dream had the power to wreck me. Too aware I would lie in bed sleeplessly, conjuring one terrifying image after another, I'd gotten up and showered. Artie and I had waited for the sun to rise snuggled on my sofa, back-to-back episodes of *Parks and Rec* lulling me into a dreamlike stupor.

Artie was too ensconced in blankets to attend to his normal greeting duty. I checked myself in the hallway mirror as I passed. My full-length reflection didn't surprise me. Black leggings adorned with russet fur emerged from under an oversized jumper. The strawberry pattern had once prompted Ollie to call me a field in need of ploughing, a line I'd never admit worked like a charm. Fingers dragged through my wet hair in restless patterns had reduced it to wildness. Purplish bags that rivalled Paul and Juliet's hung beneath my bloodshot eyes.

I was too tired yet amped up to feel embarrassed of Paul seeing me so dishevelled. It wasn't like he hadn't seen me in a state before, or vice versa. The nature of our job meant long hours when beautifying ourselves was the least of our priorities. I opened the door and smiled grimly at his double-take.

'What's happened?' he asked, thick brows lowering.

'Had a bad night.'

He let it go. Perhaps he thought my sleep was disordered due to my shoulder and aftershocks of the attack. I'd not talked to anyone at work about my nightmares. My colleagues already knew too much, things I wished could be hidden away. I kept this one element of weakness to myself.

'This will cheer you up.' Paul passed over a plastic bag once I'd closed the door behind him.

I pulled out a card while he shrugged off his coat. Mismatched handprints brightened the front, the red and blue paint enthusiastically smudged. Inside, Paul's sons had scrawled their names. I traced the line of kisses at the bottom, each bigger than the last.

'That's from the monsters, and Joanie baked triple chocolate cookies.' Paul attempted a frown, but the twitch of his mouth gave him away. 'I told them I was mad at you for being naughty, but they didn't listen.'

'I have something to help you like me again.' I led the way to the living room and placed his family's gifts on the coffee table.

'You know I always like you, right?' Paul walked into the room. 'It's like I tell the boys; bad behaviour has consequences, but it doesn't mean I love them any less.'

Paul's steadfastness was a balm. I knew he wouldn't stay mad for long, but not that he would be kind so quickly.

I couldn't be so sure about Juliet. We'd find a way to work together again but telling her off wouldn't be allowed to fly. I anticipated many frosty weeks when we returned to the station.

I walked over to the TV. I hadn't moved the file since my run-in with Juliet. I didn't want the reminder of how we'd butted heads or the constant temptation to do as she'd said and look through its contents.

'Here.' I passed it to Paul.

He eyed the labelled evidence bag. 'What's this?'

'Yesterday afternoon I went for a walk in the New Forest.' Artie's tail thumped as I recounted seeing the hooded figure in the forest and the chase that followed, but his blanket fort was too cosy to be abandoned. 'They left this file on a log. I made sure to only touch it with gloves, and checked the top few pieces of paper to make sure it was safe.' I needed to impress I'd not tampered with it. 'It's full of articles about Juliet with handwritten notes on them.'

The residual frown lines on Paul's face cleared. 'Did you get a look at who left it?'

'The briefest flashes from far away.' I picked up the page I'd torn from my notepad. 'I jotted this down after they ran off. I swear I've seen them before, but I can't think where.'

An itch plagued the back of my mind. The person who left the file wasn't a stranger, but I couldn't place the scant images I could conjure.

'Alright then.' Paul tucked my notes in his pocket and the evidence bag under his arm. 'I'm going to need you to come in for a session with the sketch artist.'

I couldn't keep a grimace off my face. I'd sat with artists several times and always came away feeling like a massive disappointment. Years passing hadn't given me a clearer vision of the man who'd abducted me and my brother, but the artists looked at me expectantly every time he struck again.

This session wouldn't be any different. I hadn't gotten a decent look at the person who'd left the file. The rendering would be devoid of detail, since an inkling I'd seen them before wouldn't translate well into a sketch.

'Fine.' I scrubbed a hand through my hair. I couldn't get out of this. As the sole witness of someone of interest in Paul's investigation, he wasn't going to allow me not to come in. 'Can you give me an hour?'

Paul grinned. 'Will it take that long to make yourself presentable?'

'Piss off.'

'Make sure to eat breakfast. Cookies cover all the major food groups.' Paul pointed his stick at the plastic bag before heading for my front door. 'Consider yourself officially forgiven,' he called over his shoulder. He grabbed his coat and let himself out.

I wondered if his forgiveness would extend to allowing me to look at the case again, or persuading Angela I could work on Henry's. Not likely.

I pulled the tin out of the bag and popped it open. My mouth filled with saliva as the rich smell of chocolate filled the air. Artie's head rose from his nest of blankets.

'These are not for you.' I grabbed a couple of cookies and jammed the lid back on the tin. Artie sighed as I tucked it on top of the fridge.

In my bedroom, I searched one handed for something loose and vaguely professional to wear while shoving bites of cookie into my mouth.

I hadn't told Paul about Juliet's visit or how she'd wanted to look at the file. I was easily forgiven for stepping out of line, but I didn't think he would extend the same kindness to her.

Paul didn't need to know he was right. Juliet had encouraged me in exactly the way he'd said she would.

That wasn't a lesson he needed to learn. It was one for me.

Unknown number. Sent 9:02.

Get rid of this phone. Use our real numbers from now on, but don't you dare mention anything to do with this. It never happened.

From: James Knowles **james.knowles@police.gov.uk**
To: Paul Willis **paul.willis@mit.gov.uk**
CC: Nicole Stewart **nicole.stewart@mit.gov.uk**
Date: **29 April, 9:37**
Subject: **Operation Orion – surveillance**

Paul and Nicole,

This is an overview of the surveillance ordered for Alcaeus, Tsambikos, and Giannis Galanis, and Terence Dunlow.

Alcaeus Galanis has spent the bulk of his time at the spa the brothers were in at the time of the shooting. He has been managing day-to-day activities and has had several meetings about a potential renovation. His wife – Cora Galanis – has been at their home for the bulk of surveillance. Alcaeus has not met with anyone of interest at the spa or at his home.

Tsambikos Galanis has visited a number of properties registered to his name. These are a mixture of residential and businesses across the city. None have been associated with any criminal activity. He has not met with anyone of interest at these addresses or at his home.

Giannis Galanis had been frequenting family-owned restaurants across the city, but since 26 April at around 4:30 p.m. he has not left home. He has not met with anyone of interest.

Terence Dunlow has infrequently left his home. He visited a nearby supermarket twice. His boyfriend – Benedict Hogan – is also in residence and has not left the property without Terence. No one of interest has visited Terence at his home.

I hope this is helpful,

James

Gabe

The sketch artist's office was situated on the second floor of the station, one I avoided when possible. The bulk of the space, sectioned off into offices and labs, was taken up by the forensics team. Any visit here ran the risk of bumping into David Rees. Despite the mellowing of his arsehole tendencies since Melanie Pirt's case, I didn't relish talking to him.

Nodding at the few people I passed in the narrow corridor, I kept my back straight. My shoulder ached, a familiar accompaniment. I would move, and so I would hurt. At least my loose jumper didn't tug at my wound.

I knocked on an open door, startling the young man inside. The last time I'd worked with the station's sketch artist, thankfully on a case rather than dredging up my own history, a middle-aged woman had sat in his chair.

'You're new, right? I'm Gabe.'

He stood and pushed thick glasses up his nose. His fingers danced through his spiked white-blond hair. 'I'm Gunter. Take a seat.' He pointed at a plastic chair rammed into the only free space left in the tiny room.

A window spanned the entirety of one wall. It looked out over the street below, currently busy with a mixture of stationary traffic and tourists over-excited by the brief presence of spring sunshine.

I was learning the rhythms of a coastal town. While Southampton wasn't a top tier holiday destination, it had its charms. Once the sun held real warmth, each car journey would take a few minutes longer and cafés would overflow with fresh business. Attention would turn to finding pickpockets and solving disputes between holiday home owners and the fleeting residents who trashed their Airbnbs.

I sat down on the unyielding plastic while the artist folded his long limbs back into his chair. His desk, stretching from wall to wall in front of the window, was dominated by three screens.

'Morning,' Paul said as he walked in.

'Sir.' Gunter shot up from his seat, his knobbly knees practically shaking in his black skinny jeans.

I stood as well, intending to offer my chair to Paul, but he waved us both back down.

'Let's get to it,' he commanded.

Gunter fiddled with his mouse and the screens changed from blank blackness to blank whiteness. I glanced at Paul, wondering when would be the best time to ask about the file. He had to have opened it, had to know whether the contents would help him find mine and Juliet's shooter.

His expression was hard to read as he leant against one side of the doorway. His stick tapped as we waited for Gunter to get ready. I'd seen a few of the articles, but I itched to read them all. Not just the printed words, but the cruel notes as well. There had to be a clue about the shooter between the red covers.

Paul gave nothing away. I was off the case. Maybe I wasn't allowed to know if he had a clear lead.

Gunter swivelled his chair to face me. 'How are you feeling today?'

'Can we not do this bit?' Artists worked through a series of stages to get the best results. The first was rapport building, but no amount of friendliness between me and Gunter would make helpful details materialise. 'Let's go straight to recall, please.'

I didn't want to be mean, but this would be painful enough without prolonging it. Gunter didn't protest. He turned back to his computer, the tips of his ears pink.

'It's best if you close your eyes,' he said. 'Watching the screens can muddle things.'

All sketch artists had slightly different methods. In my experience, they all yielded nothing.

I obediently closed my eyes. Gunter was new and young. He couldn't know how many times I'd already disappointed others like him. I'd play along so he knew he'd done everything he could to make this a success.

'Tell me big things first.' His voice was gentle, like he was attempting to lull me into a false sense of confidence and security. 'Can you remember their height and build?'

I pictured the hooded figure from the New Forest. 'They were a little taller than me. Maybe 5'6 or 5'7.' Aggravatingly average. 'They wore a bulky hoodie. Black. I couldn't see much about their upper body.' I thought back to them running away. 'Their jeans were tighter. I'd guess from their hips it was a woman, and medium build. Not too fit, since I was able to catch up with them and my shoulder wouldn't let me run properly.'

Not that I was especially fast normally. Short legs and a natural disinclination toward exercise left me just about able to pass the annual fitness exams.

'Do you remember anything about their footwear?' Gunter asked.

I scrunched my face. 'Trainers, I think. Nothing distinctive about them.'

'You said they were in a hoodie. Was the hood up or down?'

'Up.' I thought hard. 'They must have longish hair. It spilled out around their face.'

'What can you tell me about their hair?' Gunter coaxed.

'It was brown. Not as dark as mine.' I focused on the glimpse I'd caught of their face both times I'd shouted. 'Curly, or frizzy. Tangled around their hood.'

'What could you see of their face?'

'They were white. As light skinned as you.' Both the file leaver and Gunter would burn on a mildly pleasant day like today. I sighed, squashing the urge to open my eyes and glare at screens that no doubt held the least helpful image possible. 'I can't tell you much about their face. They were a fair distance away.'

'That's alright,' Gunter reassured me. 'They had brown hair. How about their eyes?'

Wide. Panicked.

Oddly familiar.

'I think,' I tailed off. That persistent sense of their identity being inches out of reach tickled at the back of my mind.

'Gabe?' Paul piped up from the doorway.

I opened my eyes. 'I really think I know them.'

Paul's eyebrows shot up. 'You said that before, but where from?'

'I'm not sure.' I grimaced. This was when trusting my gut was frustrating. It screamed I knew this person but provided no context. They could be someone I'd seen once at the supermarket or an old co-worker I'd forgotten.

Gunter nudged one of the screens to face me. 'Is this any help?'

The sketch was woefully incomplete. A hood stretched over wild brown hair. The basic eyes, nose, and mouth filled spaces my memory refused to fill.

Gunter tapped his mouse, and the eyes changed colour. Watching my reactions, he cycled from blue to grey to brown.

'Stop.' I squinted at the screen. 'Can you make them lighter?'

A couple of clicks, and the irises became a distinct hazel shade. The sense of familiarity intensified. I'd seen those eyes before they whipped away at the New Forest.

I closed my eyes again and pressed my teeth into the sides of my cheeks. Methodically, I thought through the various strangers and new faces I'd encountered in the last few days. For this sense of recognition to be so strong, I had to have seen them recently.

Henry's mum's eyes behind thick glasses and his dad's narrowed in suspicion. Ollie's rich brown eyes brought a pang of guilt, as did Douglas Frey's skittish gaze. His son had worn sunglasses. I knew Alice's near black eyes far too well to not recognise her, same with Maddy's brown and Juliet's grey.

No one matched. But still, my gut shouted these hazel eyes belonged to someone I knew.

The Galanis brothers had mocked me from the wall of my living room until Nicole cleared the evidence away. Their eyes were all unremarkable shades of dark brown, like mine.

I got my eyes from my dad. My mum's were grey-blue. Barnabas's had been too.

The bad man's eyes were never clear.

I mashed my palms over my face. The answer sat out of reach, taunting me.

'You alright, Gabe?' Paul asked.

'I know them.' I dropped my hands to my thighs, fixing my gaze on the screen. 'I just can't think how.'

'Perhaps it's someone you've recently been in contact with?' Gunter suggested. 'Try working through all your recent interactions.'

What did he think I'd been doing? I pressed my mouth shut rather than snap at him. Another way I wouldn't allow myself to be like Juliet.

'I've thought through everyone I've seen since I came home from hospital.'

Gunter swivelled back and forth in his chair. 'Think about while you were in the hospital, or before.'

A barrage of faces, blurred by medication and pain. Doctors, nurses, healthcare assistants.

At least I'd gotten out of there quickly. The ward sister hadn't been happy about my quick release. Her brown hair had been tied into a messy bun on top of her head. I'd found her attractive, though she'd barely looked at me. Her gaze had darted between my bandaged shoulder and the chart in her hands.

'Shit,' I breathed. 'I know who it is.'

DATE

29 April

NAME OF PATIENT

Mr Terence Dunlow

NHS NUMBER

8906386654

NAME OF DOCTOR

H. G. Reddecliff

PAYMENT METHOD

Mr Dunlow's treatment is covered by Mr Benedict Hogan's family plan

CONCERN

Low mood over a number of months

BACKGROUND

Mr Dunlow has been feeling sad for a number of months. Just over six months ago, his sexuality was shared publicly without his consent and as a result he became estranged from his father and moved house. He also started a new job around this time, which has become increasingly stressful.

Mr Dunlow describes himself as a social smoker. His alcohol consumption is moderate, at around five to ten units per week. He does not use social drugs.

CONSULTATION

Mr Dunlow said that although his general health is good, he has been feeling more tired than usual and his appetite has been low. He has little interest in his daily activities and hobbies he previously enjoyed.

I assessed Mr Dunlow via PHQ-9 mental health and depression criteria – his score was 10 to 14 (moderate depression).

TREATMENT

We discussed a number of options. Mr Dunlow was eager to recover soon, so medication was proposed and accepted. He will trial Sertraline 50mg once daily. Mr Dunlow has been advised of the side effects of this medication and possible transient exacerbation of symptoms during the initial trial. He has no known allergies or interactions with other medicines.

A referral for counselling has been completed. Mr Dunlow has been advised and encouraged to establish a good sleep regime, exercise regularly, avoid social isolation, eat regular healthy meals, avoid/minimise alcohol, and ensure adequate hydration.

A review appointment has been booked for three months' time.

From: David Rees **david.rees@forensics.gov.uk**
To: Paul Willis **paul.willis@mit.gov.uk**
CC: Nicole Stewart **nicole.stewart@mit.gov.uk**
Date: **29 April, 10:32**
Subject: **Operation Aster – forensic results**

Willis,

Attached are a number of forensic findings from HENRY GARSIDE'S room at university and his body. There is also a report from the pathologist.

Foreign DNA was found on HENRY GARSIDE'S BODY, mainly on his FACE and HAIR. These are primarily from one individual, but there are small amounts from one other. They are not a match for anyone currently on the system.

Items recovered from HENRY GARSIDE'S dorm room provide no matches to the foreign DNA on his body. Most of the matches are for HENRY GARSIDE and ROWAN LOUGH, who provided a DNA sample yesterday morning. TISSUES previously discovered by Martin have been tested and mucus particles confirm the blood was the result of a nose bleed rather than self-harm.

The pathologist has confirmed the cause of death was significant trauma to the back of the head. The site and spread of the damage suggest HENRY GARSIDE fell backward onto a hard surface with more force than would have been achieved by an accidental fall. The time of death is estimated to be between eleven a.m. and four p.m. on 24 April.

Rees

Gabe

'The file was full of newspaper clippings and print outs from the police website. The annotations seem to have been added along with each of them, but occasionally they've gone back to deface them again.' Paul sat behind me. He'd insisted I take the front seat, since whoever had been shot most recently had priority. Apparently, it was a rule. 'They're all about Juliet, and date back to around the time Douglas Frey retired.'

Nicole turned into the hospital car park, then idled behind a Jeep as they reversed into a space. 'Come on, you dickhead.'

I suppressed a smile. If one thing could humanise this woman I often felt subpar to, it was her inability to sit in a car without spouting abuse at her fellow drivers.

'How does any of that link to a nurse?' Vulnerability had plucked at me since I'd made the link in Gunter's office. If the nurse left the file, then potentially someone who wanted to hurt me had been around while I was at my most defenceless.

'No idea,' Paul said. I could tell he was grinning without painfully twisting to check. Even if this step proved faulty, it at least gave the case forward momentum.

I'd felt less sure of my leap of recognition since Paul called Nicole down from the seventh floor to drive us over to the hospital. I'd felt certain of where I'd seen those distinctive eyes, but doubt flickered. My gut had been wrong before. I'd vowed not to trust it too blindly again.

I hated to think a possible wild goose chase was distracting Nicole from finding Henry's killer but her presence was necessary. Neither me nor Paul would be any use if the nurse was the person who'd left the file and she ran again. She may not be fast, but she could outrun the two of us.

So there were two witnesses to my potential humiliation instead of one.

'For fuck's sake,' Nicole muttered as the Jeep driver edged back and forth to slot their car into an ample space. She zipped past as soon as they pulled in far enough.

Restlessness jangled through me. If I was right about the nurse, a lot of questions lingered unanswered. Too much of the picture would remain blank.

'One thing is sure,' Nicole said as she parked up, reverting to her usual calm once the car was no longer in motion. 'Whoever compiled the papers had been building up hatred toward Juliet for a long time.'

I unclicked my seatbelt, swallowing a question about whether there had been any articles about me, whether there had been horrible notes encouraging me to die too. Paul would have said if there was. He wouldn't sugarcoat the truth, especially not if I was in continued danger. I dipped my hand into the pocket of Ollie's coat, my fingers brushing the smooth plastic of the panic alarm.

'We were already working on the assumption Juliet was the primary target, so it doesn't change our lines of enquiry,' Paul said, as Nicole jumped out of the car and jogged over to the nearest parking machine. 'Does mean she needs to be made aware of the elevated threat, though. I've called her a couple of times but had no luck. Have you talked to her today?'

'No.' I wouldn't divulge why I was the last person Juliet would talk to unless I had to.

Paul and I eased out of the car while Nicole slotted the ticket into place on the dashboard. She kept pace with us as we meandered through the car park and approached the front of the hospital. Gaggles of smokers and gulls greeted us, each staking claim to their sections of dull concrete.

Energy raced through me. We could take a step forward with this case, or this could be an abrupt crash into a dead end.

'Lead the way,' Paul said as we stepped into the wide entrance. A café sprawled on one side, while people queued for a helpdesk and toilets on the other. Those with no visible ailments mixed with people in hospital gowns, drips hanging on long sticks above their shoulders.

I wound through the crowds to the bank of lifts. Paul lent on his stick while I rolled my shoulder, Nicole bouncing on her heels between us. The lift rose to the fourth floor where it opened onto a quiet corridor. I walked along the speckled plastic and turned onto the ward I'd woken up on four days ago.

A nurse rushed over as we stepped through the double doors. His purple scrubs strained over toned thighs, his curly hair a contrasting shade of green.

'I'm afraid visiting hours are over.' His brown forehead crinkled with concern. 'If you really need to, you can pop in for a minute and say hello.'

'We're not here for a patient.' Nicole brandished her ID. She managed to look good in the laminated photo. I looked half-asleep in mine, taken on my first disorienting day at Southampton station. 'We need to talk to one of the other nurses.'

'Oh.' He blinked, eyeshadow sparkling. 'Which one?'

Good question.

'I'm not sure.' I kept a wince off my face. 'I was here a few days ago following a shooting. I need to talk to one of the nurses who was on duty. The ward sister.'

Nicole rattled off the dates I was in hospital. The nurse extracted a tablet from a pocket in his scrubs and tapped at it.

'She was here when I left,' I added. 'She has brown curly hair.'

I didn't mention her eyes. Not everyone would find them captivating.

The nurse flicked at the screen of his tablet, then turned it toward us. 'Is this her?'

Relief flooded my veins. An ID picture filled the left side of the screen. A woman with bouncy hair and distinctive hazel irises smiled.

The nurse who had been so reluctant to see me go. There was no doubt in my mind she was the person who had left the file.

My instant relief curdled. Being looked after by someone who apparently hated Juliet and may have shot us was disconcerting.

'Mary Turner,' Paul read. Her name rang a faint bell. 'Is she working now?'

'Yes.' The nurse slid the tablet back into his pocket. 'I hope she's not in trouble?'

A figure emerged from behind a closed curtain midway across the busy ward. I tensed as Mary disposed of her gloves and a plastic apron in a bin beside the ward's central console. She smiled at a patient, then turned toward the entrance.

All colour drained from her face as her gaze alighted on us. She looked to a fire exit set between two beds on the other side of the ward. For a moment I was genuinely thankful Nicole was here, before Mary's shoulders slumped and she hurried across the ward toward us.

'This her?' Paul checked.

I nodded. Tears gathered in Mary's eyes as Nicole asked her to come down to the station. The excess water dulled their colour. Her hair wasn't caught on top of her head today. It spiralled in ringlets around her face.

Another flash of recognition tugged. There was a reason Mary's face was so familiar. I'd seen her since I'd left the hospital. But not in person, and not as she was now.

Paul stepped to my side. 'You alright, Gabe?'

'Mary?' I waited for her to blink at me. 'Is your name actually Maria? Are you Douglas Frey's daughter?'

With her hair loose and tears tracking down her cheeks, Mary looked a lot more like her teenage self.

Nicole's grip on her arm tightened. 'Is that true?'

Mary used the sleeve of her scrubs to wipe her face. Her father's eyes had always been dull, but it took a change to diminish hers. Water, or the ravages of time and neglect on the photos dotting the walls of her father's cottage.

'I'm not answering any questions until I've talked to a solicitor.' Mary's broken voice was miles away from the stern disapproval I'd experienced last time I was here.

I pulled Paul to one side as Nicole led Mary from the ward, her co-worker and patients alike gaping at her back.

'The shooter was most likely a man?' The itch at the back of my mind eased, everything falling into place. 'Douglas wouldn't have been capable, but Mary has a brother.'

Call connected at 11:32.

'Hello?'

   'Hello, this is Detective In—'

   'Hello? Hello?'

   'Hi, can you hear me?'

   'You need to speak louder. I can't bloody hear you.'

   'Sorry. Is that Mr Frey?'

   'Yes. Who are you?'

   'I'm Detective Inspector Paul Willis. I need to speak to your son, Thomas. Is he there?'

   'Tommy?'

   'Yes.'

   'He left.'

   'When?'

   'Yesterday. He's not been here today.'

   'Did he say why he was leaving?'

   'He was shouting.'

   'What did he shout about?'

   'He was cross.'

   'Can you remember what about?'

   'He had to leave. It was all very sudden.'

   'Did he say where he was going?'

   'He shouted at me.'

   'Mr Frey, could you please ask your son to contact me when he comes home? Ask him to call the station and talk to Paul Willis.'

   'I'm not a bloody answering machine. All I did for you people, and you turfed me out. You believed that blonde bitch over me.'

   'Who's that?'

   'Fuck off. Just fuck off. I'm done talking to you.'

Detective Sergeant Nicole Stewart: Informal interview commencing at 12:03 p.m. on Wednesday 29th April. The interviewee is Mary Turner. She has sought legal counsel prior to this interview. This interview is being conducted by myself, Detective Sergeant Nicole Stewart, and Detective Inspector Paul Willis. Mary is not under arrest and can stop this interview at any time. We will be discussing the shooting of Detectives Gabriella Martin and Juliet Stern on the 24th April.

Detective Inspector Paul Willis: Thank you for submitting your DNA prior to this interview. For now, it helps to eliminate you as a possible suspect.

Mary Turner: That's fine. I want to be helpful.

DS Nicole Stewart: Can you please tell us your whereabouts on the afternoon of the twenty-fourth?

Mary Turner: I was with my father. My brother usually cares for him, but he had to work and asked if I could take care of Dad. Tommy has been part of a big construction project down at the docks. He said they needed everyone to work extra shifts so they could finish on time.

DI Paul Willis: I've spoken with your father. It's unlikely he will be able to corroborate your alibi.

Mary Turner: Dad's unwell, but Tommy will tell you I was there.

DI Paul Willis: I've also spoken to Thomas. He said he was with your father that afternoon.

Mary Turner: I don't know why he's said that. He wasn't there. He was at work.

DS Nicole Stewart: How did you feel about the detectives being shot?

Mary Turner: I was upset. We don't often see shooting victims at the hospital. I was relieved they would both recover.

DI Paul Willis: Did you recognise either detective?

Mary Turner: Yes. Not the younger one.

DI Paul Willis: You recognised Detective Stern?

Mary Turner: Yes. She was, well, you know.

DI Paul Willis: You'll have to explain.

Mary Turner: She's in the file. The one Detective Martin saw me leave.

DI Paul Willis: Why did you give the file to Detective Martin?

Mary Turner: I'm a nurse. It didn't feel right to sit back and watch innocent women get hurt.

DI Paul Willis: Whose is the file?

[Long pause. Sniffing.]

DS Nicole Stewart: It's okay, Mary. Take your time.

Mary Turner: I didn't expect anyone to see me. I couldn't leave the file at her home. There were too many houses around; one of her neighbours might have remembered me. I was careful as I followed Detective Martin out to the New Forest. I thought you would come to your own conclusions without me getting involved.

DS Nicole Stewart: What conclusions did you expect us to come to?

Mary Turner: That the file belonged to my brother. Tommy.

DI Paul Willis: Can you tell us about Thomas's feelings toward Detective Stern?

Mary Turner: His file makes it pretty clear. He hated her.

DS Nicole Stewart: Your brother recently left your father's house without saying where he was going.

Mary Turner: Oh no, is Dad alright? He needs someone there, especially at night.

DI Paul Willis: I believe he's fine. We should be able to let you go soon so you can check on him.

DS Nicole Stewart: I raised your brother's absence to ask if you knew where Thomas might have gone after he left your father's house.

Mary Turner: I have no idea. He doesn't have many friends.

DI Paul Willis: Are you and your brother close?

Mary Turner: Not especially. We're very different people.

DI Paul Willis: Did Thomas ever speak about Detective Stern in a violent fashion? Do you think he could have been involved in the shooting?

[Sniffing.]

Mary Turner: No. He couldn't have. He might hate her, but I can't believe he would do that. He's never hurt anyone. At least not on purpose.

DI Paul Willis: Has Thomas hurt you or your father before?

[Sniffing.]

Mary Turner: I'm honestly not just saying this because he's my brother. I know Tommy. He might hate Juliet Stern but he isn't a violent man. Very occasionally Dad has had bruises or sore joints because Tommy had to restrain him. He always felt terrible about it, but Dad can get so angry when he doesn't understand who we are. Tommy would never purposely hurt anyone. I'm sure of it.

DS Nicole Stewart: Why did you leave the file if you don't think Thomas had anything to do with the shooting?

[Long pause.]

Mary Turner: I love my brother but it didn't feel right, after seeing those two women hurt, to keep anything from you.

Gabe

It was too much to hope that because I'd been instrumental in finding Mary Turner, previously named Maria Frey, that Paul would let me observe her interview. My part was done. James had been summoned to drop me home as soon as we got to the station, while Paul and Nicole hurried upstairs to prepare.

Paul had thrown me a bone before I was bundled off. He pressed the files he'd taken into my hands. A sign I was wholly forgiven and trusted, but the gesture was empty. I'd examined the files several times. They contained no link to Thomas.

If he was our shooter, then Juliet had encouraged me to walk into an incredibly dangerous situation when she asked me to talk to Douglas Frey.

I'd taken Artie's boisterous greeting after James dropped me home as a sign we were due a stomp. I refused to allow what happened last time we came to these woods to taint them. Walking had become an unexpected solace in the months since I'd adopted Artie. Time and repetition had softened the memories surrounding Melanie Pirt's murder that were always awakened as I walked through forests similar to the one where she'd lost her life. I could easily quash thoughts of Mary Turner.

I eyed the other cars as I pulled into the tree-lined car park in the New Forest. A two-seater convertible sat beside a silver BMW. Their number plates were uncovered and no drivers lingered with hoods obscuring their faces.

I looked at my phone before letting Artie out of the car. No one had heard from Juliet since she'd stormed out of my maisonette yesterday. That didn't mean she was in immediate danger, no matter how loud the alarm bells in my head rang. She was pissed at me, and she wasn't ever eager to answer when Paul called. Hopefully, she was using the down time to rest and recover. As much as my shoulder hurt, hers had to be worse.

Paul had told me that if Juliet didn't reply soon, he would send officers around to her flat to check on her. She'd love that.

Following Artie along winding paths through the trees, I pressed a hand over the dressing hidden under my coat. Reconciling the nurse who cared for me with someone who had anything to do with my shooting was difficult. But Mary couldn't have laid hands on that file without key knowledge about who had attacked me and Juliet.

Uncovering Mary had to mean we were a step closer to finding the shooter. The CCTV footage suggested a man. If we were lucky, Mary would rat out her brother. It was a matter of time before Paul and Nicole made a second arrest, and this would all be over. I could close my eyes at night without horrible dreams lurking.

The only thing casting a pall over the triumph of finding Mary was the lack of a link to the Galanis brothers. It seemed they had benefitted from someone acting on a years' long grudge against Juliet rather than being directly involved. With no new leads to follow, we'd have to redouble our efforts to pin them down when we got back to work.

The light had changed while Artie and I walked through the trees. I stepped out onto a grassy meadow and was temporarily blinded by bright sunshine.

While I squinted, Artie bounded off toward a group of walkers. Hopefully they weren't afraid of Alsatians, since they were about to get a non-optional greeting from one. I threw up my good arm to shield my eyes, which widened when I saw who was patting my dog on the head.

Hampered by Artie's enthusiastic bouncing as he reunited with his previous owners, Leo and Terence Dunlow made slow progress toward me. They were accompanied by a man in a pale brown coat.

Panic flashed through me, but I smothered it. Terence might have been a suspect before we found Mary Turner, but I couldn't connect the two of them.

Apart from via a grudge against Juliet, with me thrown in on Terence's end. The articles in the file dated back to way before Terence knew of me and Juliet, but he could have worked with someone who had been nursing their hatred a lot longer.

Thomas Frey may not have acted alone. He'd detested Juliet for a long time and maybe Terence was the catalyst for him bursting into action.

Inside my coat pockets, I curled my hands into fists. One closed around the panic alarm. I didn't think Terence would attack me with his brother and who I assumed was his boyfriend around, but I would at least alert the station if he did.

'Hi, Gabe.' Leo grinned at me while ruffling behind Artie's pointed ears. The months since we'd charged Karl for Melanie's murder had wrought mixed changes on Timothy Dunlow's youngest son. He'd filled out, his lanky limbs bulked with lean muscle. His auburn hair was cropped close to his scalp, his thick glasses magnifying the shadows under his eyes.

'Hey.' I offered a nod to Terence and his boyfriend. The days since I'd chatted to Terence at the gallery hadn't been kind to him. The skin around his eyes looked sore and his hair fell lankly across his face as he bent to stroke Artie. 'I didn't know you walked around here,' I tacked on. Let them wonder how much we kept tabs on them.

'I've been more anxious since the shooting. And Terence hasn't been well.' Leo paused his fussing over Artie to push his glasses up his nose. 'The doctor said walks might help.'

If Terence clenched his stubbled jaw any tighter, his face might crack in half. He wasn't happy with his brother's oversharing. His expression softened when his boyfriend rested a gloved hand on his arm. His dark hair was styled, his skin clear. It made Terence's imperfections all the more blatant.

'It can feel pointless going for walks without a dog.' Terence's expression softened further as he looked down at Artie. 'I've missed them.'

The unease swimming through me since I'd spotted the brothers eased. Terence was often cross and petulant, but easily cowed. That didn't make him incapable of shooting me and Juliet, but it made it unlikely. He would need to have been pushed to an extreme to handle Henry's body with such brutal precision.

'How are your investigations going?' the boyfriend asked. I wished I could remember his name. His coat hugged his slim frame, while Terence's flapped in the breeze.

'Fine.' I kept my focus on Terence. 'We're taking positive steps toward arrests.'

I'd accidentally bumped into Terence on an unplanned walk so Paul couldn't tell me off for talking to another suspect, but saying anything else would lead into greyer territory.

Terence's shoulders sagged. 'I hope you find whoever hurt Henry.'

'And you and Juliet.' Leo's face widened with a smile. 'It's good to see you out and about. I was so worried when you were hurt.'

I smiled tightly at Leo. 'Artie and I need to carry on before he gets bored and terrorises a horse.'

'They're ponies,' Terence muttered.

My brows drew together. 'What?'

'They're not horses. They're ponies.'

My eyes flicked between the three men. A hint of familiar pettiness had crept onto Terence's tired face. Uneven blush rose across Leo's as the boyfriend raised a smooth smile.

'Have a good walk, Detective.' His voice was as posh as Terence's. He dipped his head once before steering his boyfriend away.

Artie's allegiance had changed in the months since I'd been his primary food and head scratch provider. He ran over to my side as I set off across the sun dappled grass. I resisted the urge to look around. I didn't like having my back to the three men, but I didn't want to give Terence the satisfaction of knowing his presence discomfited me.

He was difficult to figure out. He gave the general impression of someone whose shine had rubbed off. As a person of interest in the shooting and Henry's killing, the likelihood he was involved in neither crime was small. Perhaps that was why he was so diminished. Hard to maintain good skin and hair care regimens when committing crimes.

Terence couldn't be discounted as a suspect for the shooting because he had no obvious connection to the Freys. He disliked me and Juliet, perhaps enough for that to be stoked into violent action with the right motivation and Karl whispering in his ear. Maybe Henry had gotten caught up in it all. Terence claimed they'd never met, but no one living could tell us the truth.

I blew out a breath and Artie looked up at me. I patted his head, which he took as permission to leave my side and investigate a series of rabbit holes.

A much more likely culprit for the shooting was Thomas Frey. If he'd collected and annotated those articles about Juliet, then he'd been nursing a grudge for a long time. It would be perfect if he confessed and detailed how he'd been prompted into action by the Galanis brothers. It would almost make being shot through the shoulder worth it if we could stop the misery they caused across the city.

I pulled my phone out of my pocket. No new messages or missed calls. Sending Juliet another text would alienate her further. She hated coddling. She was either ignoring me or was in a situation I couldn't help with. Paul was aware of the threat against her. He would act if necessary.

By the time Artie and I reached the other side of the field, the only living things on the grass were a couple of grazing beasts with long swishing tails.

'They look pretty horse-like to me,' I murmured.

FORM 22A – FORMAL REQUEST FOR WARRANT: PERMISSION TO SEARCH A PRIVATE RESIDENCE

REQUESTING OFFICERS:

Detective Inspector Paul Willis and Detective Sergeant Nicole Stewart

CASE NUMBER:

87049375

CASE DESCRIPTION:

Non-fatal shooting of Detective Inspector Juliet Stern and Detective Sergeant Gabriella Martin on 24 April outside Southampton Crown Court

REQUESTED SEARCH AREA:

Orchard Cottage – owned by Douglas Frey

REASON FOR WARRANT REQUEST:

Thomas Frey is a person of interest in the shooting of Detective Inspector Juliet Stern and Detective Sergeant Gabriella Martin. Upon learning we needed to speak to his father about the shooting, Thomas absconded from their shared property. We believe a search of the property could provide clues about his current whereabouts.

A file has also been recovered and Mary Turner (nee Maria Frey) has been questioned. She claims the file, containing articles and threatening notes about Detective Inspector Juliet Stern, was compiled by Thomas Frey. Both incidents have given us reason to suspect Thomas Frey was involved in the shooting. A search of the property may provide further evidence.

Douglas Frey owns the property and has Alzheimer's. Due care and consideration will need to be taken to cause him no undue distress during the search of the premises.

Call connected at 15:07.

'Hello. Detective Inspector Paul Willis speaking.'

'Hello, Paul. It's Angela.'

'How can I help you, ma'am?'

'I hear you have a lead for Juliet and Gabe's shooting?'

'Yes. We've talked to Mary Turner and she's given us lots to go on. Our main suspect is Thomas Frey, her brother. He's scarpered but I've sent in a request to search his home to see if we can figure out where he's gone.'

'I'll make sure that's processed quickly. Is there a link between Mary and the suspects you placed under surveillance? Terence Dunlow or the Galanis brothers?'

'Not at the moment, ma'am. Do you need us to pull back?'

'Only if there's no reason for them to be watched any more. I obviously want to find whoever shot two of my detectives, but resources are already stretched and if there's no clear link, then stepping back for the time being would be prudent.'

'I'm happy to call off the surveillance. It hasn't yielded anything anyway.'

'Right. How is Henry Garside's case coming along? I know it's not easy stretching across two major investigations.'

'No leads. Henry left the art block the morning of the twenty-fourth and vanished until his body was found. I've had uniforms trawling through CCTV of the area and questioning workers on the docks. Nothing.'

'That's disappointing. Hopefully you'll find something to give his family closure.'

'We'll keep searching, ma'am.'

'Good work. Give my love to Joanie and the boys.'

Al. Sent 16:02.

My tail left about half an hour ago and hasn't come back.

GG. Sent 16:02.

Do you think mine's gone too?

Al. Sent 16:03.

Probably.

Tsam. Sent 16:03.

I'll get the boys to check x

Tsam. Sent 16:27.

All gone x

GG. Sent 16:27.

Are you still coming over for dinner again?

Tsam. Sent 16:29.

Yes, but I have an errand to run first. Al, can you pick
something up and I'll meet you there? x

Gabe

For the first time since we'd met, I didn't think Ollie would welcome my touch. He'd knocked on my front door instead of letting himself in, and stood in the hallway with his jaw clenched. His hair was stiff with gel and he carried the odd mixture of other people's perfume and sweat that accompanied him after a photo shoot.

'I'm mad at you,' he said.

'I'm sorry about Juliet.' I crossed my arms, rather than reaching for him and being rebuffed. 'I didn't expect her to do that. I should have told her to stop.'

'I don't care about her.' Ollie heaved a sigh. 'I care that you kept me away. All I wanted to do was look after you when you'd fucking well been shot, and you wouldn't let me.'

I blinked at him. That was not why I'd assumed he would be cross. I thought my lack of action would push him away, but holding him at arm's length had been more harmful.

Ignoring the stiff set of his shoulders, I stepped forward and cupped his face in my hands. His cheeks were claggy with layers of foundation.

'You are a lovely man and I'm sorry.' I lifted onto my tiptoes to kiss him gently. 'I don't want you to stay away. I want you here.'

He gripped my wrists as he leant his forehead on mine. 'Can I tell you something stupid?' His voice was quiet, all anger swept from him.

'Yeah.' I nudged his nose, wishing the talking part of the evening could end. Now I knew this wasn't over, I wanted Ollie close. The jumper and trousers I'd worn to the station this morning weren't exciting, but he had shown interest in me despite them before. The chastity my injury had forced on us had to break soon.

'You know we were meant to go to the pub the evening you got hurt?' Ollie moved his face away from mine. 'I had something to tell you.'

Cool air filled the space between us. I lowered onto my heels, lengthening the distance. It didn't make sense for Ollie to break up with me after he'd said he wanted to be around, but the fear remained.

'What was it?' I asked, wishing he would let me lower my arms. I clutched at the sides of his neck.

He licked his lips. 'I've decided to stop modelling.'

I raised my eyebrows. Ollie had never been wildly enthusiastic about his career, but said it was better than the alternative. Growing up as the only son of a farmer, he was expected to take over while his sister did whatever she wanted. A chance meeting with a modelling agent on his eighteenth birthday gave him a concrete way out.

'What do you want to do?'

Ollie's eyes jumped between mine. 'I'm going to train to be a teacher.'

'Ol.' My face creased into a smile. 'You'll be so good at that. You're brilliant with people.'

He squeezed my wrists. 'I've got a placement in the city starting this September. History at secondary.'

I stretched to touch my lips to his. 'This is amazing. I'm proud of you.'

'Yeah?' Ollie's fingers trailed along the skin of my inner arms. 'Prouder than when I'm prancing around in my underwear?'

I didn't reply, but instead pressed into him. He smiled against my lips as his fingers raked through my hair, his tongue finding mine. My hands traced over his strong arms and the muscles of his chest, the twinge in my shoulder not enough to snap me from needing to be close.

I stepped between Ollie's thighs and pushed him flush with my front door. He groaned, the deep sound vibrating down my throat.

'I missed you,' I breathed, as Ollie kissed across my jaw. I let my head loll as he mouthed the sensitive skin beneath my ear, clutching at his sides. 'Sorry I was an arsehole.'

'Don't push me away again,' Ollie murmured, his breath warm on my neck. 'You well enough for this?'

I shivered. 'If by this you mean dry-humping against my front door, then yes. But I was hoping for something a little more sophisticated.'

'Dry-humping against a wall near the front door it is, then.' Ollie hooked his hands under my thighs and lifted them to his hips. I swung my arms around his neck, taking my weight on the uninjured one.

Ollie stepped back until my spine met the magnolia-coloured plaster. I arched into him, so relieved he viewed me as his girlfriend again, rather than as an injured creature.

Someone knocked on my front door.

I groaned and tipped my head to look over Ollie's shoulder. The semi-circle of misted glass at the top showed a blurred face.

'Did you order food?' Ollie bent to place my feet on the floor. He spun around and opened the door.

My heart, accelerated at the prospect of Ollie's skin on mine, thundered with new purpose. Alarm bells burst into clamorous screams. Sweat prickled the delicate skin across my upper back and under my arms.

Tsambikos Galanis stood on my doorstep. His black hair was styled away from his tanned face, his slim build showcased in a navy suit. Behind him, a towering boulder of a man looked out over the street.

I'd left my phone on the sofa when I'd heard Ollie's knock, too caught up in seeing him again to remember to be cautious. The panic alarm was in my coat pocket, slung over the end of my bed. I had to deal with this alone.

'Evening,' Tsambikos said, white teeth flashing. 'Is that Gabriella behind you?'

I grabbed Ollie's hand and he turned to me. His mouth curved in a smile, delighted to hear someone other than my mum use my full name. My expression stoppered his smile when it was half cast.

'You okay?' Ollie's eyes darted over my face.

I squeezed his hand and manoeuvred so that I stood in the open doorway. I nudged him toward the living room. 'Can you make coffee please?'

In the early hours when Ollie slept and my mind refused to stop searching for every terrible thing that could possibly happen, I'd considered developing a signal to wordlessly tell him we were in danger. But then the sun rose and Ollie woke up. The world was a better place. A coded action seemed paranoid in the presence of his warm smile.

It turned out we didn't need one. Ollie had seen me afraid, all those nights when I'd woken with dark memories snapping at my heels.

His face settled into hard lines I'd never seen before. 'Are you going to be okay?'

'Please.' I pushed him with my shoulder, the pain nothing compared to how desperately I needed him gone. 'Make drinks.'

Ollie swallowed, but nodded and slipped behind me. I listened to his heavy tread across the living room, then stepped outside and pulled the door shut.

I stood on my doormat, trying to control my breathing. Tsambikos held his ground on my front path, his shiny shoes a mere step away from my slippered feet. At least I hadn't changed into my pyjamas. A jumper and trousers formed scant protection, but they were the only armour I had.

'You're a terrible hostess.' One corner of Tsambikos's mouth tipped up into a smirk.

Ollie's initial reaction had been to laugh along with him. Nothing about Tsambikos screamed criminal. If we'd met in another context, I'd have assumed he was a flashy businessman. He was well-groomed and his clothes expensive, with no hallmarks of a hardened life of crime. No visible scars or gang tattoos, no air of barely contained malice.

Tsambikos exuded polished pleasantness. That was how he and his brothers had gotten away with building a criminal empire in a sleepy seaside city. Where drug gangs and smuggling groups had been small and easily ousted five years ago, the Galanis brothers had swept in and taken control of almost every aspect of sex work and drug trafficking across Southampton. In the past two years, they had operated unchallenged.

All without dirtying their hands. Juliet and I had dug deep into every crevice since the human trafficking ring was discovered last autumn and we always smacked into an invisible fortress around the brothers.

But all of that was irrelevant. I needed to send Tsambikos far away before he could do any harm.

'I've not seen your boyfriend before,' he said. 'He's delicious.'

'Leave him the fuck alone,' I snapped.

Tsambikos tutted, pulling at his jacket cuffs with fingernails painted the same blue as his winged eyeliner. 'Always so testy. One would think we aren't good friends, Gabriella.'

During our first interview with the brothers, Tsambikos clocked my twitch when I said my first name for the recording. He'd used it as much as possible ever since. He was always like this; slippery and overly familiar. It made me want to shower, like being in his presence covered me in a tacky layer of grime.

'What do you want?' I ground out.

I glanced at the man standing behind Tsambikos. He had no visible weapons, but that meant nothing. Anyway, public violence wasn't Tsambikos's style. Usually.

My shoulder throbbed along with the frantic beat of my heart. It had never been more evident than in this moment that he and his brothers must have been involved in the shooting. Tsambikos wouldn't be here, wouldn't take this risk, if he hadn't been. This was a message, like the bullet through my flesh.

Stay away, or you'll get taken down.

I didn't know if the plan had been to injure rather than kill, or what the timing meant. Henry Garside had been murdered earlier that day. Had the Galanis brothers ordered Juliet and I to be shot to give them time to clear up their mess?

'I wanted to check on you.' Tsambikos's dark eyes alighted on my shoulder, the padded bandage making the joint bulge. 'Getting shot can't have been fun.'

'It wasn't my favourite activity.' I balled my hands into fists inside my jumper sleeves. 'You'll be pleased to hear I'll make a full recovery. So will Juliet.'

'I am pleased to hear that.' Tsambikos's voice was as smooth as silk, his expression one of total earnestness as he nodded. I wondered if he practised in a mirror. 'Make sure you don't hurry back to work before you're ready.'

He often spoke like this, using misdirection to mask his true intent. It wasn't subtle this time. The message; stay away from the station.

Tsambikos had engineered to have me and Juliet distracted and the force occupied with finding our shooter. If I messed that up, I'd have more than a wound in my shoulder to contend with. I wondered what the brothers were so desperate to hide, and whether they knew I'd been allowed back to the station before I'd screwed it up. Perhaps they weren't as all-knowing as they liked to think.

'You've checked I'm okay,' I said. 'Is there anything else I can do for you?'

I needed him gone. Now. Every moment he was here was another second Ollie was in far too much danger because of me.

Sparks crackled inside my skull. I didn't like to think about it, but Ollie could never be safe around me. No one was.

'Since I assume you're not going to invite me inside for a cup of tea, I'll be off.' Tsambikos walked backward along my front path, deftly avoiding the cracks between the paving stones. 'Nice to see you looking so well, Gabriella. It's always best to come in person, when you're worried about a friend, isn't it?'

I wondered if he was hinting at the surveillance Paul and Nicole had placed him and his brothers under. With that parting remark, Tsambikos turned on one perfect heel and marched down the road. His henchman followed, carefully closing my gate behind them.

As they disappeared down the street, I committed everything Tsambikos said to memory. There wasn't much. Far more to infer than actual words.

He knew where I lived. He knew who I loved. He wanted me and Juliet out of the way, and he'd do whatever it took to achieve that.

I didn't know if this performance was because of the shooting or Henry, but Tsambikos coming to my home had to mean something.

The clanging bells in my head didn't quiet once I was left alone outside my maisonette. I shuddered, wrapping my arms around my chest.

Angela had talked to Juliet and I about the additional risks of Operation Juno. Openly targeting crime bosses was a dangerous business. I'd not let Ollie stay over for a week after our first press conference, certain the Galanis brothers would seek instant retribution.

Months of stagnation had lulled me into a false sense of security.

A car door slammed. An engine roared, then powered away.

The bells gave way to a high-pitched whine. It only existed inside my mind, but was no less shrill and penetrating.

My knees buckled.

Back rounded, my forehead came into contact with rough cement. My fingers threaded through my hair, clammy with sweat.

I wasn't safe. I couldn't be.

Everyone I loved needed to stay far away.

Call connected at 16:46.

'Detective Inspector P—'

'I'm on sick leave. Why do you keep calling me?'

'No one had heard from you for a while. We were concerned for your safety.'

'I wasn't aware things had escalated.'

'We've gathered new information. It looks like you were the primary target.'

'That's different to your previous suspicions, how?'

'Now we have concrete evidence someone was interested in you.'

'I see. From now on, I'll message each morning and evening to confirm my safety. There's no need to call again.'

'I don't know how I'll cope with the loss. Before you go, is there any particular reason Douglas Frey dislikes you?'

'What's Gabe said?'

'Nothing. Should she have said something?'

'No. Douglas Frey dislikes me no less than every other woman who wouldn't give him what he wanted.'

'What did he want from you?'

'That's irrelevant.'

'Look, Juliet, if something went on before Douglas retired, it's going to come out. We've already talked to his daughter and we're looking for his son. If you're hiding things, they're not going to stay hidden for very long.'

'I'm hiding nothing. Douglas Frey may have hated me or not. That's his business. I have nothing to add to what I've already said about him.'

'Fine.'

'Keep me updated on further developments via email, if you must.'

'Roger that. I'll let you get back to an evening of cackling over your cauldron and pulling legs off ants.'

'Sounds vastly preferable to speaking to you.'

Gabe

'Is she alright, mate?' an unfamiliar voice broke through the rushing din.

'Stay away,' I whispered into damp hands.

I flinched when fingertips brushed my shoulder. I hadn't moved since I'd fallen to the ground. My elbows and knees ached, but my chest was worse. My ribs felt too tight, my heart bruised.

'She's fine,' Ollie called to one of my nosy neighbours. 'Gabe, love.' His palm flattened on my back. 'It's cold out here. Come inside and we can talk it through.'

Maybe talking things through was code for breaking up. Ollie had seen the terror in my eyes on finding the crime boss at my door. Finally, the gossamer thin bubble around this relationship had broken. I'd pretended for too long that it could last.

The idea of Ollie not being in my life made my legs weaken. He brought brightness to my days. I didn't want to go back to stumbling through the dark.

Meekly, I allowed him to pull me to standing. My limbs were heavy, like I'd run a marathon rather than crumpling to the ground. Ollie wrapped an arm around my waist and I leant into him, stealing a last few moments of closeness.

Uncontrollable tears coursed down my face as he bundled me onto the sofa and tucked a fluffy blanket around my legs. He grabbed steaming coffees from the kitchen while Artie laid his head on my lap, his tail flicking in an irregular rhythm. He whined, and the sound echoed inside of me.

Ollie nudged my feet to make room at the other end of the sofa. His fingers curled around my numb toes. I wanted to memorise the sensation.

'Who was that?'

My nerves rattled, and I tangled my fingers in the blanket. Dissecting what had happened was much more painful than Ollie simply leaving. No magical words could make him stay.

I didn't want him to. That would be a death sentence.

'Tsambikos Galanis.'

Ollie's eyes flicked to where photos of the three brothers had been tacked to my wall. It had been stupid to hope he wouldn't have glanced at evidence I'd displayed so brazenly. I twisted my fingers deeper into the blanket. I'd been determined to keep Ollie separate from my work, but it infected too much of my life.

'One of the shooting suspects?'

I nodded, face itching as salt water dried across my skin. When Ollie left, I'd burrow down under this blanket and emerge once the tears stopped, once I felt armoured instead of stripped bare. I didn't know how long that would take. For the first time, I was thankful I wasn't expected at the station tomorrow.

'Shit.' Ollie squeezed my feet. 'Why was he here?'

I untangled one of my hands and used my sleeve to mop away the moisture coating my face. I rubbed at my eyes, blinking until Ollie came into focus.

He didn't look mad. More concerned.

My heart sank. He didn't understand the ramifications of what had happened. I'd have to explain the danger I'd exposed him to.

'That doesn't matter.' My voice was croaky, like I'd been shouting for hours at a concert. 'What matters is that a criminal came to my home while you were here.'

Ollie didn't stop kneading my feet. 'Isn't it better you weren't alone?'

I stared at him. He wasn't unintelligent, despite the assumptions people made when he told them his current profession. I couldn't understand how the simple concept that being around me put him in unnecessary danger was so difficult for him to comprehend.

Maybe he was willing to ignore the threat if it meant he could be with me, but I couldn't do that any more. I'd been selfish for long enough. I couldn't watch someone I loved get hurt again.

I pulled my knees up to my chest. 'I don't think we should be together any more.'

Ollie's face fell. I hadn't thought the ache in my chest could intensify but something inside me broke as he opened his mouth, then closed it.

He tracked a tear winding down my cheek. His expression hardened as he scooted into the space I'd created between us.

'You won't always be waiting for your shooter to be found.' Ollie gripped my knee. 'Paul will figure out who did this and lock them away.'

I eyed his fingers. I wanted to push mine between them, to let him gather me close. He was still thinking of me, even when he was the one in danger.

I'd allowed Ollie to care for me for too long.

'Please listen.' I bound my hands in thick layers of blanket to stop my actions betraying me. 'You're always going to be in danger when you're with me. If it's not the shooter, it's whoever else I'm pursuing. They could find out about you and hurt you.'

Ollie's perfectly sculpted eyebrows bunched together. 'Gabe, that's so unlikely. You can't hold yourself apart from everyone just in case the worst happens.' He squeezed my knee. 'I know being with a detective is riskier than getting with another model or whatever, but I want to be with you. You're worth it, Gabe.'

I shook my head, batting away his kind words. The panicked din in my brain clanged on. Under the blanket, my hands shook. 'You don't understand.'

'Then explain it to me,' Ollie urged. 'We cross bridges together, right?'

The reminder of what he'd said when we first started dating almost broke through my resolve. But figuring out how to introduce friends or managing the complicated dance of who paid for what was different. This wasn't a bridge. This was an unscalable ravine.

'No. Not this time.'

Ollie's beautiful mouth downturned. All I wanted was for this to stop, but I had to hurt him. If he stayed with me, things would get worse and worse until he was snatched away.

'I understand your job is dangerous, Gabe.'

'It's not my job,' I spat out. 'It's me.'

Ollie's hold on my knee tightened. 'What about you?'

'It's.' I bit my lip, struggling for the right words. 'I. Things happened to me. You know that. Some of it. Horrible things.'

'Gabe, breathe.' Ollie's eyes grew round.

I had to forge on. My chest heaved, but I couldn't stop. 'This can't be changed. Or fixed. I can't be fixed. I am.' I sucked in a breath. 'I'm broken, Ollie. I am broken.'

Instead of watching the truth sink in and his expression turn cold, I lowered my head to my knees. It was pathetic, but I couldn't stop the keening sobs racking through me.

I'd kept this core truth hidden for much longer than I'd dreamed I could. I'd had months of closeness with Ollie, but it was always going to end. Others saw the darkness surrounding me much quicker than him. He had always seen the light.

'I can't have people close to me,' I whispered into the cavern behind my knees. 'They get hurt. I can't let that happen to you. I can't make you broken too.'

Strong arms encircled me. Ollie must have abandoned the sofa, nudged Artie out of the way so he could gather me close. I tensed, then leant into his warmth. If these were our final moments together, I'd let myself have this. I could pretend I didn't have to push away everyone who could offer comfort. I wished I could gather this feeling and keep it for the dark times when I was alone.

'Shush, love.' Gradually, I became aware of the soft words Ollie whispered around my quietening sobs. 'I'm here. You don't have to be alone.'

That caused a fresh wave of tears. Such a kind thing to say, but it wasn't true.

I couldn't keep crying. I sagged into Ollie's arms, my breathing slowing. I felt as wrecked as when I'd woken in the hospital, my mind swimming and every limb leaden. My shoulder sparked with pain, bruised muscles groaning.

'Gabe, can you listen to me?' Ollie spoke into my hair. He held me cradled tight to his chest.

I nodded. If I let him say his piece, he'd leave. I wouldn't have to fight this desperate need to cling to him any more.

'I hate what happened when you and your brother were small.' Ollie's voice was thick. I'd never shared the details of what happened to me and Barnabas, but still he mourned for me. For us. 'If I could take it away, I would.'

I'd let him. Too many times, I'd lain in bed and imagined what it would be like to forget. For all of this to stop.

It made me feel guilty, that I would forget my brother to quiet my mind, but it had been loud for years. I didn't think Barnabas would mind. I'd lived with the ghosts of what happened for too long.

'I know it hurt you deeply. It still does.' Ollie rocked slowly from side to side. 'I want to be here with you when it hurts.'

I pressed my lips together. I wouldn't ask him to stay. I couldn't be that selfish.

'I know you want to push me away because you think that will keep me safe, but that's not what I want,' Ollie went on. 'I want to be with you, Gabe. I don't know what I'd do without you any more. I'm an adult; I accept the risks of being with you.'

This was the opposite of what I'd expected to hear. His words made my chest ache a little less, the clouds in my mind lightening. I raised my head.

Ollie smiled at me. Lines of grey webbed down his cheeks, but his eyes were bright. 'I love you, Gabe Martin. Please don't make me leave.'

My breath punched out of me. More tears blurred my vision. I sank into Ollie's chest, his words doing battle with truths I'd told myself for far too long.

I didn't believe I was lovable, that anyone should or could love me. But Ollie said he did, and he didn't lie.

Before I met him, I'd kept everyone at a distance to stop them from being hurt. To stop them from seeing how broken and shattered I was.

But Ollie was too kind. Too gentle and good. I thought I could be with him for a little while. I'd been sure he would get bored or be scared off by something I did, get annoyed by something I couldn't.

He hadn't. He'd stuck around. I'd refused to talk about my past and he didn't care. I'd stayed late at work and he kept leftovers for me. I struggled to articulate how deeply I cared for him, and he held me and didn't demand a thing.

'Please don't leave.' They weren't the three words I wanted to say. No matter how much I felt them, confessing that was too much after everything else that had happened this evening.

Ollie held me tighter. 'I'm not going anywhere.'

It wasn't wise for him to stay, but I didn't want him to go. I would keep him safe every way I could, make sure danger didn't find him.

I was irreparably broken, but Ollie saw that and he loved me anyway. He helped me hold myself together.

I didn't think I'd ever have anything like this. Now I did, I wasn't going to let anything take it away.

Call connected at 18:08.

'Hullo. Detective Inspector Paul Willis here.'

'Hi, Paul.'

'Gabe? Are you alright? You sound a bit croaky.'

'I'm fine. Sorry to call you in the evening.'

'No worries. Joanie's on story duty tonight. You're only coming between me and a beer. What's up?'

'Tsambikos Galanis came to my house.'

'Bloody hell. What?'

'About an hour ago.'

'Gabe, are you okay? What the hell is he playing at?'

'I'm fine. He didn't do anything. Said he'd come for a chat.'

'Would you believe Angela asked me to stop the surveillance for him and his brothers earlier today?'

'He alluded to that. They knew they were being followed.'

'Hold on, let me grab a bit of paper. What else did he say?'

'He wanted to check I was okay after the shooting. He said I shouldn't go back to work until I was well rested.'

'Why's he coming to your home to tell you that?'

'To scare me? Have you found any link between the Freys and the Galanis brothers? Tsambikos coming here has to mean something.'

'Mary said the file was her brother's, but she didn't seem to think he would have been involved in the shooting. Unless we bring in Thomas, I don't think we're going to find a connection. The Galanis brothers are too clever for us to find anything on their side.'

'Tsambikos must have had a reason for coming here. Maybe he's rattled. He had me and Juliet shot, and now he's warning me to stay away.'

'Could be, or he could be an opportunist. Can you think of any link between the Galanis brothers and Terence Dunlow?'

'Apart from being extreme arseholes, no. Oh, I bumped into Terence and Leo this afternoon on a dog walk.'

'What are the odds that Terence is linked to your shooting and Henry's disappearance but not involved in either?'

'I've been thinking the same thing, but it's much more likely Tsambikos and his brothers were involved in both the shooting and Henry's murder.'

'They could be. My priority for now has to be bringing in Thomas Frey. If we manage that, we'll see what he has to say. Now, you look after yourself, Gabe. It can't have been nice to have that scumbag turn up at your door.'

'It wasn't amazing.'

'Is Ollie there?'

'Yeah.'

'Good. He'll take care of you.'

'He will.'

Call connected at 18:23.

'Gabriella? Darling, are you okay?'

'Yeah, Mum, I'm fine. I wanted to say sorry. I shouldn't have kept my injury from you.'

'No, you shouldn't have.'

'I didn't want you to worry.'

'I'll worry regardless. You're my daughter. I always want to know you're safe and well.'

'I am. I promise.'

'Please tell us straight away if something like this happens again.'

'I will, but it's not likely. I've been on the force for over a decade and this is the first time I've been seriously hurt.'

'What about when you were hit by a car?'

'I wasn't at work, Mum. That was on a date. And it was years ago. I know you and Dad don't like my career, but it's what I want to do.'

'We know, love. We know.'

Leading sessions for The Refuge is never easy, but tonight's meeting was particularly hard. A woman who had previously been upbeat about her future options (if a bit closed off) was broken by her husband's latest actions. It was difficult to watch this woman, who I imagine does not normally allow herself such vulnerability, cry as she told us how her husband has been using a recent injury to manipulate her.

We advised her to continue keeping a diary of his actions but I could see she wasn't listening. I won't be surprised if she doesn't come to any more meetings. She'll join the others I have to try to forget about.

A moment at the end of the meeting made me feel hopeful. One of the young men helped the woman put on her coat. It's the only time I've ever seen either of them smile.

Feelings to acknowledge: sadness, helplessness.

Feelings to celebrate: hope.

Actions to practise healthy detachment: acknowledge my ability to help is limited by group members' ableness to be helped, acknowledge the strength of the woman I'm worried about.

Tonight I need to cuddle my cat and eat some chocolate. It's normal to feel this sadness, but I have done all I'm able to and I need to move on to be most effective for my other clients.

Day 6

Thursday, 30 April

IN MEMORY OF HENRY – NINETEEN-YEAR-OLD HENRY GARSIDE'S ARTWORK WILL BE DISPLAYED AT ART FOR ALL GALLERY...

Scroll.

NO ARRESTS, NO CLUE? – WITH TWO MAJOR INVESTIGATIONS FAILING, HAS AN ATTACK ON THEIR OWN RATTLED DETECTIVES...

Scroll.

THE IMPACT OF STAFF SHORTAGES – CUTBACKS MEAN POLICE ARE STRETCHED BETWEEN CASES AND JUSTICE IS LACKING FOR LOVED ONES...

Scroll.

Juliet. Sent 7:04.

I'm fine.

Paul. Sent 7:05.

Thanks for letting me know.

Gabe. Sent 7:31.

Maddy – can you please put together all the information Juliet and I had gathered about the Galanis brothers? I could come collect it at midday and we could go out for lunch? x

From: Madison Campbell **madison.campbell@mitadmin.gov.uk**
To: Paul Willis **paul.willis@mit.gov.uk**
Date: **30 April, 7:43.**
Subject: **Gabe**

Paul,

You know how much I hate doing this, but Gabe contacted me this morning to ask for files about the Galanis brothers.

If possible, please don't tell her I told you.

Maddy

Call connected at 8:10.

'Hello?'

'Hi, Gabe. It's Paul. I've cleared it with Angela, so do you think you could come into the station today? We've potentially got real momentum with both cases now, and I want you leading a comb-through of all Operation Juno files. You up to it?'

'Yeah, that's fine. I'll need about an hour to get ready.'

'I'll send someone to pick you up.'

'I don't need that.'

'Angela insisted. She said this is a one-day thing, so we've got to make it count.'

'No pressure, then. Does this mean you think the Galanis brothers could have been involved in the shooting or Henry's death? My gut says they could be lurking in the background of both. I know I've been wrong before—'

'I like your gut. I trust it.'

'Thanks, Paul.'

'I'll get some biscuits in.'

'Custard creams?'

'Obviously. They're essential brain food.'

Gabe

'I'll get it.' Ollie kissed the top of my head before walking to the front door, Artie winding around his legs.

My crust of toast fell to my plate. Listening intently, I rose from the sofa. Every muscle clenched in preparation to launch myself into the hallway.

Ollie's laugh cut through the tension. I shook my head, then took my plate to the kitchen. I'd been swinging between hyperawareness and a dreamlike state since last night. One knock on the door and I was posed for a fight.

My mind stilled when Ollie held me. He loved me and didn't mind that there were times when he'd have to cobble me back together.

But he couldn't hold me forever. As soon as he stepped away, I floundered again.

Switching between vigilance and stupor was exhausting, but I had no time to rest. I couldn't pass up Paul's invitation. He was sceptical the Galanis brothers were involved in the shooting or Henry's death but was willing to let me try to find a link. This was my chance to bring down Tsambikos and his brothers.

I grabbed my ID and slung it around my neck one handed. My shoulder was stiff this morning, prone to random moments of stabbing pain. Ollie had helped me take off my top before my shower, and he'd picked out a crop top afterward, his movements gentle and bland. I'd shooed him away, the pain of pulling on a loose jumper and a pair of dark jeans nothing compared to the indignity of being utterly sexless in his eyes. Tsambikos's visit had put an abrupt dampener on anything more exciting than cuddling last night.

I tugged on my coat and joined Ollie at the front door. Alice grinned at me, her petite frame bulked out by her dark uniform and stab-proof vest.

'I was pissed off about being used as a taxi service, but this more than makes up for it.' She gestured at Ollie, his tattooed arms bare and his chest covered by a thin vest.

I glared at Alice while he kissed my cheek. 'I'll be here when you get home.'

'Is that an open invite?' Alice and Ollie laughed as I pushed her bodily down my front path. 'You're a spoilsport.' She led the way to her car.

'You're a creep.' I squinted across the dormant blue lights. 'I hope I didn't get you in trouble by taking you to see Douglas Frey.' I wanted to check, but equally wanted to head off any more comments about my boyfriend.

We climbed inside the car, my movements sluggish. At least I could blame my shoulder. No one had to know my brain had reduced the world to sludge.

'It's fine.' Alice buckled her seatbelt across her padded chest. Her hair was pulled into a neat bun, her bronze skin clear of make-up. 'A slap on the wrist.'

'I'm sorry.'

'I know.' Alice pointed at my injured shoulder. 'Extenuating circumstances and all that.' She started the car. Her forgiveness was more than I deserved, but our friendship only worked if we brushed off the stupid things we did to one another. 'If you want to make it up to me, you could invite me over tonight.'

'No chance.'

Alice huffed. 'Then you can help me revise for the next detective exam.'

'Gladly.'

Alice had told me her test anxiety was a hangover from her teenage years, when her parents put her under pressure to perform well. With one brother training to be a doctor and a sister who was already an architect, failure was not an option.

That was one horrendous silver lining of what happened in my childhood. So long as I was happy and healthy, my parents didn't ask too much of me.

I frowned, looking out of the window at the houses flashing by. That wasn't quite true. Dad was unrelenting in his silent campaign for me to come home. He couldn't understand why his one remaining child would want to fly the nest. Mum hadn't mentioned talking to him last night. I didn't ask if he wanted to any more.

'Is Juliet coming in?' I asked, snapping away from my spiralling thoughts.

'No. She said she can't.' Alice executed a perfect mirror check with each turn. 'I thought she'd be chomping at the bit to get a look at the investigation.'

Alice's expression remained neutral. While almost everyone else who worked on our floor, who worked at the station, followed Paul's lead in playfully mocking Juliet, Alice kept her mouth closed. She wasn't in Juliet's circle like myself and Maddy, but perhaps Alice saw more to Juliet than her cool outer shell. She'd been curious about Juliet months ago, which seemed to have given way to quiet respect.

'I'm not sure what's going on with her.'

'She's a closed book,' Alice mused.

I leant against the headrest, my eyes falling shut. I'd float on the drive to the station, but then I needed to focus. I wasn't going to catch the Galanis brothers if I wasn't giving my all.

Juliet hadn't been shut off the night she'd stumbled into my home, or when she'd asked me to talk to Douglas. Since then, the walls had slammed back into place.

I had to hope Juliet knew, even when we butted heads, that there was nothing I wouldn't do to help her if she was in real trouble.

I kept my head down when we arrived at the station. Alice led me to a briefing room on the sixth floor. I didn't know if Paul wanted me here to avoid the curiosity of our co-workers or if he genuinely thought this would be a better space to work with the huge amount of evidence we had to sift through, but I was glad of the change. Working at my desk without Juliet opposite would have been a constant reminder of how damaged things were between us.

Wooden tables that usually sat in haphazard rows had been rearranged into two long lines from the front to the back of the room. Fuelled by a near constant stream of biscuits and lukewarm coffee, Alice and I worked through the financial records Juliet and I had compiled over the course of the investigation into the Galanis brothers.

'I wasn't sure there would be a wall display with the ice queen absent,' Paul remarked as he limped into the room a couple of hours after Alice and I started our search. He'd been using his stick to take more of his weight in the last few days. I'd make sure to update Joanie the next time they had me and Ollie over for dinner. She would convince Paul to take better care of himself.

'It's helpful.' I shoved the second half of a bourbon into my mouth.

Paul examined the information I'd taped to the wall. Alice had gasped when I'd stuck up the first piece of paper, but I'd assured her I'd pay for any further damage the walls sustained. Scuffs and chips already marred the green paint. Nothing stayed pristine for long in a police station.

Tsambikos's extravagant spending sprees took up one section, while another had the brothers' businesses lumped together. A third area tracked their properties. None had yielded anything of interest.

'Talk me through this.' Paul tapped the papers clustered around an aerial map of the city.

'That's the properties the brothers own and manage.' I refused to be ashamed of the amount of biscuit crumbs that rained down as I stood up. I pointed to a line of deeds tacked to one side of the map. 'These were all bought in the couple of months after we uncovered the human trafficking ring. It's their biggest spend on property, but none of them have any connection to criminal activities.'

'And the rest?' Paul asked, his eyes darting to documents above and below the map.

I raised my hand. 'Properties the brothers have owned for a while.' I lowered it. 'More recent purchases. They've been diversifying away from residential and spas. There's an art gallery and a mooring rental in there but, again, no links to anything messy.' Nowhere Henry was known to frequent. No connections to Thomas Frey.

I pointed at the map. 'The properties are randomly dotted across the city. At first, Juliet and I wondered if those bought after the trafficking ring was discovered were going to be used as new bases for similar operations but mostly, they've stayed empty. They're being done up for private and holiday rental.'

'Can you get me a list of which of these are still vacant or having work done?' Paul twisted his stick on the worn carpet. 'Thomas Frey worked as a labourer. We don't have any other leads for where to search for him, so we might as well start with properties the Galanis brothers were getting work done on.' He held up a hand, as though he could sense the excitement whirring through me. 'Thomas may not have known who he was working for, but we need to start the search somewhere.'

257

That wasn't the endorsement or concrete connection I was hoping for, but Paul wouldn't be able to deny there was a link if he found Thomas in one of these properties.

'I'll need to put in a request for an armed unit. We haven't recovered the gun and despite his sister's endorsement, I'm not sure Thomas won't lash out if we find him.' Paul turned, and I caught the wince as he took weight on his injured leg. 'Alice, can you help Gabe get that list of properties to me as soon as possible?'

'Will do, sir.' She already had her laptop open, no doubt motivated by the prospect of putting old bank statements to one side for a while.

Paul patted me on my uninjured shoulder before walking to the door, his stick thumping solidly with each step. 'Good work, you two.'

I hid a smile by shoving a Jammy Dodger into my mouth. Alice didn't need to know how the simplest praise affected me. Juliet valued my input but was stingy with compliments. If I worked for too long with Paul, partnering with her again would be a cruel shock to my system.

Recording started: 11:13.

Strategic Firearms Officer Ruby Douglas: We're in position and ready to go, sir.

Authorised Firearms Officer Dev Afzal: Third time lucky.

Detective Inspector Paul Willis: Fingers and toes crossed. Proceed when ready.

[Knocking.]

SFO Ruby Douglas: Armed police! We need urgent access to this property!

AFO Dev Afzal: I hear movement inside the flat, ma'am.

SFO Ruby Douglas: Armed police! Open this door immediately, or we will use force to gain entry!

DI Paul Willis: Any takers?

AFO Dev Afzal: None.

SFO Ruby Douglas: Use the ram.

[Smashing wood.]

SFO Ruby Douglas: Armed police! Down on the ground!

AFO Dev Afzal: Hands behind your head!

SFO Ruby Douglas: One man subdued.

AFO Dev Afzal: I'll check the other rooms. Bathroom, clear. Bedroom, clear. Kitchen, clear.

DI Paul Willis: Is it Thomas Frey?

SFO Ruby Douglas: We've got him, sir.

Gabe

I sat before an impressive array of screens. Each displayed a different angle of the interview room. Thomas Frey sat opposite Paul and Nicole, hunched in a plastic chair. A checked shirt strained across his broad shoulders, the pattern interrupted by smudges of plaster dust. Without sunglasses on, his eyes were the same striking hazel as Mary Turner's.

Goosebumps that were impossible to banish prickled down my arms each time he spoke. There was a high likelihood I was looking at the man who'd shot me and Juliet.

Finding Thomas in a property owned by the Galanis brothers had to support my theory that they were involved in the shooting. Perhaps the brothers had asked Thomas to take us both out. He already hated Juliet. Throw money at him, add me into the bargain, and it was mutually beneficial.

Paul and Nicole had urged me into the observation room before they began questioning Thomas. My confidence grew as the interview progressed. Interrogating Thomas was an exercise in frustration, like every other time we'd talked to someone who could lead us to the brothers. It meant we were on the right track, but it was getting to Paul. His hand flexed under the table.

'Let's go over this one more time, just in case you've decided it would be in your best interests to confess your involvement in the shooting of Detectives Stern and Martin rather than letting us come to our own conclusions.' Paul's voice was turned tinny by the speakers. 'Can you account for your whereabouts on the afternoon of the 24th April?'

'I don't know.' Thomas's wide shoulders curved toward the table. 'Probably at home.'

'Do you know anything about the file given to the police that contains numerous articles about Detective Stern?' Nicole was cooler in the face of Thomas's blunt refusal to cooperate, but in the last few minutes her lips had receded to a thin line.

'I don't know what you're talking about.' Thomas had been lying since he'd set foot in the interview room, but he squirmed every time Paul and Nicole mentioned the file.

'Why did you abscond after the police made contact with your father?' Paul asked.

Thomas looked down at his hands, the knuckles dry. 'I don't know.'

'Do you know the Galanis brothers? Did you know the property you were hiding in is owned by them?' Nicole pressed.

'I don't know them. I was employed by the site manager. None of us knew who the owners were.'

'Or Terence Dunlow; do you know him?' It was an addition Paul had tacked on each time the Galanis brothers were mentioned. Apparently, he was determined not to discount Terence.

'No.' Thomas looked up from his hands, straight into one of the cameras.

I flinched away. Those distinctive eyes were piercing. One had been pressed to a scope days ago, my shoulder filling his vision before he pulled the trigger.

Paul looked at Nicole. 'This is a bloody waste of time.'

Paul, Nicole, and myself were in total agreement that Thomas shot me and Juliet. The file was undeniable motivation to lash out against Juliet, and running didn't bolster his protestations of innocence. We hoped the search of his home would yield enough evidence that he couldn't deny any more.

Thomas wasn't what I'd expected. He was hiding the truth, but seemed more scared than annoyed. I wondered if it was fear the Galanis brothers had instilled in him, if they had used threats to make him do their bidding.

I rubbed my sore shoulder. At the moment, we didn't have enough to bring any of these men to justice. The search of Thomas's house might yield more evidence, but we needed him to talk. If he had acted on the Galanis brothers' instruction, he would have been coached into giving the police nothing that pointed to them.

Shoving up from my chair, I abandoned the observation room and marched to the lifts. I needed to get back to the briefing room. Thomas was unwilling to speak and Paul wasn't wholly convinced the brothers were involved, so I needed to find the link between them.

I wasn't going to squander my day here. I couldn't waste this chance to bring Tsambikos and his brothers down.

From: David Rees **david.rees@forensics.gov.uk**
To: Paul Willis **paul.willis@mit.gov.uk**
CC: Nicole Stewart **nicole.stewart@mit.gov.uk**
Date: **30 April, 13:22**
Subject: **Operation Orion – search of Douglas and Thomas Frey's home**

Willis,

We collected a number of items of interest from the property owned by DOUGLAS FREY, where THOMAS FREY also resides.

#1 HUNTING RIFLE

#2 ARTICLES OF CLOTHING

#3 NEWSPAPER ARTICLE

#4 DUFFLE BAG

We conducted a full search of the property and several small outbuildings. As per your instruction, the search was attended by a nurse who accompanied DOUGLAS FREY throughout. I believe he was not unduly distressed by the search.

The areas of the house that yielded items of interest were THOMAS FREY'S bedroom and a shed at the end of the garden.

The HUNTING RIFLE was found in the shed. This was covered in gunshot residue. We have been unable to lift any prints or DNA, and clear attempts have been made to clean it.

ARTICLES OF CLOTHING including a GREY HOODIE and JEANS were found wrapped around the HUNTING RIFLE. These have been recently laundered and have trace amounts of gunshot residue. This is most concentrated on the sleeves of the GREY HOODIE. DNA samples taken are a match for THOMAS FREY. There is also a small amount of material that matches MARY TURNER.

The HUNTING RIFLE and ARTICLES OF CLOTHING were found in a DUFFLE BAG. This has also been recently laundered and has trace amounts of gunshot residue on the inside and outside. DNA samples taken are a match for THOMAS FREY and MARY TURNER. It is highly likely they both came into direct contact with the DUFFLE BAG.

The NEWSPAPER ARTICLE was found during a search of THOMAS FREY'S bedroom. It was found between two books. It is JULIET STERN'S call for more information about MELANIE PIRT'S murder. It has been annotated with the words, 'you'll never find them, you fucking bitch.' A copy of the NEWSPAPER ARTICLE has been attached to this email.

The handwriting on the NEWSPAPER ARTICLE has been compared to the annotations on the articles in the FILE previously retrieved. They are a match. This was further checked against an example of THOMAS FREY'S handwriting obtained from a shopping list in his home. It is also a match.

Rees

Detective Sergeant Nicole Stewart: Informal interview commencing at 1:37 p.m. on the 30th April at Mary Turner's home. This interview is being conducted by Detective Inspector Paul Willis and myself, Detective Sergeant Nicole Stewart. This is our second interview with Mary Turner regarding the shooting of Detective Inspector Juliet Stern and Detective Sergeant Gabriella Martin on the 24th April. Since we last spoke, there have been developments in this case.

Detective Inspector Paul Willis: During a search of properties owned by the company Galanis Incorporated, we found your brother, Thomas Frey. He worked on the renovation of the building and knew it was empty.

DS Nicole Stewart: Further to this, a search of your brother's bedroom and the shed in your father's garden has uncovered the gun we believe was used to shoot Detectives Martin and Stern, plus clothing and a bag covered in gunshot residue.

DI Paul Willis: We also found a newspaper article in Thomas's room similar to those in the file you left for Detective Martin. The handwriting in both the file and on this new article are a match for Thomas's.

Mary Turner: Oh, Tommy.

DS Nicole Stewart: DNA samples were taken from the bag and clothing found with the gun. These are a match for your brother. The clothes have trace amounts of DNA that is a match for you too, while the bag has enough matches that we strongly believe you came into contact with this directly.

DI Paul Willis: We understand you may have been reticent before as you didn't want to get your brother into trouble but unless you want us to think you were involved in the shooting as well, you need to speak up.

[Sniffing.]

Mary Turner: No one wants to turn on their own family.

DS Nicole Stewart: Sometimes, family members act in ways that require us to take action. Your brother has gravely injured two detectives. We need to know how and why, and if he acted independently so that we can stop others from being hurt.

DI Paul Willis: Mary, when did your brother begin collecting materials tracking the career of Detective Stern?

[Long silence.]

Mary Turner: I can't really remember a time when he didn't.

DS Nicole Stewart: Did it begin when your father retired from the force?

Mary Turner: Maybe. Probably a little while after. At first Dad didn't tell us what had happened. One day, we were a normal family living normal lives. The next, Dad had no job and Mum was angry all the time.

DI Paul Willis: When did you find out the circumstances around your father's retirement?

Mary Turner: I'm not sure Dad's ever told us the truth. Mum took Tommy and me with her when she left, but every visit with Dad he talked more and more about a woman who forced him to leave his job. He said it was all her fault he had to take early retirement. Without her interference, we would have still been a happy family. Tommy and I moved back in with Dad after Mum remarried because Tommy didn't get on with her new husband, and ever since Tommy and Dad have been as thick as thieves. Tommy lapped up all of Dad's stories about how he was wronged. I wasn't so sure.

DS Nicole Stewart: What made you doubt your father's account?

Mary Turner: My father treated me and Tommy differently. As I got older, I could see how that would have translated into his workplace. I left home as early as I could to get away from Dad, then changed my first name along with my last when I got married. I had a feeling the truth would spill out one day. I didn't want anything to do with it. I'd barely seen Dad or Tommy until Dad's health deteriorated.

DI Paul Willis: You said Thomas lapped up your father's stories?

Mary Turner: He did. I've tried to talk to Tommy more times than I can count about how Dad wasn't what he told us he was. But Tommy won't hear a word against him. He's been worse since Dad's gotten unwell. He blames Detective Stern for that as well.

DI Paul Willis: Did your father ever tell you exactly what had happened between him and Detective Stern?

Mary Turner: Dad was always vague when I was around. I think Tommy knows, but Dad wasn't interested in telling me.

DI Paul Willis: Did you ever get the impression your brother wanted to hurt Detective Stern?

Mary Turner: I assumed it was all hot air. He'd harboured a grudge against her for so long, but he never did anything about it. In the end, I asked Tommy to not talk about it the rare times I saw him.

DS Nicole Stewart: Did he respect that request?

Mary Turner: Sometimes. So much of his energy went into hating someone he'd never met that it was hard for him to not talk about it. Recently, he'd been talking about her more again.

DI Paul Willis: When did you notice that change?

Mary Turner: Last year. It must have been in the autumn. I remember talking to Tommy about whether he wanted to come trick or treating with me and the kids, and I could barely get an answer from him because he wouldn't stop talking about Detective Stern. My husband had to ask Tommy to leave on Christmas Day. He got drunk and spouted all this nonsense about how Dad was a victim and powerful people never faced justice. It upset the children, and Dad. He was shouting as Tommy helped him into his car.

DS Nicole Stewart: Did your brother mention talking with anyone else about Detective Stern?

Mary Turner: No, but I wouldn't be surprised if half the people who go to the pub near Dad's cottage know. Tommy has never been able to hold his drink, and Dad's woes are his favourite topic when he's drunk.

DI Paul Willis: Thomas didn't mention talking with anyone specifically?

Mary Turner: No. I did wonder if there was someone or if something had happened, to get him fired up about it all again.

DS Nicole Stewart: Did your brother tell you about his plans to shoot Detectives Martin and Stern?

[Sniffing.]

Mary Turner: We barely spoke other than to arrange help for Dad. Tommy told me he had a job he needed to do that day and asked me to pop into the cottage. I was cross because it was late notice, but I wasn't working so I could do it.

DI Paul Willis: You're positive you were with your father at the time of the shooting?

Mary Turner: Yes. Dad might not remember, but I took the chance to give his kitchen a good clean.

DI Paul Willis: When did you begin to suspect your brother was involved in the shooting?

[Long silence.]

DS Nicole Stewart: We know this is difficult, but remember we just want to stop Thomas and anyone he may or may not have been working with from hurting anyone else.

Mary Turner: The first sign something was up was how quiet Tommy went after Detective Stern was shot. I would have expected him to be jumping for joy, but he barely spoke at all. I mentioned the shooting to him when Dad was out of earshot and all Tommy did was glare at me. I didn't know what that meant.

DI Paul Willis: What else made you think he was involved?

Mary Turner: I do a lot of Dad's washing. He doesn't like the way Thomas does it, says it feels wrong. I was grabbing Dad's clothes to take to mine when I found the bag with the gun in it. Thomas had left it in the kitchen.

DS Nicole Stewart: What did you do when you found it?

Mary Turner: I panicked. I didn't know what it meant. I left Dad's as quickly as possible and went home. My husband kept asking all evening what was wrong, but I told him Dad was being difficult. He has funny turns when he can't remember who we are and he gets cross. I thought about the gun all night, and I knew I had to act. My plan was to give it to the police, but the bag was gone the next morning. Tommy wasn't in, so I went up to his room and took his file instead.

DI Paul Willis: You were going to take the gun to the police; why not do the same with the file?

Mary Turner: The more I thought about it, the more I wondered what I'd seen and I didn't know if the file was going to help or not. I didn't want to think Tommy was capable of shooting anyone, no matter how much he hated them. I saw the detectives after they were shot. It wasn't life threatening, but it was terrible. No one deserved that. Not even if Detective Stern did have something to do with Dad leaving the force.

[Sniffing.]

DS Nicole Stewart: It's alright, Mary. Take all the time you need.

[Sniffing.]

Mary Turner: I began to think I had to have made it up. There couldn't have been a gun. But I don't know, I guess I didn't believe myself. I didn't want to give the file back to Tommy and I didn't want him to get another chance to hurt anyone. He'd already done enough damage. I couldn't live with myself if I'd not acted in some way. I couldn't care for people all day at work and do nothing to stop others from being harmed.

DI Paul Willis: Why did you give the file to Detective Martin?

Mary Turner: If I handed the file in at a station, I'd be dragged into Dad and Tommy's mess. I knew Detective Martin's address because I'd been one of her nurses at the hospital, so I drove over to her house after a shift. I followed her out to the forest. My plan was to leave the file and hide to check she got it, but she saw me as I was putting it down.

DS Nicole Stewart: Why did you run when Detective Martin saw you?

Mary Turner: I didn't want her or anyone to know it was me who had dropped off the file. Tommy didn't know I'd taken it. I would have gotten an angry visit if he did. I didn't want him to know what I'd done. Even though I struggle with how he is and wish he wasn't so easily led by Dad, he's still my brother. I didn't want him to know I'd handed the police something that could prove his guilt.

DI Paul Willis: Thank you for giving us such a detailed account. I just have a couple more questions. Has your brother ever mentioned meeting with Alcaeus, Tsambikos, or Giannis Galanis?

Mary Turner: No, I don't recognise those names.

DI Paul Willis: How about Terence Dunlow?

Mary Turner: Doesn't ring a bell.

Gabe

'Hey, Gabe.'

I looked up from a list of properties I'd been willing to turn into a concrete link between the Galanis brothers and Thomas Frey. Alice had left me alone in the briefing room, complaining her head hurt. I sat cross-legged on the floor, boots discarded under a table while drizzle pattered on the windows.

Paul leant on the doorframe. His eyes tracked over the documents heaped around me, every one scoured by me and Alice before being set into increasingly random piles. I'd tried ordering by date and location, by proximity to the Freys' home and the fancy flats the Galanis brothers owned. I'd considered links around the university or art galleries Henry had visited. Nothing created the connections I needed. Pink twine sat sad and useless in one corner.

'How's it going?' Paul asked.

I stood, wiggling my sock-covered toes on the carpet. 'Nothing so far, but the brothers and Thomas couldn't have worked together without leaving the tiniest paper trail.'

Paul nodded slowly. 'We conducted a second interview with Mary following the evidence found at Douglas Frey's cottage.'

'Yeah?' I wished we weren't having this discussion across half a briefing room, but picking my way through the scattered documents might dislodge them and I couldn't waste time re-sorting.

'Along with the clothes and gun, Mary has given us good reason to believe Thomas shot you and Juliet. Even if he continues to be uncooperative, we should be able to charge him.'

Relief flowed through me, but it wasn't pure. Although mine and Juliet's shooter would be brought to justice, what would stop the Galanis brothers from hiring someone else to hurt us the next time they didn't want us around? Or from killing someone else like Henry?

'We need to find out when the brothers made contact with Thomas.' I looked at the documents on the tables and piled on the floor. 'There's still time. We can do this.'

Thomas wouldn't have been found in one of the Galanis brothers' properties if he hadn't been working for them. The idea they'd plotted together to hurt me and Juliet made it feel like ants were marching over my skin, but my discomfort didn't matter. We finally had an opportunity to bring down the men responsible for too much misery across the city.

Paul shifted, looking out of the windows stretching across one wall. 'I'm not sure we're going to get there.'

His words rocked through me. I hoped it wasn't too obvious I reached for the back of a chair because I needed the support. 'What?'

'You know better than anyone how clever the Galanis brothers are. Even Terence would have avoided a paper trail.' The mingling of pity and resolve in Paul's eyes told me all I needed to know. A decision had been made without me. 'I've spoken with Nicole and Angela. We think we should take the smaller win.'

'The smaller win.'

'It's still a win,' Paul hurried to add. 'We don't think we're going to be able to catch the brothers out this time.'

'We can't let them get away with this.' My strength returned as disbelief evolved into anger. 'I was shot. So was Juliet. We can't let that go unchallenged.' I dug my nails into the back of the chair. 'The Galanis brothers have to be behind it. They probably killed Henry Garside as well. It has to all be linked. Can't you see?'

Paul pushed off the door, the toes of his polished shoes meeting the sea of paper surrounding me. 'Bloody hell, Gabe. You know I won't let this fly. If those bastards had anything to do with your attack, then we'll bring this to their door.'

Paul wanted to reassure me, but one word in his impassioned speech drowned out the rest. *If.* He, Nicole, Angela, Juliet; none of them were as sure as me that the Galanis brothers were involved.

But none of them had Tsambikos turn up at their door. They hadn't seen his smug face, heard his double-edged words.

'Can you see you might have a bit of tunnel vision when it comes to the Galanis brothers?' Paul said.

Despair wound through my chest. It wasn't that Paul didn't believe there was a link, but he thought my mind was clouded. I'd been injured

271

and had been hunting down the Galanis brothers for too long. Of course I would see them lurking in every shadow.

I'd tried not to get carried away chasing one suspect and not consider anyone else again. During Melanie Pirt's case, I'd been so focused on Timothy Dunlow that I'd only suspected Karl Biss when it was almost too late.

I didn't think that was what I was doing this time.

'Give me a few more hours.' I was too desperate to care about the pleading edge to my voice. 'At least ask Thomas about the brothers again.'

'I will. Of course I will.' Paul scrubbed the hand not gripping his stick through his thick hair. 'You've got until the end of the day. Angela won't let you come in again and we can't hold Thomas indefinitely without charging him.'

'Fine.' I sunk to the floor. 'I'll find you when I've got it.'

'Good luck, Gabe.'

Paul's parting words made me want to growl. No one wished someone luck when they wholeheartedly believed they would succeed. I thought I was searching for a needle in a haystack, while everyone else believed I was looking for something that wasn't there.

Regular thumps of his stick marked Paul's departure. I gripped the papers I'd grabbed at random and squeezed my eyes shut. I should be grateful to be here at all, but I burned with resentment. The people behind hurting me and Juliet were going to be allowed to get away with it because it was simpler to charge the man who'd pulled the trigger.

'Knock, knock,' Alice called from the doorway. 'Is it safe to come in?'

I opened my eyes. 'How much of that did you hear?'

'Everything.' Alice grimaced. 'But at least I've brought two things that will make you happy.' She held up a packet of custard creams and stepped away from the door with a flourish. 'Reinforcements.'

'Reinforcement?' James questioned as he walked into the room. 'Hello, Gabe.'

My face creaked reluctantly into a smile. I'd first met Police Constable James Knowles when working Melanie Pirt's case, and I'd made sure to request him as back-up ever since. He was a hard worker, his bulky frame at odds with his placid temperament.

He carefully picked his way across the papers toward me. 'How are you doing?'

'I'm fine.' I paused when his grey eyebrows shot up toward his receding hairline. 'Apart from being shot, obviously.'

'Like you'd ever let us forget about that.' Alice passed me the open packet of biscuits. I glared at her as I took four.

'Mainly, I'm pissed off.' I looked around at the paper covered room. 'You heard what Paul said. Unless we can find a link between the Galanis brothers and Thomas Frey in the next few hours, then they're going to charge Thomas with the shooting and let the arseholes behind it get away.'

James took a deep breath. 'Time to get searching, then.'

My eyes watered. I blamed the persistent pain in my shoulder and the various frustrations of the day. Instead of indulging in a time-wasting cry, I shoved a biscuit in my mouth and picked up the papers I'd abandoned.

Then I immediately set them down. 'These are from February. The brothers may have made contact with Thomas long before then. We need to go back further, at least to when Juliet and I first started investigating them.' We'd assumed something happened recently to kick off the shooting, but the brothers could have been planning to take out me and Juliet since we'd first stumbled on their operations.

'More paperwork to search through?' Alice grumbled. 'Goodie.'

Rowan. Sent 16:28.

Do you think it's normal that no one from the police
has been in contact with me since I found Henry and
when I've called them, they've fobbed me off?

Flea. Sent 16:32.

This may come as a shock to you, but I don't know
what's normal behaviour for the police during a
murder investigation.

Rowan. Sent 16:33.

Don't be a dick. Seriously, what do you think is going
on?

Flea. Sent 16:34.

They're probably too busy trying to find who killed
Henry to chat with you.

Rowan. Sent 16:34.

You really think that?

Flea. Sent 16:35.

Why? What do you think is going on?

Rowan. Sent 16:36.

I think they're still distracted by the detectives that got shot. They're not taking Henry's death seriously.

Flea. Sent 16:37.

If it's what you think, you should do something about it.

Call connected at 17:04.

'Hello?'

    'Is that Terence?'

    'Yes, who's this?'

    'It's Joanna.'

    'Oh. Hi.'

    'How are you feeling?'

    'Not good, I'm afraid.'

'You've been off since the twenty-sixth, and you've had a lot of other absences before that. I didn't think when we took you on that we'd have to cover for you so much. It's really affecting the morale of the other staff.'

    'I'm sorry. I'll be better soon.'

    'It's not that you're avoiding us? I know you've worked for fancy places before and we do things a bit differently here.'

    'No, not at all. I'm grateful you took me on. I've just got a lot of personal stuff going on and I've been unwell. I'll be back in the next few days.'

    'See that you are. I've got some things that need your attention.'

Gabe

'Guess who I saw at the chippy,' Maddy said as she strode into the room. She stopped short, two bulging bags hanging from her hands. Her eyes widened as she took in the explosion of paper across the tables, floor, and walls. 'Wow.'

We'd tacked Mary Turner and Thomas Frey's interview transcripts up in one corner. Despite the multitude of paperwork tracking each brother's spending over the past six months and notes detailing their movements, James, Alice, and I had not yet been able to find a link between the Galanis brothers and Thomas Frey.

'I should have got that.' I put down the papers I'd been highlighting. Concentrating was marginally easier with a pen in my hand after hours of sifting through useless information. 'I owe you for bringing over the files the other day.'

Maddy gave me a withering look and picked her way across the room. Her stomach rumbling, Alice cleared a space on the table.

'Who did you see?' James pulled out chairs without dislodging a single piece of paper.

'Our dear friend Jordan Haines.' Maddy shot me a look as she unpacked steaming chips and battered cod. 'He served me. Smiled and everything.'

Alice pointed a chip in Maddy's direction. 'Did he recognise you?'

'Jordan isn't such a bad kid.' James took a wooden fork from one of the bags. 'He's had a rough time.'

The rest of their conversation washed over me as I shovelled greasy potato into my mouth. Jordan wasn't a terrible person. He'd made bad decisions and had hurt Melanie Pirt before she died, but his home life was fucked up. It would have been a miracle if he'd made it out unscathed.

Juliet felt sympathy for the young man, had likened her family situation to Jordan's. It was one of the rare times she'd hinted at an unhappy home life.

I wiped my hand on one of the napkins James had passed around and pulled my phone out of my pocket. Ollie had messaged; he was at home watching *Drag Race* with Artie. Nothing from Juliet. I had to hope that if Keith wasn't always good to her, he would at least be kind while she was recovering.

I put down my phone and dislodged the topmost paper from an untidy pile beside me. My eyes caught on a copy of Mary Turner's work ID. Her curly hair was bound tight, her smile broad.

I chuffed out a laugh, interrupting a heated discussion over whether sausages should be battered.

'Care to share with the group?' Alice asked, before biting off the end of her naked sausage.

'Just.' I paused out of habit, but no one in this room would object to my sexuality if they didn't already know. 'I wasn't sure how I felt about being attracted to a criminal. I'm glad it turns out Mary had nothing to do with the shooting.'

Maddy craned to check Mary's picture. 'I can see it.'

Alice's neat eyebrows drew together. 'You can't find Mary attractive. You're with Ollie.'

'He told me it's perfectly normal to find other people attractive while committed to a partner.' Maybe I wasn't the only one who needed relationship lessons.

'No.' Alice set down her fork. 'Ollie's a man.'

A cold wave doused me. Alice wasn't confused about a basic element of dating. She couldn't understand how I could be attracted to a woman while with a man. The shock receded, leaving weariness in its wake. Explaining bisexuality to heterosexuals was never fun.

'Sexualities other than straight and gay exist, Alice.' James's cheeks were flushed and his jaw jutted.

I mouthed a silent thank you while Alice frowned down at her half-eaten chips.

'I assume you would have already mentioned it,' I said, slicing through the tension, 'but have any of you found a link between Thomas Frey and the Galanis brothers?'

'I've been working through the spending sprees.' Alice pointed at the far wall, as keen as I was to move on. She'd adopted Juliet's approach to laying out evidence after her initial reluctance to stick anything on the walls. Pink twine stretched between several pieces of paper. 'It seems to be wholly random. Tsambikos likes buying crazy shit. He snatches up the latest cars when they come out and more motorbikes than he can ride in a lifetime.'

A wet slap announced James's fork falling to the floor. The fish he'd heaped on top flaked across the carpet.

'Has he bought a yacht?' He stood, ignoring his dropped food and hurrying over to where I'd taped the brothers' properties to one wall.

'No.' Alice passed Maddy a napkin as she dropped to the floor to pick up the scattered fish. 'I would have noticed that.'

James pulled down a piece of paper from around the aerial map, heedless of Alice's sharp inhale. He rushed to the table and passed it to me.

'Tsambikos started renting a mooring three months ago.'

While I read, James took Maddy's place picking flecks of fish out of the carpet.

'Juliet and I checked this.' I speared a plump chip onto my fork. 'There was nothing there. When we questioned Tsambikos about it, he said he wanted it ready in case he decided to test his sea legs.'

'My parents were boatie people.' James was a few years older than the rest of us, but the past tense made me want to reach out to him. 'A lot of marinas won't let you do that. Moorings are too sought after to rent one but not use it. Sometimes the waiting lists are years long and people will riot if they see spaces free.'

'I promise there's no yacht in any of those spending sprees,' Alice cut in, one cheek stuffed with sausage.

I wrinkled my nose at her. 'Tsambikos is the kind of person who gets away with things others don't.'

James shook his head, hands stilled over the carpet. 'You don't understand what these people are like. Moorings are jealously sought after. Someone with all the money and influence in the world wouldn't be able to keep them from kicking up a fuss. They wouldn't care who Tsambikos was if he was blocking what they saw as rightfully theirs.'

I wondered if Timothy Dunlow sailed. He would fit right in.

'Alice?' I turned to her. 'Do you mind checking if the mooring is still empty?'

'On it.' She grabbed a handful of chips and her thick vest then scarpered before I could decide someone else should take a break from paperwork.

I relaxed as she left. She hadn't been overtly biphobic, but it was easier being with people I didn't have to hide from or explain aspects of myself to.

'This could possibly be a lead,' I said. If the brothers had secretly bought a yacht, it had to be worth hiding. 'Or it could turn out to be a dead end. We need to keep searching for a link to Thomas.'

James continued picking the mess of fish out of the floor while Maddy dragged a fresh box of files to her side of the table. It would take a while for the smell of cod to shift, even if James was meticulous. The next time I stepped into this room, the fishy smell would be a reminder of success or defeat.

Call connected at 18:09.

'Alice?'

    'Hey, Gabe. There's a freaking great boat here.'

    'You're sure it's the right mooring?'

    'I checked with the harbour master, but there's no doubt it's the right one. It's called *The Galanis Girl*. Apparently no one has checked on it for weeks.'

    'Classy. Right. Come back here. I'll talk to Paul and get a warrant sorted.'

FORM 22F – FORMAL REQUEST FOR WARRANT: PERMISSION TO SEARCH A BOAT

REQUESTING OFFICERS:

Detective Inspector Paul Willis and Detective Sergeant Nicole Stewart

CASE NUMBER:

87049375

CASE DESCRIPTION:

Non-fatal shooting of Detective Inspector Juliet Stern and Detective Sergeant Gabriella Martin on 24 April outside Southampton Crown Court

LOCATION OF VESSEL:

Ocean Village Marina

DESCRIPTION OF VESSEL:

Luxury gulet yacht – *The Galanis Girl*

REASON FOR REQUEST:

On 14 January, Tsambikos Galanis rented a mooring at Ocean Village Marina in Southampton. This was checked by Detective Inspector Juliet Stern and Detective Sergeant Gabriella Martin and was empty. Tsambikos Galanis's spending has been monitored as part of Operation Juno, along with that of his brothers, Alcaeus and Giannis. A yacht is now in place at the mooring, which we believe has been bought illegally to hide it from the ongoing Operation Juno.

We have strong reason to suspect Thomas Frey was the shooter, but he may have been influenced by the Galanis brothers. Evidence found on this yacht may reveal a link between them.

Detective Sergeant Nicole Stewart: Interview commencing at 7:11 p.m. on the 30th April. The interviewee is Thomas Frey. He has been offered the chance to seek legal counsel but has declined. This interview is being conducted by Detective Inspector Paul Willis and myself, Detective Sergeant Nicole Stewart. This is the second round of interviews concerning the shooting of Detective Inspector Juliet Stern and Detective Sergeant Gabriella Martin on the 24th April.

Detective Inspector Paul Willis: Mr Frey, you were reluctant to cooperate during our previous interview. However, new information has come to light that I'd ask you to consider before answering any of our questions.

DS Nicole Stewart: Since you were taken into custody, a search warrant was granted for the house you share with your father. During this search, a gun was discovered that is consistent with the weapon used to shoot Detectives Stern and Martin. The gun was wrapped in clothing covered in gunshot residue and your DNA.

DI Paul Willis: While searching your bedroom, a newspaper article was also discovered. This is consistent with a file handed in to police by Mary Turner nee Maria Frey, which contains a number of similar articles and print outs.

Thomas Frey: Maria gave you my file?

DI Paul Willis: We assumed it was yours, as the handwritten notes match a sample of handwriting taken from your home, but thanks for the confirmation.

DS Nicole Stewart: Earlier today, we spoke with Mary about the evidence found in your home. This prompted her to give a full account of her knowledge of Detectives Stern and Martin's shooting.

Thomas Frey: You spoke to Maria?

DI Paul Willis: At length. She said you've been interested in Detective Stern for a long time, and this stemmed from your father's insistence that she was the reason he left the force. Mary said your obsession rekindled at the end of last year.

DS Nicole Stewart: Mary told us she found the gun and clothes in a bag at your home when she came over to do your father's washing. She returned the next day to find them gone, but she took the file to give to the police. She didn't want anyone else to get hurt.

Thomas Frey: What? I don't understand. When did you ask her about this?

DI Paul Willis: Mary was questioned yesterday after an officer identified her as the person who'd given us the file and again this afternoon. She was initially reluctant to speak out against you but after we found the gun in your shed, she has been much more talkative.

DS Nicole Stewart: With the evidence we've collected and Mary's testimony, we have clear reason to believe you are responsible for the shooting of Detectives Martin and Stern. We would like to create a clearer picture of exactly what led to this action and identify those you worked with.

[Long silence.]

Thomas Frey: Maria didn't have anything to do with it.

DI Paul Willis: Can you clarify what 'it' is?

Thomas Frey: The shooting. Maria didn't know about my plans and I didn't tell her anything afterwards.

DI Paul Willis: Did anyone else help you?

Thomas Frey: No. I worked alone. Maria wasn't involved at all.

DS Nicole Stewart: Thank you for cooperating, Mr Frey. We would like to go back to the beginning. Please can you tell us when your interest in Detective Stern began?

Thomas Frey: When I was a kid. Dad was my hero, but suddenly he was kicked off the force for something he would never do. I didn't know why that woman would have it in for Dad, but I've figured it out since. She didn't like being told what to do by a man. Once a woman was in power, she was happy enough to take the detective job he'd offered.

DI Paul Willis: What did your father say about Detective Stern?

Thomas Frey: Not so much when I was younger, but later he told me the truth. That bitch said he came onto her, but why would he do that? You can see she's frigid. No man would want her. You have to be able to see it too. You've got my file. That bitch took every opportunity to further her career after she'd booted my dad to the side. She's rotten to the core.

DS Nicole Stewart: I would ask you to kindly refrain from using slurs for the remainder of the interview.

DI Paul Willis: Indeed. Your sister said your interest in Detective Stern waned until recently?

Thomas Frey: That's not true. Maria didn't want to hear about it. I should have kept quiet.

DI Paul Willis: But something changed toward the end of last year?

Thomas Frey: I guess I got tired of keeping my mouth shut about what she'd done to us.

DS Nicole Stewart: What had Detective Stern done?

Thomas Frey: She ruined our fucking lives without a backward glance. My dad was the boss, and he was reduced to nothing. Mum left him because of what that bi— because of what Detective Stern accused him of. Maria drew away from both of us. And then Dad got ill. He never would have gotten unwell if his world hadn't been ripped away from him.

DI Paul Willis: When did you start planning to shoot Detective Stern?

Thomas Frey: I dunno. Early this year.

DS Nicole Stewart: Can you be more specific?

Thomas Frey: I'd been thinking about doing something for a while. I can only work ad hoc around when Dad seems to be doing a bit better, so we spend a lot of time together. He was so cross at Detective Stern for what she'd done to all of us. I'd see him struggling, see him made small. I wanted to make her hurt in the way he'd been hurt. Tear her life away.

DI Paul Willis: When did you decide to shoot Detective Stern after the conclusion of Karl Biss's trial?

Thomas Frey: I'd been following her work on that case. She'd gone into court to give evidence early on, but otherwise she stayed away. I thought she would turn up to hear the verdict. She'd want to gloat. I found a good place to watch from and did it.

DS Nicole Stewart: You said you worked alone, but we have CCTV images of someone tampering with various cameras a couple of days before the shooting.

DI Paul Willis: For the benefit of the tape, we're showing Mr Frey images AT115 and AT116.

DS Nicole Stewart: Analysis of the images tells us this couldn't have been you. This person is between 5'5 and 5'8 in height.

DI Paul Willis: You've told us you worked alone, but who made sure the CCTV wasn't working before you shot Detectives Martin and Stern?

[Long silence.]

Thomas Frey: I didn't know about the CCTV. I got lucky.

DI Paul Willis: Not so lucky, as it turns out.

DS Nicole Stewart: Tell us about the day of the shooting.

Thomas Frey: I don't know what else to tell you. I watched Detective Stern go into the courthouse and I waited until the sentencing was over. Then I shot her. And the other one.

DI Paul Willis: How did you feel as you waited?

Thomas Frey: Fine. Nervous.

DS Nicole Stewart: Tell us about when Detective Stern came out of the courthouse.

Thomas Frey: She and the other detective came out. I waited for the perfect moment, then I shot them both.

DI Paul Willis: Was it your intention to shoot to kill?

[Long silence.]

Thomas Frey: I shot them both exactly where I wanted to.

DS Nicole Stewart: Your intention was merely to harm, rather than to kill?

Thomas Frey: Yeah. Exactly.

DI Paul Willis: You shot Detective Stern, which I understand your reasoning for. Why then turn the gun on Detective Martin? No articles in the file Mary gave us focused on Detective Martin. None of the notes you made commented on her. You ignored her, so why shoot her as well?

Thomas Frey: She benefitted from what Detective Stern did.

DS Nicole Stewart: Is that why you shot Detective Martin?

Thomas Frey: Yeah.

DI Paul Willis: There wasn't any other reason you shot her as well?

Thomas Frey: No.

DI Paul Willis: It wasn't that someone asked you to? They knew you hated Detective Stern, and they asked you to shoot Detective Martin as well.

Thomas Frey: I told you; I didn't plan this with anyone. No one knew what I was going to do.

DI Paul Willis: You didn't tell your father?

Thomas Frey: No. I couldn't trust him not to blab about it.

DS Nicole Stewart: How did you feel when you realised the police had questioned your father?

Thomas Frey: Angry. They should have seen, as soon as he opened the door, that there was no way in hell he could have done it. He was upset that evening, worried he'd said something wrong.

DI Paul Willis: You weren't concerned the visit would have uncovered your involvement?

Thomas Frey: I couldn't see how it would have, back then. The officers didn't do a search of the house.

DS Nicole Stewart: Why did you hide the gun and your clothes inside the house, and then in the shed? Why not take them somewhere no one would discover them?

[Throat clearing.]

Thomas Frey: I didn't know Maria was coming to do Dad's washing, otherwise I would have moved the stuff out to the shed sooner. The garden is so overgrown. The shed is hidden by brambles. I thought the gun was safe in there. I should have been more careful.

DS Nicole Stewart: What made you decide to run?

Thomas Frey: My file was missing and more police wanted to talk to Dad. I thought that if I was out of the picture, I'd be forgotten.

DS Nicole Stewart: Why didn't you take the bag and gun?

Thomas Frey: I thought they were safe out in the shed. I didn't think anyone would find them.

DI Paul Willis: How did you decide where to go?

Thomas Frey: I'd worked recently on a run-down block of flats. I knew they weren't planning to rent out the finished ones until they were all done up, so I broke into one of them.

DI Paul Willis: Are you aware of who owns those flats?

Thomas Frey: I can't even remember the name of the bloke in charge of the site. I got the job through a friend.

DI Paul Willis: Those flats are owned by the Galanis brothers.

Thomas Frey: They're the guys you asked me about before, right? I don't have a clue who they are.

DS Nicole Stewart: You've never spoken to Alcaeus, Tsambikos, or Giannis Galanis?

Thomas Frey: I'd remember names like that.

DS Nicole Stewart: And how about Terence Dunlow?

Thomas Frey: No idea who he is.

DI Paul Willis: One theory we are working with is that you didn't act alone. The motivation is there, but you hated Juliet for a long time without doing anything about it. We believe either the Galanis brothers or Terence Dunlow approached you late last year. At the time, we had disrupted all of their lives through one investigation or another. One of them heard you had a grudge against Juliet, and they proposed a plan that would benefit you both. You'd shoot Detective Stern and throw in Detective Martin to help them out. I imagine there was a financial element as well. You're struggling to work around caring for your father, so the promise of extra cash had to be tempting.

Thomas Frey: Nice theory, but none of it's true. I worked alone.

Call connected at 19:32.

'Hello, this is Detective Inspector Paul Willis.'

'Hi, Paul. It's Angela.'

'Evening, ma'am.'

'I've got your request to search a boat.'

'That's right. Gabe and Juliet have been tracking the Galanis brothers' spending. This boat hasn't shown up on any of the info we've gathered, which makes us think they're trying to hide it.'

'I agree, but how does the boat link to the shooting?'

'There could be evidence on the boat that ties the brothers to Thomas Frey.'

'You're reaching. There's crossover between Orion and Juno, but this feels more connected to the ongoing investigation into the Galanis brothers' criminal activity than a concrete lead to help find Gabe and Juliet's shooter.'

'I'll level with you, ma'am. Thomas has confessed. This boat is tying up a loose end.'

'What loose end?'

'Gabe thinks the boat could provide a link between the brothers and Thomas Frey.'

'I see.'

'A huge boat turning up off the books is worth taking a look at. It could at least help with Operation Juno. And apparently no one has been there for weeks, so there's no need for support during the search.'

'Alright. I'll okay it. Take a small team tomorrow morning and have a look.'

'Thank you, ma'am.'

'How was Gabe today?'

'Brilliant. She trawled through paperwork and watched a couple of interviews.'

'Good. If she's still in my station, make sure she goes home now. And stays there. I don't want to see her again until she's actually cleared for work.'

Gabe

I shut my front door, then slumped against it. My eyes slipped closed as my forehead pressed into the painted wood.

Paul insisted I be ferried home after I observed Thomas Frey's second interview. His confession was a giant step forward, but we needed more. I was fully prepared to continue searching through Operation Juno's files into the night, but Paul had been immovable.

I wasn't sure he was listening when I told him he should have pushed harder. Thomas was obviously still hiding the full truth. His answers were too vague to be anything other than a cover. Paul had patted me on the back as Alice walked me out of the briefing room. His insistence I'd done a great job didn't mean much. I hadn't done enough to merit being involved in the case tomorrow.

A wet nose snuffling my hand was the first sign my presence at home had been detected. The second was arms circling my waist.

'I ran you a bath when you said you were on your way.' Ollie's lips ghosted over the back of my neck.

I leant into him, threading my fingers through his. 'I missed you today.'

It was the closest I could come to returning the sentiment he'd expressed last night. If the smile he was sporting as I turned in his arms was any indication, he understood. He lowered his head to kiss me, his lips gentle on my mouth then the tip of my nose.

'Go have a bath.' He nudged me into the bathroom. 'You'll feel better once you do.'

Ollie insisted baths were the cure to all ills. As he spent more time here, my bathroom had gradually filled with scented candles and bottles.

I generally opted for quick showers, but I was inclined to agree with him as I sank into the steaming water. All the aches I'd been carrying for days eased. The dressing on my shoulder had to be kept as dry as possible but even with the epicentre of my pain held above the lavender scented water, my muscles loosened.

I wiggled my fingers and toes, bubbles hiding them from view. Although my body was being forcibly relaxed by the expert bath Ollie had prepared, my mind refused to rest.

The second interview with Thomas strengthened my conviction he'd been working with the Galanis brothers, despite his insistence he'd never met them and had worked alone. Thomas had been a changed man, almost desperate. Juliet and I might not have intimate knowledge of how the Galanis brothers conducted their business, but we suspected they used things people loved against them. The panic in Thomas's eyes when he heard his sister had been questioned had to mean she was the one he was frantic to protect.

I needed the yacht to reveal a link between Thomas and the brothers, then Operations Juno and Orion would end in success. Maybe then Paul would believe the brothers could have had a hand in Henry's disappearance as well. He would have to take back his tunnel vision comment.

'No drowning,' Ollie teased as he opened the door. He plucked a towel from the heated rail. 'I can't handle my girlfriend having two near-death experiences in one week.'

'I'm not sure I could handle it either.'

I stood and let the bubbles slide down my heated skin. Ollie wrapped me in the towel as I got out of the bath, his arms winding around my back. His chest pressed flush to mine.

I grinned up at him, rocking into the hardness at my hip. 'Anything I can help you with?'

Ollie didn't bother with a clever reply. His mouth connected with mine, and we both moaned as my towel dropped. His hands spread across my damp skin.

Paul. Sent 21:11.

Checking in.

Juliet. Sent 21:34.

I'm fine.

Paul. Sent 21:35.

Glad to hear it. Have a good night.

Day 7

Friday, 1 May

MYSTERY SURROUNDS THE SHOOTING OF TWO DETECTIVES

Detectives Juliet Stern and Gabriella Martin were shot outside Southampton Crown Court on 24 April. This followed the sentencing of Karl Biss, who shot and killed a young schoolgirl, Melanie Pirt, in October last year. Understandably, questions have been raised as to whether these two incidents are related. Both detectives are set to make full recoveries.

Police have refused to comment. While making regular statements, they have been frustratingly vague about advances in this case.

Most worryingly, they have refused to confirm or deny whether they believe this is an isolated incident. Officers on the streets could be at risk due to their senior colleagues' refusal to share vital information.

An arrest has been made. We have to hope it is the culprit. We will find out eventually, whether or not the detectives heading up this case see fit to share.

Despite the lack of momentum, this case has pulled all police focus, leaving none for the hunt for nineteen-year-old Henry Garside's murderer. Henry was a keen art student at Solent University before he went missing on 24 April. His body was later discovered at Southampton Docks on 27 April. Despite the seriousness of this case, no significant allocation of time or effort has been given to finding his killer.

Rowan Lough, a good friend of Henry's who found his body after police had given up the search, said, 'It's disgusting that the police are literally ignoring Henry's death. If they're not going to find who killed him, then we will.'

Rowan has started a social media campaign to raise awareness and put pressure on the police to step up their attempts to find Henry's killer. He is also organising a number of memorials around the city, targeting Henry's favourite cafés and art galleries.

Paul. Sent 7:01.

Still alive?

Juliet. Sent 7:12.

And kicking.

Paul. Sent 7:13.

We're following up a lead at Ocean Village Marina this morning. Want me to send a car so you can be there?

Juliet. Sent 7:17.

I can't today.

Paul. Sent 7:18.

Look after yourself.

Gabe

Despite the layers Ollie bundled me into before Alice picked me up, I shivered and tucked my chin under my scarf. Gulls screamed overhead, their grey and white wings blending with the swirling clouds. In the marina, irregular splashes on the sides of boats underscored the team's murmured conversations.

Paul and Nicole greeted Alice and I when we arrived, along with David and one of his forensic minions. No armed response team, no other police constables for added support. I chose to interpret that as confidence a search of the boat would yield quick results, rather than unwillingness to spend resources on an activity Paul considered pointless.

At least a smaller team meant fewer witnesses if this was a dead end.

David and the other forensic guy sat snug in their van while the rest of us shifted from foot to foot at the entrance to the marina, happy to let us find and secure the boat before they ventured forth. Paul clutched the warrant to search Tsambikos's yacht while the harbour master checked the roster of boats currently moored.

He seemed unaffected by the slapping cold as he drew a map, a flannel shirt his only protection. Alice kept quiet as he explained the warren of walkways. She'd visited yesterday, but it wouldn't be simple to find the yacht in the maze of hundreds of bobbing boats.

'What do you reckon we'll discover?' Nicole's fingers interlocked around a thermos of tea. 'Tsambikos thinks of himself as a flashy gent. It's not too much of a leap from that to pirate.'

I nuzzled my face deeper into a scarf that smelt like my boyfriend. 'I've always wanted to find actual treasure.'

'Would make a change from bloodstained clothes and incriminating documents,' Nicole said dryly. She walked over to Paul's side as he thanked the harbour master.

I had no clue what we would find this morning. I hoped for evidence to link the Galanis brothers to Thomas Frey, but they had been meticulously careful before. Finding a boat stashed with enough incriminating items to bring them down felt as likely as discovering gemstones and a map with a red cross.

I pushed down the doubts. Ollie had distracted me last night but as soon as I stepped outside my maisonette this morning, they'd slunk back in. My gut said Thomas hadn't worked alone, that he was protecting his sister when he claimed he didn't know the Galanis brothers, but we had no leverage to force him to tell us the whole truth. Unless we found damning evidence on this boat, Thomas could go on lying and the brothers would walk away yet again.

'Off we go, chaps.' Paul strode onto the first wooden walkway.

We wound slowly through the moored boats, hampered by the howling wind and Paul's considered pace. The vessels either side of us ranged in style between brightly painted fishing boats and sleek yachts. A few houseboats bobbed atop the waves, their roofs dotted with blooming flowers.

The wood underfoot was reassuringly solid, despite the glimpses of choppy water between each sturdy board. My parents had taken Barnabas and me to swimming lessons, but I hadn't done more than idly paddle in years. I didn't fancy testing whether my rudimentary understanding of how to stay afloat was intact so kept as close to the middle of the walkway as possible without crowding Alice, who walked at my side.

Nicole kept pace with Paul, one hand around her thermos and the other hovering near his back. He placed his stick squarely on the planks of wood, didn't let it slip into the dead space between.

'How's your shoulder?' Alice's hands were tucked under her stab-proof vest.

'It's alright. Less pain each day.'

Ollie had been unsure whether having sex was wise, but a multitude of positions put barely any strain on my injury. Not that I could share that aspect of my recovery with Alice. She was far too interested in mine and Ollie's relationship. The intrusive questions would never end if I gave her an insight into our sex life.

'I heard Angela talking to Paul this morning,' Alice murmured. 'She said she's not going to be able to keep you and Juliet away from the station for much longer.' She pumped her eyebrows. 'If I had Ollie waiting at home, I'd be milking the time off for all it was worth.'

I rolled my eyes, concealing a pang at Juliet's name. She wasn't part of our modest team. According to Paul, she'd sent him a message at the start and end of each day to confirm her safety, but she hadn't wanted to come along to search the boat.

It was so unlike her. I wanted to call and demand to know what was wrong, but it would be pointless. She wasn't answering her phone. Even if she did, she wouldn't tell me anything.

Juliet might have accepted refuge at my home for one night, had opened up enough to give me reason to suspect Douglas Frey, but she'd clammed up right after.

I should have expected it. It was naïve to think someone as closed off as Juliet wouldn't retreat after enforced sharing. She needed time to build up her high walls again.

Paul reached the end of one long stretch and turned right. The view was unchanging, boats in various sizes and colours lurching on the waves.

I'd been iced out by Juliet for much less than this. She hadn't spoken to me for a week after I'd asked what her daughters' names were, and she'd ignored my cheery message at Christmas.

Maybe Juliet would suggest a shake up, that it was time she and Nicole have a go at working together. Nicole wouldn't be as accommodating as me, but she didn't join in with the banter around Juliet being an ice queen.

I thought I would be working with Paul when I first moved down here. I didn't know why the prospect of it now felt so dismal.

'Apparently *The Galanis Girl* is on the left,' Paul called over his shoulder.

Tsambikos must have been confident we wouldn't discover his yacht to give it a name that could be so easily linked to him and his brothers. Or maybe he rated his powers of persuasion so highly that he thought he could talk his way out of this too.

My eyes drifted despite my reluctance to look away from the wooden walkway and constantly shifting slices of sea.

Above the rocking boats, there was movement. Dark and solid. Not a waving sail or flashing window.

I tripped over my boot.

'You okay, Gabe?' Alice's hand was instantly firm on my elbow.

I used it to drag her to her knees on the wooden planks.

'Get down,' I whisper-shouted.

Nicole ducked into a crouch while Paul fell to one knee with his other leg straight out in front. Despite the pinched grimace on his face, he shuffled to look at me.

'What's up?' he whispered.

I pointed in the direction of Tsambikos's yacht, blocked from view by a bobbing fishing boat painted a garish shade of orange.

'Someone's on the boat.'

Benny. Sent 7:42.

Hello, love. I've got the breakfast things, are you ready for me to pick you up? Did you say you'd be down at the marina? I hope a walk has made today seem brighter x

Gabe

Nicole dropped to her hands and knees. She crawled past Paul to peer around the fishing boat. My ears strained, but all I could hear were metallic clinks from chains on the swaying boats, the calls of hungry gulls overhead, my loud breathing.

I raked over the glimpse I'd caught of the person on the deck of the huge yacht. It could have been any of the Galanis brothers, or one of their lackeys. A thick hat hid their hair and a bulky coat swathed their body.

Catching any of the brothers here would be a massive boon, but I hoped it was Tsambikos in a compromising position he couldn't wriggle out of. He was the ringleader, the one who'd come to my home to scare me.

Nicole returned to Paul's side. 'It's Giannis.'

The youngest Galanis brother. I pressed my lips together. Giannis had been the least active when Paul ordered surveillance on the brothers and was always quiet during interviews. The worst of the three to find here, but his presence had to mean we were onto something.

'How likely is it he's armed?' Paul winced at the awkward position of his leg as Nicole crawled behind him to spy on Giannis.

I frowned at the water splashing beneath the wooden slats. 'Highly likely. The brothers have guns legally registered under their names.'

'I've got my taser, sir.' Alice patted the bulge on her hip.

'Would he turn on us?' Paul asked.

'I don't know.' I squinted in Giannis's direction. 'All our dealings with the brothers have been low stakes. I'm not sure how any of them would react if cornered, but I wouldn't put money on Giannis remaining calm.'

Nicole appeared at Paul's side. 'He's filling a bag and it looks like he's almost done. If that's all he's here for, I reckon we've got less than a minute before he's headed this way. If we want to catch him in the act, we need to move now.'

'Right.' Paul's eyes darted between us. 'Alice, I want you with me as I approach from where the boat is tied up. Nicole, you circle around. Cut off his other escape point in case he tries to scarper over the other side.'

'Give me thirty seconds to get into position.' Nicole folded into a low crouch. Alice and I squeezed to one side to let her pass.

'Gabe, you need to stay put.'

I whipped my head around. 'What?'

'You're not meant to be here.' Paul's voice was firm. 'Either stay out of sight, or I'll take Alice's taser while she escorts you to safety.'

I had no time to argue. Out of sight, Giannis could be zipping his bag shut and preparing to leave. We needed to catch him. If Paul was determined to disregard me as a spare part, I had to endure it.

'Fine.' I shifted to sit cross-legged, folding my arms across my chest.

'We'll shout when it's safe.' Paul used his stick to haul himself to his feet. He hurried off to confront Giannis, his limp pronounced. Alice had her taser ready in her hand as she followed.

I waited until they were out of sight, then rose onto my knees. I edged to the side, exposing as little of myself around the fishing boat as possible.

Giannis stood on the deck of a huge yacht. His black hair peeked out under a blue hat, his jeans ripped at the knees under a bulky coat. He could have multiple weapons concealed under that puffed fabric.

He bent over a stuffed backpack. He faced me, but his whole focus was on checking the bag's contents.

'Police.' Paul's shout cut across the rushing wind. 'Stop what you're doing and turn around with your hands above your head.'

Giannis's light brown skin flushed red as he snapped upright. A moment passed, my heart thumping and gulls calling and sea lapping, then he sprung into motion.

He threw the bag off the side of the yacht, then raced toward the pointed front.

'Stop.' Paul's command was faint over the wind.

Giannis leapt off the yacht and onto the back of another. Instead of escaping from Alice and Paul along the wooden walkways, he was racing across the swaying boats.

Straight toward me.

Call connected at 7:50.

'Hi. What's up?'

    'Hello, Ally. Have you seen GG?'

    'Not since last night. Is there a problem?'

    'Not necessarily. I was meant to pick him up for an early meeting. The silly sod has either forgotten or decided something else is more worthy of his time.'

    'I won't say which I'd bet on.'

    'Don't be cruel. Let me know if he gets in touch.'

Gabe

I jerked to the side, keeping the barest sliver of my face visible to track Giannis's ungainly approach. Shouts filled the air, Nicole and Paul's demands mingling.

Giannis raced along the side of a houseboat. He kicked off a plant to give himself a better position to leap onto a sleek motorboat. He was so fixated on evading the others that he didn't spot me lurking.

I shifted from my knees to a crouch, thigh muscles coiled. Adrenaline surged as Giannis jumped onto the back of the bobbing fishing boat. The thump of his boots drowned out the ache from my shoulder and the fear of a man twice my size running toward me.

He slammed onto the wooden walkway and I threw myself into his side. My uninjured shoulder crashed into his stomach. I wrapped my arms around his middle in a tackle.

Giannis grunted. He was broader and taller than his brothers. I'd launched myself into pure muscle.

He lurched to the side, but I couldn't bring him down. He planted his feet and grabbed my shoulders. One of his thumbs dug into the bullet wound.

I screamed and slumped out of his grip, the pain so consuming I couldn't find its edges.

Panting, I grasped my shoulder. Giannis stared down at me, his brown eyes wide. He hadn't expected one rough touch to fell me.

His face hardened. I tried not to cower as he lifted his leg.

He kicked me square in the chest. My back thumped into the walkway, head and neck hanging over the water. I heaved in a breath, my battered chest and shoulder warring for attention.

Giannis leered over me. Pure terror clutched my heart when he grinned. He raised his foot. My world was consumed by the sole of his boot.

'Gabe! Stay down,' Alice shouted.

A crack of static broke through the agitated calls of gulls. Giannis jerked to the side. His mouth opened on a silent scream as he crashed onto the gangway beside me.

'Fuck, fuck, fuck.' Alice raced toward me. 'Fuck, Gabe. Are you alright?'

She dropped to her knees and pulled me up. I grabbed the edges of her vest, pressing my forehead into her neck. My breathing punched out in heaving gasps.

'You're okay.' Alice rubbed up and down my spine, comforting through my coat. 'You're okay.'

I wiped at the tears escaping my eyes. Beside us, Giannis lay moaning across the walkway. The taser pad stretched from his thigh to the unit Alice had dropped.

His stick tapping announced Paul's arrival. 'Bloody hell. You couldn't help but get involved, could you?'

That forced a laugh past my sore chest. Taking Alice's hand, I rose to my feet and stood next to Paul. She detached the taser then roughly rolled Giannis onto his front. Tightening cuffs around his wrists, she rattled through his rights.

Paul's hand gripped mine as he tucked his phone away. 'You've got to stop scaring me like this.'

I leant into his shoulder. 'I'll try.'

Nicole appeared at the end of the walkway, holding a sodden backpack. 'Want to see what was worth all this bother?' Her eyes raked over me. I shot her a tight smile as she dragged the zip of the bag down.

I didn't need coddling. I'd have bruises and my wound would need checking, but my injuries weren't life threatening. What we'd come here to find was more important.

'That's mine,' Giannis moaned from where he laid face down on the walkway.

'We've got a warrant, mate.' Paul stepped over Giannis's legs to take a closer look at the contents of the bag.

Nicole pulled apart wet sheaves of paper with gloved hands, her eyebrows creeping up. She let them slap together and grinned. 'This is a whole lot of stuff Giannis and his brothers would not want us to see.'

David and his underling appeared behind her shoulder. He shook out an evidence bag as he hurried over.

'Stop touching things,' he snapped.

Nicole passed him the bag and stepped back. The dripping fabric twisted in his grip.

'Stop,' I croaked.

David paused. 'What?'

Giving Giannis's legs a wide berth, I walked to David's side. I pointed at the front pocket of the backpack. 'What does that say?'

David tilted the bag. 'HG.' Doodles of thrashing waves surrounded the black letters.

Paul's thick eyebrows shot up. 'Bloody hell.'

Not quite *you were right, Gabe* but I'd take it.

'Let's hope for more of the same in the boat itself.' Blue lights flashed over Paul's face. 'Ah, that'll be the ambulance for Gabe.'

'I don't need one,' I protested, but I'd already lost the battle. Paul wouldn't let me hang around while the boat was searched, not when I'd just been attacked.

'Tell me if there's anything to do with the shooting in there,' I said over my shoulder as Alice steered me toward land.

Paul had to be less sceptical now. The brothers wouldn't have Henry's backpack unless they were involved in his murder. One of my theories had proven correct. The other could too.

Significant items taken from the yacht belonging to Tsambikos Galanis
– for priority testing:

- Backpack (retrieved from the sea) containing:

- Bank statements

- Seven passports (various individuals)

- Photographs (check once dried for matches to passports)

- Three mobile phones

NOTE – the initials HG can be found on the front pocket of the backpack
– check for HENRY GARSIDE'S DNA

Other items found on yacht (hidden in compartments below deck):

- Photographs (many hundreds – mainly of young men and women)

- Several passports (approx. 50)

- Several thousand pounds worth of bank notes

- Several mobile phones (approx. 50)

- Several bags of white powder – possibly cocaine (approx. 100)

Significant find for immediate testing:

- Bloody fingerprints on the underside of the staircase rail leading
  from the inside to the outside of the boat

Call connected at 9:04.

'Hello?'

  'Tsam. It's me. GG.'

  'Darling, where are you?'

  'They fucking arrested me.'

  'What? Is Ezra there?'

  'Yeah. He's told me what to say in the interview. He gave me his phone to call you.'

  'That's good. I'm sorry I can't be there.'

  'Tsam, I fucked up.'

  'How?'

  'I was at *The Girl* when they caught me.'

  'What?'

  'Yeah. I'd gone down to get the things—'

  'Shut up. Shut up now. And you keep your fucking mouth closed during the interviews.'

  'Yeah, Tsam. I promise.'

  'Why the fuck did you go down to the boat? I told you not to go there.'

  'We weren't being followed any more. I thought it would be safe.'

  'From now on, you don't think. You do as I fucking well tell you.'

  'Are you going to be able to get me out of this?'

  'Of course I am. You might be a massive pain in the arse, but you're my brother. I'm not going to let anything happen to you.'

  'Thank you, Tsam.'

  'Keep your damn mouth shut.'

  'I will.'

Gabe

Whoever spent the bulk of their time in the observation room had decided comfortable seating was a must, and I was eternally grateful. I hadn't lied when I told the paramedics I could continue my day without a detour to the hospital. Giannis's grip hadn't broken the stitches in my shoulder and I'd walked away from his kick with bruises rather than broken ribs.

Only alone in this cramped room did I sink into the chair and groan, my body aching worse than when I'd first woken at the hospital.

At least the pain was worth it. David's excavation of the yacht had uncovered piles of incriminating evidence, not least of which were bloodied fingerprints I hoped belonged to Henry. It would give his loved ones a horrible kind of closure I knew too well.

I was still slumped in the chair when Giannis walked into the interview room. He had a different presence when separated from his brothers. He and Alcaeus usually flanked Tsambikos while he smarmed his way through every interview. We'd not had cause to bring any of them in for formal interviews before. I didn't imagine it would diminish the other two to the same extent.

Giannis huddled on his chair, making his muscled bulk as small as he could. His face was downcast, his lashes damp and nose red. He'd taken off his coat to reveal a yellow hoodie, as well-worn as his torn jeans.

At his side, Giannis's solicitor wore a pristine grey suit. His silver hair swept back from his wrinkle-free forehead. One arm rested on the table, showcasing a watch I suspected cost more than I paid in rent each month.

Giannis let his solicitor talk for him. My coffee grew cold beneath the screens showcasing the interview as he twitched toward the well-dressed gentleman each time Paul and Nicole asked a question. Giannis contributed the odd muffled sniff, which the microphones broadcasted loud and clear.

Giannis was pitiful in his current state, but I could feel where his boot had smashed into my chest. This was a man whose instincts turned toward violence.

On screen, Paul's frown deepened. 'You're going to have to give us more. There's no way you and your brothers are getting out of this one. This is your chance to get your version of events on record.'

Giannis opened his mouth, but his solicitor cut in. 'This is all implication. Until you have hard evidence you can put to my client, he's under no obligation to tell you anything.'

'Evidence like finding him on a dirty great boat full of illegal shit?' I muttered at the screens.

Nicole tapped one of the pictures spread across the table. She'd kept calm in the face of Giannis's silence and his solicitor's nonsense. 'When we found you at the marina, you were packing a bag.' With a pointed look at Ezra Berry, she added, 'Could you tell us where you got the bag?'

Giannis shrugged. 'It was there.'

'Why did you put these items in it?' Nicole pressed.

Giannis shifted in his seat. His bottom lip was bitten raw. I hadn't realised how much he'd sheltered under his brothers' wings before.

'It's Tsam's boat. I'm allowed to go there if I want to,' Giannis muttered at the tabletop.

'That's quite right,' Nicole said brightly. 'Why did your brother buy the boat?'

'He likes sailing.'

I gripped the chair's armrests, itching to storm into the interview room. I wouldn't do a better job than Paul and Nicole, but it would be a whole lot more satisfying than watching them wheedle Giannis into saying anything vaguely helpful.

'Do you know how your brother bought the boat?' Paul asked. 'It doesn't show up in his financial records.'

Giannis shrugged. 'I don't know how Tsam spends his money.'

What I actually wanted to do was step into that room with Juliet at my side. We worked well as a team to coax the truth out of reluctant suspects. We looked harmless, each in our own way.

I hoped we'd get the chance to work together again, that she wouldn't push me too far away. I'd still had no contact from her. I hoped she was resting.

Nicole pointed at the picture. 'What was so special about these things?'

'You don't need to answer that,' Ezra snapped.

Silence settled in the room. Paul and Nicole's expressions remained a trained neutral.

'I needed them,' Giannis said. His solicitor clenched his clean-shaven jaw.

'Why these things?' Nicole asked.

Giannis shrugged. 'I don't know.'

'You do,' I whispered at the screens. Similar frustration leaked from Paul and Nicole as they glanced at one another. Giannis might be a weak link, but he'd been coached well.

'We've dispatched teams to arrest your brothers. What do you think Alcaeus and Tsambikos are going to say when we bring them in?' Paul mused. 'Do you think they'll be as loyal to you as you are to them?'

'Why would you bring them in?' Giannis asked before his solicitor could interject.

Nicole gestured at the photos spread across the table. They documented the huge wealth of evidence taken from the yacht. 'Hundreds of incriminating items were found on the boat that link to a number of serious crimes. As the boat belongs to Tsambikos, we have many questions for him.'

'Which you can pose to him,' Ezra chimed in. 'My client has no influence over what his brother may or may not say.'

'Do you think Tsambikos will protect you?' Paul asked.

'That implies there's something to protect him from,' the solicitor snapped.

'Tsam loves me,' Giannis murmured. 'He won't say anything against me.'

Unfortunately, that was probably true. If questioning Giannis was frustrating, then interviewing Tsambikos would be the embodiment of futility. Alcaeus would be just as bad. These brothers had formed a seemingly impenetrable wall.

At least the evidence from the boat was damning. There was no way in hell they would be able to talk their way out of that. Hopefully, the blood results would come back soon. I didn't want Henry to have met his end on that yacht, but concrete evidence the Galanis brothers had killed someone was hard to come by.

They might not be taken down for mine and Juliet's shooting, but that was far from the worst thing they'd orchestrated. The Galanis brothers had degraded and dehumanised countless young men and women, had trafficked drugs and weapons. They ran a tight ship of violence so terrifying no one would speak out against them. They'd hurt hundreds of people as innocent as Henry, who we'd never find a trace of.

'What about Thomas Frey?' Paul's eyes darted to one of the cameras. 'Who hired him to shoot Detectives Martin and Stern?'

My phone vibrated in my pocket, distracting me from Ezra's outraged reply.

Call connected at 9:59.

'Hey, Ollie. You alright?'

'Yeah, I'm good. I came over to walk Artie, but he's not here. I wanted to check you've got him and—'

'Artie's not at home?'

'No. Is he not with you?'

'No.'

'Fuck.'

'Ollie, have you touched anything inside?'

'Um. I don't know.'

'It's okay. Please leave now and wait outside for the police. Is there any sign he escaped?'

'I don't think so. Let me grab my coat and I'll have a look at the door.'

'Don't touch it if possible.'

'I'll have to turn the lock. Yeah. Done. I'm looking at the door now and I can't see how Artie could have gotten out. There's no damage.'

'Nothing around the lock? On the outside?'

'I don't think— No. Actually, there are marks around the lock. Scratches.'

'Shit.'

'Do you think he's been taken? Should I call the police?'

'I'm at the station. I'll get someone to come over. Stay there and don't touch anything.'

Hey, mate. Can I show you something?

'Who's that?'

'One of your neighbours. Give me a second, I'm on the phone with my girlfriend.'

'Ollie, I'm heading out but I'll let you know when I've got Artie.'

'Stay safe, Gabe.'

'You too. Please.'

Gabe

I'd jumped out of the car and stormed up to the pretentious terraced house before Alice had a chance to unbuckle her seatbelt. Heedless of the jab of pain from my shoulder, I thumped on the misted panes of glass stretching from the top to the bottom of the red front door.

Since I'd gotten the call from Ollie, a high whine had dominated my mind. Someone had stolen my dog. For that to have been done with a minimum of fuss, it had to have been a person he knew. Someone he would go with quietly.

Terence Dunlow may not have shot me, but he wasn't above finding ways to hurt me. He'd told Paul he didn't harbour any resentment, but Terence was a liar. He hadn't been warm when I'd met him the other day. Maybe that chance meeting was the nudge he needed to take me down a peg.

And he was exactly the type to reach out and take whatever he considered rightfully his. He'd said he missed the dogs they used to own when his family lived on their ancestral estate. Maybe he'd decided he wanted one of them back.

His circumstances didn't seem to have changed too much. Terence might not live with his father any more, but he was still snug in the lap of luxury. The houses on his street were terraced, but all had wide windows on either side of front doors framed by potted plants. Trees swayed on the pavement, casting shifting shadows over cars barely a year old.

A blur appeared behind the front door. I breathed deep as locks turned slickly, but my pulse stuttered erratically under the collar of my coat.

'Where's my dog?' I demanded before Terence had fully opened the door.

His posh boy brow creased. There was an air of entrenched entitlement to Terence that Leo had escaped their privileged upbringing without.

'What?' Terence croaked, his auburn hair mussed over his forehead.

I didn't have time for stupid games. I stepped forward, which forced him to jump back. I took that as permission to enter his home.

'Artie?' I called as I rushed past a spluttering Terence. 'Artie?'

'Gabe, what are you doing?' Alice shouted from outside as I ran from a high-ceilinged living room to a shining kitchen to a dining room fit for entertaining minor royalty.

'What's going on?' Terence had switched shock for indignation in the time it took for me to search the opulent rooms of the ground floor. None showed any sign of a distressed Alsatian.

I rounded on Terence as I withdrew from a study lined with leather-bound books. 'Where's my dog? Where's Artie?'

Terence's face was set in a frown that would rival his father's, the effect ruined by his baggy hoodie and pyjama bottoms. 'I don't know what the bloody hell you're talking about.'

Alice stepped onto the welcome mat inside the door, her eyes wavering between Terence and me. 'I suggest we all take a moment to calm down, then discuss what's going on.'

Asking her to drive me here hadn't been fair, but my car wasn't at the station and I needed to get to Terence quickly. She'd asked where we were headed and had swallowed my vague excuse of running an errand for Paul. I'd have thought the shit I'd pulled with Douglas Frey would have taught her to be more wary.

'Is he upstairs?' I demanded. 'Where have you put him?'

Terence's shoulders slumped. 'I don't know what you're talking about. I haven't seen Artie since we met you in the forest.'

I'd seen Terence lie before, but I couldn't tell if his resignation was an act or a sign he hadn't taken Artie from my maisonette.

'Where were you this morning?' I asked.

A blotchy blush spread across his face. 'I went for a walk. As you know, I've not been well.'

He didn't look healthy. His skin was dry and dull, his normally posed frame slouched. I felt an involuntary spasm of pity. This had happened before, when he'd revealed his father's backward attitude to his sexuality. No matter how much I disliked Terence, I couldn't forget he was human.

If he hadn't taken Artie, then who had? My heart lurched. Terence had been the easy option, had provided an opportunity to save my dog. If he was innocent, then the chances I'd see Artie again dwindled.

'Is everything alright?' Terence's boyfriend descended the stairs in pyjamas much more dignified than Terence's.

'You.' Alice marched into the hallway, abandoning her neutral position at the door. She pointed a finger in Terence's boyfriend's face. 'Who are you?'

Terence puffed up. 'This is Benedict Hogan. My boyfriend.'

'Do you have a tan coat?' Alice scanned the entranceway. She was out of luck. Nothing as common as a coat rack resided in Terence and Benedict's home.

'Yes.' Benedict looked politely bemused, like he was watching a play he didn't understand.

Terence shoved his hands into his hoodie pocket. 'I bought it for him.'

Alice shook her head. 'Why were you at the site of Gabe and Juliet's shooting?'

'He was where?' I hadn't welcomed Alice's interruption, since questioning Benedict would in no way help me find my missing dog, but her question derailed me.

'Juliet noticed a man in a tan coat before you guys walked into the courthouse. I've been staring at his face on CCTV for days. We hadn't been able to figure out who he was, but it's you.'

Benedict blinked, his dark eyebrows rising toward his tousled hair.

Terence shifted his weight, his socks bunching on the dark wooden floor. 'He didn't have anything to do with the shooting.'

'Why was he there, then?' I asked.

Terence's tongue flicked over his chapped lips. 'I asked Benny to meet me there before he went to a spa with his sister. I had no idea something bad was going to happen there later in the day.'

'Why did you wait for so long?' Alice asked. 'You stood in the exact spot where Gabe and Juliet were shot for over an hour.'

'You did?' Terence clutched Benedict's hand. 'God. Benny would have waited there for so long because he's not a complete waste of space like me.' His voice broke on the last word, his lip wobbling.

Terence was a mess. His hair was tangled, clothes creased. His once perfect skin was marred with blemishes.

He hadn't taken my dog. It wasn't likely he'd left this house in days, apart from his medically mandated walks.

'Terence, what's going on?' I asked. He could simply be unwell, but a nervous energy emanated from him that had been absent months before.

He bit his lip. 'I've fucked everything up.'

Benedict angled toward him. 'Teddy, that's not true, but it would be helpful if you told the police what's been going on.'

Terence sniffed wetly. 'I hate my job. I thought maybe I needed to get used to it since it's different to where I'd worked before, but it hasn't gotten any better. Joanna, my boss, is horrible to me. She makes me work overtime with no pay and belittles everything I do.'

I hadn't liked the gallery manager, but I'd assumed Terence could hold his own against her. It undermined my view of him, that a squat woman wearing too many bangles could affect him, make him miserable. But then, he'd been bullied before.

'I didn't want to be there any more, but it was the first job I'd got without any help from Dad. I wanted to prove I could do it, that I could pay my own way.'

Benedict pressed his lips together and tightened his fingers around Terence's.

'Things got worse recently. Joanna asked me to do things I wasn't sure were strictly legal. Like the group of students Henry was meant to be part of; we took their work but gave them no receipt. The pieces that got the most attention would be sold, and I never saw any money making its way back to the artists. When I challenged Joanna, she told me she would drag me down with her if I said anything.'

Terence opened the drawer of a side table that could have been an antique. He handed a phone to Alice.

'Joanna gave me this so that she could communicate about all the dodgy stuff out of hours.' Terence leant closer to Benedict. 'She'd agreed to pay me for the morning I went in to take the artwork off the students but got cross when Henry didn't turn up and only gave me half.' He gestured at the phone as Alice thumbed at it. 'There's messages about it all on there.'

Deep lines formed on my forehead. 'You've been lying to us, but not about Henry or the shooting. You've been unhappy at work because your boss has been mistreating you?'

Terence nodded. His round eyes reminded me of his younger brother. 'I honestly never met Henry, and I couldn't have shot you.'

'He doesn't have it in him.' Benedict's expression was strained but fond as he looked at his boyfriend. 'Teddy's been struggling, but he's not a bad person.'

I was saved from formulating a response by my buzzing phone. Imagining a text from Ollie, I hurriedly pulled it out of my pocket.

The single word on the screen made my blood run cold.

I grabbed Alice's arm. 'We need to go.'

Juliet. Sent 11:05.

HELP

Gabe

'You're an arsehole.' Alice huffed to a halt beside me.

I'd raced out of the car when she pulled up into one of the visitor spaces. I'd taken a look at Juliet's address, both here and out with her husband, a few weeks after we started working together. I didn't want to have to search through HR documents in a crisis. My intrusiveness felt like pragmatism now.

'Noted.' I pressed the buzzer for Juliet's flat for a third time. She hadn't replied to any of my frantic messages or answered her phone. 'I don't know if she's in.'

'Remind me again why this is a good idea and, more importantly, why I should listen to anything you say.' Alice tapped the top of her new taser.

'Juliet texted me.' I interrupted myself with another long buzz on the doorbell. 'If she needed anyone else, she'd have contacted Paul or used her panic button.'

If Juliet was truly in danger, she wouldn't have sent me a message to bring me running to her side. This had to be personal, something she needed me for. She'd have to forgive Alice tagging along. After my outburst at Terence's, there was no way she would leave me to my own devices.

I buzzed again, pushing my finger into the metal button. I'd abandoned my search for Artie to come here. Juliet was more important than my dog, but I hoped this could be resolved quickly so I could revert to my hunt. Turning away from finding Artie had been harder than expected, but I couldn't let Juliet down.

One of her neighbours opened the door. I swung it wide, slipping inside before they could stop me. Their protests and Alice's explanations quietened as I climbed the stairs to the third floor.

I paused in the hallway. Number 17's door was propped open by bulging black bags. I inched along the corridor until I could peer inside.

The front door opened straight into an open–plan living room and kitchen. It was empty, the spaces where furniture would have stood marked by indentations in the grey carpet.

'Complete arsehole.' Alice was out of breath when she arrived. 'Stop fucking running off.'

'Sorry,' I muttered, leaning to take in more of the bare flat.

Alice did the same. 'Did you know Juliet was moving?'

'No.'

Juliet didn't share much of herself. I didn't know where she'd grown up or if her parents were alive. It shouldn't have been so unsettling to see her home stripped.

A short woman emerged from the section of room hidden behind the door. She promptly dropped her feather duster when she saw me and Alice. Her yellow gloved hands clutched at the front of her apron as her eyes fixed on Alice's uniform.

'No trouble. No trouble.' She pointed at the bin bags beside the door. 'I come and clean.'

Alice backed up, hands spread wide. 'No trouble.'

The woman's attention switched to me. Alice loitered out of sight, fiddling with the volume on her radio.

'Do you know the woman who lives here?' I asked.

The woman bent to pick up the feather duster. A long plait trailed down her rounded back. 'I come and clean.'

'Is the woman who lives here moving?' I wasn't going to bother her for too long, but I couldn't leave without attempting to find out what was going on.

The woman nodded vigorously, pointing the feather duster at me. 'Yes. Moving. She moving.'

'Do you know where?'

The woman's focus veered away from me. 'I clean.'

'Okay. Thank you.'

I joined Alice and kept in step with her all the way to the car. Her measured pace made me want to grab her arm and drag her outside.

'Last request,' I promised. 'Can you take me to Juliet's house?'

Recording started at 9:32.

'Hi, my lovelies. I hope the universe has brought good things for you today at the start of a fresh new month. I love you all, and I'm manifesting your dreams for you. Now, I know you've all been super keen to hear my thoughts on the new range of eyeliners from… What the fuck? What are they doing? Shit, shit, shit. They're getting away. I need to call the police. Or the RSPCA. Fuck. Dan? Who do I call about a stolen dog? Oh, shit, I'm still recording.'

Gabe

I breathed evenly as Alice turned into the U-shaped driveway. As she'd driven away from the city and toward Juliet's house in Eastleigh, the pavements had grown wider and greenery sprouted from hedgerows and neat window boxes.

'Don't you dare run off again,' Alice warned as she parked up.

My hand fell from the door handle. 'Wouldn't dream of it.'

Alice pulled on the handbrake. 'Are you sure I don't need to call for back-up?'

I looked at the farmhouse sitting peacefully behind bushes beginning to flower. If Juliet had felt threatened by whatever had prompted her message, then surely she would have reached out to someone else. She wouldn't call me into the middle of a dangerous situation.

Doubt bloomed as I shook my head. The line I would draw in the sand was miles from Juliet's. 'Let's check out what's going on first.'

Alice pushed her lips together but didn't protest as we left the car. The gravel drive widened at the front of the house. Lush gardens dotted with shrubs and fruit trees were bracketed on each side by mock Tudor cottages, the wooden beams cutting across the cream plaster far too even for them to have been built more than a handful of years ago.

Juliet's house was two storeys, the brickwork a light yellow and the roof a tidy thatch. I walked up to the front door and knocked. A minute passed without any answer.

I pushed up onto my tiptoes to peer through the clear semi-circle of glass at the top of the door. Photos dotted the walls of a cosily cluttered hallway that led to several other rooms.

A door stood open at the end. On the burnt orange tiles, a shadow moved.

'I think she's in a back room.' I stepped away from the door.

'Looks like we can get around.'

I led the way to the left side of the house, peering into the windows as we passed. In a sunny living room, a puzzle lay scattered on the floor.

I didn't think Juliet would appreciate us snooping around her home and gardens, but I couldn't leave without checking she was okay.

I moved as close to the house as the abundant but curated plant life would allow as we neared the next window. The tended lawn underfoot silenced our approach. The window showed a kitchen diner that spanned the back of the house. The room was spacious and bright. Multi-coloured wellies stood beside French doors and pictures were tacked to the fridge.

Juliet sat at a long wooden table, her head bowed. A man paced on the other side. Juliet's mouth moved and he thumped his fist on the table. His face contorted as he snarled.

Ducking, I motioned for Alice to move back. 'Tsambikos Galanis is in there with Juliet.'

The words sent a scattered pang through me. Juliet was in a room with an incredibly dangerous criminal. She shouldn't have messaged me for help.

'We need back-up.' Alice reached for her radio.

A loud smash inside was followed by a cry.

'There isn't time.'

Alice nodded once. 'Is there a door?'

I thought back to the bright room. 'Double doors. They're glass, but Tsambikos was facing away from them.'

'The key will be to get as close as possible without being seen.' Alice dropped onto her knees. 'I'll need you to open the door while I go in with the taser.'

I couldn't argue with her idea to crawl across the lawn and keep ourselves below the tops of the budding bushes surrounding the house, no matter how much my shoulder wanted me to. I'd been running on pure adrenaline since I'd gotten the call from Ollie, but it wasn't enough to block out the throbbing ache flooding my arm and one side of my back. Giannis hadn't reopened the wound when he'd pressed his thumb into it, but he'd certainly done damage.

Putting minimal weight on my left arm, I crawled forward. My progress was slow and uneven, but Alice wouldn't judge. Despite her faults, she was loyal. Her crawling across Juliet's garden behind me was evidence of that.

Keeping my torso low, I rounded the back corner of the house. Windows looked out over the long garden. A tyre swing twisted beneath a towering oak tree and a barbeque sat beside covered garden furniture.

I paused next to the double doors. Through the long panes of glass, the bottom of Tsambikos's suit trousers flashed back and forth. Shattered glass sparkled across the floor of the kitchen.

'You ready?' I whispered.

'Yes.' Alice squeezed my ankle. 'Be careful, Gabe.'

Sound advice, but I was about to hurl myself into a dangerous situation. It didn't matter. If I could extract Juliet from Tsambikos's clutches, I'd do it.

I placed one foot flat on the ground and took a deep breath. My heart thundered in my ears, drowning out birdsong and kids laughing in distant gardens. The sun shone through scattered clouds, but I couldn't feel its warmth.

I breathed out, then surged upward. Two steps on paving stones, and my hand landed on the nearest door handle. I yanked on it. It wouldn't budge.

Grimacing, I reached for the other one. Inside the kitchen, Tsambikos twirled on one expensive heel. Our eyes met as I tugged downward. The door swung out.

Alice wasn't gentle as she barged into the kitchen. Her shoulder bashed into mine.

White hot pain exploded from my arm. I clutched at it, falling against the door.

'Hands up,' Alice shouted at Tsambikos.

He complied immediately. Juliet's head jerked up. Her eyebrows lowered.

For a split second, it looked as though she was annoyed at our arrival. That couldn't be true. She'd called me here. Perhaps she was angry I'd brought back-up, but she couldn't have expected me to take down Tsambikos while injured.

Juliet's expression clouded again as her gaze shifted from where Alice was patting Tsambikos down to where I leant on the door. She stood and rushed over.

'Gabe.' She stopped an arm's length away. 'Are you okay?'

'Yeah.' Not a total lie. My shoulder was already returning from a stabbing pain to a sharp ache.

A fresh scratch cut across Juliet's cheek. I reached toward her. 'Did he hurt you?'

Juliet stepped back. My arm fell to my side.

'I'm fine. It wasn't him.'

'Gabriella.' Tsambikos inclined his head. 'We have things to discuss.'

Alice had guided him to a chair on the other side of the table. Apparently, he'd come to Juliet's home unarmed. I didn't know whether to trust Alice's frisking skills or assume Tsambikos had been creative in secreting weapons about his person. She'd taken his phone, which sat in the middle of the dining table.

Roiling energy resurged at his casual words. I stepped into the kitchen. 'What the fuck are you doing here?'

Tsambikos's eyes rolled toward Juliet. 'I needed to have a chat with our mutual friend.'

I turned away from his smug face. Juliet's was a blank slate. If she felt gratitude at being rescued or anger at a gang boss sitting in her kitchen, none of it leaked through her expressionless mask.

She avoided my gaze. 'You should hear him out.'

I stared in disbelief between Juliet and the criminal sitting at her table. 'What? How is that going to help anything? He's broken into your house. Even without that, we've found a boat full of incriminating evidence. He and his brothers probably murdered Henry Garside, amongst others. We're going to find a link between his family and our shooting.'

'There are a number of things I would like to explain.' Tsambikos spread his hands, showing off smooth palms. 'Things have not gone exactly to plan.'

Juliet wouldn't look at me. Since Alice and I had crashed into her kitchen, everything had gone sideways. Juliet wasn't meant to be a robotic shell when rescued, wasn't meant to encourage me to give the scum we'd been hunting for months the time of day.

'Fine.' I pulled out a chair and sat down heavily. I refused to give into the pleading of my tired body and lean into the back. I needed to be on edge. 'What do you have to say?'

'Let me get you and young Alice up to speed with what I've told your esteemed colleague.' Tsambikos smiled when Alice blanched, clearly not expecting him to know her name. She stepped back, her hand on her taser. 'I want to walk out of here. I want my brother released from custody. I want my family to be allowed to disappear.' He looked between the three of us, Juliet standing near the open door and Alice hovering at the end of the table. 'I'm not unreasonable. I know there are things you all need in return.'

'Nothing you could offer would change our minds about arresting you,' I said.

Tsambikos's smile widened. 'You shouldn't speak for everyone in the room, Gabriella. Juliet hadn't arrested me yet, had she?'

I whipped my head around. Juliet stared out of the open door, hands bunched at her sides. She wore a white blouse and jeans, was still significantly taller than me even though her slippers didn't add the inches her heels normally did.

Far too much of Juliet's life was a mystery to me. I had my suspicions, but something serious must be going on for her to contemplate Tsambikos's ridiculous offer.

'Young Alice.' Tsambikos purred her name. 'I know exactly what you want: top marks on the detective's exam. Surely letting three people walk away is nothing compared to all the good you can do once you're a detective. I've been keeping tabs on you. It's not fair you're penalised because you struggle with exams. You deserve better.'

Alice didn't move. She stood at the end of the table, her back straight and her hand resting on her taser. Her expression was a controlled blank. She didn't look at Tsambikos or me or Juliet.

She didn't reply either.

Becoming a detective was more than a dream for her. It was a desperate need, wrapped up in proving herself to her family and achieving what she knew she was capable of.

'And you, Gabriella.' Tsambikos turned the full wattage of his smile on me. 'There are so many things you want.'

'Nothing will sway me.' I balled my hands under the table. 'Don't bother offering.'

'You don't want your dog back?'

I couldn't stop a flinch. Tsambikos had taken Artie.

Maybe I had been so quick to believe Terence had my dog because then there was a chance I would get him back. Artie was lost if held under Tsambikos's power.

A wave of sadness so strong I wanted to fold forward and sob into the scrubbed tabletop crashed over me. As much as I loved Artie, I couldn't let the Galanis brothers go free to save him.

I couldn't remember if I'd said goodbye this morning. Artie had been bounding around as I put my boots on.

'No deal.' My fingernails pressed into the soft skin of my palms. 'I don't think you realise what charging you would mean to me.'

It marked the end of a reign of terror. Tsambikos and his brothers had held parts of this city in their grasp for far too long. Too many people would be saved by taking him in, and one lovely dog had to be sacrificed. One dream for Alice. An unknown promise for Juliet.

Tsambikos nodded, his eyes intent. 'You need something that would mean much more to you.'

'Nothing is going to change my mind.'

'What if I gave you him?' Tsambikos asked.

'Artie?' I shook my head, ignoring the pain in my chest that had nothing to do with the injuries I'd sustained over the last few days. 'I'm not bargaining with you, not even to get my dog back.'

'No, Gabriella. Not him.' Tsambikos let the silence stretch and alarm bells began ringing in my head. I'd spoken to Ollie a couple of hours ago, but anything could have happened since then.

'Who?' I demanded.

Tsambikos's eyes narrowed. 'The Barrel Man.'

All the air punched out of my lungs. The room darkened. Inarticulate shouts and thumping and grey static rang through my ears. My heart sought escape from my ribcage, my brain sparking with crescendoing alarms.

That name. Title. I didn't use it. Didn't read the articles or watch the programmes that might.

I hadn't heard it in such a long time.

'Gabe.' A soft voice whispered in my ear, at odds with the discordant maelstrom pounding over me in rushing waves. 'Gabe, breathe.'

Hard to obey when I couldn't feel my lungs. My body screamed to keep myself small and unmoving.

I inhaled sharply, the sound loud amongst the cacophony of sirens inside my mind.

I did it again, and again. Gradually, other sensations returned. The ache in my shoulder. Cold hands over my face. Nails digging into my forehead. Unforgiving tiles under my side.

I'd fallen off the chair. I lay curled on Juliet's kitchen floor. I breathed as I returned from darkness few things had the power to send me falling into.

Alice rubbed circles on my back. Wetness coated my face under my palms. Clammy sweat cooled across my skin. Birds sang somewhere outside and a fresh breeze rustled through the bushes on either side of the open door.

I pulled up my sleeve and wiped it over my face. I couldn't hide what had happened, but I could be vaguely put together when I faced Tsambikos again. My heart tripping and my limbs clumsy, I accepted Alice's help back into the chair. Her hand gripped my uninjured shoulder.

I glared across the table. 'Don't mention him again.'

Oddly, Tsambikos looked stricken. 'I won't.' He opened his mouth. Closed it. Then said in a rush, 'But what if I could bring him to justice? What if he wasn't allowed to ever hurt anyone again?'

My brain felt too big for my skull. I wanted to close my eyes and rest my head on Alice's hand. I wanted Tsambikos to be taken away and for someone to cover me in a blanket and keep all the badness at bay.

I forced myself to focus. I could rest later. I spread my clammy hands across my thighs.

'You think you'll be able to find him, when the police have been searching for decades and have found nothing?' My voice was a weak rasp.

'There are means I could employ, strings I could pull, that law-abiding officers are not able to.'

I tore my gaze from Tsambikos's cajoling face. Juliet was closer than before, her eyes fixed on me. She must have moved when I'd fallen.

Her mask was gone. Concern and sadness played on her face, with something like despair.

I wouldn't ask what Tsambikos had offered her, wouldn't force her to share anything she didn't want to. It had to be huge for her to consider letting him go. She had a demon that needed banishing. I wondered if it was lurking in her past or a more present torment.

'I can free you,' Tsambikos whispered, the only sound in the sunlit room as Juliet and I stared at one another. The high winds of the morning seemed a distant memory. 'I can free you all.'

Tsambikos promised to do away with our troubles. He would root them out and destroy their power over us.

I blinked away the hot wetness rising to my eyes. For so long, I'd lived under the shadow of what the bad man did to my family, to my brother. He'd gone on to abduct and murder other children. I couldn't bring them back, couldn't save Barnabas, but Tsambikos was offering a way to stop it happening again. I could spare families the heartbreak mine had suffered.

And maybe I would be free. The nightmares would end. I'd stop fearing the worst for those I loved. I'd finally feel safe without the bad man out in the world.

A similar war battled across Juliet's face. Tsambikos's offer would transform her life. She wanted freedom as much as me.

We stood close to the edge. I'd never been this out of my depth before. Perhaps Juliet had, but the panic in her eyes suggested otherwise.

One step forward, and we would fall.

'It's not such a terrible thing, letting me and my brothers go. We've done wrong, I admit that, but when you compare us to others out there, we're small fry. We don't operate in the ways they do.'

Tsambikos thought he was making his case more compelling, but all the words falling from his mouth did was remind me of exactly why we couldn't let him and his brothers walk away.

Our shooting was the tip of the iceberg. Juliet and I had been meticulously closing the net around the Galanis brothers for months. The extent of the pain they caused was staggering. Tsambikos might consider himself a lesser evil, but he and his brothers were rotten through and through. Thick blood covered their hands. Henry's bruised face flashed into my mind, his mutilated fingers.

Resignation settled like a hard shell over Juliet's face before I turned back to Tsambikos. His smile was tentative. He believed he'd offered enough to let him and his brothers walk free.

'What happened to Henry Garside?' I asked.

His fate wasn't as important to Juliet as it was to me, but I had to know why Tsambikos and his brothers had killed him. I couldn't be accused of messing with another detective's investigation. I was neck deep in this one, even if Angela and Paul claimed otherwise. Henry had been mine to find and return to his family. I'd failed them.

Tsambikos's smile froze. Whereas Giannis turned monosyllabic and sullen under individual questioning, the synapses in Tsambikos's brain fired in such quick succession it was almost visible. Giannis was like a hippopotamus: dangerous if provoked and prone to mindless violence. I sat across from an apex predator.

'I deeply regret what happened to Henry.' Tsambikos kept his voice low and cajoling. He'd calculated that denying his involvement was pointless. From now on, he was focused on damage control.

My face was a pained blank. I had to let Tsambikos believe there was a chance he could wriggle out of this so he would keep talking.

'What happened?' I asked again.

Tsambikos's tongue flashed across his bottom lip. 'I believe Henry was searching for the back entrance for a community gallery. I was conducting a meeting several doors down. Henry walked in on it, and he couldn't be allowed to speak about what he'd seen.' Tsambikos's face contorted with overwrought concern. 'Henry didn't suffer. I made sure of that. And I'd planned to deal with the aftermath quietly. The surveillance placed on myself and my brothers prevented that.'

I couldn't keep a deep frown off my face. I'd known Tsambikos must have a warped morality to head up his horrific businesses, but this was twisted. He pretended to care about the young man he'd killed, but really Tsambikos was sorry he couldn't dispose of the body without a fuss. No thought was spared for the grieving parents Henry left behind, the friend who would never be able to expunge the images of when he'd found his murdered friend from his brain.

Tsambikos claimed Henry hadn't suffered, but I'd seen the cuts across his face. The bruises around his delicate wrists. The blood pooled in harsh points across his torso.

'Arrest him,' I croaked. I looked up at Alice, firm at my side. 'Arrest him now.'

Over my head, Alice glanced at Juliet.

'I could end it.' Tsambikos's eyes fixed in the same direction.

Juliet stepped forward to stand next to me, her hands tightening on the back of a chair. 'Arrest him.'

'Fuck.' The word was no more than breath over Tsambikos's lips. 'Before you do, can I send one message?'

I wiped my sweaty hands on my thighs, legs weak like I'd been running for hours. 'Why would we let you do that?'

'Because I want to give you your fucking dog back,' Tsambikos snapped. It was the first time he'd spoken with anything other than smarmy calm in my presence.

My heart leapt. 'Let him do it.' I couldn't lose Artie if there was a chance to save him. 'But watch what he's sending.'

Tsambikos rolled his eyes but waited for Alice to round the table before he picked up his phone. I looked at Juliet while he typed, but she had shut down again.

'Hey.' Alice snatched the phone from Tsambikos's hand. 'What does that mean?'

A smirk quirked his lips upward. 'A typo, I assure you.'

Tsam. Sent 12:39.

Leave the dgo.

Gabe

I stood on the front step while Alice guided Tsambikos into the back of her car. Juliet leant against the doorframe, her face set into hard lines.

'Did he break in?'

Juliet sighed. 'I found him in the kitchen.'

A flash of fear wracked through me. 'Why didn't you press your panic button?'

Asking for my help had been wrong. If I'd come alone, Tsambikos could have easily overpowered us.

'I'm not sure where it is,' Juliet said slowly.

I narrowed my eyes, but let it go. It was another lesson. I would always want to help Juliet, but I couldn't trust calling on me was the right decision.

'Did he talk about the shooting before we arrived?' In all the upheaval after mine and Alice's arrival, I'd not hurled that accusation at Tsambikos.

'He didn't.' Juliet held a hand over her padded shoulder.

I licked my lips, keeping my gaze fixed on Alice. She was speaking into her radio. 'I hope he didn't say anything too upsetting.'

'No,' Juliet murmured. 'He didn't upset me.'

I gripped the sleeves of my jumper. Things between me and Juliet were delicate. I didn't want to go too far and cause them to break.

'We went to your flat first,' I ventured. 'The cleaner said you've moved out.'

'I'll be living here from now on.' Juliet's words were dull. 'Keith and I decided it was for the best. I need someone around while I recover, and I've been struggling to see the girls while living in the city.'

'Is that what you want?' As far as I could tell, Juliet had been perfectly happy with their old arrangement.

Her jaw worked back and forth. 'Why wouldn't it be?'

'You know you can talk to me, right?' Unease writhed in my belly.

Juliet turned to look at me, her eyes unchanged by the smile lifting her lips. 'There's nothing to talk about. I'm perfectly happy with how things have turned out.'

This was exactly the forced politeness she talked to David Rees with. I'd pushed her to become as closed down around me as she was with her most detested colleague. Any blank slate the last hour may have caused was already sullied.

Gravel crunched as a boxy car pulled up behind Alice's on the U-shaped drive. Keith's expression was unreadable from such a distance.

Juliet stiffened. 'You should go.'

I bit my lip, but couldn't stop myself from saying, 'You call, I'll come running.'

Maybe Juliet wouldn't always make the right choice, but I wouldn't leave her hanging if she needed me again.

Cool fingers at my wrist stopped me from walking away.

'Thank you,' Juliet whispered. Her fingers retreated.

I didn't look back as I marched over to Alice's car. Raising my hand in a vague wave toward Keith, I ducked inside.

I rested my head back once my seatbelt clicked in. Exhaustion plucked at me with clumsy fingers, but I could only take the car ride to rest. I'd watch over Tsambikos's interview once we got to the station. I didn't dare jeopardise the investigation by asking about the shooting now, but I had to know what he'd say. I had to know this was over.

I had done the right thing. I couldn't exchange this terrible man's freedom for peace from my demons. I wanted the bad man brought to justice, but in the right way.

Suppressing shivers, I wrapped my arms around myself as Alice pulled out of the drive. Tsambikos might try to lie his way out of involvement with a hundred horrible things, but I had to hope one thing he'd said was true. I hoped Artie would be returned home safe.

From: David Rees **david.rees@forensics.gov.uk**
To: Paul Willis **paul.willis@mit.gov.uk**
CC: Nicole Stewart **nicole.stewart@mit.gov.uk**
Date: **1 May, 13:04**
Subject: **Operation Aster – DNA match**

Willis,

The blood samples taken from the rail of the yacht this morning have provided a positive match for HENRY GARSIDE. As his fingerprints are not on the system, it's impossible to tell if they are his. They do not match anyone on the system.

Using the DNA sample taken from GIANNIS GALANIS this morning, we have a strong match for the trace amounts of DNA left on HENRY GARSIDE'S hair and face. The larger amounts of DNA are still unidentified, but markers suggest this could belong to a relative of GIANNIS GALANIS.

My team is searching the boat for any further DNA samples. Currently, the samples matching HENRY GARSIDE are too small to speculate as to whether they are evidence of a superficial or life-threatening injury sustained on the boat. There is definite evidence of attempts to clean the inside of the boat, using the same chemicals found on HENRY GARSIDE'S body.

Rees

Detective Sergeant Nicole Stewart: Interview commencing at 1:51 p.m. on the 1st May. The interviewee is Tsambikos Galanis. His legal representative is also present, Ezra Berry. This interview is being conducted by Detective Inspector Paul Willis and myself, Detective Sergeant Nicole Stewart. This interview is concerning the murder of Henry Garside on the 24th April, the shooting of Detective Inspector Juliet Stern and Detective Sergeant Gabriella Martin on the 24th April, and the breaking and entering of Juliet Stern's home today. We will also be asking Mr Galanis about his wider criminal activities, as we have evidence he has overseen human, weapon, and drugs trafficking across Southampton.

Ezra Berry: Before you begin, my client would like to make a statement.

Detective Inspector Paul Willis: Wonderful. Go ahead.

Tsambikos Galanis: Thank you, detectives. I would like to state that all criminal activities were committed by myself alone. I believe you have one of my brothers in custody. He is wholly innocent of every charge levelled at him. Neither of my brothers had any idea of the additional business I was conducting. Every charge can be laid on my shoulders. However, I would like to state for the record that I had nothing to do with the shooting of Gabriella and Juliet.

DI Paul Willis: That's quite the statement.

Tsambikos Galanis: I felt it best to make the truth clear from the outset of our little chat.

DI Paul Willis: The truth. Right.

DS Nicole Stewart: Can I check? You're claiming your brothers had no idea of the illegal activities you were participating in?

Tsambikos Galanis: That is correct.

DS Nicole Stewart: You and your brothers have been inseparable during the course of Detectives Martin and Stern's investigation.

Tsambikos Galanis: Not quite. We're very close. I feel terrible to have deceived them for so long.

DI Paul Willis: Confessing all of your crimes may help to alleviate your guilt.

Tsambikos Galanis: I can only hope so.

DS Nicole Stewart: Giannis was arrested this morning when retrieving incriminating items from your yacht. Why did he do this if he knew nothing of your criminal activities?

Tsambikos Galanis: Because he's a good brother. I asked him to do something, and he did it. No questions asked.

DI Paul Willis: Is there anything else you've asked your brothers to do?

Tsambikos Galanis: Anything specific you have in mind?

DS Nicole Stewart: Did you ask one of your brothers to tamper with CCTV prior to the shooting of Detectives Martin and Stern?

Tsambikos Galanis: Neither I nor my brothers had anything to do with the attack on the detectives. I was cut up when I learnt they'd been hurt.

DI Paul Willis: You certainly have an interest in the detectives.

Tsambikos Galanis: I feel they are far more interested in myself.

DI Paul Willis: If you weren't involved in the shooting, then why did you go to Detective Martin's home on the evening of the 29th April?

Tsambikos Galanis: I was transparent about the reasons behind my visit. I wanted to check someone I'd come to consider a friend was recovering from a terrible injury.

DS Nicole Stewart: For the tape, I am showing Mr Galanis photograph number TF001. Does this man look familiar?

Tsambikos Galanis: I cannot say he does. I'd remember those eyes.

DI Paul Willis: Does the name Thomas Frey mean anything to you?

Tsambikos Galanis: I'm afraid it does not.

DS Nicole Stewart: Mr Frey worked as a casual construction worker on your flat renovations.

339

Tsambikos Galanis: I employ a great number of people. Unfortunately, I do not have the time to get to know each individual.

DS Nicole Stewart: Mr Frey has confessed to the shooting of Detectives Martin and Stern.

Tsambikos Galanis: And as I have confessed, I had nothing to do with that terrible incident.

DI Paul Willis: We haven't been able to make contact with Alcaeus today. Any idea where he might be?

Tsambikos Galanis: I am not my brother's keeper.

DI Paul Willis: His sudden absence wouldn't have anything to do with the typo in the message you sent him?

Tsambikos Galanis: I have no idea how it could.

DS Nicole Stewart: Do you have another phone? This one only has the message you sent to Alcaeus. Nothing more.

Tsambikos Galanis: I lost my phone yesterday. I haven't had time to do anything but input my brothers' numbers.

DI Paul Willis: Henry Garside went missing on the 24th April. His DNA has been retrieved from bloody fingerprints on the yacht where we found your younger brother this morning. Giannis's DNA has also been found in Henry's hair, along with other DNA likely belonging to a relative. Are you going to claim Giannis and Alcaeus had nothing to do with that either?

Tsambikos Galanis: Whatever happened to young Henry can be fully attributed to myself alone. I have no idea why Giannis's DNA has shown up on his body.

DI Paul Willis: What happened to Henry? Why did you kill him?

Tsambikos Galanis: It was a necessary evil. I was conducting business when he witnessed a delicate situation. I couldn't allow him to walk away with the knowledge he'd gleaned. It was unfortunate, but there are always casualties in the pursuit of profit. If you think your so-called legal businesses aren't squashing people they consider insignificant to get what they want, then you're much more naïve than a detective inspector should be.

DI Paul Willis: What delicate situation did Henry witness?

340

Tsambikos Galanis: Dearest Paul. You're going to have to work a lot harder than that to extract details of my various pursuits.

DI Paul Willis: You're a smooth talker, Mr Galanis. Let me be frank with you.

Tsambikos Galanis: I welcome honesty.

DI Paul Willis: Your brothers aren't as good at this as you. One of them is going to slip up. My money is on Giannis. The best way forward is for you to tell the truth. Juries don't like liars.

DS Nicole Stewart: You may be determined to take the fall for your brothers, but there's no chance anyone will believe you single-handedly ran the sheer amount of criminal activities we're in the process of uncovering.

DI Paul Willis: Giannis will be charged with assaulting a police officer. He's not going to walk away from this a free man.

Tsambikos Galanis: He did what?

DI Paul Willis: And we need to talk to Alcaeus about breaking and entering a police officer's home and abducting their pet.

Tsambikos Galanis: Alcaeus had nothing to do with Gabriella's dog going missing.

DS Nicole Stewart: Why did you tell him to let the dog go, then?

Tsambikos Galanis: I dropped the animal off with him before heading over to Juliet's.

DI Paul Willis: For the tape, I am showing Mr Galanis a number of screenshots from a video taken by a neighbour of Detective Martin. Did you know she lives across the road from an Instagram influencer?

DS Nicole Stewart: It's not you in these pictures, Mr Galanis. You and Alcaeus may look alike, but not that much.

DI Paul Willis: As you can see, we have evidence linking both of your brothers to criminal activity. It's only a matter of time before we track down Alcaeus, and then we'll have lots of time to question your brothers and find out if Alcaeus's DNA is a match for that found in Henry Garside's hair. Do you honestly think your brothers will be able to keep us from uncovering their involvement in everything you've been up to?

[Long pause.]

Tsambikos Galanis: I would like to confer with Ezra.

DS Nicole Stewart: Of course.

Tsambikos Galanis: Before you switch that off, let me just say; a lot of muck is going to be thrown at myself and my brothers. I've gotten my hands dirty, and I wondered if a time would come when I would have to accept my punishment. I hoped it would be far in the future, but we can't always control the way events transpire. One thing I would like to clarify once and for all is mine and my brothers' involvement in the shooting of Gabriella and Juliet. None of us had anything to do with it. The detectives were a nuisance, but one I had a handle on. I had no reason to strike out against them. As we no doubt unpick my every move, you will see I didn't benefit in any significant way from their incapacitation. Now, if you'll excuse me, I need to talk with my solicitor.

Gabe

I walked slowly toward the briefing room. Paul had invited me to watch the second part of Tsambikos's interview, but I'd had enough of him to last a lifetime. They had him on the ropes. Continued questioning would bring out the truth about Henry and the Galanis brothers' wider criminal activities.

Satisfaction should have been ringing through me but tendrils of doubt dragged me down. Tsambikos was adamant he and his brothers had no involvement in the shooting. He'd not tried to deny anything else.

Through Thomas's interviews, it had been clear he was hiding something. If it wasn't the Galanis brothers' involvement, then what was it?

'Ah, Gabe,' Alice called as I walked through the door. 'Perfect timing.'

A faint whiff of fish hung in the air. James stacked a box on top of four others. The tabletops around him were clear. 'Alice wouldn't let me take down anything from the walls. She said if we wanted to blame you for property damage, then you had to be the one to damage the property.'

I looked at the evidence pinned to the walls. Pink twine stretched between globs of Blu Tack, connecting the Galanis brothers to various properties and outgoings.

I beelined for the corner at the back of the room where we'd stuck Thomas Frey's interviews. He'd confessed to the shooting, so had been relegated out of the way until we found a link between him and the Galanis brothers.

If I was this unsure about a case, I'd usually talk it through with Juliet. I twisted to look at James and Alice. 'Will you two help me?'

Alice raced around the table. 'Are we going to do detective work?'

'Hopefully.' My gaze roved over the evidence stacked against Thomas Frey. 'Tsambikos Galanis admitted to all the shit he and his brothers have done, including Henry Garside's murder, but he stated more than once that they had nothing to do with mine and Juliet's shooting.'

James stood straight backed beside me. 'He could be lying?'

'But why? He's spending the rest of his life in prison. Why not take the blame for our shooting as well?'

'Just because the Galanis brothers didn't have anything to do with it, that doesn't mean there's a problem.' Alice leant on the table. 'We've got your shooter and we caught the brothers for different reasons. Doesn't matter if they're not related.'

Apart from this churning unease caused by Thomas's fear and Tsambikos's denial. 'In the interviews with Thomas, he was hiding something. I thought he confessed because he wanted to protect his sister but if she wasn't in danger from the Galanis brothers, why did he suddenly get talkative?'

James tore the two interview transcripts from the wall, ignoring Alice's outraged huff. 'I'm going to read these. I've not had a chance before.'

He left Alice and I before the remaining evidence. 'Let's talk it through.'

'You and Juliet were shot,' she said.

'Before that, someone vandalised key CCTV cameras on the shooter's route,' I corrected.

Alice pushed away from the desk and daintily pulled the stills of the tamperer and the shooter from the wall. 'They didn't get them all.'

I took the picture of the vandal. 'This can't be Thomas Frey; he's too tall and broad.'

'He says he got lucky,' James piped up from behind us.

I shook my head. 'That's too much luck for my liking.'

'Could be the truth.' Alice passed me the other photo. 'Someone intent on not getting caught would have been more thorough.'

'Or they could not have known this camera existed. It was inside a pub. They might not have clocked it as they made plans for the shooting.' I looked down at the still. 'This picture is terrible, but does it look like Thomas Frey to you?'

Alice frowned. 'It has to be. He was the shooter.'

Juliet would have joined me on this path. She could believe Thomas was guilty while wondering if he might not be. Without her, I had to consider it alone.

'Let's say another individual ruined the CCTV. That means Thomas didn't work alone or he got extraordinarily lucky.'

'Okay.' Alice bumped her hip into the table. The jolt sent a flash wave of pain through my weary body. 'Who was he working with if it wasn't the Galanis brothers?'

'I'm not sure. I don't think Terence Dunlow was involved in any of this. He was an unlucky bystander to it all, no matter what Karl says they talked about when Terence visited him.' Once again, someone of Dunlow blood had lied. I tried not to let frustration leak into my voice. 'Let's work through what else we know.'

'What's the sister's name?' James asked.

I looked over my shoulder. He was halfway through Thomas's second interview. 'Mary.'

'Mary Frey?'

I resisted the urge to clench my fists. I didn't have the energy to clarify basic details. 'Mary Turner. She changed her name when she got married.'

James's eyes widened. 'There might be something.' He jumped up and tore the lid off one of the boxes he'd stacked.

'Small detour over.' Alice pointed toward Thomas's corner. 'What else is making your Spidey senses tingle?'

My legs protested, but I crouched to read the documents stuck to the lower half of the wall. 'This.' I pointed at the picture of the bag in the shed. 'Why wouldn't Thomas take it with him when he fled?'

'He said he thought no one knew about the shed.'

I shook my head. 'Thomas freaked out because his sister took his file and we wanted to talk to his dad, but he didn't think to take the most incriminating evidence away with him?' I tried not to groan as I rose to standing and mostly succeeded. 'Thomas isn't an idiot. He wouldn't have left it there.'

'Why would the gun be in his shed if he wasn't the shooter?' Alice's eyebrows drew together. 'Why would he confess?'

'Aha.' James jumped up and placed a piece of paper on the table between me and Alice. He pointed at the list of names. 'This is the sign-in sheet from a local shooting range.'

My eyes drifted over the scrawled names and dates. Timothy Dunlow's jumped out.

I had to read it a second time before I clocked another.

'M. Turner.' I grabbed the paper. 'How did we miss this?'

'We weren't looking for it.' James shrugged. 'We were more focused on the Dunlows, then Thomas and the Galanis brothers. I didn't know about Mary's name change.'

Gears turned in my mind. I gripped the copy of the sign-in sheet. 'When did Thomas get talkative? When we mentioned his sister.'

'You thought he was hiding something. Protecting Mary,' Alice said slowly. 'What if it wasn't from the Galanis brothers? What if it was from us?'

'Exactly.' New energy thrummed through me, banishing the clawing tiredness. 'Who else's DNA is on the clothes and bag? Who would have had the perfect opportunity to plant the gun? Who is the right height to have tampered with the CCTV?'

I suppressed a shudder. I'd been far too vulnerable around Mary Turner. 'She wanted a solicitor straight away. I thought it was caution, but what if she thought we knew more than we did?' I started for the door. 'I need to talk to Paul.'

'Gabe, hold up.' Alice slotted her hand into the crook of my elbow. I slid out of her grip, the small amount of pressure she'd exerted grinding through my shoulder. 'Before you go, answer me this. Thomas has a brilliant reason to want to hurt Juliet. There's evidence he hated her guts. Did Mary give the impression she disliked Juliet at all?'

'She didn't, but we didn't ask. By the time Paul and Nicole questioned her, we were already thinking about Thomas.' We'd jumped right over the other Frey sibling, dismissing the possibility the CCTV showed a woman bulked out by a man's clothing. 'She grew up in the same house as Thomas. She has as much reason to want Juliet out of the picture as Thomas.'

Alice let out a long breath. 'You're the detective.'

'I could be wrong,' I admitted, 'but I have to follow this. Thomas confessed, but it feels off.'

'Go find Paul,' James urged.

I grabbed the still of the shooter, then hurried away from Alice's doubtful face.

My gut had been proven wrong before, but I needed to share this with Paul and Nicole. They were the detectives on this case. I wanted to work with them, be part of the team. They deserved to know everything and put the picture together themselves.

You have one new voicemail. Voicemail left today at 2:39 p.m.

'This is another thing that needs to change. Now you're living with me and the girls, you can't wander off whenever you please. You have to tell me where you're going. You need to be more honest. If you'd thought for one second before you left, you'd have taken your coat and you'd have found the panic button in the pocket. I have no idea why you think I would have moved it. Anyway, come home soon and bring garlic bread for dinner with you.'

Gabe

'You go on ahead.' Nicole pulled in at the drop-off point outside the hospital. 'I'll be with you as soon as I can find a bloody space.'

Paul and I had sat quietly as she'd wound through the multi-level car park four times. Without us in the car, Nicole could freely vent her frustration.

'See you up there.' Paul slammed the door, and we walked toward the hospital entrance. He and Nicole insisting I accompany them had been an unexpected invitation, one I couldn't refuse despite the growing litany of complaints from almost every inch of my body.

'Right.' Paul walked through the front doors and limped toward the lifts. 'It's best if you don't speak once we're with Mary, so run through it one more time.'

It was testament to Paul's trust in my judgement and Nicole's respect for me as a colleague that they'd temporarily abandoned questioning Tsambikos and traipsed out here. I hoped I wasn't about to let them down.

'Thomas wouldn't speak to you and Nicole until you told him his sister had been questioned,' I said, as we waited behind a crowd for the lifts. 'I assumed he was protecting his sister from the Galanis brothers, but Tsambikos has said he and his brothers had nothing to do with the shooting, despite being honest about his other crimes.'

'Could be lying,' Paul said, as we shuffled closer to the lifts.

'Could not be,' I countered. 'If he isn't, then there has to be another reason Thomas started talking at that moment.'

'He might have thought keeping quiet would get Mary in trouble too.'

'That's true.' One thing I knew the power of was a brother's instinct to protect his sister. Barnabas's battle cry as he took on the bad man echoed through my nightmares. 'Thomas could have confessed simply because he didn't want Mary to be dragged down with him.'

'But you don't think that's the case.' Paul stepped forward as another dozen people crowded into a lift.

'A lot of things need more robust explanations,' I hedged. 'I don't understand why Thomas would be so concerned about protecting his sister if she didn't have anything to do with the shooting. The person who destroyed the CCTV isn't a match for Thomas Frey's build, but lines up with Mary's. I'm not convinced the picture we've got of the shooter is a good match for Thomas either.'

'That shot is terrible.' Paul gestured for a young woman in a wheelchair to cut in ahead of him. His frown reflected in the lift doors as they closed. 'There's an argument for Mary being the one to destroy the CCTV.'

'There's also the question of how her DNA got on the bag and clothes concealing the gun, and why Thomas would have left such damning evidence behind when he ran.'

'Why would Mary have handed in the file if she had anything to do with this?' Paul shuffled into a corner of the lift. He kept his voice low in the crowded space as we rose floor by floor. 'If you hadn't clocked her, then all we would have had was a file full of incriminating articles. We wouldn't have had any idea who they belonged to.'

'That's true.' I leant on the wall beside him, shoulders aching as I pressed into the cool metal. 'And why leave them at all if she was involved in the shooting?'

Paul scoffed as we wove through the crowd to escape the cramped lift. 'Sounds like you're talking yourself out of Mary having anything to do with this.'

I shook my head. 'Something doesn't add up.' We rounded a corridor toward the familiar ward. 'Don't forget the sign-in sheet at the shooting range. What are the odds someone with the same surname and first initial had been practising their marksmanship?'

'Markswomanship?' Paul mused as we paused at the entrance to the ward.

I couldn't tell if different patients lay on the beds, their pinched expressions the same as the last occupants. This time, no nurse greeted us at the door. Curtains blocked off a couple of beds. Low murmurs emanated from behind them.

'Let's wait,' Paul suggested. 'It'll give Nicole a chance to catch up if she's not still roaming around the car park.'

Not every detective would be so considerate of patients' privacy when chasing a lead. Paul had once been stuck on a ward like this, waiting until he'd recovered enough to go home. I'd been on one for a night, but there was no real sense of dignity.

The curtains around one of the beds whisked back, revealing Mary. Her scrubs were creased, her hair in a frizzy ponytail. I'd thought her pretty before. She hadn't changed, but her being potentially violent put a dampener on my desire.

She froze when she saw us, hands half out of plastic gloves. I followed Paul's lead as he walked across the ward. Hazel eyes darted between the two of us. She twitched and freed her fingers.

'Why are you here?' She dodged sideways to deposit the gloves in a clanking metal bin.

'We have a few things to clarify with you.' Paul followed her over to a sink.

She flicked on the water and scrubbed her hands. 'I don't know anything about what Tommy did. I'm sorry.'

'We're not actually interested in Thomas. We have a few things to ask you about.'

Mary's eyes skipped between us again. She shut off the water with her elbow and grabbed a paper towel. 'Do I need a solicitor?'

She could be overly cautious, but Mary's dependence on legal counsel twanged a cord. It didn't mean she was guilty, but wholly innocent people didn't often immediately demand representation.

'We just have a couple of questions. It shouldn't take more than a minute or so.' Paul winced at the full roster of beds surrounding us. 'I don't want to take up too much of your time.'

Mary's nostrils flared, but she gave a short nod. She crossed her arms over her chest as Paul extracted a Dictaphone from his pocket and rattled off the pertinent information. He didn't mention my presence, which I took as a reminder to keep my mouth shut. I'd told him everything he needed to know. I had to trust he would dig out the truth.

Paul pulled the picture of the CCTV vandal from his pocket. 'Can you identify who this is?'

Mary didn't take the picture. She stood still, her teeth digging into her lower lip. 'No.'

'It's not your brother?' Paul checked.

'It's hard to tell.' Mary's eyes were glued to the grainy photograph. 'Could be him.'

'Thank you.' Paul tucked the photo away and showed Mary another. The still from the pub. 'How about this one? Is this Thomas?'

Mary's arms had to be restricting her breathing with how tightly she pressed them against her rib cage. 'I'm not sure. Maybe.'

'Okay.' Paul returned the photo to his pocket and pulled out the sign-in sheet. 'Have you been going to the shooting range?'

'Fuck.'

The breathed word was the only warning before Mary aimed a sharp kick at Paul's stick. As he stumbled, she punched his hip. It sent him sprawling.

I threw up my hands. She batted them out of the way and smacked her palm into my injured shoulder.

I cried out as my knees crumpled. A kick to my stomach threw me onto my back.

Struggling for breath, I turned my head toward the ward entrance. Mary raced for the wide double doors, her hair escaping its binding.

She'd almost made it when Nicole appeared. She had a split second to take in me and Paul on the floor and the nurse charging toward her.

She dropped into a crouch with one leg stuck out to the side. Mary had gathered too much momentum. Her legs tangled with Nicole's.

The thump as she hit the ground blended with the beeps of machinery and gentle voices of those on the ward who hadn't caught up with what was happening yet.

'Stay down,' Nicole warned.

Mary had risen to her hands and knees. She struggled as Nicole pulled her arms back but was cuffed before she could lash out again. I turned my gaze to the ceiling as Nicole recited her rights.

'Gabe?' Paul levered himself onto his elbows. 'You okay?'

Gingerly, I sat up. It was hard to tell which hurts resulted from Mary's rough treatment and which had already been with me before we stepped onto the ward.

'I'm fine.' I used my good arm to push into a crouch, then stood. 'You alright?'

The green-haired nurse we'd met before hurried out from behind a curtain. 'What on earth is going on?'

I picked up Paul's stick and carried it over to him. Pain shot down from my shoulder as he used my hand to stand.

'We're arresting your colleague for assaulting police officers,' Nicole said from over by the door. Mary stood beside her, arms pulled behind her back. Clumps of hair stood out unevenly around her face.

Her eyes narrowed as we neared, her rage fixated on me. 'I should have known you're a bitch like her.'

My mouth fell open. I might have thought Mary was involved in the shooting, but until now I'd not understood why. I didn't know if her collusion was prompted by loyalty to her brother or fear of what he might do if she didn't help.

She glared at me, all gentleness fled. 'I actually tried not to kill you. I shouldn't have bothered.'

'You shot me and Juliet?'

Mary laughed mirthlessly. 'I wish I'd done a better job and offed the both of you.'

Nicole placed a hand on Mary's shoulder and turned her toward the ward doors. 'That's enough.'

Paul and I watched them disappear down the corridor. Around us, the normal rhythms of the ward resumed. Nurses rushed between beds and bells chimed. Patients sighed and visitors fluttered at their sides.

'I would say that's a job well done.' Paul nudged my elbow. 'Could do without being used as a punch bag next time, though.'

'That would be preferable.'

I breathed deep as we walked off the ward, even slower than when we'd entered. My mind, distracted by the protests of a body pushed too far, struggled to wrap around this new information.

Thomas Frey wasn't the shooter. The Galanis brothers weren't involved.

Mary Turner shot Juliet and me.

RSPCA – Animal surrender form

NAME OF ANIMAL

Artie (owner provided name)

AGE OF ANIMAL

Unknown

TYPE OF ANIMAL

Dog

BREED OF ANIMAL

Alsatian

CONDITION OF ANIMAL

Good weight and no signs of injury or neglect

REASON FOR INTAKE

None given. Dog was left at the door. CCTV has been copied and sent to the police

PREVIOUS OWNER/S

The collar has no tag – looks like it was cut off. The dog has a microchip. Have called the owner – Gabe Martin. She will come to collect soon

OTHER NOTES

The dog is incredibly friendly

Detective Sergeant Nicole Stewart: Interview commencing at 4:26 p.m. on the 1st May. The interviewee is Mary Turner. She has been given the chance to seek legal counsel prior to this interview but declined. Should she change her mind, then legal counsel will be sought for her. The interview is being conducted by Detective Inspector Paul Willis and myself, Detective Sergeant Nicole Stewart. This interview is concerning the shooting of Detective Inspector Juliet Stern and Detective Sergeant Gabriella Martin on the 24th April.

Detective Inspector Paul Willis: For the benefit of the tape, I am showing Mary a still of the person who tampered with several CCTV cameras before the shooting. Picture AT02. Is this you?

Mary Turner: Yes.

DI Paul Willis: When did you make the plan to take out the CCTV cameras?

Mary Turner: At the same time I decided to give Detective Stern what had been a long time coming for her.

DS Nicole Stewart: You've been going to a shooting range several times a week for months.

Mary Turner: I wanted to make sure I could get the job done.

DI Paul Willis: Was it your plan to merely injure Detectives Stern and Martin?

Mary Turner: I wanted Detective Stern dead. I got unlucky. If I'd aimed an inch lower, she'd have been finished.

DS Nicole Stewart: And Detective Martin? Comments made on your arrest gave us reason to believe you did not intend to kill her.

Mary Turner: I didn't. Don't know why I bothered. Anyone who could stomach working with Detective Stern for so long must have something wrong with them. The world would be a better place today if the both of them were gone.

DI Paul Willis: I see. In your previous interview, you said you didn't feel any ill will toward Detective Stern.

Mary Turner: I couldn't exactly tell you I hated her, could I?

DS Nicole Stewart: You previously said you didn't believe your father's account of what happened when he retired from the force.

Mary Turner: I knew that version of events would appeal to you. You're all 'me too' mad here. It's the same at work. Women can't possibly be responsible for the terrible things that happen to them. They have to be innocent victims. I bet Detective Stern never thought to herself there had to have been a reason my dad propositioned her. I bet she thinks she did nothing wrong, when if she hadn't been so flirty and had dressed appropriately, my dad wouldn't have gotten the wrong end of the stick.

DI Paul Willis: You blame Detective Stern for your father leaving the force?

Mary Turner: She's the root of everything wrong in my family. If my dad hadn't met her, he and my mum would still be married. He wouldn't be cared for by my useless brother, and Mum wouldn't be off God knows where with an arsehole who isn't interested in letting her talk to her kids.

DS Nicole Stewart: Can you pinpoint when your anger toward Juliet became a plan to kill her?

Mary Turner: There wasn't a definite moment. I don't suppose you can imagine for a second what it was like growing up in that house. Our lives were perfect, and then everything fell apart. We barely saw Dad for years, but then Mum ditched us and shunted us back to him. He was twisted up with hate. He hated Detective Stern and Mum. He hated me. I couldn't blame him. Women had been terrible to him.

DS Nicole Stewart: That must have been difficult.

Mary Turner: It was horrible. I couldn't wait to get out. I went to university and snatched up the first guy who showed an interest. I changed my name, didn't go home, and I tried to forget the mess I'd escaped from. But she wouldn't let me.

DI Paul Willis: Detective Stern?

Mary Turner: She was everywhere. Her name always in the paper, her voice always on the radio. She gave birth at my hospital. I didn't work on maternity, but

I could feel her presence like a black cloud. That's how it's always felt, like she's hovering over my life. She's always made it dark.

DS Nicole Stewart: Speaking of the hospital; why didn't you use your position there to further injure Detectives Martin or Stern?

Mary Turner: It was too risky. Detective Martin was on the ward, and back then I didn't want to cause her further harm anyway. Detective Stern was in a private room, but in a hospital there are too many chances to be caught out. Not that I got a moment alone with her. Until she was conscious, her bloody husband wouldn't leave her side.

DI Paul Willis: What made you start planning to shoot Detective Stern?

Mary Turner: A lot of little things came together. I'd managed to cut Thomas and Dad out of my life for years, so Detective Stern was more of an annoyance. But then Dad got sick. I had to see him and Thomas more. All I'd left behind was thrown in my face. I cared for Dad in a hundred ways, and he never did anything but glare because I'm a woman. Thomas wouldn't shut up about Detective Stern, kept showing me his pathetic file. I thought things might get better as Dad forgot, but Thomas kept the fire burning. He wouldn't let Dad leave Detective Stern in the past, told him she was the reason our lives had gone to shit. In the end, killing her seemed like the only way to get them to both shut the fuck up.

DS Nicole Stewart: You shot Detective Stern to silence your father and brother?

Mary Turner: If she was gone, they would finally stop talking about her. We'd be left in peace. And I can't say the thought of ridding the world of her wasn't appealing.

DI Paul Willis: What made you decide to shoot Detective Martin as well?

Mary Turner: That was the first part of my plan to not get caught. Someone who hated Juliet would surely just shoot her. Why would they bother with her partner?

DS Nicole Stewart: What other steps did you take to keep us from suspecting you?

Mary Turner: You know them.

DI Paul Willis: It would be helpful if you talked us through them.

Mary Turner: The CCTV was the next step. I didn't realise I'd been captured trashing them. I made sure to have an alibi that was hard to check. Dad couldn't be trusted to know who was with him at any time, and I didn't give a shit if I messed up Thomas's alibi. I made sure to clean the clothes and bag, and wipe all the prints off the gun.

DI Paul Willis: Why did you drop off the file for Detective Martin to find?

Mary Turner: I was worried when Dad was questioned. I needed to get out ahead, to make sure your attention stayed fixed on anyone but me. And Thomas's attitude pissed me off. I'd done what he was too chicken-shit to attempt, and all he did was mope around Dad's house afterwards like Detective Stern getting hurt wasn't what he'd wanted for years. If I'd told him what I'd done, he wouldn't have uttered a word of thanks. So I stole his silly articles and left them in the woods. I thought they would confuse you. I didn't plan to be seen. That changed things.

DS Nicole Stewart: In what way?

Mary Turner: I'd been turning over the idea of letting Thomas take the fall since I started planning. I used his bag to carry the gun, wore his clothes. I hoped you wouldn't sniff around too much and I wouldn't have to do it, but once you'd questioned Dad more suspicion was bound to come down on us. After I was seen leaving the file, I knew you'd ask more questions. I moved the gun into the shed that night.

DI Paul Willis: What would you have done if Thomas hadn't confessed?

Mary Turner: I knew he would. He's always been protective. He didn't like how Dad treated me. Thomas would take the blame because he would feel guilty. The fool. He'd think of my kids being without a mother and how he was the one who kept talking such a big game about hating Detective Stern and wishing something bad would happen to her. I bet he's half convinced himself he did shoot her. He didn't pull the trigger, but he probably thinks he pushed me to do it in his stead. Like he could make me do anything. Moron. I did it to shut him up, to cleanse Detective Stern from our lives.

DI Paul Willis: There's a lot to unpick here and we need to ask a lot more questions, but let's take a short break for now.

DS Nicole Stewart: I couldn't agree more.

MARY,

   THE DETECTIVES SAID I'M ALLOWED TO WRITE A NOTE TO YOU BEFORE I LEAVE.

   I DON'T KNOW WHAT TO SAY. I DON'T KNOW WHY YOU DID THIS.

   YOU OF ALL PEOPLE KNOW HOW MUCH I HATE DETECTIVE STERN, BUT I NEVER WOULD HAVE HURT HER. I'M SO SORRY I MADE YOU THINK YOU SHOULD.

   I DON'T KNOW HOW THEY FIGURED OUT IT WASN'T ME. I DIDN'T TELL THEM ANYTHING.

   I'LL LOOK AFTER DAD, AND CHRIS AND THE GIRLS. YOU DIDN'T KILL ANYONE, SO YOU SHOULDN'T BE IN PRISON FOR LIFE.

   LOOK AFTER YOURSELF. I LOVE YOU.

   TOMMY X

Gabe

'I can wait until Ollie arrives,' James offered as I undid my seatbelt.

'It's fine,' I reassured him, but paused with my fingers on the door handle. 'If you've got a minute though.'

I dug into my coat pocket and retrieved the Twix Paul had given me as I left the station. He said he didn't have time to share it and that his and Nicole's waistlines would be grateful if I took it off his hands.

'Paul has this tradition.' I tore open the shiny plastic and eased out one of the sticks of chocolate covered biscuit and caramel. 'Whoever is instrumental in closing a case gets to share a Twix with him. He gave this to me, and I'd love it if we could share it.'

Pink blush spread across James's face, but he took the offered chocolate with a smile. 'Thank you, Gabe.'

'Finding Mary's name on the sign-in sheet for the shooting range was incredibly important.' I took a bite of Twix, which I then spoke around. 'You've got a brilliant eye for detail. Noticing the mooring was essential for finding the yacht as well.'

James polished off his Twix in two bites, but chewed and swallowed before speaking. 'I got lucky both times. My parents were the boat lovers, and I happened to remember the surname Turner from the register.'

'I don't like blaming luck too much.' I tugged at the door handle. 'You've accepted the Twix, so you also have to accept the compliment.'

James's blush grew as I climbed out of his car. 'Thank you,' he called, before the door swung shut.

I chewed on the rest of my Twix as I walked toward the entrance of the RSPCA. I wasn't sure I deserved the Twix of Glory, but Paul was insistent. Forcing James to acknowledge his value as a police officer made it worth it.

Paul considered my input essential in finding evidence to bring down both the Galanis brothers and Mary Turner, but he'd conveniently forgotten I'd been a hindrance too. Juliet and I had been tailing

Alcaeus, Tsambikos, and Giannis for months, and neither of us had spotted the empty mooring. A yacht packed with illegal materials had sat right under our noses. Without James's help, we would have had nothing to pin on the brothers. Henry's death would have haunted his friends and family, whereas now they would have a chance at mournful peace.

Although I'd helped Paul uncover Mary's violent streak, I'd also jeopardised his investigation. Loyalty to Juliet had seen me question a person I should have been nowhere near. If Douglas had been dangerous, I could have been badly hurt.

I would always respect Juliet, but I needed to trust myself. My gut didn't often steer me wrong. If I thought I shouldn't do something, then I couldn't let her persuade me otherwise again.

Tsambikos's offer refused to budge from the forefront of my mind. I'd barely considered letting him go, but the prospect of seeing the bad man locked away was appealing. I could have let the brothers go to give myself a full night's sleep.

Not that nightmares would keep me from falling into bed as soon as I got home. My whole body whined as I pushed through the front door of the animal centre. The smell of damp fur greeted me, along with a familiar booming bark.

I walked over to the reception desk set in one corner alongside racks of animal toys and packets of medication. Two paws scrabbled beside the hip of a woman standing at the desk, followed by a snuffling black snout.

Tears spilled down my cheeks. The receptionist smiled fondly between us as I offered my hand for Artie to lick. She clucked at him, an RSPCA jumper stretching over her generous curves.

'It's alright, duck.' She patted my spit-covered hand after Artie got distracted by sniffing around behind the desk. 'He's right as rain.'

I pulled my hand back and wiped the drool on my coat, using the sleeve to mop at my face. Ollie would not be pleased if I ever returned it to him. 'It's been a long day.'

'Looks it,' she said, confirming I looked as shit as I felt. She flicked a greying ponytail over her shoulder and passed me a clipboard. 'Take a seat while you fill in the paperwork. I'll bring him around.'

I settled into a plastic chair against the far wall framed on one side by a stack of old blankets and on the other by a teetering pile of cat beds. I'd written my name at the top of the first form before Artie bounced over. I sunk my hands and face into his warm fur, more tears eking out as he wriggled in my embrace.

'I bet you went willingly, you great lump,' I said into his neck. Alcaeus hadn't been picked up yet but Paul had promised to add animal theft to the charges he'd be facing.

Artie licked my ear, then played with a knotted rope while I completed the paperwork. My phone vibrated in my pocket as the receptionist checked the forms, Artie leaning against my legs. I glanced at the message.

'My boyfriend is outside.' I scratched the soft fur behind Artie's ears.

'Lovely. This is all done.' The receptionist grinned as she passed over Artie's lead. My hand shook. I'd get a new one, and a new collar. Ones Alcaeus had never touched.

'Thank you for looking after him,' I said, as the receptionist took one last chance to fuss Artie.

He dragged me out of the doors. His tugging increased when he saw Ollie, the boot of his Mini flung open. Artie jumped in and rubbed his head against Ollie's jumper until he gently closed the boot.

'Hard day?' he asked.

I stepped forward and pressed my face into his chest. Ollie's arms instantly looped around my back, his hands rubbing soothing patterns down my spine. I didn't care that hugging him awakened the mile-long list of pains across my body. As I breathed in the scent of his expensive body wash, something screwed tight inside of me loosened.

'Move in with me,' I said into the fabric bunched around my face.

Ollie leant back. 'Pardon?'

I wriggled a hand between our bodies to wipe my face but didn't step away. 'We should move in together.'

I didn't want to keep doing life alone. I didn't want to be like Juliet, too scared to let anyone in. I might not be able to form the words yet to tell Ollie how I felt, but I could show it.

Ollie kissed me, his smile firm against my lips. 'I would love to move in with you.'

'Let's find a new place,' I said, as Ollie touched his forehead to mine. 'Somewhere that can be yours and mine.'

I'd found the maisonette when I was reeling from being separated from my parents for the first time. It was the perfect hideaway while

I figured out how to live alone, but it wasn't a home. I wanted somewhere new with Ollie where we could start living our lives together.

'Sounds grand to me,' Ollie murmured, dimples poking into his rounded cheeks. 'You're my favourite person, Gabe.'

I lifted onto my tiptoes to kiss him. 'You're mine too.'

Call connected at 17:48.

'I assume this is important?'

'Hello, Juliet. How are you? I'm fine, thank you for asking.'

'Don't piss around, Paul. I haven't got time for it.'

'You'll be pleased to hear we've charged Mary Turner, who was born Maria Frey, with your shooting. She's made a full confession.'

'That's good news.'

'Why didn't you tell me the circumstances around Douglas Frey's departure from the force?'

'I didn't think my personal history was pertinent to the case.'

'Juliet, you know people don't get to keep secrets when they're involved in an investigation. Even the smallest detail can lead to a conviction.'

'You got there without my help. I don't see what the problem is.'

'Of course you don't. Well, I also wanted to apologise. I know I've not always been the most patient—'

'I don't need your pity.'

'I'm trying to say—'

'This is exactly why I asked for the circumstances around Frey's departure to be suppressed. I don't need you treating me differently because I'm a poor woman the horrible man tried to oppress. Either treat me as you would have before, which includes zero apologies, or stay out of my way.'

'Wonderful. Always a delight to speak to you.'

'Was there anything else?'

'Since we've concluded the case, that means you don't need to check in any more.'

'The babysitting can stop.'

'Exactly. Enjoy the rest of your sick leave, Juliet.'

Call connected at 18:02.

'Detective Inspector Paul Willis.'

'Hello there, Paul. This is Nathan Faulkner, from UK border force. I hope you're having a good day?'

'I suspect you're about to make it better.'

'I'll have a go. We apprehended Alcaeus Galanis as he tried to use a fake passport to board a boat to France leaving this evening. I'm sorry I've not called sooner, but we had trouble identifying him. He was being uncooperative.'

'It's a family trait.'

Three months later

Call connected at 8:02.

'Gabriella, how are you?'

'Hi, Mum. I'm fine. Sorry I didn't call last night. I was at the station until late. I didn't want to wake you.'

'I wouldn't have minded.'

'I'm not sure I would have been worth chatting to.'

'Is the search not going well?'

'You don't want to hear about this.'

'If it's part of your life, then I want to hear it.'

'Then yeah, it's not going well. It's been a week and we've found nothing.'

'Gosh. His poor, poor parents. And that poor little boy.'

'See, Mum. I didn't want to upset you.'

'This kind of thing will always set me off, love. I know you'll do your best for them, but you must look after yourself as well.'

'I try. It's hard when a case like this comes in. If we don't get any leads on where Max is soon, we'll have to start winding down.'

'You'll have done everything you could to bring him home.'

'Thanks, Mum. I'm sorry, but Juliet's pulled up. I've got to go in. I'll call again soon.'

'Love you, darling. Give my love to Ollie.'

'Will do. Love you.'

From: Leonard Dunlow **leonard.dunlow@police.gov.uk**
To: Hannah West **hannah.west@policehr.gov.uk**
Date: **23 July, 9:10**
Subject: **Change of details**

Hello Hannah,

Thank you for such a great one month review last week. I'm enjoying this job so much and I'm looking forward to learning even more.

I'm sorry I couldn't tell you about this then, but my situation has changed in the last few days.

I'm now living with my brother – Terence Dunlow. I would also like him to be my next of kin. I've attached the form to this email.

I had been living with my father, which I mentioned has been difficult as he doesn't like me working for the police. Nothing major happened, but my brother and his boyfriend offered me a room and a change felt right. I hope my dad will mellow if we're not living in each other's pockets.

Thank you,

Leo

Call connected at 10:05.

'Hello?'

    'Hello, is that Keith Stern?'

    'Yes, who is this?'

    'It's Sally Bull. We spoke a few months ago about concerns you'd had about your wife. I'm returning your call from yesterday evening. How are things going?'

    'To be honest, they're amazing. Juliet has been living with us full time for a few months now, and it's like she's a different person. No anger, no coldness. She's working less and spending more time with the girls. Things have really turned around. I just wanted to let you know there's no cause for concern at all.'

    'That's so good to hear. Are you happy for me to leave it to you to get in touch if anything changes?'

    'That's absolutely fine. It's good to know you're there if I ever need you. Thank you so much for all your support at a difficult time.'

SHARP AND LINK GARDEN CENTRES

Allington indoor and outdoor furnishings

sharpandlinkallington.co.uk

1 Large Barrel	£59.99
Subtotal:	£59.99
TOTAL:	£59.99
Cash	£59.99
Potential Garden Points earned:	5

Ask in store or sign up online for our loyalty card to make savings with every purchase

23/07   11:36   Store: Allington   Cashier: Lily French

ACKNOWLEDGEMENTS

Writing the acknowledgements for book two is a weird thing, since there's a whole load of people who also need to be thanked for things to do with book one after it flew out into the world. I hope you'll indulge my outpouring of gratitude for all the people who made publishing *Shot in the Dark* a joy, and those who have worked incredibly hard to make *Close to the Edge* a successful sequel.

Always, my first thanks have to go to you – my readers. It still absolutely blows my mind that you are interested in my stories. Thank you for the love you've shown *Shot in the Dark*, and I hope *Close to the Edge* is everything you were hoping for. I write all alone (with Odie) and for so long a book is shared with a handful of people. You have made one of my stories being read by a much larger group of people wonderful, and I am so excited for even more readers to meet Gabe and Juliet in this book. Thank you also to anyone who has come along and listened to me natter about my writing, especially at some brilliant libraries – Yate Library in Bristol, Camberley Library in Surrey, and Freshwater Library on the Isle of Wight.

A massive thank you to all the bloggers and bookish folk who read *Shot in the Dark* and shouted about it. It has been such a joy to read your reviews, watch your videos, and see your love for my story. Thank you to the authors who read *Shot in the Dark* and said such kind things. Thank you to all the wonderful bookshops who stocked *Shot in the Dark* and all the booksellers who welcomed me in to sign stock. Many Waterstones branches made me feel like a real author and not just some weirdo coming in to scribble in a book – Lymington, Southampton West Quay, Portsmouth, Ringwood, Bournemouth Arcade, Bournemouth Castlepoint, Winchester Brooks, and Camberley. Particular thanks have to be given to Jonathan and the rest of the team at Waterstones on the Isle of Wight – you took *Shot in the Dark* and hecking championed it. Huge thanks to all the independent bookshops who have let me potter in to sign stock – The Imaginarium, Medina Books, Babushka Books, Westbourne Bookshop, P&G Wells, and Gulliver's Bookshop.

If possible, I have fallen even more in love with my glorious agent, Saskia Leach, since *Shot in the Dark* published. Saskia – thank you for keeping me sane! You are brilliant at calmly explaining the MANY things I don't understand about publishing and your unflagging enthusiasm for my writing buoys me up when my confidence is low. You continue to be a brilliant human being and I look forward to many more cat vomit stories in the future. Thank you to the wider Kate Nash Literary Agency team – there are lots of you working behind the scenes to make this process as bump-free as it can possibly be.

Siân Heap – thank you for continuing to be a brilliant and passionate editor. Your feedback never fails to make my stories stronger, and I love how meticulous you are about whipping my books into shape. Working with someone who makes me feel excited to jump into edits is such a joy. Thank you for bearing with me as I've taken my first steps into publishing – you and the rest of the team at Canelo have made it such a wonderful journey. I've felt so supported by you all.

Some chums read *Close to the Edge* to reassure me that it made sense and vaguely followed on from *Shot in the Dark*. Natalie Jones – thank you for your kind encouragement and bookish chats. Chris Reddecliff – your thoughts were all brilliant and I loved hearing your theories. Chloe Ford – thank you not only for reading my book, but for dealing with all my ramblings. Ben Britton – your feedback is always spot on and I value your honesty so much. Mum – you'll probably have read *Close to the Edge* two or three times before it hits shelves and your cheerleading always makes me smile.

A lot of other people helped me to make *Close to the Edge* as accurate as possible. Anything that is vaguely factual is thanks to them sharing their life experiences and wisdom with me. A massive thank you to my Uncle Mark, who worked for many years as a police officer and helped me with everything procedural. Thank you to Mike Wigley, who chatted to me about bullet wounds and blood loss at great length. Thank you to April Newton and Liam Mennel, who advised me on family law. Thank you to Toby Smith, who helped me to understand children's social work. Thank you to Sally Doherty and Sean Hassall, for answering my questions about moorings. Dad – thank you for chatting to me about prison visitors.

Thank you to my family of writers – Marisa Noelle, Sally Doherty, and Emma Bradley. You are all fantastic individuals, and I love authoring alongside you. You inspire me, and thank you for putting up with long spells of silence interspersed with SHOUTING. Thank you also to the lovely 2023 debut group – having people to cheer/lament with as our books publish has been such a support. Thank you for answering all my questions.

I'm terrible at naming characters, and a couple of people suggested names I fell in love with. Tsam Potts, thank you for letting me use your name. I hope you don't mind that Tsambikos is a bit of a turd. Jenny Mattern – thank you for suggesting the name of your father. Gunter felt perfect for my sketch artist.

Social media continues to be a blessing to me – it's where I chat about books (and cinnamon rolls) and SO MANY readers have gotten in touch to let me know they enjoyed *Shot in the Dark*. I love chatting with you all and I'm so grateful whenever you reach out. Weirdly (as I'm very much not a cool kid), there are far too many people who chat to me online for me to name you all. But if you have ever sent me a kind word or exclaimed with me over the wonder that is baked goods, then I am so so grateful to you. Online spaces can be toxic and harmful, but I love the people I meet on Instagram and Twitter.

Thank you so much to my friends and family who have read and raved about *Shot in the Dark* (although I now expect the same for *Close to the Edge*, so you better be ready). I am genuinely blown away by the support you've shown me and my story. I was so worried about people I know reading it and also terrified that no one would, but the amount of you who have read my book and then SHOUTED about it is incredible. Thank you for celebrating writing books with me – it's hard work but you make it feel worth it.

Special thanks must go to my dad. He hadn't read a book since before I was born, but after *Shot in the Dark* published he read a little every day. It made me so happy that you made such an effort to read my story, and made me even happier that you enjoyed it so much. I can't wait for you to read *Close to the Edge* – I look forward to hearing your theories. Thank you to you and Mum and all my family for being a constant well of support.

This whole book is dedicated to him so he probably knows I'm rather thankful, but the biggest thank you to my lovely husband. Ben, you've not only cheered me on as I've written *Close to the Edge*, but you've also ferried me around to events and signings. Your support for my writing and the publicity stuff that goes alongside it is constant – thank you for being proud of me. You are with me when my brain is struggling and you are with me in the brilliant times too – thank you for being my best friend and for being my biggest cheerleader.

And finally, thank you to Odie. You haven't yet figured out why I spend hours staring at a screen each day but you take your job of sleeping nearby very seriously. Thank you for always being up for a walk after a long day of typing and a cuddle when needed. You are a very good dog.

Do you love crime fiction and are always on the lookout for brilliant authors?

Canelo Crime is home to some of the most exciting novels around. Thousands of readers are already enjoying our compulsive stories. Are you ready to find your new favourite writer?

Find out more and sign up to our newsletter at canelocrime.com